Pictures Don't Lie

Pictures Don't Lie

ACE BRYANN

Charleston, SC
www.PalmettoPublishing.com

Pictures Don't Lie

Copyright © 2020 by Ace Bryann

First Edition

Hardcover ISBN: 978-1-64990-212-2
Paperback ISBN: 978-1-64990-725-7
eBook ISBN: 978-1-64990-655-7

Prologue

My darling, I can no longer suffer, living with your harsh words and cruel dismissal of me, even if you have decided that you no longer love me. I need you to know that our last night together in New York, right after the business conference, was both my happiest memory and the most sadness I have ever felt. I thought that you had finally agreed to acknowledge our love, only to discover afterward that I was just a game to you. If you had just asked me to stay quiet about the affair, I would have, because regardless of how you've treated me, I still love you. But attempting to buy my silence drove your knife that much deeper into my heart. I've left behind with this letter your check for $1,000,000. If you'd be so kind, please donate the money to a suicide prevention charitable cause in memory of me.

Once she had finished writing, she paused to reread her note. Yes, she thought, it was perfect. She took another swig from the bottle of whiskey, having already gone halfway through it. Her mind was now completely made up. This was the only way. Her only way out of the dark depths of her misery, and the only way to make him experience the pain in the way she had.

Taking the note, she continued into her bedroom, where she removed an envelope from her purse, lying on the desk. In the envelope was a check written to her for $1 million, as well as a picture of her and Derek, the one she had shown Paul. The picture had been taken during the charity event. His arm was around her, and they were both smiling for the camera. It had been the happiest day of her life, and he had made love to her that night. She stared at the picture, his sapphire eyes sparkling. On the outside of the envelope she wrote the name Derek Landino.

She thought of how her scheme to ruin his life would die now with her, and it brought a slight smile to her face. This was her only solace, and her only sense of peace, however minuscule it was. She staggered through her small room, from the desk over to the mirror that hung above her bedroom dresser. As she gulped more whiskey, she took a last glance at her reflection. Her long, dark hair was limp; her brown eyes were dull and sunken, making them look abnormally large. Although James had been making her eat some, she was still extremely malnourished and pale.

Her eyes were blurry, and her head was still spinning as she sat down on the bed. She needed to finish this now. She knew that with his power and resources, it would not take long for him to return with authorities and charge her for what she had done. The note she'd left, along with the check, was the only way left to ruin him. Without him, there was no point to this world anyway, and a fleeting smile crossed her face as she thought that maybe one day she'd see him again in hell.

She heaved a sob, and with despair consuming her, she reached for the pill bottle sitting on the nightstand—the pills she used to help her through sleepless nights. She twisted the cap off and proceeded to swallow the pills three to four at a time, washing each handful down with the other half of the bottle of whiskey, until both were gone. She was taking no chances, and her decision to end her life was resolute. She had chickened out once before, but this was different. There was no going back. Dizzy and nearing unconsciousness, she collapsed onto the floor. Her eyes felt heavy and dark, she could no longer see, and she was simply slipping away into nothingness. She was cold. The last image in her mind was of his face.

Chapter 1

20 Months Ago

The iPhone buzzed on the desk. "Incoming Call: Mattia." Derek made a face at the screen, then sent it straight to voice mail. *He's not going to leave me alone*, he thought, wondering how long he could continue to avoid him. He ran a hand through his raven hair, pushed up his shirtsleeves, and returned to staring at his laptop, his dark brows coming together in concentration. This charity benefit was important; he had to make an appearance. He would simply have to move the dinner with the investor for the downtown project.

"Sir?" The disembodied voice of his personal assistant, Gregory, interrupted his scheduling dilemma.

"Yes, Gregory," Derek answered the intercom sitting on his desk next to his computer, his eyes not moving off from the screen.

"Abigail Steiner left you another message," Gregory said. Derek groaned softly. Again? "This is the third time today, sir."

"I'm not here," Derek replied absently.

"Yes, sir." There was a pause. "Luca Mattia—you know, from Calina—is also on the line."

Derek sighed. "I'm not here," he replied again, losing patience.

"Sir…" Gregory hesitated. "I don't think he's buying that anymore." Derek blinked and glanced at the intercom, raising an eyebrow.

"Remind me why I pay you, Gregory," he responded.

"Yes, sir." But the intercom didn't click off; Gregory was still there. Derek knew when his assistant was afraid to give him bad news.

"What else, Greg?" he asked.

"Your ex-wife called you again." Derek stared at the intercom. *Unbelievable*, he thought, realizing that his bad day was about to get worse; he really didn't have the energy to talk Cynthia off a ledge today. He rubbed his brow with one hand and leaned back in his chair.

"Get rid of Mattia," he told Gregory with a finality to his tone. This time he heard the intercom click off.

Derek stood up from his desk and stretched his broad shoulders as he had been sitting too long. He strode over to the view from his office, which looked out over New York City. On the twenty-third floor of his headquarters, foot to ceiling was glass. His office was styled simply to his tastes, large and spacious with minimal color. There were few furnishings—he did not hold meetings or spend much time here. New York City was technically where he lived, where he hung his hat. But he spent so much time traveling he did not consider any one place to be "home."

Derek was born in a European Latin microstate called Calina. When he was four years old, however, the country went through a revolution, and he, his mother, and his younger brother, Nicola, were forced to flee. His father had not been lucky enough to escape. The three immigrated to the United States, and after many years earned their dual citizenship legally. Their mother had ensured that the family's wealth was intact when they fled Calina. Even though resources were available, Derek was awestruck by the United States and grew up admiring the earning potential, wanting to chase after the American dream. He was ambitious to a fault and began to build his own fortune. Throughout school he had a knack for business and was purchasing real estate by age eighteen. He attended Columbia for business, and upon graduating, he married his then sweetheart, Cynthia, at the young age of twenty-two.

As he built his enterprise by dabbling in any entrepreneurial opportunity that turned a profit, Derek Landino and his core company, Land Corporation, became household names. By thirty he was gracing the covers of *Forbes* and *Time* and claiming he was the youngest multibillionaire in the United States. After he achieved such status and fame, his marriage began to fall apart. Cynthia was struggling to adjust to the constant charity benefits, ribbon cuttings, magazine shoots, and beautiful models throwing themselves at him around every corner. Even though Derek was forever faithful, he could not blame her for her unhappiness. He could tell they were growing apart, and Cynthia did not share his passion for building his business. He had no intentions of stopping, regardless of her constant begging for him to settle down. After nine years of marriage, he asked her to divorce him. He knew he was making her miserable, and in all honesty, he loved his work more. It was messy, but Derek had made sure she was set for life. The tabloids had a field day with his divorce, and soon after he became the "it" bachelor. With his chiseled features, muscular build, black, silky hair, and uncharacteristically Latin sapphire blue eyes, every woman wanted him, and every man wanted to be him.

Now, at thirty-four, Derek stayed devoted to his work. Continuing to build his empire and Land Corporation, he expanded back into his roots in Europe. When asked what motivated and drove him in interviews, Derek humbly stated he needed to build so he could give back. True to this philosophy, he began spearheading several philanthropy projects, including shelters and medical and education facilities across the United States and Europe. Not turning a blind eye to the arts, something he truly found passion in, he purchased and resurrected a failing art gallery in Paris and financed many art education programs in low-income districts.

A sharp knock interrupted his gazing out at the city, and Gregory walked in.

"Sir, these items needs you final signature." He walked over to where Derek stood. Derek took the folder and opened it flat on his desk. "Abigail," his assistant offered, "isn't she that strawberry blond model from Austria?" Derek stopped midsignature and looked up to narrow his eyes at Gregory. Gregory just raised his eyebrows in innocence and gave a slight shrug. After a silence, Derek finished signing, folded up the paperwork, and handed it back to him. "She called for you three times today," he continued hopefully. Derek realized he wasn't going to let it go and suppressed a sigh.

Gregory had been with Derek since his divorce almost three years ago, and he sometimes wondered how he had managed prior. He was the younger brother of his divorce attorney and best friend, Timothy McKenzie, and it had been Timothy who recommended Gregory for the position. Although young, just twenty-eight, Gregory was a borderline genius, computer whiz, and extremely efficient at handling all of Derek's appointments, meetings and priorities, both business and personal. In short, Gregory was Derek's right hand, and he knew more about Derek and his business than any other employee in the company. And he seemed appropriate by Derek's side during events. Slightly shorter in stature at an even six feet, Gregory looked the part of the intellectual assistant—attractive with light brown, wavy hair, warm brown eyes, a clean-cut look, and glasses, which added a touch of sophistication.

Having known Derek personally for some time now, Gregory knew when he could be pushed and when to back off. Apparently, right now, Derek supposed, he was in need of explanation.

"I'm not interested," he told Gregory evenly, "she was a date. That's all."

"You did invite her to a couple different events," Gregory countered. "I thought you might be serious about this one."

Serious. Derek let the word play over in his head. He was very serious. Just not about women. Images of two nights ago flashed in his mind: strawberry blond hair falling around him, her legs for miles intertwined with his, her supple bare breasts, fucking until the early morning hours. But that's all it was to him.

"She was a good time," Derek replied, concluding the conversation with a dismissive look that told Gregory the discussion was over.

He turned back to his computer as the iPhone on his desk buzzed again. "Incoming Call: Cynthia." He couldn't help but roll his eyes.

"I'll take it," he said to Gregory when he saw the uncertain look on his assistant's face. Gregory offered a consoling glance, then promptly took the folder and left. "Hello, Cynthia," Derek answered once Gregory had gone.

"Derek," she began, almost breathless, "finally, and just in the nick of time." He waited for more. "I've been trying to reach you, but I suppose you've been too busy running around with that new model girlfriend of yours." He clenched his jaw in irritation, a vein throbbed in his temple. He knew she was trying to bait him. She was well aware that he was not in a relationship, but she just couldn't help herself. Staying silent, he waited, knowing it was best to let her go on and not argue. "Are you?" She asked now quietly. "I saw the tabloids of you two—you and what's her name? Ariel?"

He sighed loudly. "Abigail." He corrected her, losing his patience. "And no, if you need to know, I'm not running around with her. Cynthia, you know I'm busy, is this really why you called?"

"No," she responded curtly. "I actually have a favor to ask you." He smirked.

"If you need me to do something for you, maybe you shouldn't start by insulting me."

"I'm sorry," she replied, sounding sincere, and continued. "Really though, Derek, I don't know why you feel the need to escort a different socialite around town every other night. You know you're seen as a playboy, right? Is that the image you're trying to portray?" A tone of sadness came into her voice, "I know you're not like that."

Feeling perturbed and unwilling to hear a lecture on his social life, he couldn't help the edge to his voice.

"No, Cynthia," he responded coldly. "This is not the brand I'm going for, and my social image is not my top concern. But, as you are well aware, this is my lifestyle. I'm expected to show up at events with a date, and I prefer not to be tied down to any relationship. What I don't understand is why we are talking about this. I don't owe you an explanation, and frankly, darling, this is none of your business." He inhaled slowly, calming his nerves. She was the only one who could rile him. "Do you have something to ask me or not?" She became quiet, backing off.

His words stung.

"Yes," she replied slowly, knowing that he was close to ending the conversation completely. "I have a new client," she started, "the dean of academics at the University of North Carolina. Not only am I doing his house, but he's also hinted that I might be able to do some work for the university as well." As she spoke, excitement rose in her voice.

Derek knew Cynthia loved her job as an interior designer, and she was very talented. "Well," she continued, "I could land the job at the university if…" She trailed off, hesitating to speak further.

"If?" Derek prompted her.

"You see," she continued, "the dean is looking to fill his lecture series on business entrepreneurship. When he found out I was the ex-Mrs. Derek Landino, he practically begged me to ask you to appear."

Derek scoffed. Part of the divorce agreement had been for Cynthia to resume her maiden name of Masterson and give up the Landino name, but he knew she used the angle of her connection to him whenever it was convenient for her. Usually he didn't mind, but this was an annoyance.

"Cynthia. Really?" he replied. "The University of North Carolina? You know this isn't something I would schedule."

"Please, Derek," she begged, "it's just an hourlong lecture at one. You've given plenty of motivational speeches and talks. This wouldn't be any different. Hell, you could probably rattle something off half-asleep!" She took a breath. "Plus, appearing at a smaller university will do good for your brand."

"When?" he asked. There was a brief silence.

"Next Tuesday." she finally said timidly, knowing what his reaction would be.

"Tuesday!" he exclaimed sharply, "are you crazy?" He could practically hear her wincing through the phone. "Cynthia," he said more calmly, reasoning, "there's just no way I can schedule something on such short notice." He heard a slight sigh.

"It's ok, I understand." She sounded defeated now. "I just really needed the work."

He knitted his brow in confusion. "Why?" he asked incredulously, "didn't you make out well enough in the divorce? You shouldn't need to worry financially."

"It's not that," she explained, "it's just that my business isn't doing so well, and I needed to land this client. I just wanted to know that I could make it on my own."

Derek considered this. He understood how that felt, and he respected her feelings of independence. Deciding not to point out that she needed his favor to "make it on her own," he consented to the lecture.

"I'll move some things around." He exhaled, hoping Gregory could work some magic on his already packed schedule.

"Oh my God, Derek!" she shrieked excitedly. "Thank you, thank you! I'll let the dean know."

Derek rubbed his eyes, immediately regretting the decision. "Have them contact Gregory to set it up," he instructed.

He ended the call, then pushed the intercom button on the desk.

"Greg, can you come in here for a second?" A moment later, there was a sharp knock and Gregory reentered. The aftermath of a conversation with the ex-wife was never favorable and usually left Derek in a foul mood. Not daring to pry into the phone exchange, Gregory waited for direction. "I need you to clear Tuesday," Derek told him, clearly annoyed. "The dean of the University of North Carolina will be contacting you about setting up a lecture there."

Gregory blinked at him, attempting to digest the instruction. "Sir, you are canceling two board meetings, lunch with your brother, overseeing the final work on the downtown project, and the charity benefit for a lecture in North Carolina?"

Derek grimaced; he hadn't realized it was that much. "Yes, I committed to it as a favor for a friend." Gregory made a face, knowing that the "friend" was Cynthia.

Derek paced over to the window, knitting his brow. The boards could wait, he decided, and his downtown project manager could handle the last details there; he trusted him. Lunch with Nicola...this was supposed to be a big-brother, get-your-act-together speech he had all planned out. While Derek had built an empire for himself, his younger brother had preferred to live the life of a true playboy, using up his trust fund as well as the other family wealth his mother had left.

Nicola was thirty years old now and needed to grow up. In addition to the obligation he felt as his older brother and the need to preserve what was left of his family legacy, Derek had major motivations for kicking Nicola in the ass to see the light and become a responsible human being.

"Apologize to the boards for me," he said, turning back toward his assistant. "Get Pete on the phone to oversee the details downtown, and reschedule with Nicola as soon as I'm free." His instructions were precise and made with confidence. Gregory nodded, making mental notes.

"What about the charity benefit?" He asked.

"It's at seven p.m.," Derek replied. "The lecture is at one, I can be back in time. Make sure the jet is waiting." He paused, checking off a mental list. "I'll bring the tux with me and prepare on the plane; have the Armani pressed, please. Timing will be crucial, but we can manage."

He closed the lid to his laptop. "I'm calling it," he said, then looked at his watch; 8:00 p.m. Scooping up his computer, he passed Gregory as he walked toward his office door, then stopped, remembering a last-minute detail. "I'll need a date for the benefit, won't I?"

The assistant nodded. "Abigail?" He suggested hopefully.

"Absolutely not," Derek replied quickly. "She's definitely way too attached."

Gregory thought for a moment. "Courtney?"

"Courtney." Derek echoed, placing the name with a face. A pretty face came to his mind—dark eyes and long, dark hair. "The concert violinist," he recalled, remembering their last, and only, date about a month ago, which had also been a good time. She was talented, intelligent, and presented well, and enough time had passed that he felt confident she wasn't attached. "Yes," he said, "go ahead and extend the invitation."

"Sir, are you sure you'll be able to make it back in time for the benefit?" Gregory asked as Derek was about to leave. He shrugged.

"I don't see why not," he replied. "I can't imagine anything that would keep me in North Carolina longer than necessary."

———————◦———————

She smoothed back her long, dark hair, smiling slightly as she indulged in her daydream. Closing her eyes, she thought again of that evening a little over a month ago now. She bit her lip, suppressing a slight giggle. Out of all the women, he had chosen her. From her bedroom in her small apartment in the Upper West Side, she walked into the living area, picking up a recent tabloid from the coffee table. His face was on the cover, a dashing grin for the camera and a beautiful strawberry blonde at his side looking up at him with a much too wide a smile on her face. She reread the headline: "Derek

Landino's New Love Interest?" Smirking, she shook her head as she studied the cover. She felt sorry for the model, who clearly adored him, knowing that she was just a "convenience" for him. *Poor thing*, she thought to herself, *I hope she doesn't think she actually has a chance with him.* She knew in her heart that Derek loved her. After all, they had spent that amazing night together not so long ago.

He had picked her up himself, had not even sent a car for her, and had chosen to escort her to the most wonderful charity gala. She had felt just like a princess, having chosen a beautiful midnight blue formal gown. When they arrived at the gala, the press couldn't get enough of their entrance. As he helped her out of his red LaFerrari, the flashes from the photographers nearly blinded her. She was swept up by the glamour of the experience and loved the attention. Attention she was receiving from the press. But mostly she loved his attention. He was so concerned that she didn't become overwhelmed, so he had wrapped one strong arm around her and quickly ushered her into the event.

After the presentation, there was champagne, a fabulous dinner where more pictures were taken of them together and dancing. He had held her so close, and she could still hear the sweet music, still feel the silky fabric of his tuxedo jacket beneath the palms of her hands, still see his beautiful smile as he looked down on her and the twinkle in his sapphire eyes. "Are you enjoying yourself?" he had asked her softly, near her ear.

"Oh yes," she had answered; the feeling of his arms around her was the most wonderful feeling she had ever known. She knew she had fallen in love, and it felt so perfect being with him.

After the event ended, he drove her home. As they stopped outside her door, he reached for her face with one hand. Bringing her face to his, he placed a soft but firm kiss on her lips. She was awestruck by his affection toward her and could not believe how lucky she was. *Of course*, she told herself as he pulled back from the kiss, *the way he holds me and smiles at me, it is clear we are falling in love.* "Why don't you come in," she whispered.

She raised her eyes up to meet his and bit her lower lip in anticipation. His eyes gleamed, and a wicked grin crossed his face. But his expression quickly became serious.

"I'd like to," he said, narrowing his eyes, "but I must be completely honest with you. I don't have relationships, and I don't get involved. Affairs must remain uncomplicated for me. I travel frequently, and it's not only inconvenient for my work, but it would also not be fair to you." He paused, then added, "You see, my business will always come first. Are you ok with that?"

She nodded. *How sweet that he wants to protect me*, she thought. *He's trying to downplay his feelings so I won't push him away.* She knew she needed to show him that she felt as much for him as he clearly did for her. Yes, this is fast, she knew, but she loved him, and she was certain he loved her too.

She took a deep breath and opened the door to her apartment. Taking his hand, she led him inside. Once they were inside, he immediately pulled her flush against him and kissed her urgently on the lips. His mouth parted open, and he let his tongue find hers, caressing it with his own. The intensity of his kiss rocked her core. She had never known such exhilaration, the feeling reinforcing her love for him and her belief that this was right.

As she continued to reminisce about that night, she thought again of how it felt to have him inside her, owning her completely. Shivers shot through her body as she indulged in the memory, and an aching and longing coming over her. The release she had had with him was in a different league. No man had ever or would ever compare. Afterward, when he smiled at her, she knew he felt the same. He did not stay with her all night. Having spoken of a very early meeting the next day, he had kissed her gently one last time, dressed, and bade her good night. Left alone, she didn't feel dejected. Knowing how important his work was to him, she vowed right then to be patient and understanding. She was sure that he would love her even more for this and appreciate her acceptance of his priorities. She resolved to wait for him. He would come back to her; they would be together again. After all, they loved each other.

Her phone buzzed, bringing her out of her daydreams. She grabbed it quickly in anticipation, as she always did, knowing each time it was him. "Incoming Call: James." Disappointed, she rolled her eyes. She had told James, her colleague at the concert hall, that she was deeply involved with Derek Landino and would not be interested in any invitation out. But at least once a week, he would ask her again. She was annoyed by his persistence, but she did appreciate his friendship, so she took the call.

"Hi, James," she said.

"Hiya, Courtney." James's tone was light and friendly. "Look," he started, "I saw the recent tabloid. I know you must be feeling hurt. After all, I know you thought he was into you. My offer still stands. Why don't you come out with me tonight and have some fun for once?"
Courtney paused confused, then laughed. "Oh really, James!" she exclaimed. "You actually believe that headline?"

"Courtney, look…" he started, but she cut him off.

"I already explained this to you," she said calmly, "he's just protecting me. If he took me to every event, he knows the press would be all over me. He can't let anyone know whom he really loves. Trust me."

"But you haven't even seen him in over a month," James countered slowly and gently. "As a man, I think I can tell you that if I really loved someone, I would make efforts to spend as much time as I could with her."

"He can't, James," Courtney said in defense. "He's too busy to spend all his time with anyone! He has too many obligations, and I admire his ambition. It's what I love most about him, I think. And he knows I would not feel as comfortable in such a spotlight." She paused, thinking again of how protective he had been over her that night at the gala, and she smiled. "He will come see me at first chance."

As she said that last sentence, her phone beeped, indicating she had another call coming through. Holding the phone away so she could glance at the screen, she saw "Incoming Call: Private." A huge smile came to her face, and she couldn't control the excitement in your voice. "I have to let you go,

James!" Not giving him a chance to respond, she clicked to end the current call and accept the incoming one. "Hello?" She answered, attempting to keep an evenness to her tone.

"Ms. Metcalf?" came a cool and professional voice.

"Yes," she responded, curious now.

"This is Gregory McKenzie, the personal assistant of Mr. Derek Landino."

Courtney's heart raced at his words. "Oh! Yes, of course!" She exclaimed, joy running through her body. She just knew it!

Gregory continued. "Mr. Landino would like to extend an invitation to you to join him in attending the Morrison Mercy Foundation charity benefit this coming Tuesday evening. He hopes that you will be available at six-thirty p.m., and this is a formal occasion." The assistant was concise and to the point.

"Yes, of course," Courtney responded quickly. "Derek knows I'd love to join him. I'll be ready at six-thirty."

Gregory raised his eyebrows at her confident response then shook his head slightly, dismissing the comment.

"Thank you very much, Ms. Metcalf; enjoy your day," he responded.

The call clicked off, and Courtney put her phone down slowly, daring to believe that all her waiting and patience was finally going to pay off. Day after day of dreaming about their next time together, and now here it was, only five days away! Unable to control herself, she squealed slightly and fell back onto the sofa, feelings of utter elation passing through her. Her stomach flipped, and she couldn't wait to begin planning her attire for Tuesday. Now she only had to wait five more days until her dreams would come true.

Her spirits now soaring, Courtney picked up her violin from where it was resting next to the side of the couch. Placing it underneath her chin gently, she closed her eyes as she slid her bow across the strings. Letting the sweet music fill her up, she played expertly through a complicated piece she knew well, enjoying both the challenge and her perfect execution. She loved music more than life itself, and her skilled fingertips caressed the strings in a fluid motion as she allowed the melody to take her away to a far off place; a place where she and Derek were together, forever.

Chapter 2

"Christine!" Christine looked up from her mail. She recognized the shriek as the voice of her best friend, colleague, and neighbor, April, who was currently storming through the front door. Christine lived in a small apartment right off the university campus, where she worked as art program director and instructor. April taught art history at the university, but their shared passion for art was where the friends' common interests ended. Christine threw herself into her work and aspired to be a renowned painter. April's hobbies included going to clubs, partying, fashion, and shopping for designer brands she could not afford. April was extremely intelligent, having secured the position of art history professor at a major university, but Christine knew her lively green-eyed, red-haired friend deeply dreamed of the fashion industry and becoming a model and designer.

Regardless of their differences, Christine and April had become fast friends shortly after April had moved to North Carolina from New York City and taken up the position almost two years ago. They lived next door to each other, but April spent most of her time at Christine's. As April preferred to act more like a roommate than a neighbor, Christine was used to her friend's coming and going as she pleased, usually unannounced.

Christine now smiled at April as she burst in, grateful for the distraction from the mail, which included mostly bills.

"Christine, how could you not have told me?" April demanded, waving a blue flyer in the air.

"What is that?" Christine asked curiously. "Where did you get it?"

"It was in your mail," April responded absently, studying the flyer in her hand.

"In my mail?" Christine looked down at the stack of bills, not for one second putting it past her friend to go through her mail. "Then why isn't it *with* my mail, April?" she emphasized, but April didn't respond, continuing to be engrossed in the flyer. Christine shook her head impatiently, "What is it already?"

April finally looked up, her eyes glinting. "Derek Landino is lecturing, here, tomorrow!" She squealed.

Christine tilted her head in thought, frowning slightly. "Oh yeah," she said casually, kind of disappointed in April's news, "I did hear that on Friday." She turned back to her stack of bills.

"Christine," April said as she looked at her incredulously, "aren't you excited? I mean, to see him in person? To hear him speak?" April took a seat next to Christine at the breakfast table, placing the flyer down in front of her. "Aside from being named *People*'s Hottest Man Alive for the last two years," she continued, "he's a self-made billionaire and a powerful philanthropist who's graced the cover of every major business magazine out there." She paused, looking for a reaction from Christine. "I've read his articles. He's very down to earth and motivating. The entire campus is buzzing about his coming here."

Christine looked up at April, expressionless. Of course her friend would be stoked about something like this, but Christine couldn't care less.

April was looking at the flyer again. "I mean," she said, almost to herself, "how did we even secure his booking? He must cost a fortune!"

Christine finally broke into an amused grin. "Are you starting a fan club?" She laughed. *April gets so worked up sometimes*, she thought to herself.

April rose from her seat at the breakfast table, frustrated with Christine's lack of enthusiasm. She rolled her eyes and flopped onto the sofa in Christine's main sitting area just off from the kitchen. She stretched her long, bronzed legs out in front of her.

"Really, Christine?" she called out. "You're not the least bit excited? You're at least going to go to the lecture, right?"

Christine followed her friend into the sitting area, abandoning her bills for the moment. She wrapped the thin cardigan she was wearing more tightly around her body and crossed her arms. "I don't follow the celebrity tabloids, April; I don't care about those things," she stated matter-of-factly. "Besides, I have a class during that time."

Christine really had no interest in celebrities, and that was all she thought of Derek Landino as—a celebrity. She had heard plenty of motivational lectures and felt that if she had heard one, she had heard them all. Why would this one be any different. She supposed the only reason people were excited to see him was just that, to see him. And based on April's reaction, she was guessing that the audience would be mostly female. Christine wrinkled her nose in faint disgust and adjusted her reading glasses. She would not be jumping on that sort of bandwagon of shallowness.

April, however, was very intrigued and determined to make her friend see the light.

"Come on," she said now, as she worked her light red hair up into a ponytail with her hands. "Aren't you curious to know how much of his pictures are photoshopped? Are his eyes really that color or enhanced?" She paused, biting her lower lip, thinking. "Also, you have to have heard the rumors, right?" She said in a sly tone, making Christine raise an eyebrow. "The tabloids are saying it was leaked that he's a prince, as in royalty!"

Christine couldn't help but smirk at her friend's big reveal but recovered quickly when April's excited expression quickly turned to annoyance. She narrowed her eyes at Christine. "And anyway," she continued, "no one will be at your class. Everyone will be at the lecture."

Christine smiled slightly. "We'll see," she replied, taking the seat next to April on the sofa. She folded one leg up underneath her. "Even so, I'm not canceling class so girls can drool over Derek Landino. And as long as one student shows up, it's my job to instruct." She lifted her chin a little in confidence. "And really, April," she added, a completely skeptical look on her face, "a prince? Haven't you ever heard, 'Don't believe everything you read'?"

It was April's turn to smirk and shake her head. "It's no fun being practical all the time, Christine," she said. "I'm canceling my class at that time and going for sure. I think my students will be grateful for the chance to attend."

Christine remained quiet for a moment. Now that April had forced her attention on such frivolous matters, she began to recollect on certain articles. She rested her elbow on her leg and dropped her chin in her hand. "Besides," she said, more thinking aloud than anything, "he escorts around a different socialite every night. One bimbo on his arm after another. What kind of character could he possibly have? Prince Charming? More like playboy."

April eyed Christine keenly, a slow smile forming on her lips. "I thought you said you didn't follow him!" she declared.

Christine's head jerked in April's direction, her hazel eyes flew open wide, and she felt embarrassed heat rising in her cheeks. "I…" she stammered, "I mean, it's difficult not to see it; he's absolutely everywhere," she finally mumbled. A strand of her chestnut hair fell free from her loose bun. She tucked it behind an ear—a nervous habit. Not meeting April's eyes, she stood up promptly and made her way back to the breakfast table and her mail.

April smiled knowingly after Christine. She could read her friend like a book; she was not so immune after all. She rose from the sofa and stepped toward the front door. "I've got to go," she called out.

"Where?"

"I've got to figure out what I'm going to wear tomorrow. You never know—maybe I'll get to actually meet him!"

———◦———

The next day, a little bit after two in the afternoon, Christine stood in her classroom studio frowning at the painting in front of her. She took her work seriously, and oftentimes she became so lost in her art that she was able to completely shut out the world so that nothing existed except her brush and the message it was trying to portray on the canvas. She squinted through her glasses at the strokes. She sighed. Alas, this was not one of those magical moments. She knew she was distracted and looked out at her empty classroom, her frown deepening.

April had been mostly correct. Only one of her students had bothered to show up today for her course. Being an advanced class, it was small, and seven out of the ten students were female. She pursed her lips in annoyance. After she had mentored her one loyal student, Grayson, on his current work, she went ahead and dismissed him early. She then spent the remaining half hour mulling over her own project, simply called *Loneliness*. It was a subtle array of colors in grays, whites, and deep shades of blue. Having mastered the typical landscapes, still lifes, and portraits, Christine now preferred to paint emotions.

Prior to following her heart's desire toward art and painting, Christine had earned a degree in psychology. She understood deep-seated emotions and was intrigued with the inability to identify and communicate complex emotions properly. Art gave her a means of communication, and in painting an intricate and elaborate emotion, Christine was able to marry her knowledge and passion around human psychology with her love for art.

Unfortunately, her concepts and style seemed to go over most heads. Her work was the kind one had to think through, and most wealthy buyers just wanted pretty pictures that matched the colors of their rooms. Her last three exhibits at the local city gallery had bombed, the final one coming with the news that the curator refused to show her work again.

Christine grimaced as she thought of that day. She had been told she was a talented artist with much potential and that if she were to pick a more accepted style with subjects that were understandable, her work would sell. But Christine could not sell out to herself. She wouldn't change what she felt most passionate about and knew to be her calling. *At least I have a day job*, she thought now, the dejected feeling no longer foreign to her.

"Hi, Christine." A knock and a voice brought her from this depressing thought. "Didn't catch the lecture, I see." Christine turned from her piece and smiled warmly at her colleague, Nick. Nick was a humanities professor, and they shared common interests. He had asked her out on several occasions, but Christine just didn't feel anything more than friendship for him. He was attractive, she supposed. He had a boyish grin, short auburn hair, and an athletic build. She had played tennis with him once or twice.

"No, I didn't go," she responded, putting down her paint brush.

Grateful for the interruption, knowing that she lacked inspiration, Christine wiped her hands on her artist's jacket, keeping her clothes safe from stray paint, and placed them in the front pockets. She made her way toward him and noticed a satisfied smile on his face.

"Are you heading to the staff meeting?" he asked. "Shall I walk with you?" She saw him studying her, and she hoped this wasn't another one of his attempts to ask her out, but she decided to give him the benefit of the doubt.

"Ok, sure," she answered. "I'm going that way." He moved to the side to allow her to pass by him into the hallway. "You didn't go to the lecture either?" She asked as they began to walk together.

Nick scoffed. "Are you kidding?" he exclaimed. "I wouldn't be caught dead listening to that arrogant, superficial philanderer."

Christine raised her eyebrows. *Wow,* she thought, *Nick seems pretty passionate about his dislike for Derek Landino.* She eyed him curiously, his face growing slightly red.

As if reading her expression, Nick stopped walking and looked down sheepishly.

"None of my students showed up for my last class," he explained. "I don't feel like this one lecture should take precedents over valuable class time."

Christine nodded; she couldn't help but agree with him as she remembered her own frustration. "I had one whole student," she offered solemnly at first, but then she couldn't help but smile at the ridiculousness of the situation. Nick grinned back, and she burst into laughter. In her efforts to control her laughter, she placed one hand on his shoulder. He smiled broadly at her.

"You have the most beautiful eyes," he said quietly, looking at her intently. "I wish you wouldn't always hide behind those glasses." Christine's smile faded, and she felt immediately awkward. *Why did he always have to cross that line,* she wondered, her previous annoyance returning.

"I wear them so I can work," she replied seriously.

"You're not working now," he countered, trying to hold her gaze. But Christine turned from him, feeling uncomfortable, and continued to walk down the hall, her eyes cast down. Nick fell in step beside her but didn't say anything more.

———————

The thunderous applause was beginning to die down, and Derek could still hear the deafening buzz in the lecture hall where he had just concluded his presentation. Now behind the stage, he looked down at his lecture notes, and feeling confident it had been a success, he tucked them back into his jacket pocket. With Gregory right behind him, he opened the back door to the lecture hall, having been informed previously that this route would be less crowed, and he was hopeful about making a hasty and uneventful exit. Cracking the door open at first to peer into the hallway, he breathed a sigh of relief. There was no one. He stepped out into the hallway and held the door for Gregory.

"Let's get out of here," he said, turning to his assistant. "Make sure the jet is ready. It's already getting late." Gregory nodded and looked down at his smartphone.

"Sir," Gregory began, but a sudden sound of laughter broke the silence and caught Derek's attention. He turned in the direction of the musical laugh coming from the other end of the hallway and noticed a man and a woman standing together, sharing what seemed to be a rather humorous moment.

Dismissing the man completely, Derek zeroed in on the woman, the source of the musical laughter, the sound still ringing in his ears. He watched her as she placed a hand lightly on the man's shoulder in a friendly gesture. Admiring her from afar, he immediately determined that she was beautiful. She had a casual, graceful way of moving, and her smile lit up her face. She was slender and tall—Derek supposed she was around five-eight, even though she had on flats. Her thick, chestnut-brown hair was tied loosely at the base of her neck. Strands kept coming loose, and she tucked them behind one ear. She was wearing what appeared to be a paint-splattered lab coat over a button-up blouse and pencil skirt, and her legs were long, toned, and tan. She had very fine facial features, defined cheekbones, and large eyes behind framed reading glasses. He became fascinated looking at her.

The pair began walking in his direction. Derek stood frozen, and he followed her with his gaze as she walked down the hallway. She had not noticed him; she was looking down now, as if lost in thought, and Derek saw that she was no longer smiling but appeared uncertain or uncomfortable. As they moved closer, she glanced up, and he caught her eye; their gazes locked. Her eyes widened at the sight of him, and her mouth opened slightly in surprise. She missed a step in her stride but recovered and kept walking by him, finally looking away.

It hadn't escaped Derek's attention that the man she was walking with had also noticed him watching her. He caught the glare in his direction, which somewhat amused him. As they passed, the man put his hand on the small of her back to lead her around the corner. Standing by, Gregory had witnessed the encounter.

"Sir," he said again to call his boss's attention back. Derek was still staring at the corner around which she had disappeared, and Gregory could practically see the wheels in his head turning.

"Find out who she is," he said quietly.

"Yes, sir." Gregory left his side quickly and ducked back into the lecture hall, certain that the dean of academics was still there.

Left to his thoughts in the now-empty hallway, Derek couldn't get the woman's face out of his mind. He kept seeing her smile, hearing her laugh—he had to know who she was. Gregory reappeared a moment later.

"Sir, that woman is Ms. Christine Dayne, the art program director here at the university," the assistant reported. "She has been the director here for five years and holds degrees in both fine arts and psychology." He paused. "She is also an aspiring oil painter who seems to specialize in a more modernized style using colors and techniques to express emotions. She lives locally, just off campus."

Derek raised his eyebrows at the information Gregory had rattled off. "The dean told you all of this?" he inquired.

Gregory smiled. "Google," he replied.

Derek chuckled. *Of course*, he thought. "I never aspire to be the smartest man in the room," he said.

"That's why you are the smartest man in the room," his assistant replied faithfully.

Derek smiled at Gregory, appreciative of both his resourcefulness and loyalty. His eyes drifted back to the corner. "I'd like to see her work," he said thoughtfully. "Set up a meeting with her."

Gregory knitted his eyebrows in confusion. "Sir, will there be time?" He glanced at his phone to check the time. "We really need to—"

But Derek cut him off. "Could you do that now please?" he instructed, ignoring the time concern completely.

"Yes, sir," Gregory immediately responded then promptly left Derek's side to follow Christine around the corner, hoping to catch her.

Christine was about to follow Nick into the staff meeting when a tap on her shoulder caused her to pause.

"Excuse me, Ms. Dayne?"

Christine turned to see a young man with wavy brown hair and glasses. He had a pleasant but confident tone and held a smartphone in his hand. "Yes, can I help you?" she asked, curious.

"My name is Gregory McKenzie. I am Mr. Derek Landino's personal assistant." Christine's eyes widened. *So, that* was *Derek Landino in the hallway just now,* she thought. She waited for Gregory to continue, perplexed as to why he was now addressing her. Gregory cleared his throat slightly.

"During Mr. Landino's time here today, he has been very impressed with the university. As you may have heard, he has a very strong interest in the arts, and he wishes to explore the programs here more. In the past he has been known to make very generous charitable contributions to the programs he feels are in need and worthy. Upon inquiring with the dean about who would be the best person to speak with regarding such matters, the dean recommended you, as the program director, of course. Mr. Landino would like to arrange a meeting with you, as well as a tour of the department."

Christine stared at the assistant for a moment, attempting to process what was being said. Derek Landino wanted to meet with her? To discuss a possible donation to her department? She blinked.

"Um, right now?" she asked, glancing toward the meeting, realizing it had already begun.

"At your earliest convenience," Gregory offered, picking up on Christine's hesitation. "However," he added, "I must say that he is flying back to New York this evening. After that, it will be virtually impossible to get back on his schedule." He spoke the last sentence with a finality that told Christine if she wanted to capitalize on this opportunity for the university, it was now or never. Unwilling to be pushed, however, and perturbed at being asked to drop everything on the spot for a meeting, Christine raised her eyebrows slightly. "I must attend this meeting," she replied. "It will be over by three-thirty. I would be more than willing to meet with Mr. Landino at that time if he wishes. He may meet me in my office then."

Gregory pursed his lips; he knew Derek would not be pleased with the counteroffer. However, he had been very adamant that this appointment take place. Gregory wasn't sure yet why, but his boss's mind had been made up about meeting Christine Dayne.

"I feel confident that three-thirty will be acceptable," he replied tensely. He was not used to someone demanding terms. Usually when Derek Landino asked for a meeting, the other party made it happen. "Thank you very much, Ms. Dayne." Gregory then turned to allow Christine to join her conference. He walked back toward Derek, not looking forward to telling him that this meeting he desired would push them back over an hour behind schedule.

———•———

Once the staff meeting was over, April scanned the sea of employees looking for Christine. Spotting her on the other side of the room, already almost to the door, April called out.

"Christine, wait." She pushed her way through the other professors to catch up to her friend. Catching her elbow as they left the meeting room,

April fell into step beside her. "So," she said smiling, "do you want to hear about the lecture?" Christine could hear the eagerness in her voice; April clearly wanted to share her detailed description of Derek Landino. Christine bit her lip and her face flushed.

"Um, I can't right now, April," she said, "I have an appointment in my office." She looked down at her watch. "And I'm already running late." She quickened her pace as she had gotten the impression that Derek did not like to be kept waiting. April matched her stride.

"Who are you meeting with?" she asked, curious.

Christine hesitated and didn't glance at April as she kept walking. "Derek Landino," she said meekly.

April's jaw dropped. She then grabbed Christine by the shoulder and steered her toward the nearest ladies' room, shoving her through the door.

"April!" Christine exclaimed, "What are you doing! I have to—"

"You have to tell me what's going on!" April finished for her, crossing her arms to face Christine.

"He's interested in making a donation to the Art Department," Christine explained. "That's all." She understood her friend's shock and possible jealously, but she didn't have time for this drama right now, and she hoped April wouldn't make a big deal out of the circumstances. After all, she hadn't requested the meeting, and to her it was more of an inconvenience than anything. April was now pacing in the ladies' room.

"I can't believe this," she said, throwing her hands up in exclamation. She suddenly turned to look back at Christine, studying her. "Well," she said in appraisal, "you're not meeting him looking like that." Christine knitted her brows, but before she could even protest, in a matter of seconds, April had ripped the bun loose from her hair, letting her long waves fall around her shoulders. Then she plucked Christine's glasses off her nose, and finally, pulling out a tube of lip gloss, smeared some on her lips.

Christine rolled her eyes. "Ok. Can I go now?" she asked hurriedly. "I'm late."

Trying to stay relaxed, Christine was finding that the more she attempted to maintain her indifference to meeting Derek Landino, the more nervous she became—April wasn't helping either. The image of him standing in the hallway came to her mind, and she cringed as she couldn't keep her stomach from fluttering.

She turned to leave the bathroom, but April still stood in her way. She held out her hand and crossed one arm over her body, giving Christine a pointed look.

"Give it here," she demanded. Christine sighed and removed her artist's jacket, handing it to her friend. "There," April said with a satisfied smile, "now you look presentable. You're gorgeous, Christine. Show it off once in a while."

Christine wanted to point out that how she looked did not and should not matter to any potential investor, but she knew she didn't have time to argue. As she turned to leave, April called after her. "Oh! Find out if he's really a prince."

Christine shook her head but half smiled, knowing full well that April was being completely serious.

She left April in the ladies' room and made her way to her office. She was by now running about ten minutes late. Would he even still be there, she wondered. Hoping that she hadn't blown the opportunity to secure funding for the department, she quickened her pace. If he really was interested in donating, this could be huge for her students. The student gallery was in desperate need of an upgrade.

Approaching her office, she saw Gregory McKenzie standing outside her door. Christine let out of breath of relief; he was still there. Gregory's expression was unreadable, and he didn't smile as she approached. He looked pointedly at his watch with one raised eyebrow, and his gesture was sufficient in expressing his annoyance at her tardiness. She managed an apologetic smile at the assistant but hesitated as she placed a hand to turn the door knob. She inhaled, trying to calm her nerves. Why was she so anxious? Besides, it was her office! Letting her breath out slowly, she opened the door.

"I'm so sorry to have kept you waiting, Mr. Landino," Christine said as she entered the office.

Her office was small and simple. It was furnished with a desk with two chairs facing it. She kept a large bookcase in the corner stocked with books on art of all eras and styles. There were several unfinished pieces in multiple mediums stationed throughout, and specialty homemade items rounded out the decor.

Derek had been standing near her desk peering out the window, and he turned when she entered and addressed him. He did not appear to be angry or annoyed at her timing. Smiling warmly, he extended his hand to her.

"Derek," he offered. She took his hand; it was warm, and his grip was firm. Ignoring the mix of nerves and flutters that ripped through her, she smiled back. Was she imagining it, or did he hold onto her hand a moment too long?

"Christine Dayne," she responded in a professional, polite tone. Now that she saw him up close, she felt very confident that she could answer April's questions: no, his pictures were not photoshopped and yes, his eyes really were that color. His features were flawless—his jaw and cheekbones cut to perfection, his dark brows expressive. He was easily the most handsome man Christine had ever encountered.

Afraid that she might be staring, she turned toward her desk, breaking eye contact with him. Then, shaking her head slightly, she turned back to face him.

"I understand you wish to learn more about the Art Department?" she asked, attempting to appear confident. "Are you interested in investing?"

Derek's smile widened, a dimple appearing on the left side. His smile exhilarated her, and she felt a sudden rush run through her body, her knees giving slightly. "Straight to the point, I see," he replied.

Christine flushed, realizing that discussing money first thing was awkward, most likely rude, that additional pleasantries were more appropriate. However, Derek's manner did not indicate awkwardness at all. He was very relaxed, and it struck Christine that he held meetings and had conversations like this many times a day.

She couldn't help but admire him. His attire was simple and elegant, dark gray tailored slacks, belted low on his narrow waist, and a fitted, black-collared dress shirt that he wore tucked in. He had rolled up the sleeves to a three-quarter length and wore no tie. He was put together and very self-assured, giving Christine the image of a man who knew what he wanted and how to achieve his targets. But her first impression of him had caught her off guard. Expecting arrogance or pompousness, she was rather surprised to find him congenial and approachable.

"Well," he said casually now, "why don't you tell me about the programs here, what the goals are, and I'd very much like to see some of the student's work as well." He smiled as he spoke. "Perhaps you can show me the gallery as we talk?"

Christine nodded. His direction seemed natural, and she almost didn't mind him taking control of the meeting agenda. "Yes, of course," she replied.

As she turned to lead him out of her office, Derek studied her. It hadn't escaped his attention that she had altered her appearance from before. Without her jacket, her curves were more noticeable, and he appreciated her fit, slender form. Her hair fell in loose waves just past her shoulders, and now that she no longer wore her glasses, he noted that she had large hazel eyes—turquoise and warm brown—with thick black lashes framing them. She was feminine yet strong, and he concluded that she was indeed a very stunning woman. As she passed him going into the hall, he caught her scent. The perfume he couldn't place, but he also breathed in a mix of shampoo and coconut. Entranced and anxious to learn more about her, he fell into stride beside her and began asking questions about the university, her position, her career, the classes offered, and the ones she taught. His questions were relevant, not too personal, and brought about much information.

At ease with the safe dialogue, Christine found herself opening up and never felt uncomfortable answering him. She also rather enjoyed following his lead, which she found surprising; he just made it so effortless. As she showed him around the student gallery, she was impressed with his commentary on the artwork. She had been skeptical about his knowledge of art, but proving her wrong, he noted different styles, mediums, and expressions and spoke very intelligently of color and composition. He moved gracefully, studying each piece, his hands placed casually in his pants pockets.

"The work here is very impressive," he said as he admired one of her own student's pieces. "Clearly, the director here must also be extremely talented." He looked directly into her eyes, and Christine felt color rise in her cheeks. She had never been comfortable with compliments.

"Well, I'm not the only instructor," she replied. She couldn't look away from his gaze, and she felt her face grow even hotter. *Why is he looking at me that way*, she wondered, and she saw in his eyes a mixed look of curiosity and admiration. But she knew she had to be imagining it.

"Even so," he said as he turned back to the piece, "this work seems very advanced. You mentioned you instruct the advanced students," he paused, looking back at her, "I'd love to see your work as well."

Christine looked up at him sharply. "My work?" She brushed her hair behind an ear and bit her lower lip. Her work was very personal to her, and frankly, she had experienced such an unfavorable reception to it, she was embarrassed to show it to him. "I'm sorry," she replied, thinking of the one mediocre piece back in her classroom, "my work isn't here at the university. I have a studio at home, and it's all kept there."

Derek appeared thoughtful; a slight frown came across his face. "I don't donate substantially without knowing exactly what I'm investing in," he said seriously. "The personal work of the director is always a very heavy indicator of the strength and talent of the program." He met her eyes. "However," he continued, "I don't mind coming to your studio this evening. You can show me your work then?"

Her eyes opened wide; she was unsure whether she had heard him correctly. She had naturally assumed he was in a hurry to go back to New York. "My studio?" she asked, surprised. "You mean, you wish to come to my apartment?"

"Isn't that where you said you kept your work?" he asked, eyebrows knitted.

Before she could answer him, he stepped closer to her, a grin playing at his lips. Almost invading her personal space, he locked his eyes on hers. "Would you have dinner with me tonight?" His voice was soft and sure. Christine's mouth opened slightly in shock, and she caught her breath. Her mind raced. Incapable of believing that she had just been asked out by Derek Landino, she immediately rejected the idea of any kind of pure motive and responded with the first thing that came to her mind.

"Oh, I see," she said shrewdly, unable to hide her disappointment. "Exactly what are you expecting me to do to secure funding for my department?"

Derek's eyes widened at her assumption. He stared at her for a second, then a moment later, burst into laughter. "I assure you, Ms. Dayne," he said catching his breath, "that your agreement to my dinner invitation has absolutely no bearing on my decision to donate." His eyes twinkled in amusement. "I simply wished to enjoy your company; however, if that makes you uncomfortable, we can just leave it at viewing your work at your studio"—his tone grew serious—"because that is something I would require before investing here. Shall we say seven?"

Christine glanced quickly at the floor, and she felt like kicking herself. Why would she offend him in that way? She didn't know him, and he had been nothing except generous and professional toward her. Coming to a sudden realization that she did indeed want to have dinner with him, she wondered if it was too late to accept. But how could she say so now without further embarrassing herself?

She met his eyes, and he was looking at her expectantly, waiting for her response. Deciding that the moment had passed, she felt she had no choice. "Seven is fine," she replied quietly.

He smiled at her. "Good," he stated, "I will meet you at your studio then." He turned to walk away, then paused. "By the way," he added, looking back at her, "you never answered my question." Christine looked up at him startled, then confused. What did he mean? "Would you have dinner with me tonight?"

She blushed and her stomach flipped. "Um, yes," she responded, exerting great effort to control the evenness of her tone. "Sure."

A satisfied expression came over his face. "In that case," he said, "I will see you at six-thirty." He looked intently into her eyes, then turned and walked out of the gallery.

———•———

Having ignored the buzzing of his phone, Derek now checked it as he made his way back to meet up with Gregory outside the lecture hall. "Missed Calls: 2." The first had been from Mattia (sigh); the second was from Gregory. As he approached his assistant, he saw him pacing, and he appeared extremely anxious. It was already 4:45 p.m.

"Sir, we need to leave now," Gregory said emphatically as Derek walked up to him. "And even then, you'll be arriving late to the benefit. The car is waiting just outside."

Derek seemed thoughtful, a small smile on his face, and he was clearly not concerned about the time.

"Hanger the jet," he instructed simply.

The assistant's jaw dropped. "Sir?"

"I'm staying here this evening," Derek continued. "I'll need you to find me a hotel room and pick up some personal things." He paused. "Also, I'll need a car."

Gregory blinked rapidly, attempting to process the information. "Sir, the car service that picked us up from the airport can take us to a hotel," he explained. "Do you wish me to send notice that you won't be attending the benefit?" He was in disbelief.

"Send my apologies, yes," Derek replied, seemingly unbothered by the disruption of plans. "I'm sure the chief financial officer can represent Land Corporation. Give him a call, will you? Daniel will make a fine presentation."

Derek began walking toward the exit, continuing to think through and relay instructions. "He can have my date too," he continued. "Send word to her as well, please. Explain that Daniel will escort her to the benefit in my place." Gregory matched Derek's stride as he began to make the necessary calls. As they approached the Mercedes, the driver opened Derek's door for him. "I will still need a car," Derek told Gregory after the assistant hung up with the hotel concierge and made his way around to the other side. "Have one sent to the hotel."

Eyeing his boss over the roof of the car, Gregory could no longer maintain his obedience without an explanation.

"Why are you doing this?" He suddenly exclaimed. Derek was missing a key event and most likely important investor contacts. Not to mention meetings that were already scheduled for first thing in the morning. His rash actions could cost millions is lost opportunity. Derek didn't answer but climbed into the back of the car, and Gregory took his place by his side. After a thoughtful silence, looking out the window, Derek replied.

"I have a serious date," he said slowly. Gregory opened his mouth to respond but stopped. Realizing what Derek was saying, a smile crept up onto the assistant's face.

————•————

Gregory secured a swanky, elegant hotel suite in the downtown area near the university. Registering Derek under an assumed name, he offered to reward the concierge handsomely for extreme discretion. As he returned to the suite after running errands necessary to Derek extending his stay in North Carolina, Gregory couldn't help but continue to smile. He had never known Derek to act in this manner. Always schedule-oriented, on time and precise, Derek did not miss appearances or meetings. For anyone. He had a very hands-on way of running his business and preferred to oversee everything himself. He did not cancel important events for a date.

Although Derek was extremely successful due to his ambitious and relentless drive, Gregory knew that his boss's life was lacking. He did not laugh or have fun, unless it was for show. He did not take breaks or vacations. In short, he did not enjoy living. He had built an enterprise of wealth and power and had absolutely no one to share it with. This was sad to Gregory, and more than anything, he wanted to see his boss, mentor, and friend happy and have a sense of fulfillment. For he knew, more than even Derek did, that what Derek truly lacked was purpose. He kept building and working, looking for his purpose. Gregory theorized, however, that Derek had been looking in the wrong places. Until now.

Now entering the hotel suite, he found his boss, arms folded across his chest, looking out the window of the main sitting room, appearing lost in thought.

"Sir, this was all I could find on such short notice," Gregory said as he held up a suit hanger. He had been pleased to find a Brioni. It was not tailored, as was Derek's preference, but Gregory knew which labels would fit him best as is.

Derek turned from the window. "That's fine," he said casually as he checked his watch. "Is the car here?" He took the suit from Gregory and walked toward the bedroom.

"Yes, sir, it's waiting out front. The black Audi A6."

Derek wrinkled his nose. It was not his taste. "I suppose that'll do for just tonight," he replied.

But before Derek could turn away again to change, Gregory spoke again. "Sir, the woman you were to meet tonight to take to the benefit—Courtney" Derek waited for him to continue, and Gregory hesitated. "Well, she didn't exactly take the news of a replacement escort too well. It was a rather uncomfortable conversation, if I'm being completely honest. I think she was crying."

Derek frowned. He was disappointed to hear that someone had taken a broken date hard. It seemed she had been more attached than he had originally thought, and the way this had worked out was clearly for the best. *Well,* he supposed, *she was still going to an exclusive event with Daniel, and Daniel is handsome, rich, and high status. Honestly, she can't be all that distraught.* But he still felt uneasy.

"Remind me to send her a note of apology," he told Gregory, certain that would be more than enough to smooth over any temporary hurt feelings or minor inconvenience.

"Yes, sir," Gregory responded, "as long as I don't have to call her again."

Derek smirked, dismissing any further thought of the matter. "That's why I pay you the big bucks, Greg."

Chapter 3

Christine glanced at her cell to check the time: 6:00 p.m. Having showered and blow-dried and styled the natural waves in her hair so they fell gracefully down her back, she now examined her reflection in the mirror. She had applied a little more makeup than usual, adding eyeliner and lipstick, contouring her already-high cheekbones, and giving her large hazel eyes a smoky evening look replete with burgundies to bring out their natural turquoise. Lucky that she was an artist, Christine thought to herself, and she half smiled at her reflection, pleased with what she saw. As self-doubt got the better of her, her smile faded. Her stomach was a mass of nerves. Why had she thought this was a good idea? She shook her head, knowing that this "date" was pure insanity.

At the time the thought of possibly spending an intimate moment with Derek Landino had been irresistible, but she now regretted the decision, and again she questioned why on earth he would even want to have dinner with her. After all, Derek was Derek. And she was just an average art program director, as well as an unsuccessful painter. As she thought about her work, she wasn't sure what made her more nervous, showing it to him or having dinner with him. If he didn't like her art, as so many others hadn't, she was afraid it would ruin any chance of him contributing to the university.

She took one last glance in the bathroom mirror, and no longer feeling very confident, she pursed her lips and made her way to her closet. Having not yet decided what to wear, Christine had thrown on her bathrobe. Now, as she pushed aside racks of clothes, she realized she didn't have anything near good enough. The only things close to what she was looking for were the Christian Louboutin black stilettos. She pulled them out and slipped them on her feet, the signature red soles having never been scuffed. She had bought the shoes as a present to herself for landing the director position five years ago. She had never purchased anything quite so extravagant, and afraid to wear them, she never had.

She took a few timid steps to attempt walking in the four-inch, thin heels when she heard the front door open. Knowing it was April, she breathed a sigh of relief. Of course April had cornered her after her meeting with Derek and asked for every detail. Shocked but elated to find out that he had asked her to dinner, April had immediately offered her in-person support and assistance. Christine had gratefully agreed to let her friend help her, even if she knew that April had an ulterior motive of meeting him. She was happy to accommodate April and take advantage of her keen fashion sense at the same time. Needing a friend right now, Christine called out to her.

"In the bedroom, April."

April came striding into the room holding a garment bag over her shoulder. "I approve of the shoes, but the dress has got to go."

April smiled at her joke as Christine looked down at her bathrobe. "It's getting late, and I have nothing to wear," she sighed. "I guess I can just wear that skirt and blouse." She gestured toward the attire she had had on earlier, which was now flung across the bed. "After all, I don't even know where he's taking me."

April shook her head and knitted her brow. "Well, you can bet it'll be somewhere elegant, and no," she said, tossing a glance of disgust at the outfit on the bed, "you can't just wear that." She held out the garment bag. "I knew you were going to struggle with this, so I decided to make it easy for you." April opened the bag and displayed a short, black, designer-labeled dress. Christine took the dress and fingered the luxurious fabric. It was simple, tasteful, and sophisticated. The perfect LBD.

"Wow, April," she said, holding it up against her, "this is beautiful, but I don't know that I'd feel comfortable in this."

"It's perfect," April replied decidedly. "Try it on."

Christine took off her robe and stepped into the dress to slide it up her body. "Oh," she said as she examined the dress, "this won't fit me; it's a four. You know I'm a six."

April grinned. "It'll fit," she assured Christine. "You have just the right figure for that dress. Plus, it's completely backless, so the fabric will give a little." April was right—the dress fit Christine like a glove.

Turning now to admire her reflection in the mirror, Christine felt a little more self-assured. The dress was striking. It was modest, with a higher neckline, yet her totally bare back made her look incredibly sexy. *Well*, she thought, *if he's not impressed, at least I tried.*

April studied Christine, as if reading her mind. "He is going to fall over when he sees you," she said with certainty. Christine gave her a small smile. "Do I get to meet him finally?" April suddenly asked, grinning.

"Just don't ask him if he's a prince," Christine responded, a slight roll to her eyes. "Besides, he should be here soon." She glanced at her cell again: 6:25. Would he be on time? She wondered. Would he even show up at all? Maybe she was just fooling herself; the self-doubt creeped back, and the momentary stress-relief that April had provided subsided. Anxiety now flooded through her. She took a deep breath and grabbed her clutch, about to head out of the bedroom.

A knock at the door made Christine catch April's eye. A mix of nerves and excitement shot through her. She gave her friend a look that told her to answer the door, and April nodded without a word and left the bedroom.

Seconds later Christine heard the confident, easy tone of his voice as they exchanged pleasantries. She smiled to herself when she heard April stammer. Even April, ever so cool and collected, couldn't contain herself around Derek Landino. Deciding it was time to make an entrance, Christine opened the door to the bedroom and stepped into the living area. As she attempted to maintain her grace and hold her head up, her nerves got the better of her, and she stumbled slightly in the narrow high heel. Recovering, she worked to keep the smile on her face.

"Good evening." She greeted her guest, clearing her throat slightly.

As she came into the room, Derek looked past April and reached his hand out toward her.

"Hello again, Christine," he replied softly. She took his hand and approached him. He inhaled slowly. "You look absolutely stunning." He beamed at her, the dimple appearing in his left cheek. His eyes glinted as he took in the sight of her. Holding her gaze for several seconds, he let his eyes roam across her face, the beautiful curve of her cheek and jaw down the line of her neck where they rested on her prominent collar bone just visible above the neckline of her dress. Close enough to her, he breathed in her perfume, this time recognizing the Dolce & Gabbana scent. He looked back up into her eyes. Christine noticed him taking her in, but instead of feeling self-conscious, she began to feel flattered, realizing that his praise came with the utmost sincerity. She blushed slightly.

"Thank you," she replied.

She wanted to return his compliment as she admired the way he looked this evening. The solid black suit fit him perfectly, outlining the silhouette of his broad shoulders and chest to his narrow waist and hips. His dress shirt was dark blue, setting off his eyes, and he again wore no tie, keeping the look casual with the collar open, but still he appeared distinguished and sleek. His raven hair was naturally tousled, and although he was clean-shaven, he appeared to have a hint of a five-o'clock shadow.

Struck by how alluring he was, the words caught in her throat. She turned to April. "I see you've met my friend and colleague, April." As Christine looked at April standing by the door, she gave a look that said it was time for her to make her exit. Derek reacknowledged April's presence with a smile.

"It's been my pleasure," he said to her.

"Oh, the pleasure has been mine," April gushed. "As I mentioned, I absolutely loved your lecture today." She paused, as if debating something in her head. "By the way," she started, and Christine's eyes grew wide knowingly and fearful, "are you really a prince?"

"I'll walk you out, April," Christine offered quickly, not allowing Derek to respond to the absurd question. She touched April lightly on the arm and guided her out the door.

Leaving Derek momentarily by himself in the apartment, Christine closed the front door behind them as she stood with April on the porch.

"I can't believe you did that!" Christine quietly hissed at her.

April looked at her with innocence. "What?" She whispered back, "I want to know!" Christine clenched her jaw. "It's none of our business, and it's just a dumb rumor anyway," she replied, "not to mention embarrassing…" she trailed off, fearing now he had a shallow impression of her.

April just smiled. "He couldn't take his eyes off you!" she exclaimed quietly, ignoring Christine's comment. Her smile quickly turned to a frown. "I'm jealous," she said with a slight pout.

Christine gave a small laugh. "Don't be," she said. "You know this is nothing, right? He's here to see my work; hopefully he'll donate to the university, then go back to New York, and I'll never see him again."

April's smile returned. "Never say 'never,'" she said slyly. "I want to know everything later!" she said as she hopped off the porch in the direction of her own apartment. Christine swallowed the last of her nerves, straightened her shoulders and turned to reenter.

"I'm sorry," she said as she opened the door.

Having been left alone in the apartment while Christine bade good night to her friend, Derek had taken the opportunity to glance around. Yearning to know more about her, he took in her preferred decorating style, noticed books she had laying out, and deduced that she was a very organized person. Her furnishings were more shabby chic, and Derek recognized a few key designer pieces that set the tone for the room. However, most of the decor seemed handmade, painted, or refurbished, and it was all very well done, giving the apartment a put-together and elegant look with an artsy twist. There was character, warmth, and a feminine vibe.

He turned to her.

"Not at all," he said as an amused expression crossed his face. "Did she say 'prince'?"

Christine felt flushed. "April's a little dramatic," she explained, a dismissive tone to her voice. "She reads the tabloids." She cast her eyes down, then back up slowly to meet his. Feeling somewhat intrigued, she hoped that he might actually answer the question, and she looked at him expectantly. But Derek's amused expression turned thoughtful, and he changed the subject.

"I made a reservation for us at seven-fifteen, if that suits you," he began. "I thought you could show me your work first."

Her stomach knotted. *This is it*, she thought. Taking a deep breath in, she nodded.

"It's this way," she said, gesturing toward a repurposed barnwood sliding door off the other side of the room.

"You have a nice apartment," he mentioned as he followed her across the room. "I really like that accent table by the sofa, very stylish."

"Oh, that?" she questioned, shrugging slightly. "That's just an old table I found at a local resale shop. I just refinished and painted it."

Derek raised his eyebrows. "It's very nice; it has character," he replied.

"Thank you." *At least he likes something I've done*, she thought.

She paused just before sliding open the barn door adjacent to her work room.

"I must tell you first," she began, "my work is pretty unconventional." Finding it impossible to look at him, she continued. "It's not your typical landscapes, portraits, or even modernist abstraction. I guess I'm trying to create a new style of art, using both the science of psychology and emotional expression…however, it hasn't been too well received." She added the last sentence rather timidly, and Derek could tell she was nervous.

Having done some research on his own, he was aware of her failed attempts to exhibit her work, and her need to explain made him all the more curious. Appreciating that she was extremely anxious and vulnerable but still willing to let him see what she was working on, Derek concluded she was prepared to go to great lengths for her students and her department. This was very personal to her, and he admired her integrity and courage.

Christine held her breath and slid open the door. Stepping to the side, she allowed him to pass her into the studio. She watched him closely as he entered and made his way into the room, afraid of what she might see on his face: disappointment, confusion, surprise? These were all typical reactions to her work. But Derek's face showed none of these; his expression was unreadable as he wandered further into the large, open room. Her paintings were separated in different groupings throughout the studio according to each emotion that she had worked through. Because she had chosen to bring to life complex emotions, each series contained four paintings to summarize a theme.

Standing tense, she waited for him to say something. He observed quietly for several minutes, moving from one series to the next, his eyes studying each piece. She had never before felt so exposed, as if he were using her art to glimpse into her soul. With his silence becoming unbearable, she felt the need to explain more, but she held her tongue, twisting her hands slightly.

Finally, he crossed the room back toward her.

"I *feel* your paintings," he said, looking into her eyes. His face was serious, his eyes narrowed pensively. Christine's heart skipped a beat.

"R...really?" She stammered quietly, her voice catching in her throat. He nodded and turned back toward her first series, which she called *Accomplishment.* She followed him this time toward the paintings.

"When I look at these, the colors, brush strokes and composition," he explained, "I get a sense of worth, excitement and maybe..." he paused thoughtfully, "a thrill of success." He nodded, then turned to the next series. "However, looking here," he continued, "I can't help but feel angry, upset, or discouraged."

Turning from the current painting and gazing back again around the studio, Derek took a mental inventory of all the different emotions expressed: elation, grief, passion, lust, peace, rage, and solitude. Each emotion physically ripping through him as he looked at the works' representation of it.

"Each painting brings back to me a memory of when I felt the emotion it's representing," he said slowly, coming to the startling realization.

Christine stared at him, daring to believe that he understood, that someone understood her vision. Her tense shoulders relaxed a bit, and she felt a wave of relief wash over her. She reminded herself, however, that understanding and liking were two different things. Did he actually "like" her work? Did it show that she was worthy, as art program director, of securing his investment?

Before she could ask, he turned back toward her, interrupting her thoughts.

"You're missing one," he said, locking his eyes on hers.

Now realizing he had been contemplating her last series, which only contained three paintings, her heart rate sped up. "I realize it seems as though this series is unfinished," she explained. "However, I believe the theme here is well represented with three emotions: passion, lust, and devotion."

"You've never been in love," he concluded quietly, not looking away from her.

She inhaled sharply, and her mouth opened slightly in surprise at the personal assumption. As she overcame a momentary loss of words, the scientific part of her brain kicked into life. "I paint emotions," she replied coolly and evenly. "Love is not an emotion."

He raised an eyebrow, and the corner of his mouth tugged upward in a half smile at her response. He was completely mesmerized by her. She was talented, intelligent, strong-willed, and passionate. Not to mention absolutely beautiful. He could not anticipate her next move or what she would say. The unpredictability was not something he was used to, and he had never felt more intrigued or interested.

"We should probably get going," he told her, his face breaking into a full smile. Taking her lightly by the elbow, he escorted her out of the studio and to the front door.

Once they were outside the apartment, Derek led her to the black Audi parked out front.

"What a beautiful car," she stated as he opened her door. She climbed in and after fastening her seatbelt, placed her clutch in her lap.

"It's not my preference," he replied as he took his seat behind the wheel, "but, it'll do for tonight." The engine came to life in a low purr. "You really are beautiful," he repeated, regarding her again with a tempting smile. Christine returned his smile shyly and tucked her hair behind her ear.

As he started to pull the car around, she closed her eyes briefly, again asking herself what on earth she was doing with the most eligible bachelor in the country and why he even wanted to take her out.

"Where are we going?" she asked, glancing in his direction.

"I hope you don't mind the Bellamy Club," he answered. "I was hoping to go somewhere a little bit under the radar." Christine blinked. She had never been to the Bellamy Club. It was terribly exclusive, expensive, and swanky, and really more of a speakeasy than a restaurant. But she had heard that the food was great, and they played live music.

The club was around twenty minutes away, and as they drove, Derek chatted easily with her, asking her more about her classes, students, and interests. He was easy to talk to, and again Christine found herself feeling grateful for his natural ability to take control. Although he put her at ease, she was not feeling bold enough to ask him questions. When he did mention his work in conversation, he was always specifically vague, giving just enough detail without being detailed. The subjects of politics and religion never came up, and Christine realized that even in his public life, he was very careful never to divulge these personal preferences. None of his charitable contributions ever seemed to favor a side or belief. *Why did it matter anyway*, she thought. After tonight she'd never see him again; she didn't need to know what religion he believed in.

Burning to ask him if he was still interested in donating to the art program at the university, Christine kept looking for the right moment in the conversation to bring it up. But it never seemed to come. Not wishing to make the dialogue awkward, she kept quiet. Derek seemed like the kind of man that would say what was on his mind and reveal his intentions when he deemed it necessary. As such, she continued to allow him to direct the conversation.

The car pulled up to the club's valet, and both their doors were immediately opened for them. Derek handed over the keys and quickly stepped around the car to take Christine's hand as she climbed out. As he gently placed her arm through his, they began walking toward the doors.

A quick flash, then another, caught Christine's eye as they neared the entrance. She glanced around, unsure of the source of the bright lights. As she looked back, Derek quickened his pace, staring straight ahead. She had no choice but to keep up with his stride, almost speed walking to do so. She stumbled once in her heel, and he wrapped one arm around her waist to keep her steady on her feet, using his other hand to grab the door handle. Ushering her quickly inside, the maître d' immediately greeted them.

"Mr. Landino, so nice to have you join us this evening," he said professionally. Derek's eyes darted, appearing to look for someone. Then he focused on the manager and nodded curtly, raising one eyebrow at him. Picking up on the urgency, the maître d' cleared his throat. "I will personally escort you to your private table. If you'll follow me please, sir."

Derek's arm dropped, and he grabbed Christine's hand to quickly follow the manager, leading her through several rooms as they headed toward the back. Christine surmised she was being rushed, and not expecting this, she was struggling to digest why she felt like they were running from someone.

Finally arriving at their table in what appeared to be a reserved and exclusive room, the maître d' pulled her chair out for her. She placed her purse on the table to the side and took her seat.

"I apologize," Derek said, taking his place opposite her once the manager had left them. "I should have told you that your picture might be taken tonight." He caught her eye. "Since I wasn't expected to be here, I thought you'd be safe from any press." Christine looked at him in surprise, then understood what was going on. Of course, she thought, paparazzi were most likely following him. It suddenly dawned on her that she would probably appear in some tabloid tomorrow. She was unsure how she felt about this. Meeting his gaze, she could see a worried expression on his face. *Does it bother him?* She thought. His public image was important. How did it look that he was out with some nameless art program director? Feeling self-conscious and small, she dropped her eyes to the table in front of her.

"Christine," he said, "if this bothers you, I will make sure you stay out of any headlines." He reached for his phone in his jacket.

Looking up quickly, she shook her head, not wanting him to feel put out. He didn't need to worry for her sake.

"No," she said. "I mean, I don't think it'll bother me..." she trailed off, then, having decided to ask rather than wonder, she added, "does it bother you?" He placed his phone back in his pocket. His face relaxed, and a grin appeared.

"Normally it does," he said. "Tonight, not so much." He looked at her intently, his smile fading slightly. "You know," he continued, "since my divorce, this is the first time I've been out with someone outside the context of business or some kind of charity event."

Although surprised by this, she was intrigued—it was the first personal comment he had made since she had met him.

"It's nice to be with someone for me," he finished. He held his hand out to her across the small table. The low lighting in the club made his smile more inviting and his eyes bluer. Her heart beating strongly in her throat, she gently placed her hand in his. His hand was warm and smooth as he closed his thumb over the tops of her fingers.

Christine wasn't sure how long she had been staring into his eyes; all she knew was that she wasn't aware of the waiter, who was suddenly standing beside them, having seemingly appeared out of nowhere. The entranced spell she was caught up in broke, and she took her hand back from him. She blinked and looked up at the waiter, who apparently had asked if he could place their order.

"May I make a wine recommendation?" The waiter now asked.

Christine glanced at Derek expectantly. She assumed he would want to choose for them. But Derek was looking at her. Silence followed, and it hit Christine that he was waiting for her to select the wine.

"Oh!" she said, surprised. "Um, how about a semidry Riesling?" She looked from the waiter back to Derek. "Is that ok with you?"

"Whatever you would like," he replied, smiling.

"And for the entree?" The waiter prompted. Again, Christine hesitated. Did he wish to order for them both? She had kind of expected that, considering he appeared to like being in control. But, again, he waited in silence for Christine to choose.

"I've heard the shrimp risotto here is amazing." She passed the waiter her menu. "I'll try that, please."

"Same," Derek added, not taking his eyes off Christine. She got the impression that he was not at all interested in the food and wished the waiter to leave, which he did promptly, also picking up on Derek's nonverbal cues.

The music for the evening was simple live piano. The array of beautiful ballads was expertly played. They were seated in a section of the club that included both dining and a small, intimate dance floor. There were very few other diners in the section with them, and one couple was dancing nearby. Christine could hear only very faint laughing now and again and the tinkling of silverware and glasses clinking along with the sweet, slow melody of the piano. The lighting was low and subdued with lit candles atop crisp, black table linens. Christine felt almost alone with him.

Feeling that the opportune time would never come, she decided that she needed to ask him about the university contribution.

"I'm sorry if this isn't the right time," she said honestly, "but I was curious if you had made a decision regarding your offer to invest in our art program." She forced herself to make eye contact with him as she asked the question, refusing to feel intimidated. Her cheeks were burning hot, and she only hoped that the low lighting camouflaged her blush.

Before Derek could answer, however, the waiter had reappeared to pour the wine. Pouring swiftly, not spilling a drop, he placed both glasses in front of them and again departed. Christine didn't take her glass; she wanted Derek to answer. His eyes glittered in the candlelight, and he finally broke into a full smile.

"Oh, that?" He chuckled softly, waving his hand casually. "Christine, I made that decision the moment I first saw you in the hallway."

Her eyes flew open wide in shock. "What?" She demanded. "What do you mean?"

"It's already done," he responded naturally. "The dean will have the paperwork on his desk in the morning. I'm sure he'll be pleased with you; you were in desperate need of a new gallery." He leaned forward, a thoughtful expression on his face. "Pretty sure the roof had leaked, and your students' work cannot be properly shown with that kind of lighting. I'll see to it a new one is built." He paused, mentally calculating. "I think $20 million should cover it."

Christine gaped at him. She could not believe what he was saying or that he had assessed the state of the gallery in the brief time he was there. *Then what was all this for?* she asked herself.

"Then why—" she began, but he cut her off, looking directly into her eyes.

"I had to meet you," he said softly. Unsure of how to respond, Christine kept quiet. Her mind was racing at his revelation.

Derek picked up his wine glass and held it out toward her. "Saluti." He toasted. She blinked at his choice to toast in Italian, but quickly dismissed the occurrence, picking up her own glass and touching it gently to his, the crystal making a faint ringing.

"Cheers," she replied, noticing that he took a very small sip, then set his glass deliberately out of reach. She frowned. *Maybe he didn't like the selection after all*, she thought.

"Is it too dry for your preference?" She asked.

"No, actually it's quite good," he responded. "I just don't drink."

Christine raised her eyebrows at this news, a skeptical look crossing her face. Of course her preconceived notions of him, like those of most others, included drinking, parties, and maybe even drugs. After all, wasn't that the life of a celebrity? Derek laughed at her expression.

"Don't worry," he said easily, "I'm not a recovering alcoholic or anything like that." He lowered his tone, "I just prefer to stay in control of my senses." He paused as he met her eyes. He held her gaze, and his face turned serious. "Will you dance with me?"

He offered his hand to her again. Mystified, Christine nodded. She took his hand, and he rose, pulling her gently to her feet. Leading her to the dance floor, he positioned himself with her in perfect form.

"I don't really dance well," she admitted nervously.

"It's ok," he said softly, focusing on her face.

He gently held her right hand in his out to the side and placed his other around her lower back. His broad shoulders were set square in precise posture. As he began leading, swaying her gracefully, she was able to follow his moves easily, noting that he danced effortlessly. She was acutely aware of his hand pressed firmly on her bare back, and the feel of his skin on hers heightened her senses, sending shivers running through her.

"You're a beautiful dancer," she said breathily, feeling absolutely entranced.

He smiled. "My mother taught me to dance," he said warmly. Christine smiled back, surprised to find herself enjoying the personal information he volunteered. Almost as if she were unearthing hidden treasures.

As the song ended and another began, he slowed his pace. Continuing to sway, he pulled in her hand, enveloping it as it rested against his chest. Simultaneously, he pressed on her back, bringing her body closer to his, very nearly connecting. He bent his head down to hers, his cheek almost touching hers, his breath near her ear. He was so close, and she felt his warmth. She inhaled deeply, taking in the scent of his aftershave. As she closed her eyes, her mind felt dizzy and her senses were on overdrive. She could dance like this forever, as though she were floating away with him into another world.

Stop this, she suddenly commanded herself, *remember who you're with.* Snapping out of it, she opened her eyes, refusing to be swept away by him.

"I want to see you again," he said suddenly near her ear, his voice low. She pushed back slightly to look at him, a look of bewilderment in her eyes, her brows coming together in confusion. *How can he say that?* she thought.

He gave a half laugh at her expression. "You're right," he smiled, "we should have dinner first." Breaking apart from her, he took her hand again and led her back to their table.

No longer in his arms, Christine felt cold. She hadn't wanted the dance to end, but how could she even begin to allow herself to have real feelings right now? Assuming that this was his way of enchanting every woman he went out with—and she admitted he was very good at it—she knew she needed to stay guarded. She would not become one of his one-night stands.

Derek could tell by Christine's face that she was surprised by his words, and he shared her astonishment, having not planned to say them. But he found himself in uncharted waters now, unsure of his next move. Being with her made him feel reckless, and he had never wanted a woman as much as he wanted her. Yet he knew he needed to refrain from acting on his desires. At least for now.

As they sat back down at the table for dinner, Derek tried to piece together how the rest of the evening should go. *This night should end with me in her bed*, he told himself. Then he should be on a plane first thing in the morning heading back to New York. But looking at her across the table, he just couldn't sell it to himself. He needed more than that. Suddenly, he felt very panicked at the prospect of not seeing her again. Derek didn't panic. *What is she doing to me?* he asked himself.

Realizing that he had been lost in thought for too long, he noticed she was grinning at him, a playful expression on her face. "You appear to be thinking about something very intently," Christine said.

Regaining his composure quickly and pushing all complex thoughts aside, he returned her smile and knew it was time to change the subject. "I'm sorry," he replied. "Won't you tell me where you studied?"

Throughout the rest of the evening, Derek continued his typical effortless chatting. He learned that Christine was originally from Nashville, Tennessee, and she had one sister, Emilia. Her mother had passed away, but her father still lived there. She had studied at Vanderbilt, where she earned degrees in both fine art and psychology. After practicing psychology for a couple of years, she learned that it was not her passion. When the opportunity came to work for the University of North Carolina as an instructor, Christine jumped at the chance to bring art to others. After two years of working as an instructor, she earned the position of director. Through his line of questioning, he was able to piece together that she was thirty-three. He never asked a woman her age, so he had figured out other ways to learn the information.

Derek kept the conversation light and flowing throughout dinner, as they left the club, and during the car ride back to her apartment. Although he listened, took in information, and responded appropriately, questions continued to burn in the back of his mind. *What should I do?* he kept asking himself.

As he pulled up to her apartment and parked the Audi, he made a decision. Having never felt so conflicted, he nonetheless knew this was the right thing to do. He got out of the car and stepped around to open Christine's door. Offering his hand to help her out, he led her back up to her front porch. Tightening his grip on her hand slightly, he stopped on the porch and looked into her eyes.

"Can I see you again?" he asked her quietly. Having debated his next actions carefully, Derek could not accept going back to New York without knowing where this could lead. He had never before experienced the intensity he felt with her, and he was not able to simply walk away and forget her.

Christine knitted her brow at him and frowned, looking confused and almost sad.

"I don't understand," she said. "You're leaving. How can you ask me that?" She paused, as if debating what to say. Derek waited for her to continue. "I'm not a fool, and I don't play games." She finished firmly.

Unable to resist her any longer, he reached for her face with both hands, his fingers just threading through her hair behind her ears. The boldness of his touch left Christine stunned, unable to move or breathe as she searched his eyes.

"Let me be clear." His voice was low, almost a whisper, as he brought her face close to his. "I'm completely captivated by you. I don't know what you're doing to me; all I know is I don't want to go back to New York. So, will you see me again?" he repeated.

Unwilling to fight to keep her resolve any longer, she let her guard drop. As she nodded slowly in answer to his question, he placed his lips on hers, barely grazing them at first, then pressing against her mouth firmly. An exhilaration ripped through her and down her spine as he kissed her. Her mind was racing so fast, and the only thought she was able to put together was how good he felt. His mouth parted hers slightly, and he let his tongue sensually find hers. No longer concerned with the consequences, she returned his kiss eagerly, wrapping her arms around his torso and up his strong back to pull him in more tightly to her.

Derek knew in an instant that if he wanted to, he would have received no objection to pushing her into the apartment and throwing her onto the nearest soft surface. His body moved instinctively to do just that but he caught himself, halting the urge. *No*, he told himself, *not now. Don't ruin this.* Instead, he pulled back from her slightly, ending the kiss good night. Continuing to cradle her face in his hands, he brushed one thumb lightly over her lips. A smoldering smile came across his face as he looked into her eyes.

"Paint that," he said. Then he turned away from her and placing his hands in his pockets, walked back to the car. He flashed her one last smile before climbing in and driving away.

Dazed, a wave of emotions running through her, Christine stared after him until he was gone. Her lips were still tingling, and her heart was pounding in her ears. Turning slowly, she opened her front door and entered. She was suddenly feeling very drained and fatigued. Walking in, she wasn't at all surprised to see April sitting at the breakfast table waiting up for her. She got the impression that her friend knew what had transpired on the porch, and Christine walked over collapsing into the chair next to her.

"So," April began, "when is Prince Charming going to call you?"

Christine's eyes flew open at the obvious question that she hadn't even considered asking. Her heart fell. "I don't know," she answered slowly with heavy realization.

Chapter 4

Courtney slammed her apartment door shut. Daniel had just dropped her off following the charity benefit, and having refused to allow him to walk her to her door, she had exited the limo as soon as it had pulled up without even a goodbye. She decided that this had to be the worst night of her life, and tears stung her eyes again. She had never cried as much as she had today—and crying was totally unlike her.

She thought back on the evening and what it should have been. Hoping that the caller who had told her Derek was sending a replacement had been mistaken, she had prepared for the event only to be crestfallen when that other man had gotten out of the limo to pick her up. Confused and hurt, she knew she had to find out what had happened to Derek, so she had agreed to go to the event with Daniel. After all, there had to be a good explanation as to why he wasn't coming; was he hurt or ill? But Daniel wouldn't tell her why and just kept repeating that he was "detained" or he had "another engagement."

However, Courtney knew full well that Derek would not have passed her over for another priority. Not tonight. Infuriated by Daniel's dismissive attitude toward the situation, Courtney had refused to speak to him.

"You could have at least made conversation with some of the investors," he told her once they were back in the limo after the event. "I don't know why you even agreed to come; you clearly made up your mind not to enjoy yourself." He sighed, taking in her long hair, slender figure, and form-fitting gown. "It's too bad," he continued, "we could have had a good time."

After his remark Courtney finally responded. "With *you*?" She sneered. "You don't compare to Derek, and he knows I'll always be true to him." She paused, desperate to learn his whereabouts. "Why can't you just tell me what happened to him?" She pleaded.

Daniel rolled his eyes at her. "How many times do I have to tell you?" he said impatiently. "He decided on another engagement this evening. He's not even in the state right now!" Seeing the devastated look on her face, and though he had surmised she was crazy, he took a bit of pity on her. "Look," he said more calmly, "I don't know what you were thinking, but this is common for Derek." He reached over to pat her shoulder, but she flinched away from him. "He has many engagements," Daniel explained, "many business dealings, and he just can't make them all. As long as Land Corporation is represented well, he will send a replacement when necessary." He caught her eye as she finally looked at him. "You're just the escort," he added.

Courtney remained silent; she knew that this was just what Daniel had to say, the "rehearsed speech" he had most likely given to dozens of other women. But she was different. Daniel just didn't understand that. The limo had pulled up to her apartment then, and Courtney had gotten out as fast as she could without even giving Daniel a last glance.

Now in her apartment, she ripped off the peach satin gown she had chosen to wear for her magical evening and threw herself on the bed sobbing. She grabbed a pillow, and holding it close to her body, she cried until her head was pounding in pain. Her face tear-stained, she reached for her phone to check the news tabloids for what seemed like the hundredth time for any update on what had happened to him. Surely, something had to be coming through any time now stating that he had been in an accident or something. She knew he had traveled to North Carolina that day; there was news about the lecture he was giving at the university. But that was the last thing that any tabloid had reported. They just hadn't reported anything yet, she thought. Attempting to calm down and pull herself together, she convinced herself that she'd know everything by tomorrow. Maybe he would even call her and apologize, rescheduling their time together. She smiled weakly at the thought.

———◇———

"Really, Greg, it was easily the worst date I have ever had." Gregory was in the main sitting area of the hotel suite simultaneously making calls and working off a laptop. Trying to keep up with reschedules, conflicts, arising questions, and delegating now urgently needed leadership tasks, he found himself on the other end of an awkward conversation with Land Corporation's chief financial officer, Daniel.

"I'm sorry to hear that, Daniel," he responded. "You know Derek is very particular about his escorts for important appearances. I'm sure he would not have recommended Ms. Metcalf if he had had any knowledge of that kind of behavior." He turned the phone on speaker and placed it on the table. As he listened, he continued to labor at the keyboard, sending notice to one of the project managers.

"I know, Greg, and I don't know what her deal was, honestly," Daniel replied. "The moment the limo arrived and picked her up, she was moody, wouldn't talk to me, and kept her arms crossed." He sighed heavily. "Really, I don't know why she agreed to go! She kept asking me about Derek—was he ok, was he in the hospital, what had kept him from coming. Almost as if she couldn't believe that he just simply chose a different engagement and couldn't make it…" Daniel trailed off and paused. "I think the girl's a bit unhinged, Greg. You might want to consider that she could be a stalker for him down the road."

"Thank you for the information, Daniel," Gregory replied. "I'll make sure Derek is aware. By the way, how did everything go at the benefit, given the circumstances?"

"Oh, it was fine," Daniel said confidently. "I gave the presentation. My date didn't do anything to charm anyone, so no new leads for future investors or connections from that, but I was able to do some valuable networking."

"That's good to hear, at least," Gregory said. He glanced toward the suite door at the sound of a key. "I will touch base with you tomorrow, Daniel. Good night." He ended the call just as Derek walked through the hotel door.

Surprised to see him at all this evening, Gregory checked his phone for the time: 11:15 p.m. Feeling disappointed, he assumed that the date had not gone well.

"I didn't expect you, sir," Gregory said. Derek walked into the sitting area and took off his jacket, his expression pensive. Placing the jacket over the back of the chair, he sat opposite his assistant. He didn't respond to Gregory's comment, his mind attempting to digest the evening and how he felt about it.

Gregory waited for a reply, and feeling the need to know what had transpired, he fished for more information.

"I trust dinner was good?" he asked. "The venue was satisfactory?"

Knowing what his assistant was up to, Derek narrowed his eyes at him slightly, but then half smiled. If anyone knew Derek's typical habits, it was his assistant. He assumed Gregory would not have expected him back until at least 3:00 a.m., after having spent most of the night with his date. Not that he slept with every woman he went out with, but it was clear to both men that Christine had captured Derek's attention and interest. Deciding to not let Gregory suffer any longer, Derek responded.

"Yes, dinner and the venue were perfectly fine," he said. "In fact," he continued, "since you're still up, I need you to take care of a couple of things."

Gregory raised his eyebrows in curiosity.

Having made the decision to stay near Christine until he knew where their relationship would lead, Derek now needed to figure out some details as to how. "I can't drive that Audi any longer," he started. "Can you have my car brought down, please?" Gregory gaped at him. Derek didn't trust anyone else to drive the $4 million 2016 LaFerrari.

"I will make the arrangements," Gregory replied, knitting his brow. "You are intending to stay in North Carolina then, sir?"

"Yes, I think so," Derek said slowly. "I think I'm due for a break." As he said the words, they felt very foreign to him, and a wave of guilt threatened to flood him.

He looked at his assistant, and he could tell that Gregory's mind was racing through the schedule, the meetings, the investors, the projects, and the lost time and money a delay would cause. But then he remembered Christine's laugh. Her smile, and those eyes. Suddenly the guilt vanished, and he knew he was where he needed to be. He smiled at the thought.

"It's ok, Greg," he said calmly, "I will reschedule what's necessary." He rose from the chair and strolled over to the window, looking out onto the balcony. "But I can't continue to stay at this hotel," he added. "The press knows I'm here; they followed us to dinner tonight." He pulled the curtains shut and scowled. "So much for the discretion of the concierge." He turned back to Gregory.

"I can find us another hotel," the assistant offered, attempting to wrap his head around this massive shift in immediate plans.

"No," Derek said firmly, "no more hotels. I cannot completely stop working, you know that, but I need to be able to free up some of my time while still keeping an eye on things remotely and securely." A thought occurring to him, he looked sharply at Gregory. "Where's the yacht?" he asked.

Following his train of thought, Gregory understood what Derek wanted-ed. Yes, the yacht would be a viable solution that provided security and freedom, a floating office, and Derek could stay as long as he liked. Realizing where the yacht was, Gregory frowned.

"It's in Florida," he said. "It would take a couple of days to get it here."

Derek was quiet for a moment, then made a decision. He didn't want to wait.

"Buy a new one," he said.

"A new one, sir?" Gregory asked in astonishment. Derek was acting very reckless, and he looked at it as part of his job to question unnecessary, costly decisions. "That's about ten million dollars in expenses that's not really necessary."

"I will determine what is necessary," Derek replied firmly, meeting Gregory's eye. His tone told Gregory additional questions were futile and the decision had been made. "I'll call the marina personally first thing in the morning," he stated. "You just get my car down here." Gregory nodded.

Derek walked back toward the sitting area and picked up his jacket from the chair.

"Call Christine tonight, please," he said, smiling to himself. He had deliberately not told her when to expect his call. Not being sure of what arrangements he needed to make at the time, he was unwilling to make any commitments. He knew, however, that she was most likely wondering. Not wanting to make her feel anxious, and impatient to see her again anyway, he wanted her to hear from him sooner rather than later. "Ask her if she'll come to the marina tomorrow, say one?" he continued. "You can pick her up. I'm reluctant right now to go back to her place. I don't want the press following me there. Take the Audi." Leaving Gregory to make the call, Derek headed to the bedroom to change.

Gregory stared after his boss for a moment, amazed at both the decisions being made and the swift manner in which they had come about. Derek was making major changes to his entire life for a woman he had just met. Seeing that it was clear the call was to be made now, Gregory picked up his phone, disregarding his instinct that it was much too late in the night, and prepared to dial Christine's number.

ACE BRYANN

It was 11:30 p.m., and Christine was still sitting in her breakfast area with April. Having filled her friend in on most of the evening, Christine now poured out her concerns that she would never hear from him again.

"I feel like such a fool," she told April. "I played right into him. But he seemed so sincere…" she trailed off, not meeting April's eyes.

"Christine, you don't know that he won't call you," April replied comforting her.

As soon as the words left her mouth, Christine's phone vibrated on the table. Curious, she picked it up. Who would be calling at this hour, she wondered. The screen read, "Incoming Call: Private." She gave April a puzzled expression and answered the call.

"Hello?" she asked.

"Hello, Ms. Dayne?" Christine recognized the polite voice of Derek's assistant. "This is Gregory McKenzie; I trust you remember who I am?"

Her heart rate increased. "Yes," she replied, keeping her tone even, "I remember you, Mr. McKenzie."

"Gregory." he corrected her. "Mr. Landino hopes you will join him tomorrow at one at the marina."

Christine's mouth opened in surprise. "Um, can you hold for a moment, please?" She staggered. Placing her hand over the phone, she looked at April. "He wants me to go with him to the marina tomorrow," she whispered.

"Go." April mouthed the word emphatically back at her.

"How?" Christine hissed. "I have classes tomorrow!"

April rolled her eyes dramatically. "Go!" she mouthed again, giving Christine an astonished look.

Christine took her hand off the phone. "I'm so sorry about that," she told Gregory. "I'd be happy to join him." She looked at April, who was now smiling triumphantly. Christine felt guilty knowing she'd have to cancel or find another instructor for her classes, but excitement at the thought of seeing Derek again soon took over.

"Excellent," Gregory replied. "Mr. Landino has asked that I escort you to the marina to meet him as he will be busy tomorrow morning. I don't know if sailing is possible yet, but you may want to dress accordingly and bring a swimsuit with you as well. I will see you at twelve-forty-five tomorrow, Ms. Dayne."

"Um, Christine." She corrected him in turn.

"Good night, Christine," Gregory said as he ended the call. He smiled as he put down his cell, and although this change in plans was stressful, he approved of Derek's choices.

Having changed into just a pair of gray flannel pajama pants, Derek walked back into the main area. Placing his hands in his pockets, he looked at Gregory with expectation.

"She's coming." The assistant reassured him. Derek smiled appreciatively, and Gregory could see the relief on his face. "Derek," Gregory suddenly called after him as he was about to return to the bedroom. Derek turned around. He knew Gregory was about to ask him something personal. He always did when he addressed him informally. "You like her," Gregory stated. "You've gone to great lengths, not to mention expense, to stay here and see her again."

Derek remained silent, waiting for Gregory to continue, expecting the third degree on schedules, irrational costs, or deadlines. Not wishing to explain yet what he was feeling or why he was doing what he was doing, he gave Gregory a poker face in anticipation of the next question.

"Why are you here now instead of with her?" he asked Derek finally.

Out of all the questions Gregory could have asked him, he had decided on the most difficult to answer. Derek wandered back over to the chair opposite Gregory and sat down. Folding his hands in front of him casually, his elbows resting on his knees, he looked at the floor.

"I don't want to ruin this," he answered after several seconds. "I mean, whatever this is." He looked up at Gregory. "I've never felt this way before, and I've never wanted someone so bad in my life." He paused, glancing at his hands. "But I wouldn't dare go there, not until…" he stopped.

"Until what?" Gregory prompted him.

Derek thought of how to answer. "Until I'm ready," he concluded.

Gregory nodded in understanding. "Good night, sir," he said.

Derek rose, gave a wave along with a yawn, and retired back to the bedroom, closing the door.

———◦———

Gregory pulled up to Christine's apartment at exactly 12:45 p.m. the following day. Recognizing the black Audi, Christine walked out to greet him. Unsure if the butterflies in her stomach were nerves or excitement, she tightened her grip on her tote bag and smoothed the folds of her dress. She had again begged April to help her find the right outfit to wear. April had selected a flowing, yellow maxi sundress in a large floral print, assuring Christine that the color matched her skin tone perfectly. Although Christine felt that April had also chosen the dress for its thin spaghetti straps and low neckline. But the fabric was breezy and flattering, so Christine had agreed to the recommendation.

Fighting to stay confident, she smiled at Gregory, who stood outside next to the car. He returned her smile and opened her door.

"Hello, Christine. I'm sorry Derek isn't here personally," he said as she climbed in. "He had some matters to attend to this morning." Shaking his head slightly with a smirk as he walked to the driver's side, Gregory knew that those "matters" included finding, buying, and preparing a yacht with a small crew. Due to the expedited nature of the situation, the whole affair ended up costing closer to $15 million, which made Gregory's stomach lurch, and he made Derek personally call Daniel to tell him the unpleasant news, claiming that no, Derek did not pay him enough. However, Derek had consented to selling the current yacht in Florida. It wouldn't be a wash, but at least the net cost would be sustainable.

Spending money freely was not in Derek's nature. He invested only in what would benefit and turn a profit, and he had an uncanny knack for always choosing the right ventures. Considering his choices as of late, Gregory could only deduce that Derek had decided to invest in Christine. Or maybe, Gregory realized, he was finally investing in himself.

As Gregory drove her the short distance to the marina, Christine found herself conflicted. She had agreed to this "second date" without thinking it through. Having tossed and turned most of the night, she almost regretted accepting the invitation and had even thought about calling it off. Yet she had realized that she had no means of contacting Derek and so had no choice but to proceed.

She had come to the conclusion that the only thing he could possibly want from her was a casual fling, and the sheer possibility of that kept her intrigued but also scared. Scared because the truth was she liked him. She liked him far more than she felt she should. Scared because she was not the one-night stand type and this could only end one way for her—painfully. She knew, however, that even if she had thought through seeing him again more carefully, she would not have made a different decision. She was drawn to him like a magnet, and she almost hated herself for it.

Not knowing that she was battling her emotions internally, Gregory talked freely with her, choosing easy topics and simple pleasantries. Christine hadn't been sure what to expect from being with the assistant, and after their first encounter, she wasn't sure what he thought of her. But Gregory was very relaxed and smiled at her, which put her more at ease. As they pulled up to the private dock and parked the car, he suddenly turned to her.

"Christine," he started, "I've known Derek a long time now. I want you to know that I think you're good for him." He said the words slowly, as if debating if he should be saying them. Christine gave him a perplexed look, unsure of how to respond. What did he mean? "I've never seen him like this," Gregory continued, now gripping the wheel and staring out the windshield of the car. "It's a good change." He said the last words seemingly more to himself, and Christine looked out too and noticed they were parked in front of a large yacht. Gregory glanced at her, smiled, and proceeded to exit the car.

Looking around as Gregory held the door open for her, she noticed a beautiful red sports car also parked in front of the luxurious yacht. Realizing they were headed to the superyacht, Christine couldn't help but feel way in over her head, and a sinking feeling dropped in the pit of her stomach, her nerves almost making her feel sick. Noticing that she had turned a bit pale, Gregory eyed her curiously.

"Are you ok, Christine?" He asked with concern.

Embarrassed, Christine forced a smile at him. "I'm fine," she almost choked. Taking a breath to calm herself, she gestured to the car, wishing to take his attention from her. "Is that a Ferrari?"

Gregory turned. "It's a LaFerrari, actually." He corrected her. "It's a limited edition."

"It's his, isn't it?" she asked quietly.

Gregory nodded. "Yes. He had it brought down here this morning," he replied, then smirked. "He didn't care for the Audi."

Who would, compared to that, Christine thought to herself. "It suits him," she remarked under her breath.

Gregory started walking toward the yacht.

"If you'll follow me, please, Christine," he said as he led her to the gangway. "Derek should be waiting for you on deck."

She felt overwhelmed, and refusing to let it engulf her, Christine followed Gregory in silence.

"This is really beautiful," she murmured in awe once they had boarded. She had never been on a yacht before, but she knew there were different varieties and sizes. Since this was as superyacht, no expense nor luxury had been spared, and it rivaled the feel and amenities of a small cruise ship. The colors and decor consisted of muted earth tones with splashes of dark blue. As she passed through the interior, she saw cozy, cushioned sitting areas and an electric fireplace.

After they had climbed a flight of stairs up one deck, Gregory led her toward the stern of the vessel. They walked through a door that opened up onto a large deck with a welcoming sitting area that overlooked the ocean off the very back of the boat. She saw Derek by the rail, his back toward them as he faced the ocean. As they approached, Christine heard he was talking on the phone to someone. But it wasn't in English. It appeared he was speaking in perfect, rapid Italian—however, not knowing the language, Christine wasn't sure. She felt awkward walking in on his conversation, and she glanced at Gregory, who had a concerned look on his face. Clearly, this was not an opportune time.

Derek turned then, and having seen them enter, he spoke one more quick sentence and ended the call. Now walking toward them with a smile, he reached out for Christine's hand.

"Thank you for joining me today," he said to her. Turning to Gregory, he greeted his assistant. "Greg, why don't you take Christine's bag to one of the state rooms."

Christine looked at him in surprise. "State room?" she asked.

Derek nodded. "In case you'd like to change later," he replied simply. "I haven't tried out the pool yet. I thought we could go for a swim?"

"Of course," she responded.

Derek looked back at Gregory. "Thanks, Greg." It was a polite acknowledgment and also a dismissal. Gregory glanced at Christine, gave her a smile, then left as she handed him her tote bag.

Christine turned back toward Derek; the way he smiled at her made her shiver. He motioned toward the seating area.

"I had a spread brought up," he said, not taking his eyes off her. "Have you eaten yet?" Her mind only on the kiss they had shared last night, Christine tore her gaze away from his to the low table in front of the sectional. It was covered in a beautiful charcuterie display with different meats, cheeses, breads, and fruits. It was meant to be an informal luncheon, yet it was still elegant and impressive. Having been too nervous to eat that morning, Christine realized that she was indeed hungry.

"Excuse me, Mr. Landino?"

Derek turned at the interruption to a man who had appeared on the deck through the same door through which she and Gregory had entered. "The captain needs a quick word, sir," the man said, his tone sounding urgent.

Derek nodded, then turned to Christine. "Please," he said, "sit down and help yourself. I should only be a moment."

Christine took a seat and watched as he strode over to the man who had addressed him. She assumed he was a member of the crew, and soon another man—seemingly the captain—joined their conversation. As she watched from afar, she couldn't help but admire Derek's stature and his commanding yet casual presence. He was dressed down today, and she enjoyed his more relaxed attire, which consisted of a sky-blue button-up shirt paired with linen khaki pants. His shirt was made from an airy fabric, and he wore it untucked, with the sleeves rolled up, which seemed to be his signature style. His constantly tousled hair and soft brown loafers completed the image of a man who belonged on a yacht out at sea.

Realizing that she had been watching him too long, she looked back toward the table and selected a piece of cheese. Nibbling it, the solid food helping to calm her nerves a little, she looked out over the ocean. The water was a beautiful deep blue, and sailboats and other yachts dotted the horizon in the afternoon sun. There was a slight breeze that ruffled her hair, but it was warm and relaxing. It was a perfect day, and although Christine had been to the coast numerous times before, she couldn't recall appreciating the beauty or peacefulness of it as much before. Even if her time with Derek was short-lived and ended painfully, at least she could enjoy being here now.

Reaching over to take a piece of fruit, she noticed a tabloid sitting on the table next to the spread. Her eyes opened wide as she saw that the front page had her picture on it. Picking up the tabloid, she stared at the picture in shock. Christine remembered the moment the photo had been snapped, and she shook her head in disbelief. It was while they were dancing; they had been captured looking into each other's eyes. They were close; he was holding her hand against his chest. It was the exact moment at which she had looked at him after he had said he wanted to see her again. She narrowed her eyes, inspecting the expression on his face in the photo. He looked genuine, sincere. Confused, she set the tabloid in her lap and scanned it.

By now Derek had ended his conversation and was walking back to her. He took a seat next to her, and having noticed what she was looking at, he waited for her reaction.

"Derek Landino Seen With Pretty Art Program Director After Lecture," the headline read. Having read through the article, Christine saw that her actual name was not even mentioned. Instead of feeling relieved, however, she felt uneasy. She was not anywhere near his league, and she didn't belong with him. She placed the article back on the table and slowly lifted her eyes to meet his.

"I'm sorry," she said quietly. "I'm sure you're not ok with this."

He knitted his brow, his gaze intense. "Of course I'm not ok with it," he said, watching her closely. He leaned toward her and touched her cheek lightly. "You're so much more than 'pretty.'" He let his hand caress her face, then he brushed aside a stray strand of her hair, tucking it safely behind her ear. His touch made her heart race, and suddenly, giving in to her desires, she wanted nothing else in the world except for him to kiss her again.

Letting the moment pass, Derek looked away from her to reach across the table. "How about some wine with lunch?" he asked, handing her a glass. "Semidry Riesling? I think you'll find this to be a very good vintage."

Feeling slightly disappointed, Christine took the glass from him. Holding up his own glass, he clinked hers lightly in a toast, took a small sip, then set his glass to the side away from him.

"So you really don't drink at all?" she asked; it still struck her as funny. He shook his head, smiling.

"No," he replied. "I've seen too many bad decisions made because someone lost control." Christine thought about his response for a moment. She had drunk plenty, but she had yet to make any real devastating decisions because of it.

"Are you afraid that you'd lose control?" she countered, interested in his response.

"I have yet to lose control," he replied simply, seeming slightly amused by her question. "I see no reason to ever tempt that." He shrugged. "It's just not something I feel I need."

She raised her eyebrows at his explanation, taking a sip of her own wine. It really was delicious, one of the best she'd ever tried. She was always appreciative of a good Riesling. And it suddenly dawned on her that there was a reason he knew of her favorite; he had simply asked her to choose last night at dinner. The simple cleverness of the move made Christine uneasy, and she felt again the need to guard herself, vowing that she would also not be losing control.

Throughout lunch Derek noted that Christine seemed quiet, reserved. Setting down a napkin, he stood and offered her his hand.

"Would you like to walk around?" She accepted his hand, and he pulled her to her feet. Placing her arm through his, he escorted her to the deck, leading her toward the bow. As they walked along the starboard rail together, Christine slid her hand along the smooth surface of the wood, thinking again how beautiful the boat was. She stopped when she heard the engines kick into life and felt a small lurch.

"Oh, we're moving," she said, startled. She really hadn't expected that they would actually be going anywhere.

"You don't mind a short cruise, do you?" Derek asked.

She hadn't really given much thought to how much time she would be spending with him today. Thankfully, she had had the foresight to secure a substitute for all of her classes.

"As long as you get me home by a decent hour," she teased, smiling playfully at him. Truth be told, the thought of being secluded with him aboard his yacht out on the ocean exhilarated her.

He returned her smile.

"What do you consider decent?" He winked at her, and not expecting an answer, he turned to look out over the water as the yacht pulled away from the docks.

Christine studied him for a moment, the breeze fluttering his shirt and hair. Feeling brave, she decided to ask him about the phone call she and Gregory had walked in on.

"I didn't know you spoke Italian," she offered. Derek didn't respond or turn to look at her, and she could tell he was pondering something. "Actually," she continued, "was that Italian?"

Still looking ahead, he finally answered her. "It was Calean, a dialect of Italian," he said truthfully.

Christine looked confused. She had never heard of it before. "You must pick up languages pretty easily," she observed. "You spoke it very well. But that seems a rather odd language to learn," she paused. "Why not simply study Italian?" He turned to finally face her, his expression appearing a bit defeated.

Looking at his face, Christine feared she had overstepped. She opened her mouth to apologize, but he spoke first.

"Calean is my native language," he said, having made the decision to share certain information with her.

Christine stared at him. "You're not American?" she asked incredulously. She had never considered that he was from a foreign country; his English was perfect, and he held no trace of any accent.

Derek frowned. "Of course I'm an American," he replied quickly, honoring his love for the United States. In response to her perplexed expression, he explained further. "I hold dual citizenship," he shared. "I moved to the United States when I was barely four years old, but I was born in the European microstate Calina."

"I've never heard of Calina," Christine said thoughtfully. "What about your family?" she asked, attempting to take advantage of him finally opening up to her. "Do they still live there?" He leaned against the rail.

"It's just me and Nicola," he replied. "We moved here with our mother, but she passed away when I was twenty."

Christine remembered the expression of fondness on his face when he had spoken of his mother the night prior. He must have been close with her, she thought.

"I'm sorry," she said softly. "And your father?"

Derek hesitated and quickly affected a slight grimace on his face. "He died in Calina," he stated.

Christine could tell he wanted to say more, but he didn't, and she knew it was best to not ask further. She turned to watch the waves as the yacht moved effortlessly, the sunlight dancing off the ripples in the water. She could smell the fresh scent of the ocean and enjoyed the wind blowing her hair.

"It's glorious out here today," he said now, changing the subject, as if reading her mind. He caught her eye and smiled warmly.

She nodded her agreement. "Yes, and it's a beautiful yacht," she added. "You mentioned you haven't tried the pool?" She paused, thinking. "How long have you had it?"

Derek glanced at his watch. "About four hours," he replied. "I think she'll do."

Christine wasn't sure if the appropriate response was to laugh or act astonished. "You bought a yacht today?" she asked, eyebrows raised. "But why?"

She struggled to follow his train of thought as to why he needed a yacht in North Carolina; she couldn't imagine any purpose for it. Derek stood up straight from the rail and looked thoughtfully at her.

"Well," he replied, holding her gaze, "I've never been a fan of hotels, and it really is more private here. With the marina security, I don't need to worry about the press." He reached for her hand and held it warmly in his. "I can manage my business remotely from here."   Christine looked down at her hand in his. "Why would you want to do that, though?" she said cautiously. This didn't make any sense to her. "How long are you intending to stay in North Carolina?"

"How long do you want me to stay?" he asked softly.

She looked sharply back up at him. "I have nothing to do with your plans," she stated, shaking her head. A brief look of frustration crossed Derek's face, and then he gently cupped her chin in his hand, bringing her face close.

"I keep trying to tell you," he said, "I'm here for you. I'll be here as long as you'll let me be."

With that, he brought her lips to his. His kiss was soft and sensual, and it took her breath away. He pulled back from her, ending the kiss too soon for Christine's preference. He smiled as he looked into her eyes. "How about that swim?" he asked.

Chapter 5

"I don't know how else to say it," Derek said, running his hand through his hair in frustration. Having escorted Christine back to the state room where Gregory had placed her tote bag, he had proceeded to his own room to change. Gregory sat behind a laptop on the sofa in the spacious two-room cabin suite. He stopped typing midsentence and looked up at Derek, who stood with his arms crossed. He knew Derek would struggle with this; he could tell the girl was scared to death of him, and Derek's reserved nature did not make it any easier for either of them.

"I think you just need to be patient," Gregory responded, looking back at the memo he was currently working on. "You just met her, after all; she doesn't know you." He squinted at the computer. "Sir, Scott needs an approval to review the financial statements for Osgood Inc. It seems as though their profits are down from last month."

Derek narrowed his eyes at Gregory in thought. "I approve," he said dismissively, unconcerned about the financial well-being of Osgood, his mind elsewhere. "Why does she always have to have her guard up?" he pondered out loud.

"Why do you?" Gregory answered back, not taking his eyes off the computer. Derek opened his mouth to respond, but his phone buzzed. "Incoming Call: Cynthia."

"Just answer it," Gregory said, still typing, after the phone had buzzed several times. Derek looked pointedly at his assistant, then hit the accept button.

"Hello, Cynthia," he answered, walking toward the bedroom for privacy.

"Hi, Derek," his ex-wife replied politely. "I wanted to thank you again for agreeing to do the lecture yesterday. The dean was so pleased; it had the best attendance of any guest lecture yet."

"You're welcome," Derek replied suspiciously, anticipating an ulterior motive for her call.

"And the donation too!" Cynthia continued. "You can imagine my surprise when the dean told me you'd agreed to build their art department a new gallery." Derek flinched. *And there it is*, he thought. Cynthia was not stupid. Clearly she had seen the morning tabloid and put two and two together.

Feeling the familiar throb to his temple, the one he got whenever Cynthia confronted him about any other woman in his life, Derek felt he needed to put an end to this game.

"Cynthia," he said calmly, deciding straightforwardness was best, "I think I've met someone." Silence followed, and he instinctively cringed, waiting for the guilt trip or snappy remark.

"I realize that," she finally said quietly. Derek raised his eyebrows, surprised by her unemotional response. "It's really why I called," she added and sighed. "I called to say goodbye. I won't call you anymore." Stunned, Derek had no reply and waited for her to continue. "I hope you're happy, Derek," she said. "That's all I ever wanted—your happiness. I thought I could give you that, but I accept now that I can't."

He listened intently to her, hearing the sincerity. "Thank you, Cyn," he replied softly, "I wish you the best as well."

She clicked off, and Derek sat on the edge of the bed staring at the phone. He understood that he may never hear from her again. Relieved that she finally had the closure she needed to move on from him, he couldn't help but feel a twinge of grief. He cared about her; after all, she had been a large part of his life for many years. Knowing now that a new chapter had begun and a weight was being lifted, he smiled slightly, the beautiful curve of Christine's face invading his thoughts.

Having changed, Derek emerged from the bedroom minutes later sporting black swim shorts, Versace sunglasses, and a towel draped over one shoulder. As he prepared to exit the cabin, Gregory called his attention back.

"Sir, what did Mattia say?" He know that Mattia had been on the other end of that phone call he and Christine had walked in on. Shocked to have found Derek actually having a conversation with the diplomat from his native country, Gregory could not contain his curiosity.

Derek paused, his hand on the door handle. He sighed. "The prime minister is pushing to restore the Landino family back into power," he said seriously. He turned to face Gregory. "The country is in shambles and simply doesn't have the resources to install a different form of government. Not having a true monarch or leadership for so long hasn't helped any in rebuilding the economy. They've been struggling since the revolution." He shook his head gravely. "Virtually no progress has been made." Gregory opened his mouth to ask questions, but he couldn't think of the right one. "I knew this was happening," Derek continued, meeting his assistant's eyes. "It's been going on for a while."

Gregory's face showed no emotion as he took in the weight of what Derek was saying. "How much time do you have?" he asked, finally deciding on the question he cared most about.   Derek's face turned hard.

"As much time as I need," he stated with finality. Gregory could see anger rising within him. "My father was assassinated," he said, "and my family was forced to flee, all for the good of Calina. Now the country is in no better shape than it was in before the revolution, and they just expect me to…"

he stopped, unable to finish. "Parliament is split anyway," he said, taking a breath. "It could be months before they reach a decision, if they ever reach a decision." Gregory knitted his brow and studied Derek. He had never seen such stress in him before. "Leadership in Calina is seriously lacking," Derek continued. "Unfortunately, it's the citizens who have been suffering." Giving Gregory a last glance, he opened the door and left the cabin to meet Christine.

In her own room, Christine peered into her tote bag looking for her swimsuit. Expecting to find the modest blue one-piece that she knew she had packed, she was shocked to pull out instead a cherry red bikini. *April,* she thought. She wasn't sure whether to be mad or amused at her friend. Inspecting the suit, she was relieved to see that it wasn't a thong, and at least it had two straps to hold up the top around each shoulder. Still she felt self-conscious about changing into something so revealing.

She could not deny how she was feeling toward Derek, and she hated that every passing moment she spent with him made those feelings stronger. His demeanor, look, touch, and smile enthralled her. He was charming but took control, which was sexy as hell. But the more she felt for him, the more afraid she became. She knew she wasn't nearly enough for him, and she didn't dare believe the things he said to her. Regardless of what he had suggested, he had to see this time with her as something only casual, noncommittal. Eventually he would hurt her, and she was fearful of not being able to recover. Never had she wanted to embrace something so bad and run from it at the same time. She shook her head, sighed, and wrapped a large towel around her entire body, vowing to stay guarded—for her own protection.

She left the cabin and made her way to the pool. It was a small pool on the very top deck, just large enough for a lap or two. It was partially enclosed, and large, white-cushioned lounge chairs lined each side. The water was crystal blue and illuminated with LED lighting. The space felt private and exclusive. A waterfall on one side added a touch of elegance to the sleek design.

As she emerged onto the deck, she saw that he was already there. He placed a towel and sunglasses down on one of the lounge chairs in the sun, then turned back toward the pool, walking to where she had entered under the enclosure. As he approached her, she couldn't help but let her eyes roam over his physique. Every line was cut and edged to perfection, and she found herself longing to explore the hallows and grooves, from his muscular shoulders and smooth chest down to his six-pack abs and his narrow, defined waist. His shorts rested low on his hips, and Christine couldn't stop her eyes from tracing his flawless abdominal V. She watched him move with confidence and ease, and subconsciously she clutched her own towel against her chest.

"Hey." He smiled as he neared her, his eyes practically illuminated by the sun.

Her breath caught in her throat, and she half hated he had this kind of effect on her. She suddenly wondered what kind of effect she had on him, if any. "Hello," she replied. "It's a perfect day for a swim." She tried to sound casual, but she knew her voice had come out slightly higher than usual. His smile broadened, and she got the impression he enjoyed making her nervous this way.

"I'm really glad you're here with me," he said softly. Christine's eyes widened slightly as he locked his gaze with hers, and she wondered if he would embrace her. "Come on," he said, breaking eye contact and motioning toward the pool.

He sauntered over to the far side of the pool. Having walked quickly toward the edge, he entered the water in a perfect swimmer's dive. He was an excellent swimmer, she observed, and he glided gracefully, using a freestyle stroke. Christine took a deep breath and removed her towel, dropping it on the nearest chair. Tucking her hair behind an ear, she approached the edge.

There would be no dramatic pool entrance for her. She knew how to swim, but not to Derek's level.

"How's the water?" she called out to him.

Derek made his way over to where she stood. Running a hand back through his now-soaked hair, he looked up at her, one corner of his mouth turning upward in a wolfish grin as he admired her. He gazed on her face, letting his eyes follow the curve of her neck down to the cleavage of her full breasts. Taking in her toned stomach, hips, and long legs, he couldn't help but feel desire. Her hair fell softly around her shoulders, and the cherry red she wore set off her touchable tanned skin. Unable to keep the urge to feel her close to him at bay, he reached up quickly, grabbed her arm, and pulled her into the water, almost making her fall on top of him.

"Wait!" was all she got out before she was submerged, a look of shock on her face.

Her head bobbed up, and she brushed the water out of her eyes.

"You tell me," he answered, giving her a playful smile. She looked at him in astonishment, then couldn't help but smile back. Feeling a bit more at ease, she splashed water at him with her hand in return, then turned to swim in the other direction. He reached for her, but she was already gone, swimming toward the other side of the pool to the waterfall. Christine did enjoy swimming, and the water was cool and refreshing. The waterfall was in the sun, and she tilted her face up, letting it warm her skin. Standing upright, the water lapping around her waist, she closed her eyes briefly and smoothed her wet hair back with both hands.

Enjoying their game of cat and mouse, Derek followed her to the waterfall, deciding it was time she was caught. Christine noticed that he was gliding toward her, and her instinct was to swim away again, but she didn't. As he stood before her, she looked up into his eyes, almost breathless in anticipation. His eyes dilated as he searched her face, and she recognized a hungry look of wanting. He reached for her waist and pulled her to him. Unable to resist touching him any longer, she placed her hands on his chest, feeling the firmness of his muscles as they tensed beneath her fingers. Letting her hands wander, she wrapped one around the back of his neck, pulling him closer. Encouraged, he bent his head toward her and claimed her mouth with his own. He kissed her softly at first, but his desire soon took over. As he brought one hand up to her face, his fingers cradling the back of her neck, he pressed firmly on her lips, parting them so he could taste her fully. Heat rising up through her body, Christine sensed an urgency in him she had not yet felt. She was unable to catch her breath as he sucked slightly on her lower lip, and she felt her knees go weak. As he held her securely, his arm wrapped around her waist, she felt his support was all that was keeping her from melting into the water.

He ended the passionate kiss, and his lips left hers, desiring to explore her neck just below her jawline. He devoured her soft skin, and she couldn't help but sigh. She tilted her head back to give him easier access, which he took eagerly, kissing every inch of her jaw and throat, his tongue massaging her. Bringing his lips back to her mouth, he let his hand slide from her neck down her breast and back around her waist to her firm ass, pressing her body hard against his. She brought both her arms up around his neck, enjoying the feeling of her fingers in his hair and her skin flush against his. As he continued to kiss her, she longed for more and her heart pounded; she wanted him to never stop.

He broke their kiss suddenly, an insatiable look on his face. Moving his hand up her arm to her shoulder, he gripped her swimsuit top strap. Christine inhaled sharply, thinking he was going to rip it off her. But Derek froze. Composing himself, he softened his eyes. Releasing her strap and bringing both hands back to her face, he rested his forehead on hers briefly. He closed his eyes in an attempt to slow the blood coursing through him.

"Mr. Landino, sir?"

The sudden interruption made him let go of her completely and turn toward the voice, which seemed to have appeared out of nowhere. A man had emerged on deck and was approaching the pool. Derek didn't say anything but made eye contact with the man, giving him the go ahead to continue.

"The captain wishes to inform you of an urgent situation," the man said seriously. "He asks to speak with you."

Derek raised his brow. "Of course," he stated. The man nodded in return and then left promptly.

"I'm sorry to have to cut our swim short," Derek said, turning back to Christine. "Feel free to stay at the pool as long as you like though. Hopefully, this won't take too long." Reaching for her, he touched her cheek and smiled. Then, wading over to the steps of the pool, he climbed out. Grabbing his towel and wrapping it around his waist, he headed to the stairs leading to the lower deck.

Now left alone, Christine's mind was reeling. Her heart still pounding, she hugged her arms, suddenly feeling cold. What had just happened, she thought frantically. Unsure whether she was more frustrated that she had let it happen or that it had stopped, she made her way to the steps and exited the pool. She began to dry off after finding her towel. Then, having wrapped it around her body, she wandered to one of the sun-drenched lounge chairs and sat down. Her head spinning slightly, she leaned back in the chair, letting the sun warm her skin from head to toe.

She felt emotionally drained and attempted to calm her body down and think clearly. She realized she had little to no control when near him, and it was exhausting trying to maintain any resolve. However, what happened in the pool left her confused too. It was obvious he was also holding back. *But why*, she wondered. Isn't that what he wanted? Wasn't that what she was here for?

She closed her eyes, attempting to block out the questions and get off this mental roller coaster. The warmth of the late afternoon sun felt good, and the sound of the rushing ocean all around her was soothing. She heard faint sounds of sea gulls in the distance. She couldn't think further about what she was doing or going to do, and she was regretting now only getting those couple hours of sleep last night. *I'll only rest for a couple of minutes,* she told herself.

———————◆———————

After a forty-five minute chat with the captain, Derek returned to his cabin to rinse off from the pool and change. Now having a moment to think, his mind wandered to being with Christine. He vowed to maintain better restraint around her, but God, how he wanted her. And he knew she wanted him. The thought made him smile, and he could see her starting to open up to him. She was starting to believe what he already knew.

Anxious to find her, he donned his linen pants and selected a white tailored shirt for the evening. Running his hands quickly through his hair and rolling up his shirtsleeves, he made his way out of the cabin. Unsure if she'd still be there, he decided to head for the pool first, figuring it was a good place to start.

He found her lying down on one of the lounge chairs, sleeping, her towel wrapped around her. He sat down on the chair beside her as strands of her hair fluttered across her face. He smiled as he brushed them back with his fingertips, then shook her shoulder gently.

"Christine," he said quietly.

After a moment, her eyes flew open. She looked at him confusedly at first, then realization hit her and she sat straight up.

"Oh my God," she said, touching her head. "I'm so sorry!"

He laughed softly. "It's perfectly all right," he replied, reassuring her. "It is pretty peaceful and warm out here; no wonder you dozed off." He held her eyes. "I'm sorry for leaving you. There was something I needed to take care of." His expression changed to a grimace as he looked away from her, thinking of the news he needed to relay.

"I hope nothing's wrong," she said, noticing his face. But before he could answer her, she changed the subject, clearly still embarrassed. "How long was I sleeping for?"

His smile returned. "Well, I don't quite know," he answered. "I guess it depends on when you fell asleep. I've been gone a little over an hour." She appeared mortified. "It's really ok," he added quickly, wishing to put her at ease.

He reached for her hand, and she looked at him, returning a small smile. "Are you hungry?" he asked. "Come on, let's have dinner?"

She nodded. Looking down, Christine realized she was still wearing her swimsuit and towel, both now completely dry. She instinctively touched her hair, not even wanting to think about what it looked like. He stood and still holding onto her hand, pulled her to her feet. "Why don't you go change," he said, sensing her insecurity. "I'll come and get you in a half hour, if that's ok with you?"

She gave him another nod.

"Of course," she replied. Her head still felt a bit fuzzy, and she was grateful for the opportunity to freshen up and regain her bearings. He squeezed her hand slightly, then released her. Catching his eye one last time, she turned and headed for the stairs.

Attempting to shake the feeling of being completely humiliated and in disbelief that she had just fallen asleep on a date, Christine walked quickly to her state room. As she entered the room and started toward the bathroom to rinse off, she almost didn't notice the large vase of roses on the accent table. Doing a double take, she knew they had not been there previously. She touched one of the delicate red buds gently. They were absolutely beautiful, arranged in a gorgeous crystal vase. She picked up the accompanying card. It was a plain, white, heavy-paper card with an elaborate "D. L." on the front, embossed in ebony black. Inside was his personal note to her: "Yours, Derek." She read and reread the two words over and over again, intrigued by the elegant slant to his penmanship. She put the card down slowly, trying to digest what it meant, if anything.

Heading now back to the bathroom, she turned on the shower. As she let the warm water wash over her, she realized one thing was for sure—the nap had done wonders for clearing her head. She was ready to surrender to her feelings toward him; whatever was going to happen was just going to have to happen, and she would need to cope with the consequences. She accepted that he was mostly likely going to break her heart, but she had to take that chance. She was drawn to him, and feeling like a fool, she knew she was falling for him.

After rinsing, washing, and blow-drying her hair, Christine redressed and was about to head out of the cabin when there was a knock. Opening the door, she smiled as she saw Derek there, admiring his extreme punctuality, noting he was a man of his word.

"Hi," he said, grinning back. He leaned against the doorframe, crossing his arms casually. "Ready?" he asked. Christine had the sudden urge to pull him into the cabin and pick up where they had left off in the pool. She found herself aching for him, longing to have him touch her. But she was not bold. And she wasn't sure how he'd react.

As her eyes searched his, Derek could see the thoughts running through her mind. Knowing what she was thinking as the tension between them mounted, he placed his hand on her shoulder to guide her out of the room and into the hallway before either of them could act on their desires. He closed the door behind them firmly, and realizing that the moment had passed, Christine refocused. He placed his arm around her waist and led her down the hall, back toward the stern of the yacht.

"I had dinner set up on deck out back," he explained as they walked. "It's a beautiful place to watch the sunset."

"That sounds amazing," Christine replied, attempting to slow down her heart rate. Now that she'd decided how she felt, she burned to ask him a million questions. Afraid of his answers, she kept her mouth shut, however, and she allowed him to guide her to the deck in silence.

As they approached the place where they had lunched earlier, she noticed a dining table had been set up. He pulled her chair out for her, and she took her place, noting that dinner had already been set out. Christine recalled Derek's standoffish demeanor toward the waiter last night and surmised he did not appreciate interruptions.

"Dig in," he said, taking his seat opposite her. "Pan-seared salmon, lemon butter, and asparagus." He paused. "Or, if that doesn't suit you, I can bring you whatever you'd like."

"No," she replied quickly. "This looks wonderful." She smiled at him, then looked out over the water, immediately mesmerized by the colors. "You were right," she murmured, "this is truly beautiful."

"I couldn't agree more," he said quietly, but Christine didn't notice that he wasn't looking at the sunset but her; his eyes had never left her face.

The sun, shining bright yellow, was setting close to the horizon and gave a postcard perfect view with an array of oranges, pinks, and purples. The ocean was calm, almost still, and settling into a dark, deep blue. The last rays of light danced on the surface as the sun appeared to kiss the water.

"I wish I could paint it," she said, thinking aloud, more to herself than to him.

Derek smiled warmly at her. "You are extremely talented, Christine," he told her. "I'm sure you could paint anything you want to."

She looked at him sharply, not realizing what she had said. She half smiled, pausing to take a bite from her meal. "Well, what I meant was that I wish I could paint how it makes me feel."

"I stand by my previous statement," he replied, a twinkle in his eye. His face grew more serious, and his eyebrows came together. He leaned forward slightly. "Why do you paint emotions?" he asked.

She could detect the sincerity in his voice, but she hesitated to answer. Chewing slowly, she pondered how much she wanted to share. Telling him the truth would make her feel exposed.

"Art is my world," she finally said, meeting his eyes. "But I'm a failure at it." She struggled to find the words as her internal torment threatened to overwhelm her. She sighed. "I never felt like I could truly capture the essence of anything else I tried to paint," she started. "I always feel so many things when painting—passion about the work, fear of not getting it right, disappointment, accomplishment. But each time I finished a piece, none of those emotions were conveyed. In the end, it was just a pretty picture. The work left me feeling…empty."

She could tell he was listening intently, taking in her every word. She had never actually verbalized the stress she felt over her work and life to anyone before.

"Having a clear understanding of emotions through my background in psychology, I decided to try to paint the emotion itself instead," she continued. "My work now gives me the fulfillment I need." She paused to take in his expression, which was now unreadable, and she wondered if he thought her crazy. After all, she chose to be a failure, making art in her own way, versus being a successful artist and complying with the norm. She squared her shoulders, ready to defend her position. "Others may not like it," she now said firmly. "But I feel validated. I would rather have that sense of personal accomplishment than sell meaningless art."

Unbeknownst to Christine, the reasons behind her choices only made Derek admire her more. He eyed her curiously for several moments, taking in the weight of her integrity and passion and how much he related to her in that moment.

"I think your work has great promise," he said genuinely. "You are very forward-thinking in your field, I believe, and the brilliance behind what you do is clear." He paused, the wheels turning as the entrepreneur in him took over. "You just need to find the right angle, the right opportunity…" he added thoughtfully. His eyes gleamed as he instantly recognized the profitable and impactful venture.

Christine laughed, smirking at her own disbelief to his reaction. "Well," she said, "maybe."

Derek refocused on her and smiled, reminding himself he was not at work right now. However, he vowed to revisit this train of thought in the future.

Although she didn't buy into his compliment, she appreciated it all the same. Meeting his eyes, she decided it was her turn to ask questions. Still fearful of questions pertaining to her or what he wanted from her, she chose to ask about his work.

"So what about you?" she said, stabbing an asparagus with her fork. "What's the driving force behind your business?" He looked surprised by her sudden change of subject. "And don't give me the interview answer," she added quickly with a knowing smile.

The corner of his mouth upturned, his mind having already chosen one of the many prepared speeches he was accustomed to giving. But she had opened up to him and chosen to be vulnerable. Perhaps it was time he did the same.

"I understand what you mean about feeling fulfilled," he started. "And you're anything but a failure. You're actually more ahead than you realize, uncovering already what you're destined to do and working toward that." His face held a wry expression. "The rest of us are wandering, feeling lost, continuing to search." He gazed out onto the water and narrowed his eyes. "We're all just looking for something..." He glanced back at Christine, his eyes locking on hers. "I'm no different," he continued quietly. "I'm still searching too." He dropped his eyes, and for the first time, Christine saw past his assured exterior. He had fears and doubts; he didn't always have the answers.

"What are you looking for?" she asked intently.

"Purpose," he said plainly, reconnecting his gaze with hers.

Christine nodded, understanding all too well the vacant feeling of having no direction or reason for existing. She found her own inspiration in the art she painted, reassured in knowing that only she had the power to create it. Derek had chosen to build his company, creating a massive wealth and enterprise, thinking he would eventually feel satisfied, that he might fulfill his destiny. Only, he was beginning to understand that his current path was not leading him to where he wanted to be.

He was not the man she had once assumed he was. The complexity and depth of his thinking stimulated her, and she was fascinated by his strength of character. He wasn't the greedy, shallow playboy the tabloids sensationally represented him to be.

"Maybe," she said slowly, staring into his eyes, "the reason you're still searching is because you're meant to do something else. Something more."

She said the words so simply, and unknowingly she had nailed the truth. He was amazed at how clearly she could see him and how unwilling he was to admit she was right. Suddenly, flashes of his mother's face, of Calina, his father's crown, all came to the forefront of his mind. His heart began to pound with the intense imagery, and he needed to stand.

"Excuse me, please," he said as he rose.

He walked over to the stern and stared out on the now dark blue water, the horizon turning gold. He leaned his forearms against the rail and laced his fingers together in thought. A moment later Christine approached his side.

"Derek," she said tentatively, "I'm sorry if I said something I shouldn't have." Her voice was tender and apologetic.

Feeling guilty at causing her uneasiness, he turned toward her. "Of course not," he said reassuringly, placing his hands gently on her shoulders. "It's me. I should apologize. It's difficult for me to talk about my personal endeavors." He winked at her and smiled. "Maybe I should see a psychologist."

She smiled back at him in spite of herself. "I could make a recommendation," she replied teasingly.

"Unless it's you, I'm not interested," he said quietly. The way he looked at her caused her stomach to flutter.

He slid his hands off her shoulders and around her back, bringing her into him, his strong arms enveloping her against his chest. She sighed under her breath as she felt his warmth and took in his scent. She looked up and locked her eyes with his, getting lost in their depths. It was still and quiet, and she was entranced. Her brain suddenly kicking into life, she realized it was too quiet.

"Um, Derek," she said, a quizzical expression now on her face. "Why aren't we moving?" He pursed his lips and knitted his brow, giving her an almost sheepish look. He had deliberately procrastinated giving her the news.

"Why don't we finish dinner," he said, releasing her from the embrace and gesturing back to the table.

Christine didn't like not being answered, but she thought it best to sit down. Taking a bite of her salmon, she looked at him, eyebrows raised.

"The captain has informed me there is an issue with the engine," he explained. He paused for a reaction, but Christine remained still. "As I shared with you earlier," he continued, "this is my first time taking her out. Apparently her maiden voyage has given us a few surprises."

"What are you saying exactly?" she replied, almost cutting him off, trying to keep the panic from her voice.

Not unaware of her tenseness, he sought to put her at ease. "I realize this isn't ideal for you," he said, choosing his words carefully. "You were not expecting to stay aboard tonight." Her eyes widened as the situation began to register with her. "The crew is working to fix the problem," he added, "and I feel confident you'll be home first thing tomorrow morning."

"You mean, I have to spend the night here?" she stated slowly, unable to meet his gaze.

"I'm very sorry," he answered. "I know this isn't convenient."

Her only response was to pick up her wine glass and take several sips, her mind now coming to grips with the fact that she would be staying here all night. With him. She finally brought her eyes up to his, recognizing the desire within them as the same images ran through both their minds.

Chapter 6

Courtney's eyes burned, her lids tender and swollen to the point that she could barely open them. Her head ached, and she sat up from where she had collapsed on her bed, reaching for the bottle of vodka she remembered setting down on the floor. As she took a swig, she glanced down at her pillow, stained with black and brown from her eye makeup. She swallowed the liquor hard, and it got caught in her throat; she checked her phone for the time: 8:05 p.m. Having spent most of the day drinking and crying, she realized she must have passed out at some point. The room was still spinning, and she felt like vomiting, but she didn't care as long as it kept her from thinking about him.

She had gone out that morning to get her usual coffee on her way to rehearsal and had seen the tabloid at the stand next to the coffee shop. At first she felt a fleeting moment of relief, seeing him in the news—at least she knew he was safe. But then her eyes focused on the photo itself. She snatched up the tabloid, paid for it, and forgetting about her coffee as well as rehearsal, she headed back to her apartment.

Poring over the article once back home, she stared again at the photograph. Derek and some other woman—except, she quickly realized, this was different. She had gotten quite used to seeing him in the news with other women, but it never concerned her. In every picture, he never looked at the woman he was with; he always smiled for the camera. This told Courtney that he didn't care who was on his arm, and it was nothing but show. But this—not only was he gazing at the woman in this picture, he was smiling adoringly at her, not even aware that his picture was being taken. *Why was he looking at her that way?* she asked herself, in shock. Then a slow understanding dawned on her. *This is where he was last night instead of with her...*

This can't be, though, she told herself, *he loves me*. Knowing that there had to be a reason for this, she racked her brain trying to come up with something feasible. Swapping out coffee for vodka that morning, she set down the tabloid and poured a drink straight. As she sipped the liquid, she crossed her arms, still staring at the photograph where she had left it on the counter. Her face twisted in fury as she looked from Derek's expression to the woman. *Why was he looking at her like that!* she screamed inside her head. She downed the rest of the vodka in her glass and quickly poured herself another, slamming that one as well. Her disbelief now subsiding, she was flooded with anger.

Unable to accept that Derek had passed her over for another woman, Courtney could only conclude that he had to be some kind of victim, seduced or forced to be with that art program director in the picture. She hated that woman with him. Feeling the need to act out on her rage, she grabbed a kitchen knife from the block next to her bottle of vodka. Walking over to the tabloid still on the counter, she viciously stabbed the woman in the picture, slashing right through her so-called "pretty" face. She sneered as she admired her work. *There*, she thought, *now he has nothing to look at.*

She missed her rehearsal, and she did not answer calls or texts. She didn't care about those who seemed to care for her, those who were wondering where she had been all day. All Courtney cared about now was numbing her senses so she didn't have to feel the anger or pain that was consuming her.

Now evening time, after she had crashed for all of the afternoon, she staggered with her bottle back toward the kitchen, the effects beginning to wear off. She began to shake and tremble, grasping the kitchen counter to steady herself. Suddenly, nausea washed over her and she doubled over. She squeezed her eyes tight, willing the sensation to pass.

A knock at her door distracted her, and she wearily raised her head.

"Courtney?" came a man's voice from just outside. "It's James. Are you in there?" She grimaced and gulped a dry sob, sliding to the floor of her kitchen, tears spilling down her face along with the last of her mascara. Not wishing to speak with him, she stayed quiet as she hugged her knees. "You missed rehearsal," he continued. "Henry was furious." He paused, but Courtney didn't care about their conductor. He knocked again. "I know you're in there, Courtney. I saw the tabloid." She heard him sigh. "Please let me in."

Courtney didn't move. She knew that last swig of vodka was about to reappear. Finally, she heard his footsteps fade away as he left her door. James couldn't help her, she knew, her senses fully back as waves upon waves of pain coursed through her. The only thing that could help her was getting Derek back.

The photograph of him gazing at that other woman burned in her mind. She allowed herself to think for a brief moment how it would feel if he were here now. With her, holding her. But the pain and longing those thoughts brought on made her sick. Barely making it, she crawled the few feet to the bathroom, finally retching out the now almost finished bottle of vodka. Her stomach empty, she continued to dry heave until her energy was spent, and she broke down and sobbed as she collapsed onto the bathroom floor.

———————

Christine stifled a yawn as she leaned her head back against his chest, pulling her knees up to her on the sectional, his arm around her shoulders. They had finished dinner, during which she had drunk three glasses of wine in an effort to deal with the anticipation of what may or may not happen tonight aboard the yacht.

Afterward he had asked her to stroll with him about the boat. As they walked hand in hand, she talked easily with him, pausing occasionally to stare at the stars or into his eyes. Feeling as though their dinner conversation had been heavy enough for one evening, she asked him simple questions and discovered he enjoyed the theater, spicy food, fast cars (of course), and a good cappuccino. She learned that he never took vacations and could not say where he'd even like to go if he ever did. Pausing at that comment, he had added that the only place he wanted to be was wherever she was.

Now, as it neared midnight, she found herself snuggled against him at the stern of the ship. The night air out on the ocean had turned chilly, and she couldn't help but find comfort in his warmth. As she leaned against him, he toyed with a strand of her hair. The evening had seemed almost magical to her, and she gazed out, enchanted by the moon and its perfectly reflected counterpart in the black ocean.

"It's getting late," he said softly, "we should get some rest."

Happy where she was, Christine felt as though she could have fallen asleep right there on deck. She did not want to do that again, however, and so consented and nodded her head in agreement.

"Oh," she said, frowning slightly as a thought occurred to her, "I didn't bring anything with me. I have nothing to wear."

A smile played on Derek's lips, and his gut response was to say, "Nothing is quite all right." But he bit his tongue. "I'll make sure to find you something," he replied. "Come on." He lifted his arm from around her and stood, offering her his hand to help her up. As she accepted his hand, she looked up and caught the glint in his eye and dreamy smile. She swayed slightly, feeling a bit dizzy. *Maybe that third glass was one too many*, she thought, wondering if it was the wine or something else that made her feel light-headed. He gave her a concerned look.

"Are you ok?" he asked, grasping her arm to steady her.

"I'm fine," she responded quickly. "I guess I'm just tired."

Still holding her hand, he led her back toward the cabins. He headed to his own first and stopped outside the door.

"I'm pretty sure I have something you can borrow," he said. "I can't imagine that dress would be very comfortable to sleep in." His eyes lingered on her face, then he let them trail to the spaghetti straps on her shoulders, following the plunging neckline down to the curves of her breasts. Her heart began to pound as he opened the cabin door, stepping aside to let her enter.

Being in his room made her stomach tie in knots. It was a two-room suite, and the door opened into the sitting area, with the bedroom off to the left. She watched him closely as he entered behind her, then proceeded toward the bedroom.

"Wait here," he instructed. A moment later he came back holding a T-shirt. "I'm sorry," he said, looking apologetically at the shirt. "I don't have a lot of things here yet. Will this work for you?"

Christine took the shirt from him. It was black and soft, as if it had been washed numerous times. Holding it up, she saw it said Rolling Stones. "You're a Stones fan?" she asked curiously, not picturing Derek as someone who enjoyed rock and roll.

He smiled. "Doesn't get much better than 'Paint it Black,'" he replied. "Just be careful with that," he added with a playfulness. "That shirt's been with me a while now; it's one of my favorites."

She laughed. "I'll guard it with my life."

He caught her eye, his smile turning to a smoldering look as the image of her in just his T-shirt with sexy bed hair came into his mind.

"Come on," he said, clearing his throat slightly, casting the image from his mind. "I'll walk you back to your room." He walked toward the cabin door and opened it for her. Christine hesitated for just a second before departing, not wanting to leave his room.

She walked in silence with him down the hallway as her heart continued to race. The tension was almost too much to bear, and suddenly feeling rather anxious at the prospect of nothing happening between them, she bit her lower lip attempting to keep any anticipated disappointment from consuming her.

As they arrived at her cabin, she remembered the roses.

"Thank you so much for the flowers," she said, stopping in front of the door. "They are truly beautiful."

Derek leaned toward her, bracing one hand on the door frame. "Not as beautiful as you," he replied softly.

She smiled at his comment. "That was very cheesy," she said with a hint of laughter.

"But very true," he responded seriously. Her smiled faded, and she couldn't help but get lost in him again. *How are his eyes that blue?* she thought absently.

"Christine," he said after a pause, "do you want me to stay here, in North Carolina?"

She diverted her gaze, knowing that she had to be honest with him but still afraid to do so. "I don't want you to leave," she admitted.

He smiled slowly. "I'm glad to hear that."

He leaned closer to her, still bracing himself against the door frame. He brought his other hand up to caress her cheek lightly with the backs of his fingers, and she lifted her eyes to his just before he kissed her gently. The feel of his lips on hers, even just the subtle touch, ignited the already burning embers within her, creating an intense heat. Knowing that he was about to pull away from her and unable to accept that this was all he was going to give her, Christine slid her hand behind his neck, pulling him toward her, enabling a firmer and prolonged kiss.

Forgetting his resolve to simply kiss her good night, he responded to her need, returning her kiss vigorously, parting her mouth open against his. Her knees gave slightly; she had never wanted anyone as much as she wanted him. Blaming her bravery or foolishness in imbibing that third glass of wine, she reached behind her for the door handle to her room. She turned the handle, and the door opened quickly as her weight leaned against it causing her to stumble backward. His reflexes sharp, Derek wrapped his arm around her lower back, catching her easily. He smiled mischievously at her, amused by her sudden boldness. Still leaning over her, he pressed his mouth back on hers, kissing her now with a fierceness that disabled her breathing. Bringing her back upright, he brushed her hair back away from her neck and shoulders and let his lips wander down her throat.

Unconcerned now about what he might think and following her desires, Christine slid her fingers down from around his neck to the buttons on his shirt. She moved from one to the next until his shirt was open; then tracing her fingers back up his cut abs and chest to his shoulders, she pushed it off him. He released her briefly to allow his shirt to fall to the floor. Then, reaching behind him, he closed the cabin door and seized her back around the waist, pulling her to him.

Derek's mind was wild with lust, and it was clear she wanted him. Having vowed to not take this step until he could come to terms with what he felt for her, he now found it easier to just throw caution to the wind and give into the inevitable. Effortlessly, he lifted her off her feet a couple inches and lowered her back onto the bed behind them. Now hovering over her, he brought his hand up to her face, letting his fingers brush across her lips then thread through her hair. Claiming her mouth with his, he slid his hand gently down her throat to her breast. She moaned softly as he squeezed lightly, his thumb massaging her nipple underneath the thin fabric of her dress. As his lips followed the trail down her jaw and neck to her ample cleavage, he continued to explore her curves, moving his hand down her stomach and back around her hip.

She grabbed his head with her own hands, her fingers weaving through his silky hair. Her back arched slightly as she allowed his touch and kiss to take control of her body. Grasping the flowing skirt of her dress, he hiked it up so he could feel the soft skin of her bare thigh. He ran his palm along her hip, then gripped her ass firmly, pushing her into him. She could feel he was rock hard, grinding against her in an erotic simulation that made her insides ache and her body throb. She guided his face up to hers and pressed her mouth back onto his, pulling sensually on his lower lip as she kissed him.

Everything about her sent his senses into overdrive—her soft skin, the smell of her hair, the taste of her lips. Her dress was now bunched up around her waist, and as he moved to pull it off over her head, he realized how much more he wanted than this. This would not satisfy him. At least, not for long. Releasing his hold on the fabric, his brain began to function. If he slept with her now, this would be no different than any other affair. Suddenly conflicted, he raised himself up from her slightly and locked eyes with hers, searching for answers, wondering what this even meant to her. Taking a deep breath to slow his heart rate, he could tell she knew he was drawing back as a confused expression crossed her face.

"Derek?" she questioned. He sighed and sat up. She followed suit, working to catch her breath as she straightened her dress.

She sat quietly next to him for several moments, nervously smoothing her hair, unable to look at him. As he watched her in her clearly discouraged state, he could see she was mistaking his caution for rejection. Knowing that he needed to explain himself but unsure how, he took her hand in his.

"Christine," he began, uncertain if she would understand, "you are unlike any other woman I've ever been with." She turned toward him, finally daring to meet his eyes, constantly seeking out the sincerity within them. "I'm finding myself feeling things I've never known before," he continued, cringing internally at her broken expression. "And I need what we have to have meaning. I hope you can be patient with me."

Stunned and frustrated at the unexpected turn of events, Christine struggled to process what he was telling her. She felt dismissed, but there were no options for her at this point. She had basically thrown herself at him, and harboring what little pride she had left, she wasn't about to beg. He was looking at her expectantly; his face seemed to truly hold concern.

Suddenly she needed him to leave. Afraid of letting her emotions show, she refused to fall apart in front of him, and she had to be able to think clearly.

"Um, sure," she responded quietly, nodding slowly, "I understand." The truth was she didn't understand at all, but she wanted to be alone. He narrowed his eyes, realizing that she was pacifying him.

He didn't wish to leave her in a dejected state, but pressing her to open up to him was probably not the best course of action right now. Tomorrow would be a better time to talk, he decided.

"Hey," he said softly, gaining her attention. She lifted her eyes to his, and he gave her a small smile. "I'll see you in the morning."

She managed to force a smile back. "Ok," she replied. He stood up from the bed and picked his shirt up from the floor. Opening the door to leave, he turned back to look at her.

"Good night, Christine." Then he left her cabin, closing the door behind him.

Now alone, Christine sat still for a moment, expecting a wave of emotion or tears to come. But, surprisingly, they didn't. She couldn't help but feel foolish, and at the same time, she couldn't help but trust him. Completely bewildered by the contradiction, she yawned as exhaustion took over her body and mind.

She stood up from the bed and pulled off her dress, tossing it onto a chair. As she slipped into his T-shirt, the feel of the fabric against her skin took her back to being in his arms only a few minutes ago. Her stomach flipped over at the thought. She drew the sheets back on the bed, and slid into them, her mind burning with questions. As she considered the things he said to her, she wondered what his true intentions were. Was he pushing her away because she didn't mean anything to him? Or was it because she meant something more…

Turning over on her side, she made the decision that she would not play his games. It was time he gave her a straight answer, and she needed to stop feeling afraid to ask him a straight question. It would be the first thing she asked when she saw him in the morning. She closed her eyes, her brain beginning to shut down and find sleep. She thought of him, his room just down the hall. As she drifted off, feeling restless, she couldn't prevent her mind from dreaming of what it would be like if he did, in fact, want a relationship with her.

———◇———

Having slept lightly, Christine awoke easily the next morning to a knock on the door. She assumed it was Derek, and she jumped up, brushed out her hair quickly, and opened the door. Surprised to see Gregory instead, she managed a smile.

"Good morning," he said in greeting, taking care not to notice that she was only wearing a T-shirt. But Christine was immediately aware of her attire and attempted to conceal a blush. "Christine," Gregory continued, "Derek asked me to inform you that he was detained by business this morning, and he regrets he cannot join you for breakfast." Christine bit her lip, unable to hide her slight disappointment.

Having slept on how she felt and her next actions, she was rather anxious to discuss both matters. Now she wasn't sure if she'd ever get the chance. Picking up on her displeasure, Gregory spoke tentatively.

"He asked that I escort you to the deck, where breakfast is set up, and then, when you're ready, I'm to drive you home."

Christine opened her eyes wide. "Home?" She questioned. "You mean, we're back?"

"Yes," the assistant responded pleasantly. "The crew worked through the night, and we sailed back very early this morning, arriving at dock about an hour ago. It's currently 7:00 a.m." She mouthed the time to herself, her class schedule registering with her.

This overnight adventure had not been planned, and out on the ocean, with no cell phone signal, she had not been able to contact anyone.

"I'm sorry," she said. "I cannot stay for breakfast. Can you take me home now, please?"   Gregory raised his eyebrows. "Of course, if that is your wish," he replied.

"Please just give me two minutes to change." Not waiting for his affirmation, she closed the door. Pulling the T-shirt off, she slipped her dress back on. She smoothed out the covers on the bed; she felt like she couldn't leave the room a mess. As she folded the T-shirt neatly, she considered having it laundered, but unsure of how to return it to him, she decided it was best to leave it on top of the comforter. After all, she didn't even know if she'd see him again.

She glanced at the roses, considering them. She couldn't take the heavy vase with her, so she settled on keeping the note and placed it in her tote bag. Opening the door, she stepped out into the hallway, where she had left Gregory waiting.

"I'm ready," she said, falling into step next to him as they walked down the hallway toward the gangway.

"Don't worry about the vase," Gregory smiled. "I'll make sure they're delivered to you."

"Oh," Christine replied, surprised that he knew about the flowers. "Thank you."

As they disembarked and Gregory led her to the parked Audi, she pulled out her cell phone and turned it back on. Climbing into the car as her phone kicked into life, she noticed the LaFerrari sat in its space, telling her Derek was still somewhere on board. She glanced one last time at the yacht, and she couldn't help but feel a bit sad to be leaving, wondering when or if she would hear from him.

She looked at her phone and caught up on the missed calls and texts. As Gregory took his seat behind the wheel and started the car, Christine smiled to see that April had tried to reach her three times. She also had a text from Stephanie, the instructor who had filled in for her yesterday and a missed call from—she stared at the number. *Really?* she thought in shock as she recognized all too well the number that appeared on the screen. Noticing that a voicemail had been left, she threw Gregory a cautious glance, knowing it was not safe to listen to the message with him within earshot.

Placing her phone back in her bag, she turned to him as he drove.

"You mentioned Derek was detained?" She questioned casually, trying to not let on that she was at all concerned. Gregory smiled, understanding entirely what Christine was asking, and he knew the last thing Derek wanted was for her to feel apprehensive.

"Yes, he had some business to attend to this morning via teleconference," he replied, more than happy to explain. "He did, however, want me to tell you that he hoped to be in touch with you later this afternoon or early this evening." He glanced at her. "Assuming you'd be inclined to accept his call then?"

"Of course," she replied slowly, feeling the rush of relief flood through her and becoming instantly irritated by it. "My last class ends at four today," she added, refusing to be at his beck and call. "I'll be available after that." Gregory nodded, mentally noting the time offered.

As they drove back, Christine made a call to Stephanie asking her to again sub for her morning class. Knowing that she was now indebted to her colleague, Christine began to feel guilty for blowing off her students a second time. Derek Landino had come into her life so suddenly and swept her away, but it was time for her to come back to reality. She had a career and responsibilities, and she couldn't put everything on hold for him. Especially when she didn't even know where she stood with him.

They pulled up to the curb in front of her apartment, and Christine's eyes flew open wide as she spied a familiar black truck. Gregory parked the

Audi directly behind the truck, and she couldn't help but curse under her breath. It would have been in her best interest to have heard that voicemail—but it was apparently too late now. Not wishing for any awkwardness, she turned to Gregory.

"Thank you so much for everything," she said, forcing a smile. She then quickly exited so he would not have the opportunity to respond or stay longer than necessary.

Picking up on her agitation, Gregory watched Christine as she hurried up the sidewalk to her apartment. As she approached the front porch, a man emerged from just out of view. He seemed to have been waiting for her. The assistant continued to watch them closely, noticing that Christine's body language indicated that she was not happy to see this man. He was very tall, with sandy blond hair and a broad, football player's build. Eyeing the black truck and recalling her reaction upon seeing it, Gregory decided action was best. Grabbing his cell, he made a call.

———◦———

"Jackson, what are you doing here?" Christine said as soon as she saw him.

The man she had addressed gave her a brilliant smile. "You look more beautiful than I remember." Unamused by both his presence and his comment, Christine crossed her arms as she narrowed her eyes at him.

"What do you want?" she demanded.

Jackson spread out his hands in a mock surrender and knitted his eyebrows. "I was hoping to catch you before class, and I wanted to talk to you," he said simply. "Please, Christine, can't we just talk?" His voice sounded pleading, and his boyish smile returned. "How about some coffee?"

Christine tucked her hair behind her ear, then looked over her shoulder at the curb, well aware that the Audi was still there. She sighed.

"Ok," she said grudgingly. "But only for a minute." She moved to the front door and turned the lock.

"Are you just getting in?" Jackson asked, keenly following her inside.

Annoyed by the question, Christine turned to face him. "That's not your concern," she replied tensely. Jackson shrugged but raised his eyebrows at her. "Give me a minute," she instructed him. "I need to change. You can wait at the breakfast table if you want." She gestured to the kitchen area, then turned toward her bedroom. Jackson wandered over to the table, his hands placed casually in his pockets, but he didn't sit.

"Mind if I make some coffee?" he called out to her. Now in her bedroom, Christine rolled her eyes. She pulled off her dress, irritated that he had the nerve to still feel at home in her apartment.

"Whatever," she called back. In reality, she needed coffee too. And the sooner it was made, the sooner he could leave.

Cleaning up quickly, she washed her face and brushed her teeth. She did not want to look "pretty" for him, so she threw on a pair of gray cotton drawstring shorts, a faded green T-shirt, and put on her glasses. Piling her hair up in a messy ponytail so it was out of her face, she emerged to face him. He smiled at her when she entered the kitchen.

"It's no use, Christine," he said, adding coffee to the coffee maker. "You're beautiful no matter what you do." She opened her mouth to give a retort, but he continued, now opening an overhead cabinet. "I left you a message," he said, peering into the cupboard. "I had hoped you'd call me back. When you didn't, I thought it best just to come over and see you," he paused. "Did you move the sugar?"

"Yes," she snapped, beyond frustrated. "A lot's changed since you left." She brushed by him and retrieved the sugar from the far cabinet. Unfazed by her icy tone, he continued to smile, seemingly amused at her attitude, as if he were accepting her challenge with an arrogant sense of being victorious.

As she set the sugar bowl and a spoon on the breakfast table, he followed her out of the kitchen. She then turned to face him as she sighed, looking expectantly, waiting for him to say what he had come to say. Approaching her, he placed his hands on her shoulders, and she automatically stiffened at his touch.

"I miss you, Christine," he said softly, locking his eyes on hers. "I know I was a jerk. I want us to be together again."

She shrugged out of his grasp and paced to the other side of the table, walking toward a wall. "You should have thought about that before you slept with Avery," she said with a cruel smile, turning back to him.

Three months ago now, Jackson had walked out on her for another woman. Christine had never even been given the opportunity to confront him, and their relationship had ended without actual closure.

"I'm so sorry," he pleaded now, moving toward her. "I know I hurt you, and I made a mistake." He looked at her intently, but she refused to meet his eyes. Crossing her arms in her insecurity, she stared at the floor. She admitted to being devastated when Jackson left, wondering what she had done wrong or why she wasn't good enough. But she had come to terms with his betrayal and had moved on. She was over him, and she knew she was stronger for it. "Besides," Jackson said, stepping closer to her still. "You can't be serious about this guy. This *celebrity?*" He emphasized the word in a condescending way, and Christine looked up sharply at him. He knew about Derek; the tabloid came to her mind, with its picture of them dancing two nights ago.

"It's none of your business," she said quietly, scowling at him.

As he invaded her personal space, Christine instinctively stepped backward toward the wall. Taking another step back, she realized she could go no further. She met his eyes now, challenging him with a glare.

"Christine," he said, and his tone was smooth as he placed a hand on her shoulder. "Why don't you come back to me before you get hurt again?" He slid his hand down her arm to her waist, sending shivers up her spine that made her feel dirty.

"Jackson," she said in warning, giving him a look of disgust. But he braced his other hand on the wall by her head. He leaned over her, trapping her, her back almost to the wall.

"He can't mean anything to you." His face was near hers now, and he was almost touching her forehead with his own. She dropped her eyes and tried to turn from him. "We have history, me and you," he continued. "You know you love what I do to you." She cringed as his hand on her hip crept around to her lower back, then down her ass.

She turned back to look in his eyes, contempt filling them. "Get your hands off me," she said through gritted teeth. She raised her arms to push against his chest in an effort to get away from him, but he quickly grabbed both her wrists.

Gripping her tightly, he pushed her back flush against the wall, his face hardening as frustration took over at her hostile and standoffish response to him.

"What's your problem?" he said sharply, his voice rising in decibels. "You know he's just using you, don't you? You're just some publicity stunt." A sneer crossed his face, and his lips curled as he bared his front teeth. "You probably let him fuck you too, didn't you?"

He was practically shouting at her now, and Christine attempted to twist her arms away from him, striving to get free. But as she struggled, he only clamped his hands down harder on her, causing stabs of pain in her wrists and arms. At the same time, he pushed her back more firmly against the wall.

"Let go!" she cried at him, now irate but also fearful. "You're hurting me."

Chapter 7

Derek wasn't concerned with the consequences as he shifted gears in the sports car, pressing his foot firmly on the gas. He had received the call from Gregory stating that a man had been waiting for Christine when he dropped her off and was now inside her apartment. Furthermore, Gregory had relayed that Christine did not seem pleased, and her reaction had caused enough alarm that the assistant had felt the need to inform Derek. Gregory was not someone who overreacted or dramatized, and his intuition was spot on.

Fighting emotions that were foreign to him, Derek had hastily gotten off the conference call and left the marina. He had accomplished what he needed to with the meeting anyway, and although they had been necessary, his decisions were not ones that he was anxious to share. The personal visit to Christine would be killing two birds with one stone: relaying his news and finding out who this man was.

As he drove, the image of Christine with another man made him boil, and he scowled, pressing harder on the gas. Derek didn't get angry, and he was startled by his feelings and how they were controlling his actions. Always composed, he did not ordinarily allow his emotions to hijack his thinking or behavior. This was new, and for the first time he understood jealousy. The idea that Christine could be seeing someone else had never even occurred to him. Why wouldn't she have said something?

He pulled up slowly to her apartment, parking behind the black truck. Narrowing his eyes at it, he exited his car and walked up the path leading to her front door. Pausing on her porch, he contemplated if he wanted to knock or just burst in. He decided it was probably best to maintain civility, and he raised his hand to rap on the door, but voices inside made him stop. Unable to hear whole conversations, he could definitely make out Christine speaking with a man. Feeling slightly guilty about eavesdropping, Derek waited. He shook his head as it got quiet, preparing to knock again, but then he heard shouting and Christine cried out. No longer worried about being polite and knowing she was in distress, he instantly grabbed the door knob and shoved open the door, letting himself in.

He did not greet them, only taking in the scene before him, a hard look on his chiseled face. Christine was backed against the wall by the breakfast table, the man grasping onto both her wrists in what appeared to be a struggle. They were both now looking in Derek's direction, surprised at the interruption. He sized up his ostensible rival, noting that the man was taller than he by about two inches, with a broad chest and shoulders. Not the least bit intimidated, Derek glared at him.

"Do you want to let go of her?" he asked coldly, breaking the silence. "Or shall I make you?" His tone was even and menacing.

Jackson immediately dropped Christine's arms, and as he was distracted by Derek, she pushed past him.

"Derek?" she said, moving toward him, shock on her face at his sudden appearance. "What are you doing here?"

Focusing on her now, he studied her face. He saw relief in her expression, along with concern, and he softened his eyes at her. "Are you all right?" he asked her, avoiding her question for now. She nodded, casting her eyes to the floor as she rubbed her wrists lightly.

Jackson swaggered over to them, refusing to be upstaged.

"You must be that celebrity I keep hearing about," he remarked contemptuously. Derek turned his attention back to Jackson, his eyes clouding immediately. "I'm Jackson, Christine's boyfriend." He placed his arm casually around Christine as if he owned her. Jackson was indeed bigger, but it was Derek's commanding presence that held control. He folded his arms, his face set in a scowl as he eyed Jackson's arm around her.

"*Ex*-boyfriend," Christine said emphatically as she squirmed away from him.

With the atmosphere unbearably tense, Christine held her breath and glanced between the two men. She had no idea what to expect from Derek, but it was evident he was not pleased, and she could almost feel the power radiating from him. Fearing that he had the wrong idea, she sought to defuse the situation.

"Jackson, I think it's time you left," she said calmly.

"Oh come on, Christine," Jackson said in exasperation, almost with a whine. He gestured toward Derek with a look of apparent disrespect. "You honestly prefer this rich, superficial rake?" Derek clenched his jaw, reaching his limit. "He won't be there for you," Jackson continued, looking at Christine now. "He's using you, and when he gets what he wants, he'll go back to where he came from and forget you ever existed." He placed his hands on her shoulders. "I'm real, and here now. You can't just throw away everything we had."

Deciding to give Christine the opportunity to respond instead of punching this guy out, Derek waited. He needed to hear what she was going to say.

As she listened to Jackson verbalize very plainly the fears she had been harboring, she locked eyes with Derek for a moment, aware of the clear choice. She pulled herself out of Jackson's reach.

"*You* threw away anything we ever had, Jackson!" She spat at him, losing her composure. "Which wasn't much, I realize. Derek has shown me more respect and consideration in two days than you did the entire time we were together." Resisting the intense urge to slap him, she hugged her arms. "It's over, and you need to go," she told him with finality.

"Fine," he responded harshly, pointing his finger at her, anger on his face. "But don't come running back to me after he discards you like yesterday's trash." He turned toward the door, but Christine wanted the final say.

"Yeah," she replied quietly, "'cause I don't know what that feels like." Jackson looked back at her sharply and glanced at Derek but said nothing else. Having walked out the door, he slammed it behind him.

Derek immediately turned to the window and watched him leave down the path to the curb. *If he touches my car...* he thought, but something else caught his eye as Jackson approached his own truck.

"Oh, hell," he said under his breath.

"What is it?" Christine asked, worried.

He closed the drapes and turned back to her. "Paparazzi." He sighed. "They followed me here. I wouldn't be surprised if your boyfriend makes the news tomorrow." She winced slightly at the term. "It's not good for you that I came here," he continued. "I don't want them disrupting your life."

She stared at him for a moment, still in a little bit of disbelief that he was physically standing there. He was wearing a black button-up shirt and slacks, and the all-black ensemble gave him a mysterious but regal appearance.

Her heart was still beating fast with adrenaline from the encounter with Jackson, and Christine realized how grateful she was that Derek had showed up. Although his intentions were still doubtful to her, she could appreciate his efforts to ensure her well-being today. Did he care about her after all? Wanting to feel his embrace, she suddenly approached him and wrapped her arms around his neck. He complied, holding her to his body.

"Are you sure you're all right?" he asked her again, and then his features hardened. "I didn't like seeing him grab you like that."

"I'm fine," she said, her voice muffled against his shoulder. Then she let go, and turning from him, she headed back to the kitchen, still needing that cup of coffee.

Grabbing the handle to the coffee pot as he followed her, she held it out to him in offering. He gave her a half smile, shaking his head slightly. After pouring herself a cup, Christine sat down at the breakfast table, afraid to meet his eyes.

Still eager to discuss their relationship and possibly even last night, she now hesitated to bring it up. As he took the chair opposite her, she waited for the questions or third degree about Jackson. She frowned into her mug as she wondered whether he was even bothered by past or present boyfriends, thinking that he most likely had a woman waiting for him in every state. But Derek remained silent, studying her as she took a sip from her cup.

"Why did you come here?" she curiously asked again, breaking the silence as she raised her eyes to him. As usual, his expression was unreadable. "Did Gregory call you?" The fact that he'd arrived only fifteen minutes after Gregory had dropped her off wasn't a coincidence.

Derek thought for a moment, unsure which question he wanted to answer first. He decided on the former.

"I wanted to speak with you," he began. "I thought it would best to tell you in person that I need to fly back to New York early this afternoon." Christine cast her eyes down, then nodded slowly, feeling as though the wind had been knocked out of her as the news hit her hard. She knew at some point he would have to leave.

She let out a heavy breath and shut her eyes briefly as she processed the information. At least he had the decency to tell her face-to-face that this was the end of the road. After all, he didn't owe her an explanation. He could have just left without a word.

"I see," she said, and although she felt like bursting into tears, she forced a small smile at him. "Well, I had a good time, and thank you for everything you've done for me and the university." She prepared to stand to walk him to the door with a final goodbye, but Derek remained where he was. He shook his head and regarded her with confusion.

"Christine," he replied, "I know it's short notice, but I was rather hoping you'd come with me."

Her eyes opened wide, and she opened her mouth to respond, but unsure of what to say first, she closed it again, instead settling on giving him a bewildered expression. She sat back down and took a deep breath in an attempt to calm her growing frustration.

She hated that Jackson had already set her off emotionally, and with these constant fears surrounding Derek, she came to the conclusion that she needed to end this before he did. Maybe it would hurt less that way.

"I can't go with you to New York," she responded quietly. "In fact, I don't think it's good for me to see you again." The words tumbled out of her mouth rapidly, and she practically choked on them as regret immediately began to consume her. She felt her face grow hot, and the tears began to sting. She stood up quickly to move away from him into the living area, unable to bear crying in front of him.

Derek sat quietly for a moment, hearing her words but unable to digest them. Had she just rejected him? He stood and followed her.

"I don't understand," he said with her back facing him. "Are you saying you feel nothing for me?"

His question startled her, and she turned to him, her eyes wide with both fear and wonder, glassy from the threat of tears that she now controlled and kept at bay. True to her promise to herself to be direct with him, she answered him honestly.

"I feel too much for you," she said quietly, knowing this was the moment of truth. "I can't continue to hope that my feelings are returned, that there could be anything real between us."

Derek's eyes fell to the floor, then went back to hers. For a rare moment, his emotions betrayed him and a hurt expression crossed his face.

"Real," he repeated. "You don't think this is real?"

She blinked her wide eyes at him, unwilling to believe the course of the conversation was going in the desired direction. "I don't know what your intentions are," she said cautiously, guarding her heart more than her pride now. "And your life is in New York with your business and your fame and press." She attempted to keep her voice steady, but her mind raced through their differences and lifestyles, rational thought clearly telling her it could never work. "I'm nobody," she said, looking down, "and you're…" She trailed off, unable to find a word worthy of his power. She swallowed her insecurity and met his gaze.

Suddenly it dawned on Derek that she needed him to define their relationship—a new concept for him. He approached her, and not waiting for an invitation, he wrapped his arms around her shoulders, pulling her to him.

"You are everything," he said softly into her hair. "I don't ever remember feeling anything more real." He pulled back to look at her. "My only intention," he began, "is to be with you. However and whenever I can." She opened her mouth to object, but he refused to let her. "Christine, you're all I've thought about since I met you." His eyebrows knitted together. "I've put projects on hold, canceled meetings, delayed investors, and bought a yacht so that I could be near you." He paused, thinking. "I donated $20 million to the university just to get your attention." Taking a deep breath, he knew he needed to be clear. "I don't do relationships. I haven't since my divorce," he said. Crestfallen, Christine looked down and nodded. He lifted her chin gently, making her look at him again. "Until now," he continued. "I don't want anyone else. I will do whatever I can to make this work between us." He looked at her with intensity. "Is that what you want too?"

Of course she wanted that too, and the thought of finally determining her place with him immediately sent a rush of exhilaration through her. But if he wanted a relationship with her, why did he continue to pull away from her? Pushing her embarrassment aside, she chose to address it.

"Last night—" She began to speak, but he cut her off, alleviating her from having to ask.

"Last night," he explained, "was not a rejection. You're not a conquest to me. I want much more than that." His eyes darkened with desire. "Rest assured," he said in a low voice, "I want you more than I've ever wanted anyone, but when I do take you to bed, it will mean something." Her heart thumped in her throat at his directness, and her breath caught as she stared into his eyes, reading within them his needs, which matched her own. "You didn't answer my question," he said softly, his face only inches from hers. Feeling entranced, she shook her head in confusion. "Do you want to be in a relationship with me?" The very straightforward question caused her breathing to stop, and she could tell he was ensuring she understood his objective completely.

This time she nodded, unable to hold back the smile that was forming on her lips. She managed a soft "Yes," right before he lifted her chin again and kissed her deeply. Letting herself get lost in him, she ran her hands up his back, pulling him closer, relishing the feel of him against her.

A thought occurring to him, he broke from her suddenly, catching her off guard. She looked at him quizzically as a concerned expression crossed his face. Holding her now at arm's length, he narrowed his eyes, his mind drifting back to the encounter with Jackson. "Is there anyone else I should know about?" he asked, releasing her. He had not liked how the thought of her with another man had made him feel, and he needed to ensure this was not a repeated situation.

Christine bit her lip to keep from smiling at his apparent jealousy. She shook her head.

"No," she assured him, "there is no one else." She could see the relief on his face, but her own tendency to smile faded. Should she ask him the same? She hesitated. She had always just assumed he was involved with many other women.

"And you?" she asked, coming to the conclusion that if he could inquire, so could she. "Are you seeing anyone else?" She said the words timidly, un-sure what she would do if he answered affirmatively. She was made curious, however, by his amused response.

"I don't 'see' people, Christine," he said, his eyes twinkling.

"You're saying I have absolutely no competition?" She faltered. His face grew serious.

"For my affection? No," he replied. "for my attention?" He sighed. "Yes. There will always be competition." He took her hand and regarded her apologetically. "This is the nature of my work," he explained, searching her face. "It's demanding, and I travel a lot." He pulled her back toward him, wanting her to be clear about what she could and could not expect from him. "I cannot give you my undivided attention, but I am willing to adjust how I do business to the extent that I'm able to build a relationship with you." He smiled at her, adding, "And only you."

Christine looked at him thoughtfully. Allowing herself now to be completely free from the fears of rejection and heartbreak, she could admit to herself just how much she did care about Derek. She wasn't sure how he would be able to find a balance within his work to make time for her, or how she would accommodate him within her schedule. But she did know she wanted to try. The fact that he was willing to adjust anything in his life for her confirmed what she needed to know.

"I understand," she told him sincerely. Needing to feel him again, she reached up and placed her mouth on his, knowing she could never get enough of how his lips felts on hers. The kiss was tender and served as a symbolic seal to the bond between them.

He ended the kiss and smiled broadly at her, the dimple appearing in his left cheek. "Sure you won't come to New York with me?" he asked hopefully.

She wanted nothing more than to follow him anywhere, but guilt crept up on her.

"I really can't, Derek," she said, thinking about her students. "I'd love to, but I have classes and work to do here. I can't just ignore it."

He gave her a defeated expression and sighed, but his smile remained. "So here I am competing for your attention," he mused. She shrugged and spread her hands. "I have to go, though," he said. "My plane leaves in a few hours, and there are arrangements I need to make." He raised his eyebrows. "I'd like to call you later this evening."

She smiled. "I'll be home."

He paused before turning toward the door, struck with inspiration.

"Why don't you walk me to my car?" he suggested, giving her a sly smile. Christine was bemused by the request but consented.

"Um, ok," she replied.

He grabbed her hand, opened the door, and walked with her down the sidewalk toward his car. Once he got to the LaFerrari, he stopped, seized her around the waist, pulling her right into him, and kissed her passionately on the mouth. She was shocked by the sudden and unexpected kiss, and waves of heat rushed through her, making her feel weak. After several moments he broke the kiss, the same mischievous grin still on his face.

"Now everyone will know," he said quietly. Christine's eyes grew wide as it dawned on her what he had just done. He knew the paparazzi were watching. They had probably just taken a picture of him kissing her; he wanted the world to know.

Derek then released her and walked around to the other side of the car. Opening his door, he looked back at her.

"And yes," he said simply, answering her second question. "Greg called me." He gave her a wink with a smile, got in, and started the engine. The car purred to life; then it pulled away and he was gone.

———◆———

That evening Christine sat on her bed with her laptop in front of her, attempting to do some research for one of her classes. Next to the array of papers sprawled out across her bed, her cell phone lay facedown and forgotten. She had not felt the need to stalk her phone waiting for his call. She had not felt anxious or concerned that he may not call. In fact, she had no doubt that she would hear from him, and she knew that if he said he'd call, then he would. She sighed with a small smile as she yet again became distracted from her work, the image of his face floating through her mind. Small flutters of excitement invaded her body, the kind only the prospect of a fresh romance could bring.

Giving up on her work, Christine allowed her thoughts to stay on Derek. Even though he was a public figure, he was still such a mystery to her. What did she really know about him? She knew he was rich, famous, divorced and, by his own admission, not of American birth. Becoming increasingly intrigued with his past and hoping to learn more details about his life, Christine stared at her open laptop, suddenly struck with a thought. Feeling only slightly guilty, she clicked open a Google search and typed in "Derek Landino." She clicked first on the Wikipedia link and began to scan his biography.

She read through the list of his accomplishments, amazed at just how many businesses he owned or shared ownership in; many of them were familiar to her, but she had had no clue he was involved with them. He was thirty-four years old and labeled as an entrepreneur, philanthropist, and billionaire. He was the president and CEO of Land Corporation and held many other corporate titles and positions on multiple boards of directors. In short, he was a very powerful man. He had graduated from Columbia with honors. Marital Status: divorced. Ex-wife: Cynthia Anne Masterson.

Christine paused over the link connected to his ex-wife's name. Curiosity getting the better of her, she clicked on the link, and several pictures of Derek and Cynthia together appeared. As she had suspected, Cynthia was gorgeous, tall, and blond. Clicking back to Derek's biography, she continued to read until she came to his citizenship and place of birth. Citizenship: American. Place of Birth: New York City, New York. She stared at the screen in confusion. Derek had told her he had been born in Calina and carried a dual citizenship. Calina, it appeared, didn't exist in his history at all.

Following her natural progression of thought, Christine closed the current search and opened a search for "Calina." Again clicking on the

Wikipedia entry first, she read through the information on the European microstate. It was indeed small, only 165 square miles, with approximately sixty thousand citizens. As she read on, she was disturbed to learn that the microstate had gone through a revolution thirty years prior; however, due to lack of resources and continued corruption, a new form of government had never been put in place. As such, the country had been without stability for decades. The prime minister, Luca Mattia, had been overseeing operations in the country for the past eight years.

Christine read on, hoping to gain more insight into the revolution, but all that was mentioned was that the then monarch had been assassinated by revolutionists due to his harsh, dictator-like policies and lack of concern for the people. Christine had read that the current government structure in Calina was indeed a monarchy, but there was no one currently holding that title. Furthermore, she could find no information on the previous monarch, who had been assassinated…thirty years ago. Derek had fled from his country with his family when he was four. Christine couldn't help but remember the way his demeanor had changed when she had asked him about his father, who had died in Calina.

Her heart began to race, and suddenly April's ridiculous tabloid rumors came to her mind. Was it so far-fetched to consider…

Christine's intense train of thought was interrupted by the buzzing of her phone, and she nearly jumped at the sound, having been so focused on the information in front of her. Or rather the *incomplete* information in front of her. Reaching for her phone, she looked at the screen. "Incoming Call: Private."

"Hi," she said, knowing it was Derek.

"Miss me yet?" he replied, skipping the "hello" altogether. Christine smiled, realizing that the reason he had been invading her thoughts nonstop was that she did miss him.

"I do, actually."

She cleared her throat, feeling somewhat shy and unsure where to take the conversation. But, as usual, Derek took the lead easily, asking her about her day, her classes, and her plans for tomorrow. She laughed at his dry sense of humor and felt enchanted listening to the soft, low tone of his voice. Before she knew it, twenty-five minutes had passed.

She glanced at her laptop, which was still sitting open on her bed, the screen now black.

"You know," she said to him, setting the stage for the question she wanted to ask. "It occurred to me today how little I really know about you."

"Oh?" he said. "My life is pretty public, and you actually already know more than most."

"Well, to be honest with you, I never really paid attention to your life prior to now," she replied.

He laughed at her comment. "Good," he said and paused, foreseeing where she was going. "You Googled me, didn't you."

She hesitated. She wasn't sure how he would feel about her researching him, but she noted the amusement in his tone, which made her relax. "Well…yes," she answered.

"You don't have to go through all that trouble, Christine. Anything you wish to know, just ask. I will never lie to you." Christine could hear his sincerity. He then asked, "Find anything interesting?

"I don't know if it's interesting," she said, "but did you know that Wikipedia has your birthplace listed as New York? Weren't you born in Calina?" She held her breath, waiting for his answer.

"I was," he said.

She decided to push further. "Calina seems like an interesting country," she continued, "but it's sad really—it doesn't seem like it's being run very well. Funny that there's not much information available on it. Not even too much about the revolution that happened thirty years ago." She stopped for a moment, waiting to see if he would interject with any information, but he remained quiet. "Isn't that when you said you left?" she asked. "You said you were four, right?"

"Calina is very small," he explained. "I'm sure information on it is going to be limited. Not much goes on there, and from what I have heard, the country is in shambles. It doesn't surprise me that the information is inaccurate. Yes, my family left during the revolution, and I've not been back since. I have no reason to go back." He spoke with a slight defiance in his voice, but Christine also picked up on a passion he seemed to hold whenever he spoke about his home country. She burned to ask him more questions, but she chose not to press further on the subject.

She said that she should probably let him go, and he sighed and agreed, mentioning a long day ahead of him tomorrow.

"Hey." He caught her just as she was about to end the call. "I miss you too."

She smiled at his words. "When will you be able to come back?" she asked quietly.

"Tuesday," he replied. "Until then. Good night, Christine."

"Good night," she responded and clicked off.

She stared at the blank screen of her phone for several seconds. Her mind was lost in her thoughts, and she couldn't stop herself from thinking the very question she had chastised April for asking: *Are you a prince?*

Chapter 8

"Courtney, wait up!" The voice echoed somewhere in the distance behind her, but Courtney clutched her violin case tightly, making her knuckles turn white, and quickened her pace toward the backstage exit of the concert hall. Unable to bear facing anyone, she didn't want to "wait". She was now feeling the sweet numbness begin to wear off, and all she wanted to do was have another drink. It was Saturday night, and the symphony was over. Completely over for Courtney—she knew she would never play again.

Practically running after her now, James finally caught up with her about ten feet from the exit.

"Courtney, please stop." He was breathless and caught her by the shoulder. "What did Henry say?" he asked. Having not seen for her several days, James had been watching her closely throughout the evening, knowing that something was terribly wrong. Ever since news had come out that Derek Landino was possibly in a relationship, she had missed practices, would not return calls or texts—in fact, she had practically fallen off the map. Then, two days ago, the rumors were confirmed when a picture began to circulate of Derek and the other woman wrapped in a passionate kiss in front of his iconic sports car. "Local Art Program Director Wins Heart of Infamous Bachelor," the headline had read.

After that, James had become worried that Courtney wouldn't even show up for the performance. Now that the performance was over, however, he wished she hadn't. When he saw their conductor, Henry, a man who demanded perfection, address her afterward, James knew it was bad news.

She turned to face him now, and seeing her close up for the first time in days, he couldn't hide his shock at her appearance. Usually vibrant and beautiful, she now looked as though she was wasting away. Her dark hair was limp and unwashed, her skin was pale and sickly, and her eyes sunken with dark circles underneath them. Standing close to her, he was able to smell a faint hint of whiskey.

James had never bought into her insistence that Derek was in love with her, but for some reason she was smitten with him. He couldn't wrap his mind around why she refused to accept that she didn't mean anything more to him than one date. He could only conclude that Derek Landino was clearly a self-centered villain, who at liberty took what he wanted without regard for hurting others. Courtney was but a victim, led to believe that he was in love with her only so he could take advantage. It enraged James to think about how Courtney had been treated and how it was tearing her apart now.

"It doesn't matter," Courtney answered James, looking at the floor.

"Of course it matters," James said soothingly, placing a comforting hand on her shoulder. She raised her eyes to meet his. He almost cringed at the lackluster dullness within them. *That insensitive prick*, he thought. *She doesn't deserve this.*

"I'm out, James," she snapped at him. "I've been dismissed."

Sadness crossed his face. He had hoped that Henry wouldn't go to extreme measures, but he had fooled himself into thinking that Courtney's expert skill would be enough to save her place. She had missed several practices, had shown up to the concert intoxicated and unkempt, and her performance itself had been miserable. The New York Symphony was cut-throat, and one did not get second chances. Her offenses were clearly a cause for dismissal.

"Maybe I could talk to Henry," he offered hopefully. "I could tell him you've had a family emergency or that you're sick."

Courtney scoffed, her eyes wandering. "I don't care, James," she said, almost in a whisper. She met his eyes again. "I don't care about playing. Nothing matters to me anymore except..." she trailed off, and James knew she meant, "Nothing matters to me anymore...except him."

Devastated to hear her callous attitude toward her music, James felt his heart break. It was her playing that made him look forward to another day. It was hearing the brilliance and passion in her violin that made him fall in love with her. Because yes, he was in love with her. He had asked her out several times, openly blowing off each rejection in a friendly gesture, laughing at himself as if it didn't matter. But it did matter. It mattered a great deal. And now, to see her throwing away everything for *him*. A man who clearly didn't care about her, a man who had used her. James knew he had to try and make her see reason. He had to save her.

"You can't just give up on your music," he said gently. "Why are you doing this, Courtney? Because of Derek Landino?"

At the name, Courtney's eyes focused. Her mind repeated the name just as James had said it. *Yes*, she thought, *Derek. I need him back. If I could just get him back.* She swayed slightly, her mind fuzzy from her constant inebriation, the last symphony notes as well as the conductor's final words to her, still ringing in her ears.

"It's none of your business," she said coldly. "Go away, James; leave me alone." She attempted to turn away from him toward the exit, but James pressed into her shoulder, refusing to let go.

"He doesn't love you," he said firmly. "He doesn't care about you. You went on one date with him over a month ago, and he's clearly moved on." He softened his tone. "Courtney, I'm not saying this to hurt you, but because I do care for you." His heart began to pound, and his palms began to sweat. He had always wanted to tell her how he truly felt. He picked up her limp hand and held it in his. "I care for you a lot," he choked out through his nerves. "Please let me be there for you."

Courtney's eyes widened as she studied him. He looked awkward in front of her, ungracefully attempting to declare his feelings, and he seemed almost comical to her. His concert tuxedo was a bit large on his rounded shoulders. He was tall and lanky, with brown hair kept short and straight, clipped close to the sides. He wore black-framed square glasses that made his hazel brown eyes appear large. He was what Courtney would consider average, in every way. Even his cello was, in her opinion, just average. She stood motionless for a moment, then drew her hand away from his, a hurtful sneer coming across her lips.

"James," she sputtered with a laugh. "How could you actually think I would choose you over him?" James's face became stoic, her words wounding him. "You don't compare to him," she added condescendingly.

"He doesn't love you," James repeated quietly, looking down. "I do, Courtney."

She stared at him in disbelief, feeling betrayed. Tears stung at her dry eyes; he was supposed to be her friend. If anything, he should be supporting her and helping her find a way to get Derek back. Anger welled up inside her.

"How can you say you care about me?" she cried. "You clearly don't care if I'm happy! How could you be so selfish?"

Taken aback by her sudden outburst, James found strength in his voice. "Selfish?" he repeated in astonishment. "Courtney, if anyone's being selfish, it's Derek. Yet all you do is defend him. Why?" His frustration began to overpower his feelings of indignity and rival her anger. He grabbed both her shoulders. He had to make her understand. "He doesn't love you!" he repeated again, more harshly than he had meant to.

She shrugged him off her, disdain filling her eyes as she looked at him.

"That's not true," she said with malice. "He does love me, and I love him. You know nothing of what happened between us, and I don't need your approval." She turned, preparing to leave, but she looked back again to face him. She gave a contemptuous and mocking smile, jeering at him. "Did you honestly think that I could ever be interested in you, when I have him?" Not waiting for an answer, she gripped her violin case even tighter, turned, and walked out the exit door.

He didn't try to stop her this time. He watched her leave, feeling a sense of being completely destroyed. As he stood alone backstage, an overwhelming pain tore through him. Courtney hated him; he had no chance with her. He would never hear her play again. And she was ruining herself, driving herself literally into the ground, like she had ingested a permanent poison that would forever cripple her common sense. James grieved, broken, and his eyes grew dark and cold as he realized exactly who was to blame.

———•———

Derek parked the company car in the secure lot and proceeded into his building. As he entered the private entrance, he looked back and made a face at the BMW. Having made the decision to leave his own car in North Carolina, anticipating that was where he'd be spending more of his time, he had to now endure the alternative. As he walked through the door, his phone buzzed. "Incoming Call: Mattia." He sent the call to voicemail. Since his conversation with the prime minister on the yacht, he had gone back to ghosting him. Derek was not ready to have additional conversations surrounding Calina, especially after today.

Security greeted him as he passed through the atrium on his way to the elevator. Stepping inside, he used his passkey to access the button for the twenty-third floor. As he ascended, he couldn't help but reflect on his last couple of days in New York. It was strange as he had only been gone for three days, but he was finding his old routine difficult to get back into. The priorities in his life had changed.

He had arrived back in the city late Thursday afternoon, and Gregory had arranged several rescheduled board meetings and a dinner with a prominent investor. Although it had been a long and exhausting day of playing catchup, he had still found time to call Christine. Friday and Saturday were spent checking in with key partners and his CFO, rearranging several desperately needed financial plans, and finally, the unveiling of the new project downtown. His arrival at the major event solo had made headlines, and everyone seemed interested in his personal affairs.

He did not regret his decision to make his relationship with Christine public, even if it did mean enduring more press than usual for a while. He sighed, hoping that after they got used to it, everyone would cease to care so much about his love life. As his thoughts turned to Christine, he found himself aching to see her again. Wishing to keep her mind at ease while he was away, he called her daily. He looked forward to speaking to her each time and sought to strengthen trust with her; he had been pleased at her admission that she missed him. He smiled slightly as he thought of how it felt to kiss her, breathe in her hair, and hear her laugh. No wonder he was finding it difficult to concentrate.

He stepped off the elevator and entered the reception area, heading toward his office. The reception desk was empty, and Derek strode past it, again using his passkey to access the office space. Gregory's office was just before his own, and even though it was Sunday, Derek knew his assistant would be in. Derek did not acknowledge or work by standard weekdays and weekends. He worked when he needed to work, and as a result, so did his assistant. But Gregory didn't mind the strenuous schedule. The perks and compensation of being the personal assistant of Derek Landino more than made up for his time and efforts.

Hearing footfalls and sensing that Derek was walking now toward his office, Gregory called out to him.

"How was lunch, sir?" He heard a pause in the footsteps, then he heard Derek proceed into his office. Derek left the door open, and Gregory took this as a sign that he should follow him if he wanted an answer. He rose from his desk and made his way to his boss's door.

Derek stood by the window facing the city, his hands behind his back. He did not acknowledge Gregory right away, and the silence told Gregory that lunch did not go as Derek had hoped. Finally, he took in a deep breath and turned toward Gregory.

"Nicola is a stubborn, spoiled excuse for a brother who refuses to see reason," he stated, shaking his head in frustration. "I even offered him a job. His line of thinking is completely skewed. The way he spends, it's inevitable he will run out of money." He paused and walked to his desk, leaning over it to check something on his laptop. Gregory waited for Derek to continue, knowing better than to interject. "He's a disgrace to our family name," Derek murmured now, squinting at the computer. "He looks like our mother, but acts exactly like our father." Finishing what he was reading, he grimaced and stood straight, glancing back at Gregory. "He'll grow up when he has to, and not a minute before. I can't offer that to Mattia." He stopped and ran a hand through his hair. "I can't do that to Calina."

"Mattia called while you were out, sir," Gregory offered.

Derek nodded slowly. "I know," he replied. His assistant waited for him to say more, but Derek only turned his attention back to the computer screen.

Gregory remained quiet for a moment, uncertain if he wanted to ask a particular question weighing on his mind. Deciding it was best to go ahead, he addressed his friend.

"Derek," he started. Derek looked back up at him, and his eyes narrowed in anticipation of the loaded question about to come his way. "Does she know?"

"No," he responded.

Gregory took a breath and continued, knowing it was best for Derek to consider this even though he would not be receptive to it.

"Are you going to tell her?" he asked.

Derek placed his hands in his pockets and regarded him pensively. "Right now, there's nothing to tell," he said simply.

Gregory was thoughtful, choosing his words before speaking them. Well aware that Derek could rightly tell him this was none of his business, Gregory felt obligated to offer his potentially unwelcome advice. "A relationship is built on trust," he replied. "I think you need to be honest with her about who you are. She may have a decision to make. Maybe she should know all of the facts before you take this further."

As Derek listened to Gregory's opinion, which he respected, he maintained his poker face, even though countless thoughts ran through his mind. The same thoughts that had caused him much loss of sleep over the past few days. As usual, Gregory's insight was spot on, and he always seemed to zero in on the detail that mattered most. Derek too had concluded that Christine, at some point, needed to know what she may end up facing by being with him. But there were still too many variables, too many uncertainties. He could not see putting undue strain on his relationship over something that may or may not happen.

Besides, ultimately it would be his, Derek's, decision, and Derek did not reveal his hand unless he knew the outcome would be one in his favor. He needed more facts and more time before showing any of his cards.

"I don't think anyone needs unnecessary pressure," he told Gregory. "I need to know first where this is heading with her." He knitted his brow and cast his eyes down briefly. "And until I know for sure *my* decision, or course of action, I will not ask her to make one. Status quo is best for now." He met Gregory's eye and spoke in a tone that settled the issue.

Gregory pondered Derek's explanation for a moment. He knew Derek to be shrewd, and he felt confident he was making the best choices where Christine was concerned.

"What if she asks you?" he said. "It's rumored, as you know."

Derek had considered this. He had done his best to ensure that any records of his past, heritage, and birthright were nowhere to be found. But Christine already knew certain information about his past that might have caused her to suspect something was off, and thanks to her friend, April, he was aware Christine knew of the rumors.

"I will not lie to her," Derek said. "If she asks, I will be honest about it. I actually thought she might ask me the other night." He reflected on the conversation for a moment, at the time having done his best to answer her questions without revealing specifics. "But Christine is very down to earth," he added. "The reality is too sensational for her to take seriously. I don't think she could bring herself to ask me outright."

A sudden knock on the office door halted their conversation.

"Sorry, am I interrupting?" Both Gregory and Derek turned to the door to see Land Corporation's head attorney, Timothy McKenzie, enter. Timothy's presence there was scheduled as Derek had asked to meet with him after his lunch with Nicola.

Brothers Timothy and Gregory resembled each other strongly. They were of the same height and build, had the same wavy brown hair and dazzling smile. But Timothy's brown eyes were a shade darker, he wore no glasses, and although Gregory was fit, Timothy maintained a regimented workout routine and was much broader and more muscular. With a dashing face, strong jawline, and a sterling reputation as an attorney, Timothy didn't have any trouble finding company.

Having grown up in the same neighborhood as Derek, Timothy had known him longer than anyone in his inner circle. They had attended the same college. He was Derek's best friend and best man at his wedding to Cynthia, and Derek didn't trust anyone as much as he trusted Timothy. That is, until three years ago, when he divorced Cynthia. Something had changed, Derek knew, and although the precise reason was never clear or discussed, his relationship with Timothy had never been the same. Maybe it was because Timothy had represented Derek in the divorce but sympathized more with Cynthia. Derek had always suspected this was the case, but Timothy had never addressed it, and Derek had written off the personal reasons for his divorce as none of his friend's business. He did not realize it at the time, but looking back, Derek now surmised that Timothy had a conflict of interest—though he never found out why.

Smiling now at Timothy in greeting, Derek motioned for him to enter the office.

"Not at all, Tim," he said easily. "I appreciate you coming in." Gregory acknowledged his brother with a half smile and a nod, then took his leave. Timothy strolled over to one of the cushy leather chairs arranged in an informal meeting area off to the left. Derek followed, taking the chair next to him.

"It's Sunday," Timothy said, looking at Derek keenly. His tone made it clear that he did not approve of working over the weekend. "Jesus, Derek, don't you ever take a day off?" He leaned back against the leather and crossed an ankle over his knee, making himself comfortable.

Derek folded his hands, interlocking his fingers together with a calculating smile on his face.

"Now that you mention it," he said, "that's why I asked you here." Timothy looked at him with curiosity. "There are some changes I need to make within the structure of the corporation," he began. "For starters, I'm moving my main office location to the yacht in North Carolina."

Timothy gaped at him. "Permanently?" he asked in astonishment.

Derek gave a small laugh. "Well, until further notice," he answered. "Since you are head attorney and a key partner, I will require your attendance in North Carolina as well. Not daily. But over the next couple of months I expect you will be fairly busy, and your in-person presence will be necessary." He paused, taking in Timothy's reaction. The attorney didn't object, so Derek continued. "In addition to Land Corporation's contracts, there will be a particular project that I trust only you to handle." Derek spoke with emphasis. "And it must be handled with the most extreme discretion."

Timothy eyed Derek now, taking in the instructions. His mouth set in a hard line; he squared his shoulders and stood from the chair, pacing around behind it. Derek remained seated, frowning slightly at Timothy's body language. He waited patiently for a reply.

"Derek," Timothy began, bracing his palms on top of the chair, "I need to speak with you as my friend, not my employer." Derek raised his eyebrows, indicating that he should continue. "I don't agree with your decision to move Land Corporation's headquarters. You are needed here in New York, where the deals are being made and where your main connections are. You'll lose business by doing this." He took a breath. "Have you weighed out the potential losses?"

Timothy spoke quickly, and Derek saw through what appeared to be artificial concerns or reasoning. But until he was able to unearth some truths, he decided it best to address Timothy's current line of questioning.

"Potential losses are not just measured in terms of dollars, cents, and contracts," he replied seriously. "I'm aware of the risks, but I'm also aware of the opportunity." Timothy gave him a quizzical look. "New York is not the only place in the world in which to run a business," he proceeded. "Daniel will stay on here to oversee what is necessary, and I can fly back when I'm needed." He stood now and walked over to his desk. "I've been too hands on in running this company. Leveraging the talent and leadership that I have on staff will only grow Land Corporation, and I need development of that leadership now more than ever. I will be looking to restructure some key areas. That's where you come in."

Derek stopped and regarded his attorney, and again skepticism surrounding Timothy's questions grew in him. If anyone knew Derek, it was Timothy.

"I must say I'm disappointed to discover your lack of faith in me and my ability to think this through thoroughly." Timothy stared at Derek for a moment, then averted his gaze, his jaw still set. "Since we're speaking as friends," Derek continued, "why don't you tell me what's really concerning you?"

Timothy shut his eyes briefly and looked back at Derek with an almost defeated expression.

"You're only doing this because of a woman," he finally said. Derek placed his hands in his pockets in response. "You're moving your company and changing your lifestyle so that you can continue to see this art program director?" Timothy's voice rose slightly, and Derek could tell he was agitated.

"Christine." He corrected him.

Timothy took a breath to calm himself and spread his hands in front of him. "You divorced your wife of nine years because you would not make the same changes three years ago that you're making now," he said evenly. "You could have made similar arrangements then to save your marriage, but you refused. You chose Land Corporation. Why now?" he asked. "It was ok for you to break your wife's heart, but you won't walk away from this relationship?"

The increase in Timothy's emotion told Derek that he had finally gotten to the root of the matter. What he didn't understand was why he cared so much.

"You seem to be under the impression that I owe you some kind of explanation," he told Timothy. He kept his voice even and unemotional; however, Derek was not appreciative of the interrogation. Timothy sighed and knew it would be useless to continue this conversation now. Not wishing to cause more strain than was already present in their friendship, he knew it was best to drop the subject.

"Just tell me one thing," he said with finality. "Did you ever even love her at all? Cynthia?"

The question caught Derek by surprise for two reasons. First, he was surprised that Timothy had even asked it, and second, he had never considered that he hadn't, at some point, loved his ex-wife. He thought for a moment.

He thought about meeting Christine, the way he felt about her—it was different, and more.

"I was young," he finally replied. "I felt for her what I thought was love at that time in my life." He studied Timothy's expression, reading his thoughts. "Why are you so concerned with Cynthia?" Derek was not one to withhold feelings or questions, and he was curious to get to the bottom of whatever this was, believing it had something to do with the tension between them.

Timothy's face was blank as he explained himself. "We went to college together," he said. "We were all friends in the same circles. I've known her as long as I've known you." He paused for a moment. "I care about her too, you know."

Now we've gotten to it, Derek thought. Although he was desperately trying to hide it, there was far too much earnestness in Timothy's voice for Derek not to notice it, and he suddenly understood where his friend was coming from. Timothy cared for Cynthia, possibly even loved her. Maybe he was consciously aware of his feelings or maybe he wasn't, but Derek recognized what he saw.

However, now was not the time to address this, and Derek needed his head attorney focused and on board with his business plan. Besides, he had nothing to do with Cynthia any longer.

"I will need you in North Carolina in three days," he said, no longer acknowledging the cumbersomeness of the current dialogue. "Can you accommodate the travel and schedule I've presented to you?"

The abrupt change in subject told Timothy the discussion was over, that Derek's mind was resolute. He hesitated briefly, then nodded in agreement.

"Of course, Derek," he answered. "I will go where you need me to go for the company." He knew, however, there would come a day when he would be forced to tell Derek the whole truth. Today was obviously not that day.

Chapter 9

One Month Later

The tenth anniversary gala for Land Corporation was a highly anticipated event that made headlines. The gala was exceedingly exclusive and intimate, reserved strictly for key employees, their guests, and a handful of the corporation's most prominent investors. It was being held aboard the superyacht, and Christine now sat in the back of a black Mercedes passing through marina security. Wanting Christine to feel as comfortable as possible at the event, Derek had graciously extended an additional invitation to her best friend, who sat next to her.

Elated by the opportunity to attend such a prestigious affair, April had insisted on taking Christine shopping for something new and expensive to wear. Feeling apprehensive, Christine now smoothed out the delicate fabric of her emerald-green silk cocktail dress. The dress was simple and elegant, with an asymmetrical shape to the folds of the skirt and a corset-style strapless top. She had added a simple green velvet choker to the look and styled her hair down in loose, cascading curls. April had chosen a more understated glam look with a black designer gown that had all-over lace detailing and a mermaid skirt that fell just below her knees.

Admiring her friend, Christine noted that April looked particularly stunning this evening, with her red hair piled on top of her head and her bright green eyes shining as they caught the rays from the yacht lights. As the car pulled up closer, Christine peered out her window. The sight was breathtaking. It was early evening, with the stars just beginning to appear in the purple sky, but the lights aboard the yacht were luminous and blazing.

Over the past month, Derek had successfully moved his main office to the yacht, along with key personnel, and was now efficiently running the company from North Carolina, enabling him to spend most of his time there. True to his vision, the company had flourished, with the expansion enabling new opportunities and ventures. Derek had always maintained ownership in businesses across the country, but now it seemed viable to open up additional satellite offices for the parent corporation itself.

Now seen by the public as being in an exclusive relationship with Derek Landino, Christine had begun to settle into a lifestyle that included the press, tabloids, and travel to attend events by his side in New York and even, once, in France. She was not always able to follow him, and he respected her decision to continue her career and painting aspirations. Even at the university, because of her association to him, she was receiving more attention than she cared for, and although she struggled to deal with the pressures of being in the spotlight, she knew it was worth it to be with him.

Much of her time with him was exposed to the public eye, and being ushered from face to face, meeting and greeting, smiling and having her picture taken, was exhausting. Realizing the sacrifices she was making to fit into his world, Derek took care to always ensure she felt comfortable and at ease. He knew that being constantly viewed under a microscope was no situation in which to build a serious relationship, and he made certain there were occasions for the two of them to be alone. Whether he had to arrange a private viewing of a theater performance or just bring her aboard the yacht, where he knew they were safe from prying eyes, he prioritized these moments for them, and Christine had been amazed at how successfully he was adjusting his life for her.

She felt herself becoming closer to him with every moment they shared, and she couldn't deny her strong feelings of desire. But, through the past few weeks, Derek had continued to maintain his resolve to not proceed further then a kiss. With the sexual tension mounting each time they touched, Christine couldn't help but pine and wonder if and when.

Stepping out of the car as the driver opened her door, she met April around the front, and they walked together toward the gangway. As they boarded, Christine noted the black carpet that covered their path. They were greeted by attendants as soon as they entered the boat, and after Christine had given their names, they were ushered into the main gathering area, up one deck toward the stern.

Now very familiar with the layout of the yacht, Christine was surprised to find that she could hardly recognize it. Many of her intimate moments with Derek had been spent on this large deck, looking off into the sunset. Now she could hardly imagine this was the same space. All the cushy furnishings had been removed. There was a live band and small round cocktail tables covered in black silk tablecloths. Under the enclosure was an enormous and elaborate bar carved entirely out of ice. The bar itself was sculpted to include Land Corporation's logo across the front. Strands of lights were strung up, and a beautiful, gleaming black dance floor covered the middle of the deck, beneath the stars. Black silk and more lights hung from the railings, and waiters dressed in all-black tuxedos carried around silver trays of champagne and delicacies.

The celebration was already underway, and there were guests dancing, socializing, and drinking in groups. Scanning the sea of faces, Christine searched for Derek. He had just returned from a business trip, and it had been three days since she had last seen him. She finally spotted him across the deck by the rail, speaking and laughing easily with two other men. He had chosen to wear a luxurious white jacket against all black. The ensemble was striking, and he stood out from the crowd.

Watching him from afar, Christine observed the regal way he moved. As guests positioned themselves near him, clearly seeking his audience, he greeted each one with grace, a smile, and a handshake. Looking around her, she noticed most eyes were glancing or motioning in his direction; he was clearly the man of the hour, and she felt uncomfortable approaching him in such a mass with so many vying for his attention. She gave April a small smile, extremely grateful that her friend was by her side.

"What are you waiting for?" April asked her suddenly over the buzzing of the crowd. "Go on."

Christine hesitated. She looked back at Derek and felt herself melt a little when he smiled, the dimple appearing on his left cheek. Lost in her gaze at him, she didn't hear what April had said next.

"What?" she asked, leaning in toward her friend but unwilling to take her eyes off Derek.

"You're in love with him," April repeated quietly so just Christine could hear. Christine looked at her sharply. "I can tell by the way you look at him," April continued with a knowing smile. "Don't deny it, Christine."

Christine didn't immediately respond; she just stared at April for a moment. She knew that her friend was right—she was in love with him. She had known this for some time now. But she was afraid of admitting it out loud, especially to him. What if his feelings weren't there yet? What if they never were? And if April could tell, would he be able to as well? Suddenly Christine felt extremely self-conscious.

"I'm not ready to tell him," she said in a low voice. "What if he doesn't feel the same?"

April looked toward Derek. "He does," she whispered back. But Christine didn't hear her over the large crowd of people that had just passed them. "Christine, he's coming this way," April suddenly said more loudly.

Christine looked quickly back in his direction. April was right—Derek had noticed her and was making his way to them. She was impressed with the way he progressed through the masses, pausing to chat briefly with several guests. He was brilliant at networking. It was not a skill that Christine possessed; she was naturally more introverted. As he neared them, he met her eyes, his stride natural and confident, and Christine once again had the unnerving feeling that heads were turning in their direction. As usual, he made her heart flutter when he was near.

"Christine," he said as he reached her, immediately wrapping her in his embrace. "I missed you," he breathed near her ear. Christine closed her eyes briefly and unconsciously gripped him tightly. He released her and looked in her eyes, smiling warmly.

Turning to April, he held out his hand.

"I'm very glad you came, April," he said. "I hope you enjoy your evening here."

April shook his offered hand. "Thank you for inviting me." She was beaming. "And don't worry about me; I know how to have a good time." As she said the words, April began eyeing the crowd. "If you two will excuse me?" She winked at Christine and headed into the sea of people, having spied what or whom she was looking for. Christine shook her head, smiling after her friend. April, clearly, did not have trouble networking. Derek glanced after April as she left, then turned his attention on Christine, offering her his arm.

"Will you dance with me?" he asked.

"I'd love to," she replied, taking his arm and letting him lead her to the dance floor.

The band was currently playing a slow ballad, and Derek took her hand in his, wrapping his other arm around her waist, holding her close to him. Christine loved dancing with him. His moves were fluid and graceful, and she felt like she belonged in his arms. He leaned his head forward, his cheek grazing hers.

"You are so beautiful," he said softly. "You look amazing tonight." He brought his head up to look into her eyes, noting how the lighting and emerald green from her dress brought out their natural turquoise.

She smiled at him. "You clean up nice too," she said playfully.

The reality was he had never looked more alluring to her than he did now, and she couldn't stop an aching that came over her. He laughed at her reply, his sapphire eyes twinkling.

They danced through several songs, many of the guests continuing to glance in their direction. Christine was well aware of the attention, but Derek didn't seem to notice, never taking his own eyes off of her, unless it was to nuzzle close to her ear.

"I need to tell you something," he said to her now, his tone turning serious. "I've been thinking a lot over these past couple days." He searched her face. Christine could tell that he was looking for words. He clearly had something important to say, but he seemed unsure of how to say it. Her heart began to pound. Was he giving her bad news? He locked his gaze with hers.

"I think I've found my purpose," he began gently. "Christine, I—"

"Mr. Landino, sir?" A tap on his shoulder interrupted his words. Derek turned toward the interruption, halting the dance with her. He acknowledged the man who had tapped him with raised eyebrows. "Sir, Mr. Robinson is asking for you. He is looking to discuss the upcoming merger and the possible investment." Derek took in the information and sighed. Nodding to the man, he turned back to Christine.

"I'm very sorry," he said. "This is important, but hopefully it will not take long."

Christine nodded her head. "I understand," she replied, forcing a smile. By now she was used to the constant interruptions and his being called away. He lifted the back of her hand and grazed his lips over it.

"Have some champagne, and I'll be back momentarily." Giving her a last, brief smile, he turned and followed the man past the ice bar and out of the main reception area.

Now alone in the crowd, Christine looked for April. The eyes of strangers continued to look in her direction, maybe even more so now that Derek had walked away. Or maybe her insecurity was just imagining that was the case. Finally spotting her friend on the other side of the deck, leaning against the rail, Christine noticed she was talking and laughing with Gregory McKenzie.

Gregory was usually the one who was sent for Christine when Derek was in town, and he and April had met on several occasions. Christine had never considered, however, that April might be interested in the assistant, or vice versa. But, she realized with amusement, she may have been too distracted by her own situation to notice anyone else's. Watching them together now, Christine could tell that April was clearly flirting with him. Knowing that she couldn't interrupt April now, she looked around awkwardly. It was uncomfortable to feel out of place, let alone to feel out of place with people staring at you.

"Those two," a voice was suddenly by her side. Christine turned to see Timothy, relieved to have someone to interact with. He smiled at her and offered her a champagne flute.

"Thank you," she responded, taking the glass. Having met the attorney a couple of times now in North Carolina, Christine knew that he was Gregory's older brother and Derek's best friend. Timothy gestured back toward April and Gregory with his own glass.

"I've been watching them for a while now," he continued, a playful smile on his face.

Christine grinned. "I think she might like him," she replied, taking a sip. Timothy downed the last bit in his own flute, then placed it on a passing tray being carried by a waiter.

"Well, I'll tell you a little secret," he said mischievously. "I know he likes her." Christine turned toward him, her eyes widening in surprise. He laughed at her expression. Looking back at April, who was now leaning toward Gregory suggestively and appearing to enjoy herself, Christine smiled.

"They look good together," she said decidedly, sipping again from her glass.

"Yeah," Timothy agreed, "as long as she can handle his schedule. There's a reason he's single, you know. Wherever Derek goes, so does Greg." He paused, studying Christine, taking in her flawless face and curves. Still looking at April and Gregory, Christine didn't notice. "It's not an easy lifestyle," Timothy continued in a low tone. "But I guess you know what that's like." Christine met his eyes, a slow smile forming on his lips. Unsure of how to respond, she took another drink.

"Well," he said after a few moments, gently removing her now-empty glass from her hand, "we seem to be standing in the middle of a dance floor, but we're not dancing." He placed her flute on another tray going by, then offered her his hand. "Shall we?" He gave her a dazzling smile. Christine hesitated.

"But Derek—"

Timothy cut her off. "He won't be back for a while; trust me." He shook his head. "And he wouldn't want you just standing here by yourself."

Recalling how uncomfortable she felt just a few minutes ago, before Timothy graciously approached her, she consented to the dance and placed her hand in his. Grateful that the band had picked up the pace in melody a bit, she began to follow his lead to a lively rhythm. He held her hand firmly, and Christine noted that he was a very good dancer. As he brought her hand up over her head to twirl her out and then back, she laughed, struggling slightly to keep up with his pace. Spinning her out then back toward him, he ended the dance by bracing his hand on her lower back and leaning her over in a low dip. She was enjoying the friendly interaction and laughed again as he brought her back upright.

As the song ended and another began, the pace slowed. Christine pulled away from him and prepared to thank him for his time, but as she turned away, he held firm onto her hand. Looking back at him, she gave him a perplexed expression. His dark eyes gazed into hers as he placed his arm back around her waist.

"The honor would be mine," he said softly. Feeling like she had no choice, Christine timidly rested her hand on the black lapel of his jacket. He swayed her slowly, his head bent down toward her, and she found it difficult to meet his eyes. Timothy was incredibly handsome, but he was not the man who she was here with and not who she wanted to be dancing with. Just as she was feeling like they were too close together, he pressed on her back, bringing her even closer to him, her body now brushing against his.

"You're absolutely mesmerizing," he said in a low voice near her ear.

His hand slid up to the base of her neck. Brushing her chestnut hair back off her shoulder, he cradled her neck, his thumb caressing her jaw. Stunned by his sudden forwardness, Christine stiffened at his touch. He tilted her face up, forcing her to look at him. His dark eyes gleamed, and his slight smile was devilish. He shrugged dismissively.

"Too bad for me he saw you first," he told her.

Christine's eyes frantically searched his and her mind raced. She needed to put space between them. Pressing on his chest lightly, she pushed him away from her.

"Timothy, I...I need to get out of this crowd," she stammered. Breaking eye contact with him, she turned to walk away, but dancing couples everywhere were in her path. Feeling completely unnerved, she was struggling to breathe and felt suffocated. Timothy sensed her rising panic and lightly placed his hand on her lower back. He guided her safely out of the mass of people, steering her toward the exit to the promenade.

Having just witnessed the encounter between them and watching them leave the party together, Derek stood near the bar, an ominous expression on his face. In light of their conversation in New York not long ago, if anyone knew how Derek felt about Christine, it was his best friend.

As he made to follow them across the deck, he caught sight of another person who was making a beeline in the same direction. She was a pretty, slim, petite blonde in a very light pink chiffon dress. She was chasing after them in the same way Derek had just prepared to, and it only meant one thing to him. His eyes now set on the blonde, Derek strode across the room to catch up with her.

"Good evening," he said to her as he approached.

She was almost to the exit now but turned at his voice. "Hello," she replied, then opened her eyes wide, realizing who was speaking to her. "Mr. Landino! Um, good evening." Her expression held a mix of surprise and concern, and she glanced anxiously back at the exit.

He extended his hand to her in a friendly handshake.

"I'm glad you could attend tonight, Miss…?"

She blushed slightly. "I'm sorry," she responded, clearly embarrassed. "I'm Fawna, Fawna Gable."

The last name resonated with him. "Lawrence Gable?" he asked.

"He was my father," Fawna said. "The original owner of Gable Ranch." She eyed him, waiting for recognition. "You own it." As she continued to gaze at him, she was fairly certain she had never seen eyes that shade of blue before. He smiled at her.

"Yes, I know," he replied. "I was very sorry to hear of your father's passing. I understand he left the ranch in your capable hands?" A touch of sadness entered her blue-gray eyes. She nodded in affirmation. "Lawrence was a good man," Derek continued. "He was very passionate about the ranch, but unfortunately he didn't have good business sense." He half smiled, his mind recalling that particular deal and the financial mess the ranch was in two years ago.

Fawna laughed lightly.

"That's the truth," she said. "Daddy loved his horses, but not numbers." She met his eyes. "Our family was grateful for your company's assistance. If it hadn't been for you, we would have been forced to sell out completely or declare bankruptcy. The ranch would have most likely been turned into high-rise condos." She shuddered. It would have broken her father's heart if that had happened. "It was amazing what you were able to do to help turn a profit for us so quickly."

Derek waved a hand, dismissing the gratitude humbly. "It's a good business with a good vision," he said simply. "It just needed to be run properly. Really, one of the easiest deals I've made."

She beamed at him, admiring his charm. "You should come down and see the place when you can," she offered shyly. "I've made some improvements."

Derek nodded thoughtfully. "Yes, I've heard good things about the way you've moved the business forward and expanded," he replied. "I imagine I should be able to head that way soon."

"By the way," he said, now changing the subject, "did I see you here earlier with my attorney, Timothy McKenzie?" Her smile faded, a hurt expression crossing her face.

"Um, yes," she said, casting her eyes downward. "But I think I lost him somewhere." Derek's smile widened. "What a coincidence," he replied. "I seem to have lost my date as well. Why don't we go look for them together?" She knitted her eyebrows, confused by his suggestion. Not waiting for her response, he touched her elbow and steered her toward the exit to the promenade.

They walked along the outside deck path leading to the bow of the yacht. Derek spotted Timothy and Christine standing together by the rail. Timothy was leaning casually toward her, engaging in conversation, and although she was responding politely, Derek could tell by her body language that she was not comfortable. He did not imagine for a moment that Christine would respond to Timothy's advances, but he was very disturbed to discover that his friend would make advances in the first place. Again thinking back to their discussion in New York and how Timothy had unknowingly revealed his feelings toward Cynthia, it occurred to Derek that his extensive trust in his friend was perhaps misplaced. Was this the first time Timothy had pursued a woman Derek was involved with?

"There they are!" Derek exclaimed as he and Fawna approached them.

Timothy, who's back was to Derek, turned to face him. Derek looked at him with a smile that didn't quite reach his eyes.

"Look, Fawn," he said, "how convenient for us that your date and mine are together."

"Um, Fawna." She corrected him quietly, but Derek didn't acknowledge the correction, his eyes now focused on Christine. He could see the relief in her eyes at his arrival.

"Christine," he said, looking at her, then back to Fawna. "Why don't you ladies chat for a minute? I need to have a word with Tim."

He spoke pleasantly enough, but Christine could sense some aggression. She hoped he had not gotten the wrong impression. Had he seen them dancing? Recalling Derek's demeanor when he had met Jackson, Christine was not anxious to ever see that volcano erupt. She thought again about the fact that she was in love with him, and she could not imagine ever wanting to be with another man.

Derek then turned away from the group and began walking further up the promenade until he was out of earshot. He didn't look behind him, but he knew Timothy had followed. Now that they were several yards away, he stopped and turned to face his friend.

"What are you doing?" he asked bluntly. His eyes were narrow, focused on Timothy, and he placed his hands in his pockets. It was a power stance; Derek knew how to look intimidating when he wanted to.

"I don't know what you—" Timothy started, but Derek cut him off.

"Don't," he said strongly. "I saw you."

Timothy opened his mouth, prepared to argue, but he simply sighed. "I don't know," he repeated sincerely. "It was not my intention, Derek." He met Derek's eye as he closely contemplated Timothy's expression.

Knowing that he owed Derek some kind of explanation, Timothy glanced at the two women, wondering how much he should say. He knew he would not be able to hide the truth for much longer.

"You just left her there alone, like you always do," he said, looking back at Derek. "Like you always have." He paused. "Why should I think that she's different to you? That you won't do to her what you did to Cynthia?"

"I'm not asking you to think anything," Derek responded, his anger growing. "I don't recall asking for your approval. So, you think that because I chose to exit my failing marriage, it's now ok for you to disrespect any other relationship I aspire to have?" Timothy didn't respond but matched Derek's glare. "My date doesn't need to be rescued, and it's not your place to 'fill in' in my absence."

Unable to control himself, Timothy smirked at him.

"Well, I guess it's a role I've just gotten used to then." As soon as he had said the words, he wished he hadn't. His face gave the feeling away, and he knew Derek would now piece together the rest. As he had feared, Derek's eyes widened knowingly.

"What exactly are you insinuating?" His tone was low and dangerous. Timothy thought quickly about how to respond. Now was not the time to have this out, he decided.

"You're never around, Derek," he said in a factual tone, hoping to downplay the situation. "You've made your lifestyle choices, and you need to accept that. Just don't expect everyone to be ok with it." He turned to leave before Derek could ask additional questions.

Derek watched Timothy walk back over to Christine and Fawna, offer his arm to the latter, then lead her away, back to the party. He knew Timothy had blown him off, not responding with specificity to his question. He also now knew why their friendship suffered. This was not over, he realized, but he looked at Christine and refocused on what was more important to him at this current moment.

Christine turned to look out on the water as she waited for Derek to return. There was a cool night breeze, and she folded her arms as she leaned against the rail, the wind fluttering her hair. Gazing down at the black waves, she had not heard Derek walk up to her and only noticed him when she felt a sudden warmth as he placed his jacket around her shoulders.

"Thank you," she said softly, turning and smiling at him. He stood by her side and placed his arm around her. He didn't say anything, and Christine studied his ever-unreadable profile, feeling the need to discuss what had happened. "Derek, please don't think…" she began, but he interrupted her.

"I don't," he said quietly. He then turned toward her, his arm drawing her into him. She allowed her head to rest on his chest, and she closed her eyes, feeling his warmth and strength. "I trust you completely," he told her. She smiled at his words, relieved to know he felt that way. "I never had the chance to finish what I was trying to tell you before." He pulled back from her to look upon her face. Christine searched his eyes, looking for some clue as to what he needed to say, but they gave nothing away.

"Ok," she said tentatively, questioning whether she wanted to hear what he needed to tell her.

He glanced around, noting the other guests who were now strolling the promenade.

"Not here," he said. He grabbed her hand and led her through the interior of the boat, down a deck and toward the cabins. Christine was confused, her heart beginning to beat rapidly as his sudden need for privacy made her nervous. Maintaining his silence, he made his way down the corridor, arriving at the main cabin suite, his own. Christine had not been in his cabin since that first night on the yacht with him. Opening the door, he allowed her to pass him inside.

Now, where it was warmer, Christine removed his jacket and handed it back to him. Taking it from her, he tossed it casually over the back of a chair in the main sitting area. She waited for him to speak, but he appeared to be stalling, removing his cuff links and rolling up his sleeves. She couldn't help but smile slightly in spite of her nerves. She had grown accustomed to his constant need for comfort; he refused ties, and his signature rolled-up sleeves were a must. She realized it was just one more thing she loved about him, and she thought again of her fear of telling him, although she longed to confess.

As he finished rolling his sleeves, he looked at her, taking her in, awe-struck by how beautiful she looked just then. Her eyes were wide and wondering, and he knew she was anxious, seemingly always afraid of what he had to say. He knew that her fears were fueled by his status and position, and he desired for nothing more than to put to rest any doubts or questions of his feelings for her.

Having been apart from her these past three days, he had given much thought to what he wanted to say, how he would express himself completely. He had always assumed that he would feel apprehensive to say what he yearned to say, but surprisingly, he felt no hesitations, no second thoughts, no reservations. He was assured in his next course of action and also that every decision he had made up to this point had been the right one, all leading up to this moment.

He walked up to her now and took her hand in his.

"It's ok," he reassured her, noticing that she had held her breath. He watched her exhale slowly, and she looked up at him, her eyes sparkling in the dim lighting of the cabin. "I'm in love with you, Christine," he told her softly. Her mouth opened slightly and she blinked several times.

"You are?" she whispered, barely audibly. He nodded slowly, a smile forming on his lips.

"I have been for a while," he continued, then paused, thinking. "Maybe even from the first moment I saw you. I've never felt before the way you make me feel. You've ignited something within me I didn't even know was possible." He watched her eyes glisten, tears welling in them. "I can't imagine not having you in my life."

He reached for her face, and as one tear slid down her cheek, he brushed it away with his thumb. He looked at her intently, patiently waiting for her response. Suddenly she broke into a laugh and threw her arms around his neck.

"Derek," she said as more tears brimmed in her eyes, "I love you too." He hugged her tightly to him, smiling into her hair. "I wanted to tell you before," she said, "but I was afraid." He pulled back, and she released her hold on him. He shook his head and looked at her endearingly. "You don't ever have to be afraid of me," he said, locking his eyes with hers. "Christine, I will never hurt you."

She closed her eyes briefly, feeling an enormous sense of relief wash through her. This was real, she told herself, he really did love her. When she opened her eyes and met his gaze, he could see the joy shining out through them.

Part of him had known all along how he felt, and he now knew that his love was requited; it was the assurance he needed to act on his desires. Just looking at her made his breath quicken and his heart pound, and he could no longer stop the blood flowing through his body. He didn't have to say anything or ask; she read within his eyes what he wanted. He did not look away from her face as he brushed her hair back off her shoulders. Then, reaching behind her neck, he unclasped the velvet choker, removing it from her. He placed the necklace on the nearby table, next to his cuff links, then he gently reached for her face as he placed his lips softly on hers. Ending the kiss, he looked deeply into her eyes.

Christine recognized the burning passion in him as her own heart thumped in her throat. He grazed her lips with his thumb, then without warning he claimed her mouth with vigor, and she felt through him his insane fervor, an intense craving that he had been harboring ever since the very first time he had touched her. As his tongue explored hers, his hands moved to his shirt, removing it and tossing it to the side.

Breathless from his kiss, Christine's mouth left his, traveling to his ear, then down his neck to his collarbone, her mouth tickling and teasing him as he became dazed by the sensation. His hands smoothed back her hair, and then caressed the base of her neck, moving down to the back of her dress. He felt the soft silk, locating the zipper in the middle of her back. In a swift motion, he unzipped her dress, letting it fall to the floor.

She now stood before him naked except for her lace panties and heels. He drank in the sight of her as she stepped out of her shoes, her eyes never leaving his gaze. She found herself unable to breathe, her very skin feeling like it was on fire. Needing his touch to soothe the burn, she reached up around his neck, bringing him flush against her. He placed his hands around her bare back, pressing her to him as he again seized her mouth. He then let his hands glide back up the smooth skin of her rib cage to her full, soft breasts. Taking them in both his hands, he caressed his thumbs over her now erect nipples. Simultaneously, his lips left her mouth to devour her neck, addicted to the taste of her.

Her hands fingered through his hair, and she suddenly realized she couldn't bear it if he pulled away from her again.

"Derek," she said breathily, unable to keep an almost desperate plea from her voice, "please, don't stop." He looked up into her eyes and shook his head slowly. His pupils dilated, and his smile smoldered.

"No," he said softly, "not this time." With these words, he scooped her up effortlessly in his arms and carried her the few steps into his bedroom. He set her down and kissed her again, a thought running through his mind that this was the first time he would ever make love to a woman in his bed, as opposed to hers, solidifying again to him that this was right; how it was to be from now on.

She broke apart from him briefly, her hands now moving down his chest to his abs and the sex lines just above his hips. Removing his belt, she unfastened his button and zipper. Helping her out, he grabbed his waistband and shoved off his slacks and boxers in one motion. With her hands still at his waist, she reached down, grasping his now released, large shaft, the feel of his strong smoothness sending her arousal into overdrive. He closed his eyes, a soft groan from his throat escaping his lips at her touch.

With a renewed sense of extreme urgency, he pulled her panties down from her hips, and bracing his hand on her lower back, he lowered her down onto his bed. He then climbed over her, grabbing her wrists and pinning them into the soft comforter. He positioned himself in between her firm thighs; his eyes never left her face as he supported himself above her. He kissed her softly, and she longed to touch him. At last he released her hands just as he entered her slowly but not completely.

Feeling as though she would explode at finally having him inside her, she grabbed his strong shoulders and tried to lift her hips to meet him eagerly. He paused, bracing his palm firmly on her lower abdomen, preventing her from moving. He was teasing her, but allowing her to adjust to him at the same time. At last he felt her body relax and with his own now throbbing, he gave into her need. Satisfying his own hunger he thrusted fully, burying himself deep within her.

She gasped at his power, but she had never felt so alive, as if he could reach right into the depths of her soul. In control, he began to alternate between thrust and friction. She found his rhythm easily, and he gave her just enough of what she needed to climb heights she didn't even know existed, each stroke promising to be sweeter than the last. He grabbed her ass, giving himself leverage to penetrate further, and she couldn't help but squeeze her eyes tight, too breathless to scream, grasping onto the bedding as she found release, which was an eruption unlike anything she had ever felt. She knew he had come with her as his body went momentarily rigid, the warmth flowing through her along with the pulsating aftershock vibrations of complete and total pleasure.

After a moment he pulled from her gently and collapsed next to her, his breathing heavy as he wrapped his arms around her and pulled her to him. She smiled and nuzzled against his chest.

"I needed to tell you first," he said softly in her hair after a few minutes. "I needed to know you felt the same."

She lifted her head to look up at him. "It was worth the wait." He turned his body so he could face her, looking into her eyes. Caressing her cheek with his hand, he brought her face to his and kissed her gently.

"I love you, Christine," he said again.

Christine smiled, aware that they were the most beautiful words she had ever heard. "I love you, too," she whispered back.

He gave her a sexy smile. "Next time," he said, holding her gaze and raising an eyebrow, "we'll take it more slowly."

"When will that be?" she asked innocently and bit her lower lip. His grin widened. Then, taking her chin in his hand, he tilted her head away from him, giving him free access to her neck. He grazed his lips along the sensitive area below her jaw.

"Right now," he murmured close to her ear.

Chapter 10

The next morning Derek drove Christine home himself. It was early, around 6:00 a.m. She had spent all night with him, although neither of them had slept. She had put back on the cocktail dress she had worn to the gala, but the morning air was cool and crisp, so she donned his jacket over her shoulders. He had tossed back on his black dress pants, but had opted to wear his Rolling Stones T-shirt to take her home. He looked sexy as hell to her; his hair was messy, and his sleepy expression hinted at those bedroom eyes that she had been staring into all night long.

As he pulled his car up to the front of her apartment, Christine couldn't get the images of the night and early morning out of her mind. Having made her feel beautiful and desirable, he was powerful and intoxicating but also loving and tender. His appetite for her was insatiable, and without asking, he had commanded everything she had to give. She had voluntarily held nothing back from him, matching his demands with her own. Even though she felt exhausted, she continued to crave him, and she smiled to herself, indulging in the memorable sensations of how he had made her feel.

Parking the car and killing the engine, he turned to face her.

"I'd have invited you to stay at the yacht today," he told her with a grin, "but, I've already been getting grief for leaving the party last night." He laughed lightly, glancing at his phone. He had seventeen missed calls and thirty-five text messages, most of them reading, "Where are you?" He frowned when he saw he had a missed call from Mattia, and he noted that Timothy had not attempted to contact him. He knew there would be hell to pay, but he didn't for a second regret his decisions.

He caught her stifling a yawn.

"Besides," he continued, "if you stayed with me today, neither of us would get any rest."

She turned to him and gave him a knowing smile. "Sleep is overrated," she replied. But she knew he was right.

He reached his hand around her neck and pulled her face gently over to his, kissing her softly then passionately on the mouth. "Come back this evening," he whispered as he broke the kiss, looking into her eyes. A slow smile crossed his lips. "Just eat dinner first," he instructed, "'cause we won't have time for that."

The now all too familiar rapid beating of her heart began, and suddenly Christine didn't feel tired anymore. She didn't want sleep, only him. For a second, the thought occurred to her to insist on staying with him, but she dismissed it quickly, knowing he would not agree. She nodded her head, gazing at him.

"I love you," she said, her tone barely above a whisper.

He grabbed her hand and brought it to his lips. "I love you too," he replied.

He released her, and she turned to exit the car. He did not follow her out; he didn't need any pictures today, if someone was watching. But he stayed in the car as she walked up the path to her front door, watching her as she tugged his jacked tight around her, making sure she reached the apartment safely. Then he started the ignition and pulled away, already counting down the minutes until she was with him again.

Back in her apartment, Christine took off his jacket and placed it gently over the back of a chair, making a mental note to have it cleaned for him. As she looked around, she couldn't stop a strong threat of being overwhelmed. Surprised by the sudden rush of emotion, she attempted to label and understand what she was feeling. She felt restlessness, anticipating the coming evening with him again, excited but pained as well. There was also an immense amount of joy coursing through her, which caused an almost permanent grin on her face. Conflicted, she had never felt so many things at once.

Suddenly inspired and forgetting any desire for sleep, she headed straight toward her studio, not even bothering to change. She grabbed her glasses, work jacket, and a blank canvas. Pausing only for a second, she began to visualize what she was feeling. Picking up a brush, she let the state of her mind take control of her actions and swirled color on the canvas.

———•———

Just outside the Bronx, New York, off the beaten path and through a wooded area, Courtney stood in the middle of a shabby footbridge, leaning against the rail. The bridge was built over a large, dried-up ravine. Barely a trickle of water ran through the middle at the bottom of its eighty-foot depth. The bridge was made of wood, and it was terribly old and decrepit. Most did not deem it safe; the area was widely avoided. Courtney had happened upon the secluded place while wandering one day from her cousin's home on the outskirts of the city.

After losing her position with the New York Symphony, Courtney had been forced to move from her Upper West Side apartment. She had no job, and all of her savings now went toward alcohol, cigarettes, and even occasionally drugs. Anything to numb her senses or make her forget him for a brief while. Having run out of cash quickly, she had sold her violin.

With nowhere else to go, she had turned to the one family member whom she was still somewhat connected with, her cousin, who had reluctantly taken her in on a temporary basis. Courtney was uninterested in any kind of long-term living arrangement or source of income as she knew it wouldn't matter much soon anyway.

She hadn't spoken to James since their last argument, and although he still called her, she never picked up. She couldn't focus on anything except Derek, utterly obsessed with his whereabouts. She knew that he was hardly ever in New York now, save for the occasional public appearance, and she had no means of traveling to North Carolina where he spent the majority of his time. With that whore. She had no more options, the pain and rage she felt were unbearable, and she just did not have the strength or will to continue. Without him, Courtney had made the decision that she didn't need this world any longer.

Taking a long drag from her cigarette, she flicked it over the side of the bridge, watching it fall to the bottom of the ravine. It was quiet, and the only noises were certain rustlings from the dry brush around her and the tree leaves overhead. The air was dry, and the sky was cloudless. She pressed on the rail; the wood creaked and gave slightly. Clearly the bridge wasn't safe, the decaying structure not seeming to require much weight or pressure to give way. Taking in a slow breath, she stepped up onto the bottom rail, wincing slightly as it whined and wobbled. Steadying herself, she raised one foot, prepared to place her knee on the top rail before jumping over, into the void that would end her suffering.

"Don't do it," came a voice to her left. Startled, Courtney lowered her knee and foot back onto the bottom rail and looked in the direction of the voice. A young man wearing dirty jeans and a khaki jacket was standing just off the bridge. He had longer hair that looked disheveled, and his hands were in his pockets. She had no idea how long he had been standing there. She narrowed her eyes and turned back away from him.

"Go away," she said, stepping down now from the rail completely. She wasn't keen to have an audience.

The man began walking on the bridge toward her slowly. She felt the vibrations beneath her feet and heard a crack. Suddenly she wondered if the bridge would hold both of them.

"I know how you're feeling," he said in an even tone, now by her side.

She didn't say anything in response for a moment, just gazed out over the ravine. "You want to be a hero, is that it?" She sneered at him. "You want to save the poor, depressed girl from doing the unthinkable?" She looked at him now. His eyes were dark brown but held no warmth or life. Dark circles had formed under his eyes, as though he hadn't slept in days, and Courtney suspected he was younger than he looked. "You're too late." She finished staring into his unfeeling eyes.

"It's not too late," he responded. The words should have sounded caring, but his tone was only matter of fact. He stared down over the side. "I come here once a week and contemplate the same thing." He paused. "Today was going to be my day," he said quietly, "but when I saw you here first, I thought maybe it's not my day or yours."

She continued to eye him.

"I don't think I can go on," she said desperately.

"Come with me to get a cup of coffee," he suggested, looking back at her. "Tell me about it, then decide." Courtney considered his offer. Her mind had been made up, but she realized that maybe he needed someone to hear his story. The thought intrigued her, and suddenly she wanted to learn who he was.

"Ok," she said quietly. He turned to walk back off the bridge the way he had come, and she followed him carefully, ensuring that her steps were light. "What's your name?" she asked to his back.

"Paul," he replied, not turning around, and he offered no last name. Thinking that he might ask hers, she waited, but he didn't, and Courtney got the impression that he just didn't care.

After a twenty-minute walk, they returned to the streets of the Bronx. Sitting at a grimy little corner diner, Courtney stared into a muddy, black cup of coffee. She looked up from her cup to him.

"So," she said, "why do you go to that bridge once a week?"

Paul didn't smile as he stared at her. "I thought you were supposed to tell me your story," he replied stoically.

"You first," she said, "then I'll decide if I trust you enough to share."

He considered her, noting that she had the appearance of someone who was broken, disregarded. He recognized the haunted, sunken eyes, lank hair, and paper-thin form, knowing that she was most likely abusing herself with drugs and alcohol. He thought that she was probably once very beautiful, but now she was completely wasting away into nothing. He wanted to feel sorry for her, but he just couldn't muster the feelings within himself to do so. She was just another casualty of this cruel world.

"I've been out of work now for six months," he started, deciding that it really didn't matter one way or another. "I've lost everything. My house, my friends, my family. I can't get back on my feet, and I guess I just don't see the point anymore to my life."

Courtney was awed at how he said the words so bluntly, as if he no longer felt any emotion. He could have been speaking about a stranger's life for all he seemed to care about his situation. No wonder he wanted to kill himself, she thought. He was beyond pain and heartbreak. He was now just simply hollow.

"No one in this world cares if I exist," he concluded, "and those who do know I exist would rather I didn't."

She nodded as she related to what he was saying. The difference was she only cared about one person knowing she existed, and his refusal to acknowledge her caused her pure torture.

"What did you do?" she asked him.

"I was a photographer," he answered. "It was all I was ever good at. It was my passion."

He took a sip of coffee, then looked at her.

"So?" he asked. "You going to tell me now?"

She paused a brief moment. "It hurts so bad," she started, her voice barely audible. She cast her eyes down into her coffee mug, tears emerging, stinging her dry eyes.

"What hurts?" Paul prompted.

"To love someone, and to be kept away from them." She looked back up at Paul, desperation filling her expression. "If he would only come back," she choked, "if he would only remember that I'm here, waiting for him, but…" she took a deep, ragged breath, "he's with someone else."

"Why?" Paul asked.

"I think he's ashamed of me," Courtney said quietly, hanging her head. "I'm not the type of woman the public expects to see him with, regardless of how we feel about each other."

Paul narrowed his eyes in mild curiosity. "The public?" he mused. "No offense," he said sans emotional tone, "but wouldn't that make him a coward?"

"He's no coward," she replied coldly and quickly. "But he must know how much he's hurting me…" she trailed off. Paul shrugged.

"Well, then maybe this other woman has something on him," he suggested, "like leverage."

"Leverage," she repeated quietly, more to herself than to him.

The word hung in the air, and something snapped within her. She already clung to the belief that there was something keeping Derek from her, something out of his control. If this woman did have leverage, was it possible to find something to bring him back? Her heart leaped in her throat at the idea of bringing Derek back to her, but she paused. That wasn't enough, she thought. No. He needed to suffer. He had caused her more pain than was endurable, and he deserved the same. Then, and only then, would she graciously take him back into her welcoming arms. But she needed a plan. She needed to secure "leverage" that would destroy him.

She studied Paul, who was regarding her with an eyebrow raised. She took in his shabby appearance and his dead eyes—with absolutely no will left to live in them. He was a sad excuse for a human being, she decided. He was just as desolate as she was, and he was the perfect person to aid her in her endeavor. As a photographer. She just had to sell it to him.

"I think we can help each other," she said to him, taking a sip of her now lukewarm coffee.

"What do you mean?" he asked cautiously.

"If I could exact revenge on him for denying me, it would be my salvation," she began, "but the only way to possibly do that would be to enlist someone with your talents."

"And why would I care? What would be in it for me?" He crossed his arms. Courtney lifted her chin at him. "How would you like to make an easy fortune?" she asked suggestively. He stared at her, and for the first time, a light flickered within his eyes. "If you're as good a photographer as you say you are, then I'm sure you could capture evidence of a scandal if I set one up for you." She paused, thinking, placing her mental cards in order, and showing Paul what he wanted to see. "Like I said, his public image is important. He'd pay whatever price we asked to keep certain photos from the press. We'd split it fifty-fifty." A stab of pain seared through her again as she thought of his choice to be with another. If she did this right, she could annihilate that whore as well. She sat straight and squared her shoulders. "The money would be more than enough for you to do whatever you wanted, and it would bring him down for me."

Paul narrowed his eyes at her shrewdly.

"Exactly who are we talking about here?" he asked. Courtney hesitated.

She looked around, making sure no one was within earshot. "Derek Landino," she whispered.

He almost choked on his coffee. "Are you insane?" he hissed. "You've been talking about Derek Landino?" Paul waived his hand dismissively.

"You're absolutely right," he said, "he's no coward. Don't you get how powerful he is?"

"Of course I do," she said matter-of-factly. "As I told you, I know him intimately."

"He's too careful," Paul countered. "He's too honorable. You'd never be able to set him up like that."

"If anyone knows Derek," she said with an air of importance, "it's me. Don't worry. It'll be his honorable nature that will be his downfall."

Paul was quiet for some time, thinking over her risky proposition.

"Why should I believe you know him as well as you say you do?" he finally said to her. Courtney reached into her jacket pocket and removed a photograph. The picture was over two months old, and she carried it with her everywhere; it provided her the comfort and the fuel that kept her breathing day after day. She tentatively handed it to Paul. It disturbed her to hand over her most prized possession. Paul took the photo from her, a skeptical look on his face. As he studied it, he recognized the billionaire's face, his signature smile. His arm was draped over the shoulders of a pretty, dark-haired woman with twinkling dark eyes, who was also smiling broadly.

"Pictures don't lie," she said in a monotone voice.

He looked from the photo to Courtney, trying to surmise if the pretty girl in the picture was in fact the deteriorating waif now in front of him. Making the decision that she was indeed the girl in the photo, Paul nodded his head at her, sliding it back across the table. She snatched it up eagerly and placed it safely back in her pocket. Paul concluded that if Derek had driven her to be what she was today, he deserved whatever she had planned.

"Ok," he agreed. "But still, setting him up will be incredibly dangerous, with major consequences if we're caught."

"With a huge payoff for both of use that makes it all worth it." She was negotiating quickly, challenging him slightly. She sunk back into her seat and looked out the dirty diner window. "Besides," she added, staring outside, "what does either of us have left to lose…"

Back at her cousin's house, Courtney wandered into the small kitchen. The house was cheap and old, but her cousin kept the place tidy. Since moving in, Courtney had done little to help out, always knowing that she would not be there long. But now she was on a new mission. She opened the fridge and grabbed the bottle of milk. Making a disgusted face as she poured a glass and forced herself to gulp it down, she knew that if she was going to approach Derek, she needed to look the part. She couldn't let him see her this way. Now that she had a reason, she was assured she would be able to abstain from the devices she had used to numb herself.

Moving into the sitting area off the kitchen, Courtney gazed out the large picture window that faced the street. She grinned maliciously. When she had woken up that morning, she had had nothing left to live for. Now she did: hurting him. She bit her lip. *And then*, she thought, *he'll come back to me.*

Meeting Paul had given her the opportunity to form her plan, and without his even knowing it, he had sparked the idea. She only felt a tiny twinge of guilt at having to lie to him to make him agree. She hadn't lied about knowing how to set Derek up. She spent her days poring over tabloids, articles, and any information she could find on him. Really, it wasn't too difficult to pinpoint his character, and she knew precisely how to play her hand with him.

But because of this, she also knew she would never be able to outright blackmail him for money. He was too cunning, and he had enough resources to stop any public smear campaign. No, to obtain her objective, she needed a complex and covert plan. She would extort money from him, but her intention was not to use it or give anything to Paul. Besides, taking money from Derek wouldn't hurt him in the least. She had to take away something that mattered to him, something that he apparently loved—the way she loved him. But she had to promise Paul something; she needed his help. She felt confident she could pacify him later, and if not, she wasn't too concerned. Her only motivation right now was to make Derek suffer.

———•———

Derek rested against the headboard in his cabin. Half-dressed in just a pair of navy slacks, he had one knee pulled up, his arm resting over it while his other leg dangled off the side of the bed. Christine was sound asleep next to him. Her sleek, naked back faced him, with the bedsheet twisted around her waist. Her soft brown hair splayed across the pillow.

It was five-thirty in the morning, but he had not slept at all. There was too much to think about. He looked out over the room, his chiseled features set pensively. He knew some not-so-pleasant conversations needed to take place, and he was not looking forward to any of them. But certain things needed to be settled once and for all. Having deliberately procrastinated with regard to this one discussion days, he sighed, knowing it could wait no longer. He needed closure and peace of mind.

Reaching over to the stand next to the bed, he grabbed his phone and sent a text. "I need to speak with you in 10 minutes." Almost immediately, he received a response. "Fine." He frowned, not wanting to say what needed to be said nor hear what he knew he was about to hear, but ignoring it or continuing to put it off would not change anything. Derek was by no means afraid of confrontation or the consequences, but he knew this encounter would end badly, with permanent damage to something he had valued for a long time.

Leaning over to Christine, he lightly twisted a strand of her hair between his fingers. Not wishing to wake her, he brushed his lips along her ear and rose from the bed quietly. He grabbed a white dress shirt from the closet and left the room once he had finished dressing, prepared for what he knew was about to go down.

He made his way toward the bow of the boat, the location at which he preferred to handle most of his business conversations. There were plenty of seats and tables set up, but Derek would not be seated for this. A cool breeze came in, and seagulls squawked overhead as the sunrise began to make its first appearance.

He crossed his arms, and Timothy strode toward him, his footsteps echoing off the wood deck, a hard look set on his face. Timothy did not appear surprised by Derek's impromptu meeting invitation. He had known Derek now for too long and had been expecting it. Derek didn't need Timothy to confirm what he already knew, but he did need to hear him admit it out loud and own it to his face. As Timothy neared, he did not offer a greeting but rather remained silent, waiting for Derek to speak first.

Derek didn't feel like spending any more time on this than was necessary, and he usually opted to rip the Band-Aid off anyway. His arms still crossed, he looked Timothy directly in the eye.

"How long?" was all he asked, his look daring Timothy to act like he didn't know what he was talking about.

Knowing that Derek had the upper hand, Timothy sat down on the edge of a nearby sofa. "About a month," he answered, casting his eyes down.

"Before I served her with divorce papers?" Derek asked.

Timothy nodded slowly.

Derek turned away from him and looked out onto the marina, his eyes narrowed. He had been dealing with his feelings over this matter for days now, and he was ready for what needed to happen next.

"You are Land Corporation's head attorney," he began, still looking off over the boat, "and you are knee-deep in a highly sensitive project that includes a much-needed restructuring of this company, and I cannot afford to have someone else step in now." He turned back to Timothy, who stood to meet Derek's lethal gaze. "But you are not my friend," he said, "and I do not trust you."

Timothy closed his eyes briefly and sighed, knitting his brow in defeat. He cleared his throat.

"Derek," he started, but Derek held up a hand to cut him off.

"I don't care," he replied evenly. "I don't want to hear a drawn-out explanation as to why you fucked my wife." His eyes smoldered with rage, but his tone remained calm. "You can rationalize it all you like," he continued. "Convince yourself that it was ok because I was never around. Whatever helps you sleep at night. But at the end of the day, you slept with your best friend's wife."

Timothy's own anger began to get the better of him, and he now matched Derek glare for glare.

"You didn't love her," he said through clinched teeth. "Why you even bother to care now is beyond me."

"This is about betrayal," Derek replied, unperturbed by Timothy's hostility. "You both betrayed me, and it is unforgivable." He paused. "This meeting is over," he added in finality.   Seething, Timothy turned to leave, but Derek felt the need to address a final detail and called him back.

"If you think the way you look at her has gone unnoticed by me, you're very mistaken." Timothy turned back to face Derek with piercing eyes. Derek continued, "I may not have been around to see what was going on between you and Cynthia, but I'm around now. Stay away from Christine."

In response Timothy raised his eyebrows and lifted his hands up in mock surrender. Then he turned and walked away.

Once alone, Derek exhaled out the breath he had been unconsciously holding. He wasn't sure how he'd feel after having this out with Timothy, and now that it was over, he felt both relief and remorse. They had been as close as brothers once, and Derek could recall the happier times. Timothy had stood by him and helped him create his empire. Now that friendship and partnership were over. He was nothing more to Derek than an employee.

Feeling the need to tie up all loose ends, he pulled out his phone and scrolled to Cynthia's contact information. Pausing his thumb over the call button, he hesitated. What would he even say? He didn't want to hear any explanation from her either, he decided. He put the phone back in his pocket and walked to the side of the yacht, looking out over the water. In all honesty, he didn't care about the affair. Not now anyway. Maybe if he had known then it would have been different. No, what he cared about was the deception, and he cared about it more in regard to Timothy than Cynthia. His brain blocking out any emotions, he thought about the situation methodically. Confronting Cynthia wouldn't solve any hurt feelings and would only create unnecessary drama. And it wouldn't change the present outcome of past actions. Actions, he reminded himself, that they, not him, were responsible for.

Satisfied that he had gained the closure he sought and that this was now behind him, Derek turned his thoughts to Christine. Grateful for the established reliability of the relationship between them, Derek felt confident that he would never need to fear that she did not trust him. He had determined that his unwavering love for her was not something he was willing to ever give up, and his attention now turned to the second difficult conversation he needed to have. It would be short and sweet, but it would be a definitive end to a piece of his past. A past that had threatened to come and claim him, something he could not let happen. Not now. He had made his decision, and now he needed to relay the message.

He took his phone out again and scrolled through his contacts. Following this call, one last conversation needed to take place today. He punched the call button after reaching the number of the prime minister's private line in Calina, and it was answered almost immediately.

Once again ripping the Band-Aid off, Derek got straight to the point.

"Ciao, Mattia, la mia risposta e no." He paused. "I will not go to Calina; I abdicate the throne."

Chapter 11

Christine didn't want to wake up. She was snug, comfortable, and happy. She smiled as she turned and reached across the pillow for Derek, but her hand found nothing except the soft sheet. She sighed, unsurprised, as it was usual for him to rise very early, seeing to the details of his business. Starting to become somewhat familiar with his habits, she was quickly learning that he did not sleep much. She squeezed her eyes tight, willing sleep to come back but knowing it wouldn't. Admitting defeat, she sat up, pulling the sheet up around her. It was quiet and still, and not knowing when he might return, she proceeded to pull on a pair of jeans and a T-shirt and thought vaguely about coffee.

Derek had made a quick stop at the kitchen and was now making his way back to his cabin, a hot cup of coffee in his hand. He paused outside the door, thinking through this last conversation, hoping the outcome would put his mind at ease. But as much as he desired peace and the freedom to move forward, this was the discussion he was most dreading. He could only hope that she would understand. He considered everything he had lost in the last hour: a twenty-year friendship, his birthright. He had closed the door on something that he had once believed could be his destiny. Placing his hand on the doorknob, he took in a breath, knowing that despite what he had lost, he could be happy as long as he didn't lose her.

He opened the door just as she was emerging from the bedroom. Her eyes lit up, first at seeing him, then at the coffee in his hand. She smiled.

"Is that for me?" she asked knowingly. It didn't surprise her to see him with only one cup. Derek didn't indulge in coffee too much, and when he did, it had to be very particular. Referring to him as a "coffee snob" was one of her favorite taunts, and regardless of how much he rebuffed, she constantly prophesied that he would one day just enjoy a plain, black cup of coffee.

He held the cup out toward her.

"Of course," he replied. "Good morning, beautiful." She took the cup from him and sipped, letting the caffeine find its way into her being. Looking back up at him, she saw something in his eyes that resembled concern. She knitted her brow.

"Is there something wrong?" she asked.

His eyes narrowed pensively, and he motioned toward the sofa. "No," he replied, "but, there is something I need to tell you." Taking his suggestion to sit, Christine set her cup on the coffee table. "What I'm going to tell you," he began, now beside her, "changes nothing. Nothing about me, and nothing between us."

She heard his words, but immediate disbelief came over her. In her usual nervous habit, she tucked her hair behind one ear as she searched his eyes.

He watched her reaction carefully, having now memorized her body language. He questioned whether he was making a mistake by telling her. But he could not turn back now, and he knew he could no longer withhold the information from her.

"Christine, remember when I told you I was born in Calina?" Her eyes widened slightly, an instinctive feeling washing over her as she began to foresee what he was about to tell her. Images of her Google searches flashed in her memory, as well as April's constant, outrageous claims. She nodded slowly in response to his question, but the conflicted emotions rising within her held her voice.

"There was a reason my family left our country," he continued. "Thirty years ago the reigning monarch was overthrown and executed," he shook his head in disgust. "He was a terrible king. He ran the country into the ground; people were starving." Pausing briefly, a sadness crossed his face. "People are still starving." Taking a breath, he locked his eyes on hers. "Christine, that monarch was my father. Had we not fled, we also would have been executed." She stared at him for several seconds, her brain feeling numb.

So he is a prince, she thought, *a crowned prince*. Her mind went back to the Google search, and she recalled that Calina still had a monarchy but no current reigning monarch. As she began to process what he was telling her, she realized his obligation. He was a prince, and she had no future with him. How could he have kept this from her? The dumbstruck sensation now wearing off, she met his eyes, angry tears threatening them.

"H…how can you say this doesn't change anything?" she almost hissed, struggling to find her voice. "How could you not have told me this?" He picked up her hand, which was trembling, and held it between his.

"It doesn't change anything because I've abdicated the throne," he said softly. She shook her head, confused. "It is true parliament wants to restore my family back to power," he explained. "I think much of it has to do with my current status and wealth." He grimaced at the irony and couldn't help but reflect again on the imbecility with which the country was being run. They had simply replaced poor leadership with poor leadership, again to the detriment of its citizens, and they wanted his wealth and resources to fix it, whereas when he as a boy, they had wanted him dead.

It had been Prime Minister Luca Mattia's idea to initiate efforts to restore the Landino family. Mattia had good intentions, Derek knew; at least he was trying to do the right thing, but he had few allies and had unknowingly been put into power as a yes-man who would do the bidding of seedy politicians. Those who had pioneered the revolution, with greedy motivations, were now seated in high places, having spent the last thirty years inside the government. It had taken Mattia eight years to adequately persuade members of parliament that restoring Derek Landino as their monarch would be in the country's best interest. But even so, Derek knew that his reception in Calina would be anything but welcoming; it might even be dangerous.

He also knew his choice to abdicate had put Mattia in a bad spot, and his last conversation with the prime minister had not been pleasant. But Derek had been firm, and he flat out refused to be used. After all, he thought, they got themselves into this mess, they can get themselves out. He looked back at Christine, his only concern now.

"I've turned it down," he said emphatically. "I'm not going back to Calina."

"You should have told me." There was an accusatory tone to her voice. "What if your decision had been different?" She spoke quietly now, her eyes cast down, and he could tell she was trying to control her emotion. "I had the right to know what I was getting myself into"—she looked back up at him, her eyes glistening—"before I fell in love with you."

He had anticipated her reaction, and he felt guilty for keeping his secret, but knew it was a double-edged sword either way. She had been afraid of him since the beginning. If he had told her this too, she surely would have run, especially when his own mind had not been made up concerning Calina. But his decision rested heavily on her, and he couldn't have let her know that at the time. Once he knew that their love was equal, only then was he able to freely decide his path—to be with her, no matter what.

"Would it have mattered?" he asked her. "If you had known, would you have made different choices?"

The question startled her, and her eyes widened slightly. She thought of his questions to her, almost feeling like he was challenging her to think through the course of events logically. Would she have ever gone to dinner with him that first night had she known? Would she have agreed to see him again knowing there was a possibility he could become the king of a foreign country? Surely it would have been foolish to become involved with a prince. But, she realized, it was also foolish to become involved with Derek Landino, even without the extra title in his long list of accolades. She had known the risks from the beginning, and still she chose to take them. Risks that she would have deeply regretted not taking.

"No," she said slowly. "I don't suppose I would have." She took a deep breath, regarding him earnestly. "I wanted to be with you, and that mattered more to me than the probability of getting hurt because of who you are."

He pulled her toward him, embracing her.

"Who I am," he said lowly near her ear, "is nothing more than a man, in love with you." He withdrew slightly to look upon her face. "I hope you can see that by now. I could never go to Calina while you're here." It dawned on Christine that he was choosing to renounce the throne because of her.

She thought of a conversation not so long ago over dinner on the yacht, while they stared at a beautiful sunset—the look on his face, the intensity in his eyes, and the way he spoke with passion about finding his true calling were too much to not address. She couldn't stand in his way if this is what he was meant to do. He would never be happy otherwise.

"Why are you doing this?" she asked seriously. She was keeping all emotion under control, and her tone was calm and steady. She needed an honest answer. He reached up and caressed her cheek with the tips of his fingers.

"I don't want it," he said softly. "I'm an American, and I live here. Everything I've built is here." He held her gaze. "You're here."

"But what if this is your purpose, Derek? You can't just walk away from that." As she said the words, she felt her heart race. What if he suddenly agreed? As much as she wanted him to stay, she needed to know he would never resent her. "You told me you keep searching for fulfillment," she continued, attempting to breath slowly. "What if that's because Calina is where you're supposed to be?"

Derek's response was to reembrace her, holding her firmly against him as he smoothed her hair.

"Oh, Christine," he consoled, "didn't I tell you? I have found my purpose. It's you." She pulled her head back and met his eyes. "I don't need anything else," he continued. "I'll love you as long as you'll let me." She closed her eyes as his lips met hers. Their kiss intensified, and his mouth was soon devouring her vigorously. He pushed her flush against him, then pulled her onto his lap, and she now straddled him. She broke the kiss and looked down into his eyes, her soft hair falling next to his face. She bit her lower lip.

"Why don't you take me back into the bedroom," she murmured. He reached up, letting his fingers thread through her hair, brushing it back behind her shoulder. His eyes gleamed, and at the same time they narrowed slightly. She knew that hungry look well. Suddenly, with urgency, he wrapped his arms around her tightly and stood, lifting her with him. He then lowered her down gently onto the sofa, bracing himself on top of her.

"No," he whispered, reaching for the button on her jeans. "I'll take you right here."

It was late afternoon, and Christine stood in her studio mulling over her current project, the emotions from that morning providing her fuel and the inspiration to continue adding to her work. She had known from the outset that this work would be called *Love*, the emotion Derek had accused her of missing when they first met. She remembered saying to him that love was not an emotion and, therefore, she would not attempt to paint it. And she did not believe, as most psychologists don't, that love was an emotion. There were many debates over whether it was a feeling, a behavior, or an action.

She recalled Derek's proclamation that she had not painted love because she herself had never been in love. She now knew he had been right. She had never known what love was before, or even scientifically how she thought it should be classified. Now she had determined for herself exactly what love was: love was not an emotion; it was in fact *all* emotions, as well as the ability one has to make you feel all of them at once.

As her brush moved along the canvas, adding more texture and color, she could feel each stroke ripping through her as she sought to express love and all of its dimensions. Within the piece she recognized her portrayal of happiness, joy and excitement. But there was also uncertainty, fear, and lust. She put her brush down and adjusted her glasses. Tilting her head to one side, she couldn't shake the empty feeling that she was missing something. She felt satisfied with its progression, but a nagging voice kept telling her it could not be finished. Confused and frustrated, she shook her head and tore off her jacket. *What's missing?* she thought.

Lost in contemplation, she didn't hear the door to the studio open.

"Christine?" came a voice from behind her. She started slightly and spun around to see April approaching her.

"Oh, hey." She greeted her friend. "I didn't hear you."

April's appearance suddenly made Christine eager to confide in someone about her conversation with Derek that morning. Feeling conflicted over whether or not to share what he had relayed to her, Christine knew she needed to speak to a person she trusted. And, she rationalized, he hadn't told her not to tell anyone.

"Wow, Christine. That's amazing," April suddenly murmured, looking past her at the canvas. April was someone who never seemed to "get" Christine's work, and her praise surprised her, but she turned back to the piece, narrowing her eyes at it, continuing to feel unsettled. "I think it's the best thing I've ever seen you do." April continued, walking closer to the painting. "The colors are extraordinary. It makes me feel happy just to look at it." She paused, thinking. "But I guess I feel kinda sad too." She frowned, then looked at Christine. "I don't like feeling sad. I can't decide if I like it or not." She gave a small, amused laugh, and Christine smiled.

"I'm glad to see you finally understand a bit of what I'm trying to do here," she said, satisfied with April's reaction. "But it's not finished yet. I just feel like it's missing something…" She was pensive for a minute, and April stood quietly next to her, letting her think.

Remembering her need to confide in her friend, Christine turned and began to walk toward the studio door.

"Come on," she said, "let's have a cup of tea."

April followed her into the breakfast area off the kitchen and took a chair at the table.

"I trust you had a good night?" Christine asked, smiling knowingly from the kitchen as she began to heat up the kettle on the stove. Her being with Derek usually meant Gregory had the night off. She walked over to where April was seated and saw a dreamy smile on her friend's face.

"Greg is such a great guy," April said wistfully.

Christine took the chair opposite, her smile fading. April knitted her brow, noticing the serious look on her face. Christine pursed her lips.

"You were right," she said solemnly.

April raised her eyebrows. "Well, that's a relief," she replied with a smirk, "I hate being wrong. What was I so right about?"

Christine couldn't help but give a half laugh at April's sense of humor, but she quickly turned serious again. Finding it difficult to say, she forced herself to make eye contact.

"April, he is a prince," she said.

April's mouth opened slightly, and her eyes grew large. "Are you for real?" she asked in astonishment.

Christine nodded slowly. The kettle began to whistle before she could elaborate.

Rising to finish prepping their tea, Christine suddenly wondered if she should have told April, concerned now about her friend's flair for drama. A moment later she sat back down at the table with their mugs. Knowing that she couldn't bear it if April said, "I told you so," Christine sipped her tea and waited.

"Did he tell you?" April finally asked.

Christine nodded again. "Just this morning," she replied. "He is from a microstate in Europe called Calina. His father was overthrown during a revolution thirty years ago, which is why his family came to America. They want him to return now, but he said he won't go back. He's renounced his birthright to be their monarch."

"Oh!" April exclaimed, a romantic look on her face. "It reminds me of Monaco!"

Christine gave her a confused look. "What does that have to do with it?"

April ignored her question. "I think this is amazing, Christine," she continued, excitement in her voice. "You could become a princess, just like Grace Kelly."

Christine shook her head. She needed to bring her friend back to earth. "April," she said calmly, "you're missing the point. No one is going to become anything. He's not going."

"But don't you want him to go?" April asked. "It's the opportunity of a lifetime!"

"Do I want him to leave?" Christine replied in disbelief.

April stared at her puzzled. "Wouldn't you go with him?"

Christine opened her mouth to respond, but she stopped. She hadn't really thought about the possibility of going with him. She had assumed that if he left, he'd leave her behind. But now she wondered whether he would.

"He says he doesn't want it," she told April firmly. "I guess I'm just afraid that someday he'll regret that decision. I don't want to be the cause of his regret."

April smiled warmly. "You can't make decisions for him, and every decision he's made since meeting you has been geared toward being with you." She winked and sipped her tea, a faraway look in her eyes. "And I guarantee you," she added, "that if he did decide to go, you'd be going with him."

Christine half smiled, unconvinced by her friend's claims. She picked up her mug and sipped the Earl Grey. Although she completely dismissed the idea of following Derek to a foreign country, the question stayed in her mind: If he asked her, would she go with him?

Chapter 12

Three Months Later

Seven blocks away from her cousin's house in the Bronx, Courtney entered the dingy diner, setting off the faint ringing of the doorbell. Spying Paul in the corner booth, she made her way over, a tabloid in her hand. He had already ordered coffee, and she sat down opposite him, noting this was the same booth they had shared when they first had coffee together.

"Tomorrow night is the night," she said decidedly without even a hello to him first. She set the tabloid on the table.

Paul narrowed his dead eyes at her, lowering his coffee cup after being about to take a sip. "What's tomorrow?"

"He is the keynote speaker at a prestigious event," Courtney responded, tapping on the article. "All of New York's business and social elite will be there. Amid that crowd, it'll be the perfect place for me to approach him. And best of all, she won't be with him." She emphasized the word "she" as she said it, as though the word itself tasted bad.

Paul blinked at her several times. He had major misgivings about this scheme. After all, he didn't know this woman who sat across from him, and he only trusted her as far as he could throw her. He appraised her now, noting that her appearance had changed dramatically since the last time he saw her, months ago. They had continued to communicate through text, and their exchanges had always been brief and to the point. Although she was still incredibly thin, she no longer looked sick and sunken in. He assumed she had quit drinking and taking drugs as her skin and hair looked healthy. She now resembled the girl in the photograph she had shown him.

It occurred to Paul that she must have had quite the level of determination to make these kinds of drastic changes in such a short time. He knew she was crazy and delusional and that this plot would be the riskiest thing he'd ever done. But he desperately needed the money, and maybe she was just determined and crazy enough to pull it off. Plus, he had been planning on his own, and he was leery of the possibility that she might double-cross him.

"How will you even get into such an event?" he asked her, raising his coffee cup back to his lips.

"I used to travel in that circle," she replied with confidence. "I know people. Someone will get me in." She picked up the tabloid and scanned through the details, including major invitees. "I only need to get his attention for a few minutes," she said thoughtfully. She looked directly at Paul. "You just need to make sure you're outside my house ready to go tomorrow night."

"How will you get him there?" Paul asked her skeptically. "He's wouldn't just leave this kind of event to come to the Bronx."

Courtney sat back in her seat. "Oh, he'll come," she said firmly. "After all, he is in love with me."

———◆———

Derek paced behind the desk of his New York office, occasionally glancing at an object sitting next to his laptop. Having flown in yesterday evening with the purpose of giving the keynote address at a prominent annual entrepreneur conference, he now placed his hands on the back of his chair, his eyes glued on the object, his speech the last thing on his mind.

He was due back in North Carolina in three days, and in three days he intended for his life to change dramatically. He ran a hand through his hair, thinking through the conversation that needed to take place around the small item. As he continued to gaze at it, a content smile crossed his face. There was a sharp knock at the door, and this thoughts were interrupted.

"Come in," he said, knowing it was Gregory.

The assistant walked in holding his phone and a schedule. "Sir, there are several connections you need to make this evening." Gregory started approaching the desk. However, he stopped short when he saw the small blue box holding a brilliant three-carat solitaire diamond ring. "Is that...?" He asked, looking at Derek. Derek met Gregory's eyes and nodded slowly. He had made the decision to ask Christine to marry him a week ago. Having purchased the ring that morning in New York, he planned to propose to her when he returned in three days.

Gregory was quiet, although excitement was rising inside him. He was truly happy for Derek and knew that Christine was what he needed in his life. Looking at his boss, however, he could tell that he seemed uncharacteristically unconfident. As such, Gregory attempted to give him his best poker face.

"So, when are you going to ask her?" he finally said, unable to stay quiet any longer and incapable of stopping the smile creeping up on his face.

Derek narrowed his eyes in slight amusement, reading Gregory like a book. "When I get back," he responded evenly. He then reached down and snapped the box lid closed and sighed. "What if she says no?" he said quietly, more to himself.

The reality was, Derek was not 100 percent sure she would accept his proposal. Although he was sure that she was in love with him, he was not blind to the differences in their lifestyles, nor to the fact that she continued to be afraid of him. It didn't seem to matter what he did; she still feared that he would hurt her somehow. But he could not imagine his life any longer without her. Being honest with himself, he knew that if she rejected him, it would destroy him.

"She won't," Gregory replied. Derek tucked the small box in his jacket pocket and gave his friend a small smile, although uncertainty still remained in his expression. He wanted nothing more than to believe that in three days all would go to plan and he could finally solidify what he had been searching for all his life. But something kept him from believing it would be that simple.

———◇———

At 7:00 p.m. Courtney passed through security and into the business conference held at The Pierre, a five-star hotel on Central Park. Having recognized one of the security guards from concerts in the past, Courtney had been able to sweet talk her way in, using her attire and empty promises to help her cause. She had chosen a slinky, white-satin floor-length gown with very thin spaghetti straps and a plunging neckline that dipped well below her cleavage. The back of her dress also lacked an appropriate amount of fabric, and the entire ensemble left very little to the imagination. The dress had been specifically chosen for the occasion to help ensure Derek's soon-to-be compromising position.

She had been very pleased with the amount of weight she had been able to gain. She was slender but no longer looked like a waif or drug addict. With her dark brown hair, dark eyes, and pale skin, she gave off an ethereal impression in her white gown, but her intentions were anything but pure.

As she entered the banquet room and began making her way through the groups of people gathering and networking, she became aware of several men leering at her. With a look of complete indifference on her face, she ignored the stares, smiles, and raised eyebrows and pressed on, looking for

Derek. She needed to find him before his address as she knew she had no chance of getting his attention afterward.

She stopped in her tracks, having spied him in the far corner of the room speaking to a man who appeared to be the manager of the hotel. It couldn't have been a more perfect set up, she thought, scanning the space around him quickly, noticing that there were no security guards present at that moment. As she gazed at him, she realized that she had been so caught up in her plot that she had not considered how she would feel upon actually seeing him again.

He was dressed in an all-black tuxedo, and his arms were folded as he listened intently to the manager, ostensibly to finalize presentation details. Suddenly he smiled in agreement to something that was being said, and Courtney lost her nerve. She couldn't help but stare at him, and her mind went back to that night, back in his arms. Her heart fluttered with hope. What if when he saw her he remembered how much he loved her? She smiled genuinely for the first time in months. *We could just be together*, she thought wistfully. She took several steps in his direction, attempting to place herself in his line of vision. If he would just look her way!

The manager then nodded at Derek and turned to walk away, leaving him alone. Approaching him from the side, she was nearing him, within earshot, when someone else suddenly claimed his attention. She stopped as another business associate walked up to him to shake his hand. Now able to listen, Courtney caught part of their conversation.

"Where's your date this evening, Derek?" she heard the other man ask with a smile. "It's unusual to see you without a beautiful escort, especially here tonight."

Derek laughed lightly, his smile making Courtney melt. "Well, Christine couldn't make it this time," he replied. "And if she can't go, then it's no one."

His words echoed in her brain, sending a message loud and clear, and she refused to listen to any more of their conversation. Her smile had completely vanished, her resolve to destroy him returning along with her pain. *This is the only way*, she reminded herself.

She moved closer to him, eyeing him, positioning herself just beyond the other man among the edge of the crowd. She watched as he shook hands again with the man, ending the dialogue, his blue eyes looking away and finally catching hers. She held his gaze for a second. He looked confused, as though he were placing her, then recognition dawned on his face. She knew it was time. Walking toward him, she held his eyes, forcing herself to breathe as her pulse quickened with adrenaline. His ever-unreadable expression greeted her.

"Courtney Metcalf," he said with a smile that didn't quite reach his eyes.

Derek was shocked to see Courtney at the event. He hadn't been sure he recognized her at first; he thought she looked different somehow. Thinner, maybe? And this group wasn't her scene. Feeling a bit ill at ease, he remembered her actions toward Daniel during the charity benefit four months ago now, and her presence somehow made him feel unsettled. But he had also not heard from her since that incident, so maybe there was no reason to be on edge.

"Derek," she said, offering him her hand, "it's been a while, hasn't it?"

Her tone was pleasant, but he caught something else that was immediately alarming—malice? "Yes, I'm surprised to see you here," he replied professionally, taking her hand briefly. "This isn't your crowd, being all business and such. How are things going for you with the symphony?"

Courtney's smile froze. It pained her to think about the symphony. There was a time when the violin had been her life. Just one more reason why he needed to pay. At the same time, the touch of his hand sent shivers through her body, and she wanted only to embrace him.

"That's what I was hoping to talk to you about, actually," she said sweetly. He gave her a perplexing look. "What do you mean?" he asked.

Courtney took a deep breath. "Well, my music has prompted me to take on a higher cause," she said, beginning her well-rehearsed monologue. "I want to start a nonprofit organization. One that will work with at-risk youth to develop their musical skills and talents."

She paused, looking for signs of interest. She had been hoping to use her knowledge of his charitable contributions and projects, surmising that this would be the type of venture he might buy into. It needed to sound convincing and principled or he would see right through her ruse.

"The New York Symphony board of directors is even willing to sponsor my program and offer resources," she continued, "if I can secure funding to set up the foundation properly."

"That sounds like noble work," Derek replied, crossing his arms. "It also sounds like a business proposition."

"Oh, it is," she responded, a smile spreading across her face, which was as smooth as the satin of her dress. "I'm very passionate about seeing this come to fruition. You see, that's how I got my start in music. I was a delinquent, bound for the streets, and most likely jail, had I not discovered the violin. It grounded me somehow. Gave me purpose."

Derek regarded her carefully. She held eye contact with him and spoke in a confident tone. While her endeavor sounded plausible and worthy, his instincts told him something was amiss. He couldn't quite identify what it was.

"Why don't you contact Daniel, at Land Corporation," he said. "He can coordinate a meeting with you and go over the details. We have a foundation set up that can offer grants to local nonprofits, if the idea is strong enough and a proper business plan is in place."

Her eyes gleamed; she had anticipated his attempt to blow her off. "Well, that's nice of you, Derek," she said in a low voice, "but that just won't work for me. I am unfortunately leaving town tonight to speak with a prominent partner about the project, and I need funding first so I can secure the board's support."

Derek raised his eyebrows. *Is she crazy?* he thought. "Are you suggesting that I agree to finance your project right now?" he asked in disbelief.

"Yes, darling, that is exactly what I'm suggesting," she said, her voice dripping with false sweetness. "With one million."

He blinked at her slowly. Never had he been approached with such ridiculousness. "I think this conversation is over," he replied resolutely, annoyed that she had wasted his time. But she laughed at him, which caused his eyes to narrow at her.

Courtney had hoped he would make this easy, but it appeared he was going to play hardball.

"You may want to rethink that." She toyed with him, and he was practically glaring now. She took a step toward him, invading his personal space. Looking up at him, she dropped her voice low to ensure only he heard what she said next. "I haven't forgotten what happened five months ago," she whispered. "I've kept my silence till now, but I don't know if I can keep to myself any longer that you took advantage of me in my apartment." Enjoying the pure shock that crossed his face, she continued leaning closer to him still. "You're the star of the show here tonight, and there's a lot of press. I'd hate for it to come out publicly that you raped me and ruin your night. And possibly your life." She smiled slyly as she placed her hand on his arm. She could feel he was completely tense.

Anger and disbelief rose up inside him.

"You know as well as I do that what happened five months ago was completely consensual," he hissed at her. "How dare you attempt to extort money from me." His eyes flashed threateningly, and Courtney instinctively wanted to cower, knowing that he could put an end to her existence if he wanted to. But this was simply a game of the mind, and her determination allowed her to maintain control.

"Do you remember it that way?" She widened her eyes innocently. "Because that's not how I remember it. I also remember there being no witnesses. It would be your word against mine. And, if I'm not mistaken, these things never seem to work out too well for the rich playboy." She batted her eyelashes, continuing to play with him. It was time to push him over the edge. "Besides," she added, "I don't even want the money for myself. Is your refusal to help this virtuous cause worth the risk of public humiliation, months of bad press, and court appearances?"

She held her breath as she waited his response.

"You'd go through with all this knowing it's not true?" he asked her, his eyes boring into hers, challenging her with everything he had.

Refusing to show him the slightest bit of doubt, she gripped his arm tighter. She leaned in toward his ear, the front slack in her dress gaping as she very nearly flashed him. She licked her lips. "You know I'd win," she whispered. "And even if I didn't, the press would love to see your downfall. Your public image would be forever ruined. That would be guaranteed."

His rage boiled, and in a rare moment of losing his temper, he had the sudden urge to grab her by the neck. Scowling at her fiercely as she met his eyes again, he knew he was backed into a corner. Yes, he could fight this, draw it out, but what if it didn't work out well for him? Wrongful accusations happened all the time, and innocent people paid. His thoughts quickly turned to Christine and the ring in his pocket.

"I'll send you a check," he finally consented through gritted teeth.

Courtney smiled triumphantly, but it wasn't finished. "As I said," she replied, "I'm leaving tonight. I need you to bring the check to my cousin's house after the event."

"Out of the question," he said harshly, finding it difficult to maintain any composure.

She sighed. "This doesn't have to be complicated," she said softly. "You can even make the check out to the symphony if it'll make you feel any better. Like I said, I don't want the money for myself." She opened her clutch and removed a small slip of paper. Discreetly, she placed it in his jacket pocket. "Here's the address," she said, "be there by ten."

"Fine," he snarled. "Then, this is finished." He gave her one last look of disgust and promptly walked away.

Courtney stayed at the event through his keynote address, lurking just beyond the crowd. She admired his ability to carry on and deliver such an inspiring speech even though she knew what kind of pressure he was internalizing. As expected, the crowd adored him, and he was mobbed with attendees afterward. Amid the jovial networking, Courtney slipped out of the event unnoticed. Once outside the hotel, she hailed a taxi to make her way home.

It was close to 9:00 p.m. by the time she arrived, and she was eager to make contact with Paul one last time. He was supposed to be waiting outside for her, but as she made her way to the front door, he was nowhere to be seen. A slight panic began to rise. Had he bailed on her? She searched the porch and the perimeter of the house. No sign of him. She walked back out toward the street, crossing it to the brush on the other side where he was supposed to be set up. He wasn't there either. She began to fume with anger and also become panicked. If Paul wasn't here, this would all be for nothing! She would never get another chance, not now.

She made her way back to the house, pulling out her phone to check the time: 9:35. As she approached the porch again, her mind frantically trying to piece together a plan B, Paul emerged from the shadows, having ostensibly appeared out of nowhere. She scowled at him, although relief flooded through her.

"Where have you been?" she demanded.

One side of his mouth turned upward in a half smile, although there was no pleasantness in his eyes. "Just getting some extra evidence," he responded. A camera hung around his neck, and he held it up. Courtney gave him a confused look, but there was no time now to discuss his tardiness.

"Whatever. You need to get into place across the street. I will make sure you get your opportunity. Just get the shot, ok?" Paul nodded but didn't say anything. "And stay out of sight," she reminded him as he left the porch. "He won't be expecting you, but he's very aware and knows what to look for. If he gets the slightest hint that his picture is being taken, this will all be for nothing."

Paul didn't respond or look back at her, just disappeared into the darkness toward the brush.

Courtney walked back into the house. She turned off the front porch light and made sure all other lighting in the house was off except for one light in the main sitting room. The picture window facing the street needed to be illuminated but not obvious. Peering out the window, she saw no sign of Paul or a camera lens reflection. Satisfied, she turned from the window and began to pace, knowing that she was currently operating on pure adrenaline. Deciding not to change, she kept the scant satin gown on, hoping it would help the image she was trying to create.

There was a sharp knock at 10:05 p.m., and immediately her heart began to pound. She had to pull this off! She opened the front door, and Derek stood on her porch with an unpleasant expression on his face. He had ditched the tuxedo coat and tie and rolled up his sleeves.

"Why am I meeting you in the Bronx?" he asked, scowling. "Don't you live on the Upper West Side?"

She nodded and stepped aside to let him in. He walked over the threshold but proceeded no farther. She closed the door behind him.

"I thought you'd prefer to meet here," she explained, lying to him. "So no one would see you and wonder what you were doing."

He glared at her. "Oh, I see," he said, his tone laced with sarcasm. "Now you're being considerate of my position?"

His anger unfazed her; in fact, it was better if he stayed angry. He was in less control that way. She stepped around him and walked into the sitting room, stopping to face him in front of the window, but he didn't follow her. Holding up an envelope, he placed it on a nearby table.

"This is what you wanted?" he told her sharply. "Don't ever contact me again, or I'll be forced to take measures." He turned to leave, placing his hand on the door handle.

Courtney began to panic; he couldn't leave yet. She had gotten him alone with her again. Why didn't he want to be with her? Letting her emotions take over and unable to control her hysteria, she cried out.

"How could you do this to me?" she shouted at him, unable to keep the tears and anguish from her face.

He turned back to her, shocked at her sudden outburst and attack. "What I'm doing to you?" he asked in disbelief. "You're the one who's blackmailing me!" His anger began to rise further, and he strode over to where she stood in the center of the room. He had never before considered striking a woman, but she was tempting him, and he couldn't recall hating someone with this much passion.

"You were supposed to come back." She was sobbing, incapable of holding it in any longer. "I love you." She finished desperately.

His eyes widened in bewilderment, her response having thrown him completely off guard, paralyzing him briefly with shock. She knew her moment had come. Before he could react, she grabbed his neck and simultaneously wrapped her other arm around his waist. As she had hoped, the thin strap of her gown slipped from her shoulder, facing the outside window. Having no time to respond, Derek couldn't help but let her lips touch his. It was just a split second, but it was enough.

Yanking his head back away from her, he reached up and grabbed her wrist from around his neck.

"Are you insane?" he roared at her, now holding on to both her wrists. Pushing her away, he gave her one last scowl, then turned and walked toward the door. He exited the house without looking back.

Derek opened the door to the BMW, took his seat behind the wheel, and slammed the door shut. He cursed as he drove away from his parking spot a block away from the house. *She's completely unstable*, he thought to himself. Livid that she had gotten the better of him, he sincerely hoped that that was the last he ever saw of Courtney Metcalf.

"I got it," the text read. Courtney smiled as she texted back. "Meet me at the bridge tomorrow. Brings the pics so I can see, then we'll plan our next move." Of course, her only next move was to get the pictures from Paul. She wasn't too concerned about that. The hard part was over. Paul didn't know she already had the money from Derek. He was under the impression the pictures were going to be used to blackmail him.

Courtney walked over to the table where he had placed the envelope. Picking it up and opening it, she examined the check. It was made out to the New York Symphony, at her suggestion, for $1,000,000. Most importantly, he had personally signed it. She knew he would not have had the time to have one electronically printed. Keeping his feet to the fire to ensure he would not be cautious had been part of her plan. She eyed the check, scrutinizing the payee line. It appeared he had used regular ink. She pulled out her phone and Googled "check washing." She was confident she could wash the check and forge her name in place of the original payee. This was the last piece of evidence she needed to ruin his life. She grabbed her purse and pulled out a card, a card he had handwritten and mailed to her months ago apologizing to her for being unable to attend the benefit. She looked at the envelope for the note of apology that had been addressed to her. Positioning the check over the envelope and holding them both up to the light, she could just make out her name, written in Derek's penmanship, now on the payee line. After the check was washed, it would be easily traceable.

Now that she no longer needed to keep up appearances, Courtney wandered over to the kitchen and grabbed the bottle of vodka. Pouring it straight into a glass, she gulped down the liquid, and it helped to calm her nerves. As she poured another glass, she thought of how it felt to kiss him again. It had been so brief, but it had eliminated any doubt that she had had about loving him. She knew he loved her too—he was just too stubborn to admit it right then. But soon he would see clearly again. After he was broken and had lost everything, he would come back to her.

———◆———

The following day Courtney headed for the bridge where she had first met Paul. She had left the check at home; now all she needed was the picture to go with it. As she came upon the bridge, she saw him already there waiting, standing in the middle, looking out over the dried-up ravine.

Stepping onto the bridge gingerly, she made her way cautiously to him. He turned toward her, feeling the vibrations of her footsteps on the rotting structure.

Holding up a manila envelope, he smiled slightly. As always, there was no warmth in his eyes.

"I think you'll be very happy with these," he said.

She held out her hand to take the envelope from him, but he held onto it, opening it himself and producing the shots for her to see. Her eyes widened when she saw the pictures, perfectly displaying what appeared to be evidence of a scandal. The shot of her kissing him was angled well, in profile. It showcased them in embrace, right when her lips touched his, the strap of her gown having fallen down her arm, almost completely revealing her breast. The photo appeared racy, and the lighting was low enough that his expression was cast in a shadow, which worked in her favor. Paul flipped then to another photo, this one taken at the event itself. Courtney was shocked to see the picture. She had had no idea Paul was even there.

"How did you get this?" she asked, dumbfounded.

He grinned. "You aren't the only one with connections," he said. "Like I told you, I wanted enough evidence."

Courtney now understood why Paul had been late last night. She looked at the picture he had captured. It showed her talking to Derek at the event. Her hand was on his arm, and she was leaning in toward him, whispering in his ear. Again, his own face was turned away slightly from the camera and cast in a slight shadow, making his expression difficult to decipher. Courtney was facing the camera, a demure smile on her lips. Both pictures together told quite a story, and Courtney was elated with the results. She nodded her approval of the photos, and she had to admit that Paul was indeed very talented.

Refusing to let her take the pictures, however, he placed them back inside the envelope.

"You were right about being able to trap him like that," he said to her, holding onto the envelope firmly. "I have to say, I didn't think he'd actually follow you to your house."

Courtney kept her eyes on the photos in his hand. "Like I told you," she said stoically, "he loves me. He couldn't resist."

Paul narrowed his eyes. "What's next?" He asked. "Now, I guess we need to show him the photos and make him pay, right?"

She nodded slowly, again holding out her hand to take possession of the envelope. "I'll be the one who does it," she said firmly.

But Paul still didn't give her the pictures. "I've been thinking," he said now, his dead eyes staring at her. "I don't really trust you. If I just give you these, how do I know you'll split anything with me?" Her eyes opened wide as blood began to rush to her face. "Actually," he continued, "it might suit me better to just go public with these. Hey, maybe it'll even help me land a job if I'm able to break the most scandalous story of the year."

Rage, along with panic, began to rise within her. What was he saying? Her internal voice screamed. He was going to double-cross her?

"You can't do that," she said, glaring at him through gritted teeth. "I've worked too hard to make this happen."

Paul simply smiled at her reaction, clearly enjoying making her angry. "I can do whatever I want," he shot back. "In fact, if you want these pictures, maybe you'll need to pay for them too."

"We had a deal!" she cried at him.

He laughed coldly at her. "Please," he said, "if it weren't for me, you'd be dead, you'd have killed yourself months ago. Not to mention, you needed me to even make this work. You'd be nothing and have nothing without me. So, I figure you owe me."

Courtney shook her head in disbelief. How could this be happening? Angry tears began to spill from her eyes. Her tears only made him laugh again.

"You're pathetic." He taunted her. "In fact, why don't you just go back to your original plan and jump? You can't tell in these pictures, thanks to me, but I saw the way he looked at you last night." He smiled wickedly at her. "He doesn't love you at all. I don't know what you have over him, but it's not love, sweetheart. He hates you with a passion. And if you can't accept that, then"—Paul shrugged—"maybe you're better off dead."

The fury and pain building inside her caused her to snap. Why did everyone say he didn't love her?

"You bastard!" she shouted, lunging at him, grabbing for the envelope. He moved his hand, holding the envelope away from her, surprised at her sudden action. Her hands landed square on his chest, shoving him hard against the bridge rail. Her rage fueled further force, and she continued to push him as the rotting rail started to give.

"He does love me," she cried desperately.

There was a loud crack, and the top rail behind Paul's back broke away. His feet scrambled, but he was losing his balance. The whole bridge shook, and Courtney's anger turned quickly to fear, realizing that her sudden violent shove had been too much for the rickety bridge. She looked into Paul's face and saw an emotion in his eyes for the first time: horror. In a split second, she reached up and grabbed the envelope from his hand and gave him one last push, ensuring his fate. She heard him cry out in terror as he tripped over the lower rail and fell over the side. Immediately, she dropped and splayed her body flat on the bridge, distributing her weight evenly. She winced as she heard a thud and a crunch below her; then there was silence. Still afraid that the rest of the bridge would give and she would suffer the same outcome, she crawled slowly back toward solid ground.

Her adrenaline pumping, she sat on the ground by the edge of the ravine just off the bridge. She clutched the envelope to her chest, attempting to breathe and slow down her heart rate. *Paul is dead*, she thought. She mustered her courage and peered over the side of the ravine, looking for his body. She took a deep breath in when she saw him, lying facedown, his body twisted and still.

"I guess today was your day," she said quietly.

Chapter 13

Having landed in North Carolina two days later, Derek now drove the LaFerrari back to the marina. He continued to feel uneasy from the strange and frustrating encounter with Courtney; however, he had more pressing things to consider. He intended to ask Christine to marry him tonight.

He pulled into the marina and maneuvered the car toward the yacht, waving at security as he passed. As he approached, his eyes honed in on a parked black limousine bearing two flags on either side of its front end. He pulled his own car up next to the limousine and killed the engine. Recognizing the flags and understanding what this meant, he scowled.

"Oh, hell," he muttered under his breath. He donned his sunglasses as he climbed out and made his way toward the gangway. Having already arrived, Gregory was waiting for him at the entrance.

"Sir, Mattia is here," he said immediately, not bothering with greetings. Derek nodded solemnly.

"I'm aware," he responded seriously. "Where is he now?"

"I escorted him to the bow," Gregory replied. "He's waiting for you there." He paused. "He doesn't seem very cheerful." Derek sighed. Mattia was not going to leave him alone, he realized. He had been very clear the last time they had spoken, and now was definitely not the time to rehash this.

"I'm not feeling very cheery myself," he told Gregory. He strode past his assistant, climbed the flight of stairs to the upper deck and proceeded to the front of the boat. He spotted Mattia, standing at the bow, looking out over the rail.

The prime minister of Calina was middle-aged, with graying hair that had once been jet black. He was thin and had an olive complexion. His features appeared almost severe, the stress and the weight of his position showing on his face, having aged him beyond his years.

"Ciao, Luca," Derek greeted him as he walked up beside him. Mattia turned in his direction, taking Derek's outstretched hand in a firm shake.

"Ciao," he responded, unsmiling. "I am in your other country," Mattia started, "so I will honor you by speaking English." Derek nodded, appreciating the gesture. "I trust your trip to New York was productive for you?" he asked.

Derek suspected his pleasantries were an attempt at stalling. "It was... interesting," he responded, his eyes narrowing as he thought of Courtney. "What can I do for you, Luca?" It was a direct question, but it did not sound unmannerly.

Mattia eyed Derek, appraising him.

"It has been a long time since I've seen you, Landino," he observed. "You look very much like your father; you have his eyes. It is a sign of royalty, you know." Derek grimaced. He was aware of his resemblance to the previous monarch; however, he did not like to be reminded of it. Mattia looked back out over the marina. "I thought you should know that Nicola is exercising his birthright for the throne of Calina since you declined." Mattia raised an eyebrow at Derek. "Word has it that he's run out of money here, and he's looking for his next...how do you say it? Meal ticket?"

Derek was quiet for several minutes, letting Mattia's words sink in. Of course, he had been aware that this could happen, but Derek had felt confident that Nicola would not want the responsibility. Apparently, he had not considered that his younger brother did not look at becoming a monarch as a responsibility, but only as a way to secure more funding for his lavish lifestyle.

"Can't you fight it?" Derek asked. Mattia shook his head gravely.

"Not indefinitely," he said. "Parliament has already voted to restore your family to power. Obviously it was assumed you would be returning, not your brother."

Derek couldn't help but smirk. "I guess you put the cart before the horse," he commented gravely.

Mattia turned to face Derek, his expression solemn. "Derek, you know what will happen if Nicola takes power in Calina. He will set us back decades. Our resources are depleted, our economy is unstable, and our trade agreements are falling apart. You understand as well as I do that Nicola is only looking out for himself. He'll take whatever he can, and if he's lucky, he'll be able to perhaps sell our country to Italy—if they even want it, that is. If he's not lucky, well, you know what happened to your father." He gave Derek a pointed look that seemed to suggest that Mattia might take care of the latter himself.

Derek leaned against the rail, folding his hands in front of him, staying quiet.

"You are our only chance." Mattia pressed on. "You have the means and the ability to turn our country around. Running a country is no different than running a business, and it's very clear you excel there. You would potentially be saving thousands of lives, helping us prosper as a people. And"—he paused—"it is what you are destined to do. You were born to lead your country. Calina is your first country, your home."

Derek turned away, scowling at the marina, resentment filling him.

"Do you understand what you're asking me to do?" he said firmly. "My father was assassinated by the people of Calina. My family was forced to flee—we would have also been killed otherwise. I am who I am today because of my choices and the sweat of my brow." He looked Mattia in the eye, his features set with an impassioned hardness. "Now you're asking that I give up everything I've built to go back to the very people who wanted to kill my family? You want to take away my choices and options?"

Mattia sighed.

"You were born without choices or options, Derek," he replied. "It was your father's choices that got him killed and overthrown. You cannot blame the people for doing what was right! And, regardless of how it affected your family, it was what needed to be done. Think of all the families that died at the hands of your father's policies…" Mattia trailed off, and the two men stood in silence for a moment. "It was an awful time for our country," he continued, "and I agree that things have not progressed as once had been hoped. The country needs serious change to move forward, and you now have that opportunity. As you always have."

In his heart Derek knew that Mattia was right. Calina was his birthplace, the place where his mother was born, where he should have been raised as a prince who would one day take the throne. Staring at him was the chance to make a difference for thousands of people and change lives. Excitement and pride rose in him at the thought of what he could become. But then he thought of Christine. He needed her too, he knew. He was happier with her then he ever thought possible, and he couldn't leave her.

Choosing to be honest with Mattia, he made a proposition.

"I'm planning to propose to Christine," he told the prime minister. "Tonight." Mattia raised his eyebrows. "She's aware of my birthright, but she's also aware that I've renounced the throne. If I go to her now and tell her I've changed my mind, that would not be fair to her. This has to be her choice," he said decidedly. "I will tell her we spoke before I ask her to marry me. But if she does not want to come to Calina with me, I will not go either."

After a moment Mattia sighed heavily. "You are clearly very much in love with this woman. I must admit I am disappointed to hear that you would choose love over your country."

Derek's face remained unchanged, his resolve unwavering. "That is the only way I will accept," he repeated with finality.

Mattia consented. "You will make me aware of her decision, then?" he said. "If she is to come to Calina with you, she must become your wife. She is not our citizen, and she cannot stay with you under other circumstances. We will not start out the new leadership with a scandal."

Derek nodded his understanding. "I will inform you tomorrow," he said. He shook hands again with the prime minister, and then Mattia turned and made his way to the exit of the vessel.

Derek looked back out toward the marina. He knew he wanted his life to change dramatically today, but he was not expecting the magnitude of possible change. He supposed he had been fooling himself into thinking that he could sidestep what he had been born to do, thinking that he had any kind of choice in the matter.

Of course he knew all along it may come down to this, which is why he had had Timothy working on a succession plan for his company for the past several months. He would retain a fair share of ownership in Land Corporation, but he could no longer run or control his business. He would need to name someone else as president and CEO. As much as it excited him to take on a new, larger, more impactful challenge, it saddened him greatly to lose everything else he had built over the previous ten years. Then there was Christine. Would she even consider going? He wasn't sure that she would agree to marry him, let alone pack up and move to a foreign country as the wife of a king. He shook his head, thinking through her reaction. It was too much to ask of anyone, he reasoned. He pulled out his phone to call her. But he had to try.

Arriving twenty-five minutes later at Christine's apartment, Derek parked his car out front. Turning off the engine, he paused a moment before exiting, thinking through what he needed to tell her and the decision he was about to ask her to make. Realizing that he was stalling and that this wouldn't help matters, he took a breath and climbed out, making his way up the path to her front porch. As he neared, Christine opened the door in anticipation of his arrival. He smiled when he saw her.

Given the bizarre experience in New York, along with the expectations now from Calina, Derek felt like the weight of the world was on his shoulders. Seeing Christine grounded him. Not only did he want her to come with him and be a part of his new adventure, but he also needed her by his side. As long as she was with him, he knew he could handle anything.

Walking up to her now, he enveloped her in an embrace, holding her close, needing to feel her.

"I didn't think I was going to see you until tonight," she said against him. She pulled back and smiled. "Not that I'm complaining, of course." Her smile faded. "You sounded concerned on the phone."

Derek knitted his eyebrows. "Something came up this morning," he said. "I needed to speak to you about it." She stepped aside the threshold so he could enter the apartment. Looking over her, he saw April seated by the kitchen. "Hello, April." He greeted her and gave her a smile. Standing, April made her way to the living area.

"Hi, Derek," she replied. "I'm sorry; I can go."

But Derek's smile remained, and he held up his hand. "No," he stated, "it's ok. Please stay." He looked at Christine. "I'm assuming you told her about my heritage?"

Christine's heart skipped a beat, and her mouth opened slightly. She glanced guiltily at April, then looked back at Derek, meeting his eyes.

"It's ok," he said reassuringly, seeing shame cross her face. "Confiding in our friends helps keep things in perspective. I would have expected no less." April sat back down at the breakfast table. Christine looked at Derek intently. Why was he bringing up Calina, she wondered. Her eyes widened, and adrenaline started to rush through her as she began to realize what he was going to say. He had changed his mind about Calina, she concluded. He was going to tell her he had decided to go.

Unbeknownst to Derek, Christine had given a lot of thought to what she would do if this day ever came. She knew Derek would not settle for less than what he was meant to do, having spoken with such passion about finding his purpose. She had come to the realization some time ago that she simply could not go on without him and had decided that if this moment ever arrived, she would agree to follow him anywhere. The prospect of moving to a foreign country scared her to death, but losing him terrified her more. The question was, did he even want her to go? Her heart now in her throat, Christine held her breath. Would he ask her to go, or was he leaving her for good?

"Christine," he said, now placing his hands on her arms, "something's changed. My brother wants power in Calina." He searched her face, anticipating a reaction. "I didn't think he would ever want it, but he does—only to fund his outlandish behavior."

"And you can't let him do that," she finished for him, holding his gaze. An almost desperate expression crossed his face.

"I know how this is going to sound," he said gently, choosing his words carefully. He exhaled slowly. "I will only go to Calina if you come with me." He reached up and brushed her hair behind her ear for her, accustomed to her nervous habit. "I need you by my side," he continued, "wherever that may be. If you can't come with me, I'll simply stay here with you."

"You're asking me to choose?" She asked quietly, torn between excitement and fear. He wanted her with him—but how could she make this decision? It wasn't hers to make. He took both her hands in his.

"I just want you to know that you come first in my life," he stated seriously. "If going to Calina means losing you, I will tell Mattia to go to hell."

Christine's mind was reeling, and too many emotions were running through her. She needed to think, and she never could clear her mind with him around.

"I don't know what to say," she said finally. She met his eyes. "You want to go." It wasn't a question, and she knew the answer, but she needed to hear him say it.

"I believe I could make a difference for a lot of people," he replied, wording his response carefully. "I know you need some time," he said to her now. "Please come to the yacht tonight? We can talk some more." She nodded, casting her eyes away from him, attempting to digest the gravity of the situation.

"Christine," he said, lifting her chin so she looked at him. "There's something else I need to ask you." His eyes were full of an earnestness that took her breath away. With the ring in his pocket, he suddenly had a strong urge to ask her right now. But convincing himself this wasn't the right time, he fought his instinct. Instead, he tilted her face up slightly and kissed her gently. "But I have to go right now," he told her. "Eight tonight?" She nodded again. He released her, gave her a small smile, and turned to leave. He opened the door but paused, turning back to her.

"I love you, Christine," he said.

Her distressed expression softened, and she smiled back at him. "I love you," she said, returning his sentiments with sincerity. His face brightened; then he was gone.

Feeling unsteady, Christine closed the door behind him. Turning, she walked back to where April was sitting, having almost forgotten she was there. April was silent, waiting for Christine to speak first. She sat slowly next to her friend, unsure of how to even begin verbalizing the emotions running through her.

"I'm going to go with him," she finally said, taking a deep breath. Remaining still, April looked at Christine, a solemn expression on her face.

"That was a quick decision," April said quietly.

Christine shook her head. "No," she replied. "I've been thinking about this for months." She met April's eyes intently, "I knew he would someday realize that Calina is where he needs to be. I just wasn't sure if he would want me to go with him." She looked down at the table. "Now that I know he does…" She trailed off, trying to come to grips with what was happening to her life.

She looked back at April, a small smile forming on her face. "I guess you were right again."

April gave a half laugh in response. "So," she said, her eyes beginning to gleam, "he has something else to ask you?" Christine couldn't help but let her smile grow; she caught April's eye, the same thought running through both their minds.

Placing a comforting hand on Christine's arm, April spoke genuinely. "I'm really happy for you, Christine," she said. "I've never seen you as happy as you've been with him. I know this will change everything for you, but I believe it's worth it."

"Thanks, April," Christine replied, grateful for her friend's confidence. She sighed. "I have a class to get to," she said, standing up. "I'm done at four today; can you meet me here afterward, before I meet Derek?"

April's eyes lit up. "Of course!" she exclaimed. "I have to make sure you look perfect! After all, you're getting engaged to your prince tonight." She winked at Christine and laughed.

———◇———

Just before 4:00 p.m., Courtney sat in a rental car across the street from Christine's apartment. She had arrived in North Carolina that morning, having stolen her cousin's credit card to secure both her plane ticket and the rental. Unconcerned with any consequences, Courtney only had one ambition in mind.

She was pleased it had not been difficult to track down the art program director. After all, she knew her name and where she worked, thanks to the tabloids. Google took care of the rest. Christine should have been more careful, Courtney thought. Being involved with a public figure like Derek Landino, she should have known to protect her personal information. She didn't know Christine's class schedule, however, or when she might be home. Not wanting to miss her chance, Courtney had been waiting for her to show up for almost three hours.

She shifted uncomfortably in the seat of the car, anxious to put the next piece of her plan into place, and she was confident this next part would be easy. The only thing she couldn't foresee was what she would do if Derek was with Christine when she showed up. She needed to speak to Christine alone, and she could not let him see her.

In the shotgun seat next to her lay the manila envelope. She made a face as she thought of Paul, his body mangled at the bottom of the ravine. Having pored over the news the day following his death, she had been relieved to see the story of a down-on-his-luck young man who had taken his own life off an old bridge near the Bronx. *It's better this way*, she now thought. *Dead men tell no tales.* She had never meant for anything bad to happen to Paul, but now all loose ends were tied up, and there would be nothing and no one to contradict what she was about to tell Christine.

The longer she waited, the more desperate Courtney felt. She reached over and grabbed the envelope, pulling out the pictures. Over the last two days, she had stared at the images until they were burned in her memory. They perfectly portrayed a scene in which she and Derek were intimately involved: her sensual attire, their lips touching. Sometimes she found it easier to just pretend that the story the pictures told was true. It hurt a little less that way. And, after all, it was what Christine would also soon believe anyway. Why should it not be true? Courtney inhaled a deep breath. And maybe after he and Christine were through, he'd finally come back to her.

Once he was broken and miserable, the way she was now, she could put him back together, and he would love her again.

She broke from her reverie at ten minutes after four, when a car pulled up in front of Christine's apartment. Courtney watched as a brunette exited the car and made her way up the path. She stuffed the pictures back into the envelope and grabbed the door handle but stopped when suddenly a redhead appeared, greeting Christine before she made it to the porch. Courtney could tell by the way they were interacting and chatting that they were friends. She had hoped to confront Christine alone, but, she thought with a shrug, this would have to do. As long as Derek wasn't around. She couldn't count on another chance.

Pushing open her car door, Courtney exited the vehicle and hurried across the street to catch up with Christine before she entered her apartment.

"Excuse me," she called, walking up to the two women. "Are you Christine Dayne?" At the sound of her voice, Christine and her friend turned in Courtney's direction. Christine knitted her eyebrows, a confused look on her face. Courtney could tell she was searching for recognition.

"Can I help you?" she asked, pleasantly enough.

"You don't know me," Courtney started, "and I'm sorry to come to you like this, but I have information for you," she paused. "About Derek Landino." She waited for Christine's reaction and wasn't disappointed when she saw her eyes widen with extreme curiosity.

"What do you mean?" Christine asked. "Who are you?"

Courtney shook her head, her straight hair falling in her face. "My name's not important," she said impatiently. "What you might find more important is knowing what kind of man you're involved with." The redhead stepped closer to the conversation, crossing her arms as she stood next to Christine. Courtney held out the envelope for Christine to take.

Courtney held her breath, and her heart rate began to increase rapidly as she gleefully anticipated what was about to happen. Christine took the envelope and opened it, sliding out the photos. Upon seeing the images, a look of utter horror crossed her face; her mouth opened, then her jaw clenched tight. Her initial reaction didn't disappoint, and Courtney relished knowing that she had the power to destroy them both.

"I don't understand," Christine said quietly. She looked at Courtney, a mix of anger and devastation in her eyes. "You…" she said accusatorily, but she couldn't get the words out. Courtney decided to make it easy for her.

"I was really hoping that you knew what you were getting yourself into," she said, a pitying look on her face. She then rolled her eyes dramatically. "After all, he is Derek Landino. I'm sure I'm not the only one." She sighed heavily and continued, playing up sorrow in her voice. "I've been seeing him for a while now, just when he comes to New York. These were taken just three days ago." She shook her head in mock laughter. "Those darn ol' paparazzi—they're everywhere! I suppose it was only a matter of time before he got caught." She paused, enjoying this game, and the devastated look on Christine's face, immensely. Feeling no sense of remorse, Courtney felt that Christine deserved a knife to the heart for trying to keep Derek away from her.

"Anyway," she continued, "I know you're in some kind of relationship with him; I always see you together in the tabloids. I just thought you might want to know who he is before you do something stupid like fall in love with him." Christine's hands began to shake as her fingers tightened on the photos. She looked up from them to Courtney, her eyes beginning to sting. "Oh," Courtney said, "you're already in love with him, aren't you?" She couldn't resist a sympathetic, condescending tone. "You poor thing." *Honestly,* Courtney thought, looking at Christine's face, *what does Derek see in her?*

Christine knew this woman was making fun of her and was enjoying it. Refusing to let her anger, confusion, and frustration take over, Christine took in a deep breath and looked her in the eyes. There was something deeply off about her, Christine decided, and she couldn't imagine Derek with her. She looked like she was practically falling apart.

"Why should I believe anything you're telling me?" she asked now. Courtney rolled her eyes again in response.

"The pictures aren't enough for you?" she asked incredulously. Then she reached in her bag and pulled out another slip of paper. Christine saw it was a check. Upon closer inspection, her eyes widened. Her fingers trembling, she took the check from Courtney.

"You're Courtney Metcalf." She said quietly. Courtney nodded, pulling out her New York driver's license. She had been very happy with the way the check had turned out, and she couldn't keep a small smile off her face. Having washed the payee line, she had been able to trace her own name onto it from the card Derek had sent her months ago. It was simple and brilliant. She had absolutely no intention of ever cashing the check; it was just a nail in his coffin. And because it would never be cashed, no one would ever know she had altered it. The check would never go through a bank system.

Christine could see that the check was dated only three days prior to today, and she recognized his handwriting. Derek had, in fact, given this woman a check for $1 million—and if not for hush money, then what on earth for? With the photos and the money, it was too much to not add up. Christine could only conclude that he had had an affair with this woman and then paid her for her silence. A numbness came over her then, and she couldn't feel, hear, or speak. Barely registering it, Courtney had taken the check back out of Christine's hands.

"Why are you doing this?" April suddenly asked Courtney, her eyes narrowed in anger.

Courtney shrugged. "Why not?" she asked back maliciously. "He's already given me the money. I know he's not serious about me; I was just someone he fucked." She spat the vulgarity, looking directly at Christine. "I was a fool to think that he could care about me," Courtney continued. "If telling you hurts him, then I figure that's what he deserves." She tucked the check back into her bag. "You can keep the pictures," she added. "I have more if I need them." She turned to leave.

"You are a bitch," April said coldly as she walked away.

Courtney turned back to face them. "Maybe so," she said, smiling. "But I'm not stupid." She patted the side of her bag, indicating the check, then she met Christine's eyes, an eyebrow raised. "Are you stupid, Christine?"

Her taunting words echoed in Christine's mind even as Courtney walked casually back across the street, climbed into her car, and drove away. Christine did, in fact, feel stupid, humiliated, and destroyed.

"Christine," April now said gently to her, but Christine closed her eyes tight and held up a hand, not letting April say anything else.

"No," she said quietly through gritted teeth. She turned and walked to her front door, entering her apartment. April followed her.

"Christine." April tried again.

"No!" Christine shouted back, not looking at April, the tears emerging in her eyes now.

Unable to hold it in any longer, she began to shake uncontrollably.

"How could he do this?" she cried out, her tears now beginning to stream down her cheeks.

April took the pictures from her trembling hands. "Maybe they're fake," she thought out loud, squinting her eyes at them. But her words didn't register to Christine as she was attempting to control her tears. "What are you going to do?" April asked her. "You're supposed to meet him in a couple of hours. What are you going to say?"

Christine placed her face in her hands. All the moments with him flashed in her mind—all the sincerity, the reassurance, the love she had felt. Everything was ruined now. She had feared all along that he would hurt her, and now he had. Feeling like her insides were dying, she knew she could not forgive him for this. It didn't matter what she said to him or what he had to say in his defense; there was no fixing this. There was nothing to say. She turned to face April.

"I'm not going to go see him," she declared. "I'm done with him. It's over."

April opened her eyes wide. "Christine, you have to ask him about this," she said insistently. "You have to hear what he has to say for himself."

"Why?" Christine cried. "So he can give me some excuse? Tell me it didn't mean anything, it was a one-time thing?" She shook her head, the tears coming back. "I don't want to hear that, April! I can't bear to hear that! And it won't change anything."

"If you don't go there, he'll come find you," April said. "You'll have to face him at some point."

"Not if I'm not here," Christine said, making a decision. She looked up at April. "I have to leave. Now." April gave her a confused look. Feeling desperate, Christine grabbed her friend by the shoulders. "I'm going to go stay with my dad for a while," she said. "Don't tell him where I've gone."

April nodded, a sad expression on her face. "I understand. I won't tell him." Christine closed her eyes briefly, the backs of her lids stinging.

April helped her pack, and twenty minutes later, Christine was prepared to leave her apartment, and Derek, behind. Knowing that he would come looking for her, she grabbed a piece of paper and scrawled a note on it, the only goodbye she would offer: "I know. It's over. Don't ever contact me again. Christine." Her tears fell on the paper as she wrote. Taping it to the front door for him to find, she shut it behind her and headed to her car.

April followed her. "Are you sure this is what you want to do?" she asked one last time.

"This is what I have to do," Christine replied, placing her bag in the passenger's seat. "There's no going back to what we had"—she paused sadly—"or what was supposed to be." Hot tears rolled down her cheeks as she thought about what should have happened this evening. She shook her head violently. She had to stop. She couldn't keep torturing herself. It was over. Grief had overcome her, and she felt exhausted. All she wanted to do was leave. She turned to give April one last hug, then opened the door to her car and slid into the driver's seat. She blinked back tears as she pulled away, glancing in the rearview mirror to see April standing outside her apartment, the photos in her hands.

———•———

Three hours into the drive toward Nashville, it began to rain. The sky was turning dark with clouds, and Christine knew it had been coming for some time now. She blinked rapidly for the hundredth time, refusing to let the tears start again. She bit her lip and pressed harder on the accelerator. Having chosen to take a back road for this leg of the journey, knowing there would be less traffic, she now wondered whether that had been a wise move; the rain was coming, and there were no streetlights.

She had been unable to get Courtney's voice out of her mind. She wasn't sure what hurt more—his betrayal or the apparent pity Courtney, who was obviously a train wreck, had taken on her for even considering that he cared about her. Christine had never felt more humiliated. She briefly squeezed her eyes tight again, attempting to block out the pictures. He was kissing Courtney; she was practically naked in his arms. She gripped the steering wheel, again willing herself not to cry. That would make her even more of a fool.

She glanced at the clock—it was eight, the time she had planned to meet him. What would he do, she wondered, when she didn't show up? Her note had been clear. She was sure he'd go to her house, read the note, and realize that she knew all about Courtney. He'd realize it was over. She couldn't help but think about what was supposed to be happening right now. Had she been crazy to even think that he was planning on proposing to her? She felt ashamed. How could she have been so stupid?

Her phone buzzed. She saw it was April and answered.

"Christine," April said, "I had to call you."

"What is it, April?" Christine answered, her voice uneven. She knew if she said too much, she wouldn't be able to control her emotions, but April sounded concerned and had an urgent tone.

"Christine, I'm sorry," April replied quickly, "but I had to check those photos. You know, to make sure they weren't photoshopped or anything." Christine's heart raced. She hadn't thought of that. What if they were fabricated? But there was still the check he had written. She held her breath, waiting for April to continue, unable to hold back the hope swelling inside her that this had all just been a fictitious nightmare.

"I took them to the photo lab at the university," April said. "I had Mike take a look." She paused, hesitating. Focusing on April's words, Christine had sped up the car on the now slick road without even realizing it. "Christine, I'm so sorry!" April cried, her voice cracking. "Mike would know. The photos are real." Not responding, feeling numb, Christine ended the call with April. Her one hand now shaking on the wheel and her foot pressed on the gas, she finally allowed herself to release her tears.

Her vision blurred, and she let the phone drop from her hand. It was just a half second glance to see where it had landed, but it was enough for her to miss the sharp curve ahead of her. Her reactions having been delayed by shock, she realized too late that she was driving way too fast going into the bend. Panic flooded her, and instinctively she hit the break. As the car began to skid on the slick pavement, Christine, now out of control, yanked on the wheel. She didn't even have time to scream as the car spun 180 degrees. She couldn't see or think; blurry images flashed in front of her. Finally she came to a rest, the car facing the opposite direction, teetering on the edge of a ditch. It was dead quiet, except for the rain pounding on the hood. Christine was leaning forward over the steering wheel, gripping it so tight her knuckles were as white as her face.

She forced herself to let go of the wheel, her whole body now shaking violently, and placed the car in park. She sat in shock for a minute, realizing how lucky she had been not to hit anything. Then, like a tidal wave, the adrenaline and emotion washed through her. Burying her face in her hands, she sobbed uncontrollably, releasing everything she had been holding in. She cried harder than she had ever known she could. Her eyes burned and her chest ached with pain, as though a jagged piece of glass had been violently wrenched into her heart. Lifting her face from her now tear-soaked hands, she looked out the windshield into the rainy night.

Her phone buzzed suddenly from somewhere on the floor. Reaching down and picking it up, she looked at the screen. "Incoming Call: Private." She knew it was Derek, having now realized she was not coming. Her fingers trembling, she hit the decline button, then turned off her cell completely. She felt a surge of aggression, and she threw the phone in the shotgun seat and banged her fists on the wheel.

"How could you do this to me!" she suddenly screamed, her beautiful features twisted in anguish. Then she collapsed on the wheel, her chest heaving, her tears feeling like they would never stop.

———•———

At seven forty-five that evening, Derek gazed off the back of the yacht onto the darkening water. Flooded with nerves, he took the ring out of his pocket and examined it thoughtfully. It suddenly dawned on him how crucial these next few minutes would be to his life. Soon she would be here, and everything would fall into place. Although anxious with anticipation, Derek was certain the course of action he was planning was right, and nothing before this had felt so perfect.

His phone began to buzz. Taking it out of his jacket pocket, he looked down, surprised to see the number for the car service that he had sent to pick up Christine.

"Yes," he answered.

"Sir," came a man's voice on the other end, "I am here to pick up Ms. Christine Dayne, but she is not at home currently."

Derek narrowed his eyes in confusion. "What?" he responded. "She has to be there."

The driver hesitated. "There's a note, sir," he said timidly.

Derek shook his head. "What do you mean, a note?" he asked.

Again the driver hesitated. "Um, would you like me to read it to you, sir?" The tone of the driver's voice told Derek it was not good news.

"I'm coming over there," he said, then ended the call. A feeling of dread washing over him, he clutched the ring in his hand. He needed to keep his rising panic at bay, so he pocketed the ring and hastily made his way to the yacht's gangway.

Having arrived at Christine's apartment in record time, his heart sank further as he placed his car in park and noticed that her car was not there. There had to be an explanation, he kept telling himself, an emergency of some sort. But he knew if that were the case, she would have phoned him. He had already tried to call her twice en route to her apartment, and both times his call had gone to voicemail. No, something was definitely wrong.

"You may leave," Derek told the car service driver as he passed him while approaching Christine's porch. The driver just nodded, then promptly returned to his car. Continuing on up to her door, he spied a piece of paper. He tore it off, reading the note, letting the words sink in but not completely believing them. "I know. It's over…" He read them over and over again, confusion and disbelief overtaking all his senses. Without any other options, he balled the paper up in his fist, then turned to the door and pounded on it.

"Christine!" he yelled, knowing there would be no answer.

"She's not there, Derek. You need to leave." He turned quickly at the sound of April's voice at the edge of the porch.

"Where is she, April?" he asked, both strain and harshness in his voice. April didn't respond, but he could tell, even in the dark, she was glaring at him. He moved from the porch toward her, towering as he stood facing her. "Where is she?" he repeated more urgently, needing answers. "And what is this?" He held up the crumpled note. April just shook her head in response, a look on her face that held both sorrow and contempt.

"I think it's pretty clear," she finally said sharply. "You need to leave now, and don't come back." She turned away from him to head back to her own apartment, but Derek grabbed her arm, forcing her to face him again.

"You have to tell me what's going on, April!" he exclaimed, suddenly feeling desperate. "I don't understand any of this. Why is she doing this?"

April pulled her arm loose from his grasp and narrowed her eyes at him. "Let go of me," she snapped. "Christine wants nothing to do with you. Go away." She looked straight into his eyes, willing herself not to back down or feel intimidated by him. But his expression held nothing but hurt and confusion. She shook her head again, backing away from him. Why did he look so earnest, she thought. Why didn't he get it? She crossed her arms, hugging herself as she turned away from him again. This time he didn't go after her.

A numbness came over him as he watched April walk away. *She's gone,* he thought. *Christine left me.* Admitting it to himself didn't help to make the words any more real. The rain started to fall then, but he didn't even notice it. Not registering that his body was even moving, he made his way back to his car, the note still clenched in his fist.

———•———

It was midnight, and Derek sat in a chair underneath the overhang, watching the rain splash on the deck of the yacht. With the rain, a rigid coolness breezed through the air. He didn't mind the cold—anything to help him register feeling was welcome. Still numb from shock, still unwilling to accept that she was gone, he tried, unsuccessfully, to piece together the reasons and whys.

A table sat beside him, and on it he had placed the note, the ring, and a single crystal glass of untouched whiskey.

"You don't want to go down that road," a voice said, approaching and taking the seat beside him. Derek glanced at the whiskey and prepared to argue but decided against it, afraid of losing control if he exhibited any kind of emotion. He didn't turn to look at or acknowledge Gregory, who was now seated in the dark next to him.

"Go away," he said gruffly. But Gregory didn't move, knowing that his place right now was with Derek. Derek eyed the glass, but didn't take it. He was quiet for several minutes before finally breaking the silence. "I don't know what happened," he said quietly.

"What does the note say?" Gregory asked.

Without responding, and as though on autopilot, Derek reached over and handed him the note.

"I know. It's over," Gregory murmured as he read. "What does she know?" he asked out loud, perplexed.

Derek shrugged slightly in response. "I don't understand it," he said in a monotone voice. "She won't take my calls; she just left town." He paused, gazing down, staring at nothing. "She left…me." As he said the final words, he found it difficult to breathe. The numbness now wearing off, pain began ripping through him, and it was unbearable. Suddenly he longed for the desensitizing shock to come back. "Go away," he told Gregory again, his voice now a raspy whisper.

Sensing the rising emotion, Gregory stood, following instructions this time. Prior to departing, he quietly picked up the glass of whiskey from the table and removed it. Derek didn't object and sat motionless until Gregory had gone. He then placed his head in his hands, his mind reeling, not knowing how he was going to move on or what he was going to do next. He was always so confident, so sure of everything, and he couldn't recognize what he was feeling or how to respond to it. He had never suffered from a broken heart.

After several minutes he pulled his phone out, realizing that he needed to make a call. Tapping on the recent contact history, he paused over

Christine's name again, pressing call. Voicemail. He had tried her at least twenty times. Shutting his eyes briefly in defeat, he then found a different contact to call.

"Ciao, Landino," Mattia answered, almost immediately.

"Mattia," Derek said in return, "Ho bisogno di più tempo." There was a pause.

"Non capisco," Mattia said.

"I need more time," Derek repeated, switching to English as his emotions began to rise.

"I'm to assume that she said no?" Mattia asked, following Derek's language choice.

Hearing Mattia speak of his anguish in such a matter of fact manner triggered a rage within him. "I guess you could say that," he responded through gritted teeth.

Mattia sighed through the phone. "I must reiterate, Landino," he started, "I was rather disappointed in you when you stated your position on this relationship of yours. These are not the actions of a future king. I truly hope that what has happened today is not a sign of weakness."

Derek was seething now at Mattia's words.

"Excuse me?" he hissed dangerously.

"Our monarch needs to be strong, confident, and sure," Mattia responded without hesitation. "If you are to take the throne, you need to get your head on straight and become focused on your duty. This woman is distracting you, and that is unacceptable to me." Derek clenched his jaw, unaccustomed to being scolded. "I still believe that you are the right choice to lead our country," Mattia continued. "Maybe now that this is out of the way, you will be able to recommit. But if time is what you need, then take some to get it together. We will name a new monarch in a little over seven months' time, when we would traditionally hold the coronation ceremony. Whether that monarch is you or your brother is your decision."

"I understand," Derek stated. Then without another word to the prime minister, he ended the call. He put the phone down and rubbed his brow, squeezing his eyes shut tight, trying to block out the grave reality of his situation.

He picked up the ring as he stood from the chair and made his way over to the rail; he looked out over the back of the yacht. It was still raining, and it showered down on him, but he wasn't concerned as the water soaked through his jacket and shirt. With Mattia's words to him replaying in his head, he prepared to throw the ring as far as he could out into the sea. But midtoss he stopped, Christine's face coming into the forefront of his mind. He brought the ring back in front of him, gazing at the diamond, grief taking over him. As a single tear escaped down his cheek, he couldn't help but think how tonight should have been the happiest night of his life. He returned the ring to his pocket. She may have left him, he realized, but he couldn't let her go.

"Christine," he whispered, looking out at the rain falling into the black water, "how could you do this to me?"

Chapter 14

One Month Later

Jagged splashes of red and black stroked across the canvas. A stern expression was set on Christine's face as she added the final touches to the work she had been painstakingly creating over the past four months. She had never before tried so hard to capture the essence of something. She knew when she had begun this particular piece that it had been inspired by love. Her love for Derek. Having never felt satisfied with it, she had returned to North Carolina one week prior, concluding what had been missing. *Love,* she realized, would only be complete if she accurately expressed all of it, including the heartbreak and love's polar opposite—hate. She now knew through experience that love was both good and bad, beautiful and ugly. Now that she had portrayed both sides in one piece, she finally felt content, confident in the work and what it represented. She had held nothing back of herself in the creation of this painting, and now that it was complete, she felt physically drained, as if the painting itself had extracted all of the emotions out of her.

Working on the painting had become very therapeutic for Christine, and it had helped her to cope with her constant heartbreak, which plagued her daily, even now, a month after she had walked away from him. Staying true to her resolve, she had not spoken to him since that day. For the first three weeks, he had attempted to contact her daily through multiple calls, none of which she ever answered. Now, apparently finally having gotten the hint, he had stopped calling.

Choosing to stay away physically and maintain as low a profile as possible, Christine had stayed with her father in Nashville for the majority of the last month, using all her available time off. Her relationship with Derek was not a secret by any means, and of course, her leaving him was also no secret as it hadn't taken long for the media to pick up on Derek's solo appearances. She did not have any intention of being in the limelight more than she was, and she refused to give any statements or interviews regarding her relationship.

She had been home now for almost a week, and she was glad no press had been waiting for her upon her return. By now the media had moved on from her, and besides, the tabloids preferred "single" Derek; it made for more sensational news. Derek himself had also stayed away from her apartment. She knew he would not be anxious to draw media attention to the fact that she had left him, and the appearance of chasing after her would not be good for his image.

Always a media favorite, Derek stayed in the spotlight, his business dealings and public appearances making news almost daily. It seemed to Christine that he hadn't missed a single beat and the termination of their relationship hadn't phased him at all. She couldn't help but feel tormented, and at the same time foolish, over his apparent "business as usual" behavior. Curiosity getting the better of her, she followed news stories about him, waiting for the one to break that announced he was in fact royalty and moving back to Calina to take his place as its monarch. But so far this news had not come. Instead, it had just been announced earlier in the week that he had officially moved the headquarters of Land Corporation back to New York. She hadn't been able to hold back tears when reading this latest blurb; it hit her hard in the gut all over again that he was truly gone from her life. He was no longer in the state, and this time he wasn't coming back.

Knowing that she had to somehow return to her life before Derek, Christine threw herself back into her first love—art. She now adjusted her glasses on her nose and narrowed her eyes at her painting. Only when she was working could she forget him, even if it was just for a brief moment. Knowing that the pain would return, and that she would still cry out for him in the dead of the night, she relished the time spent in her studio, her only periods of peace.

Timothy McKenzie pulled up and parked his car in front of Christine's apartment. Taking a deep breath, he again second-guessed what he was doing and why he was doing it. While Derek had moved back to New York, Timothy had been instructed to stay behind at the yacht for a little while longer and see to final details. Having learned through the grapevine that Christine was back in town, he couldn't shake his curiosity about what had happened between her and Derek. As he was no longer privy to his once best friend's personal information, he could only deduce that Derek had left Christine the same way he had Cynthia and broken off the relationship because it was holding him back from pursuing his business ventures. Of course, Timothy had known all along that Derek would mess this up eventually, just like he had his marriage. Part of him just wanted the satisfaction of hearing Christine say that she despised him, but another part of him yearned to see her again.

Although he would never admit it, if he was completely honest with himself, Timothy knew that he had always been envious of Derek's success both in business and with women. Derek had risen to a level of fame, power, and wealth that other men could only dream of. His genius in his business affairs were uncanny; his charm and grace made him irresistible. Add in his ridiculous good looks, and it was enough to make any man who constantly lived in his shadow vomit—as Timothy had most of his life.

As he stared at Christine's apartment, he couldn't help but think of Cynthia and the parallels between the situations. When Derek's marriage began to fall apart, Timothy couldn't fathom why Derek was choosing his business over her, and he began to sympathize with Cynthia, ultimately becoming intrigued with the idea of rescuing her.

Pursuing Cynthia had started out as a conquest, and he had relished in the idea of enticing her away from the great Derek Landino. Not honestly believing that he could, however, he had never seriously considered that she'd submit to him, let alone begin an affair with him. His triumphant feeling was short-lived, though, and backfired on him immensely when he ended up actually falling in love with her. He had begged her to leave Derek for him, and he thought she was going to. But then she came to him, broke off the affair, and broke his heart, claiming that she would always be in love with Derek. She wanted her marriage to work. And then, because life is twisted and full of irony, Derek served her with divorce papers only a month later. Cynthia was crushed and never came back to Timothy, even after she knew the marriage was over.

Obviously, he had never been the same toward Derek, blaming him for both Cynthia's heartbreak and his own. He had lost an immense amount of respect for his successful friend when he threw away his marriage and Cynthia, and now he had done the same to Christine. A twinge of guilt passed through him as he thought about the past affair, but this was different, he reasoned. Derek and Christine were no longer together, and he and Derek were no longer friends. It was none of Derek's business if he pursued her.

He checked the time: a little after 7:00 p.m. He was hoping to catch her at home, having chosen to stop by rather than call, afraid she might ghost him. As he approached her front door, he noticed it was a bit ajar. His confidence rising, realizing that she must be home, he knocked, then pushed the door slightly open.

"Hello, Christine?" he called out, but there was no answer. Entering the sitting area tentatively, he glanced around, looking for any sign of her. A barnwood sliding door was halfway open to the left. Figuring that to be his best bet, he crossed the living room and knocked gently while sliding the door fully open. She had her back to him, standing in the middle of the art studio.

"Come in," she responded absently. Clearly engrossed in the painting before her, she didn't turn around to address whoever had entered.

Seeing her in this setting struck him. He had always before encountered her dressed up and polished at an event, on Derek's arm. Now, in her own work element, she looked very casual and raw, wearing only a pair of skinny jeans and a simple dark-green tank top with a paint-splattered lab coat thrown over her clothes. She had on glasses, her hair was down, the natural waves falling just past her shoulders, and her feet were bare. Her arms were crossed, and several paint brushes stuck out of one of her jacket pockets. He admired and appreciated her this way. She was real, down to earth, and he couldn't help but find her sexy as hell.

"I didn't mean to interrupt," he said, approaching her. "Your front door was open." At the sound of his voice, she spun around quickly, clearly startled. Her eyes flew open wide when she realized who had entered her studio.

"Timothy!" she exclaimed, "I'm sorry, I thought you were April."

"I knocked," he offered, feeling guilty for surprising her.

She looked at him with uncertainty. He could tell she was confused by his presence. Suddenly her eyes narrowed suspiciously, as though she were processing something, then her face became almost fearful.

"Wait," she said sharply, "is he here? Is that why you're here?"

Timothy knitted his eyebrows and held up his hands. "No," he said quickly.

Realizing that Christine wasn't aware of his falling out with Derek, he explained. "Christine, Derek's not with me," he paused. "We don't talk anymore." She didn't respond but continued to eye him. "Derek's in New York," he continued reassuringly. "I stayed behind to see to the last of the details here." He stopped, attempting to read her expression.

She tucked her hair behind both her ears and looked away from him, glancing around the studio, as if suddenly realizing where they were and how she must look. Her face grew red.

"I'm sorry about the mess," she said, "I wasn't expecting anyone."

"No, please," he replied, "don't be sorry. I kinda barged in on you. I should've called first." Beginning to feel nervous, he questioned again what he was doing. Feeling the need to put her at ease, he turned his gaze to her painting. "Is that yours?" he asked.

She looked back at the piece, a sense of embarrassment washing over her. She was not keen to allow just anyone to view her work, and this was a situation that she would not typically find herself in. She looked at him again and nodded in answer to his question; she could tell he was trying to make sense of the painting.

"It's nice," he said, his dark eyes shifting back to her. "It's clear you've spent a lot of time on it." Christine was used to this sort of reaction to her work, and by now she wasn't sure if she should feel amused or offended. She decided on the former as she raised her eyebrows at him, noting that clearly Timothy knew nothing about art. She offered him a small smile, feeling anxious to get him out of her studio.

"It's ok," she said, removing her jacket and tossing it onto a stool nearby. "My work's not for everyone."

She began walking toward the door, anticipating that he would follow her out.

"So, why are you here then?" she asked, leading him back into the apartment living room.

He hesitated, wanting to be honest with her but not show all of his cards. "I felt bad," he said. "I wanted to make sure you were ok."

She turned to look at him. "Why?" She asked. "I mean, why do you care?"

Timothy shrugged slightly, giving her a concerned look. "To be honest with you, I'm not sure," he replied. "Derek was my friend. I got used to seeing his failed relationships. I thought you were different to him. I guess I'm just unsettled by what he did to you." He placed his hands in his pockets. "I felt it would put my mind at ease if I knew you were ok."

Christine's mind started racing, and her eyes searched his face. Timothy knew Derek had cheated on her? He knew about Courtney? And why were Derek and Timothy no longer friends? She began to feel light-headed from all the questions burning through her. She was not prepared to think about Derek or have this discussion. Tears pricked at her eyes.

"No," she said quietly, looking at him, "I don't think I'm ok."

He could tell she was on the verge of tears. He ran a hand through his thick brown hair.

"I'm sorry, Christine," he said sincerely. "I'm a jerk, I didn't mean to upset you." He felt the strong urge to reach out to her, embrace her, but he knew she would draw back from him if he did. She shook her head and bit her lower lip, casting her eyes down now. "Why don't we take a walk?" he suggested. "You can choose to talk with me or not; it's ok either way. I just want to help." He stepped toward her and placed his hands on her shoulders; she looked up and met his eyes. "I don't want to leave you alone like this."

Christine didn't know what good talking to Timothy would do, but she couldn't keep her curiosity at bay either. She felt like he meant well enough and it might do her good to get out of her apartment for a bit. She nodded her consent to his suggestion.

"Just give me a minute," she said. "I must look a mess, and I need to grab a sweater or something."

He grinned at her. "You do have some paint on your nose," he replied. Her eyes opened wide, then bringing her brows together, she offered him an apologetic expression.

She sighed then looked away. "I'm sorry you have to see me like this."

Unable to resist, he touched her cheek. "Stop apologizing," he told her as she looked up at him. "I think you look beautiful."

She felt her breath catch in her throat at his compliment, and she was confused by the reaction. "I'll be right back," she said, holding his gaze for another second, slightly stunned by the encounter.

Ten minutes later, after she had washed the paint off her face, discarded her glasses, and pulled a cream-colored sweater over her tank top, Timothy had driven them to the nearby coast, just off campus. In the summer months at seven-thirty in the evening, this particular beach would have been crawling with students, but this time of year, as the weather was cooling, the students preferred downtown-centered activities in the evening. As such, the beach and its boardwalk were practically deserted.

As Christine stepped out of the car, a light but frigid breeze blowing in off the ocean hit her in the face. She could hear the sounds of the waves crashing onto the shore, the rhythm relaxing her. She looked up, noticing there wasn't a single cloud. As the sun had already set, there were thousands of stars now twinkling in the night sky. It was a very peaceful evening. Maybe the fresh air and the sound of the ocean waves were just what she needed, she reasoned. Timothy came around to her side of the car and placed his hand lightly on her back to guide her toward the boardwalk.

They walked in silence for several moments, but eventually Christine could no longer hold back the questions on her mind.

"Why are you and Derek no longer friends?" she asked. Timothy didn't respond right away, and she could tell he was processing the question. "I'm sorry," she said quietly. "It's none of my business."

"No, it's ok," he responded. "I'm just not too proud of myself, I suppose." He sighed. "The truth is, I had an affair with his ex-wife, Cynthia.

He didn't know about it until just recently. I never told him." Christine's eyes flew open wide, and her jaw dropped slightly at his confession. Unsure of how to respond, she kept quiet. "It's complicated," Timothy continued, clearly feeling the need to explain himself to her. "Derek didn't appreciate her; he never loved her. I did."

He stopped walking and turned to face her.

"That's why I had to come see you." His dark eyes locked with hers; they appeared jet-black, with a hint of twinkle from the moonlight. "I saw what he did to Cynthia; it devastated me. I couldn't believe it when I found out he had done the same thing to you. I couldn't believe he had just left you like that."

Christine gave him a perplexed look. *Wait, what?* she thought, realizing what he had just said. "Derek didn't leave me," she corrected him, her brows knitting together. "He had an affair. I left him."

Now it was Timothy's turn to be confused, and he frowned in the dark. Derek had been unfaithful? Regardless of their fallout, Timothy had known Derek almost his entire life. Infidelity was not something he would have thought Derek capable of. Integrity was ingrained in him, almost to a fault. Or maybe he just didn't know him as well as he thought he did.

"Are you sure?" he asked her now.

She squeezed her eyes shut tight, trying to block out the images of the photos Courtney had given her. She nodded sharply in response, again feeling the tears sting. God, she was so tired of reliving this pain.

"I have pictures of it." She choked on the words as she opened her eyes. "And pictures don't lie." She was unable to keep several tears from spilling out, and his expression turned from confusion to sympathy. He could tell she was trying to hold it together.

Before he could second-guess or stop himself, he reached for her, wrapping his arms around her, pulling her to him. She didn't resist, shivering slightly, as he held her and breathed in the sweet coconut scent of her hair.

Feeling too drained and too tired to care about who was holding her, she let her head rest against Timothy's strong chest, appreciating his warmth and comfort. She could feel the steady pounding of his heart, and it was calming. He smoothed her hair down as the cool breeze blew over them. He pulled back from her slightly, his expression soft and his eyes intense as they gazed into hers. She became fearful, knowing that he was going to kiss her.

Closing her eyes, she let his lips find hers, her tears still wet and cold on her cheek. She knew she was vulnerable and that this was reckless, but she was exhausted from her torment and needed some relief. Caught up in the moment, her eyes closed, she didn't notice the flash.

He weaved his fingers through her hair, and his hand cradled the back of her head, holding her to him. His kiss was firm but tender, and he drew back, ending the intimacy.

"I'm sorry," he said in a low voice, searching her expression. "Maybe I shouldn't have done that." Her gut agreed that he shouldn't have, but she felt conflicted. Looking into his eyes, she could see a hungry fire within their dark depths, clearly indicating that he wanted much more. Unable to respond, she simply held his gaze. "Come on," he said, releasing her but placing one arm around her shoulders as he began walking back down the boardwalk toward the car. She fell into step with him, not shrugging out of his embrace, allowing him to escort her.

He drove her back to her apartment in silence; her mind was desperately attempting to make sense of what had just happened and how she felt about it. She thought back to the night of the anniversary gala—Timothy had come on strong then too. He was clearly a man who knew what he desired and went after it. She supposed it shouldn't have surprised her that he had shown up now that Derek was out of the picture. As she thought of the gala, memories of where that evening had led floated into her mind. Derek had told her he loved her; he had made love to her for the first time. She thought she was going to be with him forever. She suddenly felt sick and wanted to scream, anger rising within her, along with excruciating agony. She glanced at Timothy next to her in the car, wondering if he was exactly what she needed right now.

Pulling up to the apartment and parking the car, he exited and opened her door for her. She walked with him up the path to her front door, thinking about whether or not she wanted to invite him in or simply say good night. Her stomach was tied in knots as she turned to face him on the front porch. She looked up at him and read the same fire in his eyes that had been present before. After a second's hesitation, she made a decision and stepped closer to him, placing her hands on his chest. His eyes gleamed at her sudden touch. His heart beginning to pound, he leaned forward and claimed her lips with intensity. She inhaled sharply as his kiss took away her breath. Meeting his tongue with hers, she let her hands wrap around his neck, trying hard not to think about anything except how good he felt.

Breaking the kiss and stepping back from him, she took his hand to lead him inside. Crossing the threshold after her, he closed the door behind them and discarded his jacket on a nearby chair, never once taking his eyes off of hers. In the next second, he seized her around the waist and pulled her into him, kissing her urgently.

His hands were at her waist, and they slipped underneath her sweater, feeling the fabric of her tank top. He grabbed the bottom hem of her sweater and pulled upward, removing it completely over her head. Refusing to think, she let his hands roam over her body, his lips now leaving hers to massage her neck and throat. He pushed against her, and she realized he was backing her into the living area, toward the sofa. She closed her eyes as he lowered her onto the sofa, bracing himself now directly on top of her, his thigh resting in between hers. He caressed her face and recaptured her mouth.

As he kissed her, her mind began to function, forcing her to realize what was happening. And what she thought about was Derek. With her eyes shut, she could almost smell him and feel him. Not Timothy. For a split second, she lost her bearings and let herself imagine that it was Derek kissing and touching her. As she thought of his face, she thought of his name. Derek...

Suddenly, Timothy stopped, pulling completely away from her. Looking down at her, he exhaled slowly, propping himself up over her. A look of complete disbelief on his face.

"What did you just say?" he whispered.

At first Christine was utterly confused; then it dawned on her that she hadn't simply thought Derek's name. Completely wrapped up in the heat of passion and oblivious to her actions, she had said his name out loud. The realization caused a look of horror to cross her face. Timothy sat up on the sofa, and she followed suit. His features now set in a hard expression, he refused to look at her.

"I'm sorry," she said quietly, knowing now that this had all been a mistake. She couldn't help but feel ashamed.

She had wanted so much to be able to move on, even in some small way. But she couldn't. Fear and sadness engulfed her. Would Derek always plague her? Timothy didn't respond right away, just shook his head slightly, as if in disappointment.

"You're still in love with him," he said, still not looking at her but rather glaring into the darkness. She nodded sadly, but he didn't see. "After what he did to you, you're still in love with him. You're just like Cynthia," he added harshly, finally facing her, "rejecting the idea of anyone else, wasting your life because you can't be with him." He narrowed his eyes in the dim lighting, practically sneering his words at her.

"I don't know Cynthia or what happened between you," Christine responded evenly, her defenses rising but her tone staying quiet. "But you've no right to judge me or how I should feel."

"I should go," he stated, rising and walking to the door. He was clearly angry, his pride crippled by her obvious preference. He grabbed his jacket, pausing to look back at her as he turned the door knob. "Goodbye,

Christine," he said, then left her apartment, closing the door with a bit more force than was necessary.

Once alone, Christine allowed all her emotions to take over. Her tears running freely now, she felt shame, guilt, and a renewed sense of grief. She fell back into the sofa, burying her face in one of the pillows. She cried until she was completely spent, finally falling asleep from exhaustion.

———•———

The next morning, Christine awoke to someone shaking her.

"Christine," came a voice, "please wake up." The voice was urgent but quiet. She opened her eyes wearily, trying to comprehend where she was. Then, remembering her evening with Timothy, she realized why she was still in her living room. Her head was pounding from having cried herself to the brink of extreme mental and physical fatigue.

Attempting to focus, she lifted her head to see April standing over her, a concerned look on her face, her eyes darting around the room as though looking for something, or someone.

"April," she murmured, "what's going on?" She rubbed her eyes and sat upright on the sofa. April took the seat next to her.

"Is he still here?" she almost whispered.

Christine rested her aching head in her hands and glanced at April. "What? Who?" she asked, confused by the random question. Who would possibly be here, she wondered.

April didn't answer right away, but held up her phone so that Christine could see the screen. As soon as her eyes focused on the image, she forgot about her headache.

She grabbed the phone from her friend, and her eyes frantically scanned the pictures and article April was showing her. "Landino's Heartbreak: Art Program Director Moves On to Other Land Corporation Men." As if the headline wasn't enough, the article was accompanied by two shots of her and Timothy, one on the boardwalk and the other right outside on her front porch. In both of them they were locked in an embrace.

"Oh my God," she whispered. She started reading, and her stomach turned, making her feel nauseated.

The tone of the article made Christine out to be a shallow, attention-craving harlot who had broken Derek's heart and then moved on to his best friend. It even suggested that she had been seeing Timothy behind Derek's back and that she had only "toyed" with the billionaire's heart to secure funding for her department at the university.

"Is he still here?" April asked again tentatively.

Christine turned slowly to face her friend, scared to see the disappointed expression on April's face. She felt hurt that April would actually believe the garbage on the phone, but then again, she thought as she sighed, the pictures were very telling. She handed April back her phone.

"He's not here," she replied, a saddened look on her face. "This article isn't true." She looked down at her hands. "I mean, he was here last night," she explained hurriedly, "but he left. I wasn't thinking. I…I just wanted the pain to stop somehow." She took a deep breath, trying to clear her mind and think straight. "I didn't sleep with him." She looked at April. "I'm not seeing him again."

"It's ok, Christine," April replied quietly, empathy on her face. "You don't have to explain yourself, especially not to me." She placed a comforting hand on Christine's shoulder, then looked back at her phone. "If anyone should explain, it's Timothy. He had to have known how vulnerable you were." Christine nodded absently, but she wasn't willing to cast blame. She was responsible for her own decisions.

The accusations in the article reverberating in her mind, Christine jumped up from the couch to grab her own phone. Checking it, she saw she had nine missed calls, multiple texts, and a voicemail from the dean of academics, along with several voicemails from tabloid reporters anxious to get "her side" of the story.

Christine groaned, realizing the scandal she now had to deal with, but regardless of her public image, she was most concerned with how this affected her position at the university.

"I need to change my number," she murmured, slumping back into the sofa next to April.

April nodded her agreement. "They're going to be all over you for a while," she replied seriously. "You need to take some extra steps in regard to your personal information. What are you going to say?"

"To the reporters?" Christine asked, her eyebrows raised. "Nothing. They won't get a word out of me." She felt very strongly about keeping a low profile.

"You should tell them something to defend yourself," April said, her eyes wide.

Christine shook her head. "No," she said firmly. "I can't talk to any press. What if they asked me why we broke up and it came out that Derek cheated on me? Then this would be an even bigger scandal." She looked at her phone again, glancing through the missed calls and texts. "It'll die down soon."

April could tell she was trying to sound confident. "You're going to have to face him at some point, Christine," she said gently. "How could you not want to confront him? Don't you want the satisfaction of telling him how much he hurt you?"

Christine gave her friend a desperate look. "I can't, April!" She cried. "I'm afraid."

April knitted her brows together in confusion. "You're afraid of Derek?" she asked, puzzled.

"No." Christine paused, trying to muster her voice. "I'm afraid that if he asked, I'd take him back." She wiped away the tears welling up in her eyes. It seemed she could not escape them. "I love him..." she whispered.

Looking back down, she continued scrolling through her texts. Reading one, she groaned. "It's the dean," she said April. "He's asking for a meeting with me and a representative from human resources to discuss the article." She sighed heavily. "I hope he doesn't believe this insinuation about the departmental funding."

"I'm sure it's just a formality," April said reassuringly. Christine nodded slightly, still not thrilled about having to discuss her relationship and break up with her boss and HR.

Suddenly she felt panic. As she looked again at the missed calls from the press and thought about the article, the overwhelming gravity of the situation came crashing down on her. She had never asked to be in the spotlight, and she had certainly never asked for any kind of fame. It was her misfortune that she fell in love with one of the most famous men in the country. Everyone was now interested in her because of her connection to him. Her business was no longer private, and regardless of whether it seemed right or wrong, she was now on center stage. Without even knowing it, she had put on a show for the world last night that had resulted in a serious disturbance to her life, her career, and her privacy.

Gregory paused just outside Derek's office door. In one hand he held a tabloid, in the other a sack from the corner deli. He knew Derek would scoff at the food, but he needed to try. With Christine gone, Derek didn't stop to breathe, let alone eat. The man had become a machine, focused on nothing except his business. This was a good thing for Land Corporation; their stock had never been higher, and Gregory knew it was only a matter of months before Derek resigned, turning the company over to a predetermined successor that had not yet been made public. But as much as Land Corporation was thriving, Derek himself was suffering and running himself completely into the ground. Having chosen not to drink to deal with his daily agony, Derek did the only thing he knew to cope—work.

Looking down at the tabloid, the assistant heaved a sigh. He was not looking forward to being the one to break this news, but he could not call himself a friend if he said nothing. He knew Derek was not following the tabloids and would not have seen it on his own. Knocking sharply on the door, he paused, then entered.

"What's that?" Derek asked him as he approached the desk. Derek was seated behind his laptop, feverishly typing. He glanced quickly at Gregory, then resumed his pace at the keyboard, clearly focused on the matter at hand. Gregory placed the deli sack on the desk next to his computer.

Most had been unable to appreciate the change in Derek since Christine left him, but because he worked so closely with him daily, it was clear and concerning to Gregory. He knew Derek never ate or slept and had lost close to twenty pounds. His already-chiseled features now held a haunting, hollowed look. Usually clean-shaven, he had missed a day or two of his grooming routine, as well as a haircut. His eyes still gleamed their brilliant blue, but Gregory could now see the sorrow they held, the grief. Although Derek still put on a show for the public, it was during these times, when he was alone, that he could be seen for what he truly was—heartbroken and falling apart. He had kept the ring, carrying it with him everywhere, always in his pocket. Gregory had caught him staring at it on a couple different occasions.

"You need to eat something, sir," Gregory replied sternly. Derek didn't look up.

"I'm not hungry," he replied dismissively.

Gregory sighed. "Derek," he said, making Derek stop and look at him. "You have to stop this." Derek didn't respond, only raised his eyebrows, allowing Gregory to continue. "You're not eating, I know you're not sleeping, and you're working around the clock. It's not healthy, and I'm concerned you're on the verge of a breakdown. Yes, Land Corporation has never been more productive, but if you don't slow down, everything that you've worked so hard for all these years will come crumbling down when you finally crash." Gregory looked his mentor in the eye. "Because you will crash."

Derek was silent for a moment, eyeing his assistant carefully. "Are you saying," he finally said slowly, "that the well-being of our company is of concern to you, owing to my behavior?" Gregory opened his eyes wide, unsure of how to respond. Was he saying that? Did he mean to accuse his boss of being reckless and not having the best of intentions for the company? He thought for a minute, then set his expression and met Derek's eye.

"Yes," he replied simply. He was sweating Derek's reaction. To his surprise, a slow smile crept up on his face.

"I'm glad you feel that way," he said. Gregory gave him a confused look, but Derek didn't explain or expand further.

He leaned back in his chair and stretched his shoulders before reaching for the deli sack. Grabbing the sandwich from the bag and unwrapping it, he flattened the sack out on the desk with his palm. "Thanks for lunch," he told Gregory, taking a large bite.

Gregory smirked and shook his head slightly. "It's five-thirty, sir."

Derek's eyes opened wide, then he stared at his computer, grimacing when he saw the time. "Well," he said, "thanks for dinner." He laid the sandwich down on top of the flattened sack, then turned back to his computer, expecting Gregory to depart. But Gregory didn't move. He could always sense when his assistant had something important to say or was about to deliver some bad news. Looking back at Gregory, Derek waited, giving him his full attention. Gregory didn't speak; his expression appeared empathetic, and his eyes wandered. It was clear he was hesitating. Finally he took in a deep breath, and set the tabloid gently in front of Derek on the desk.

Confused at first, Derek picked up the tabloid. But then his eyes immediately zeroed in on the pictures, his body turning numb as the images became clear to him. He scanned the article, his mind spinning, attempting to focus on what he was seeing.

He had spent the last month obsessing over why Christine had left him; was this why? Reading through the details, he tried to reason whether it made sense. He didn't believe for one second that Christine had used him to gain funding for the university; that had been all Derek's doing. But Timothy? As his eyes drifted back to the photos, the numbness quickly wore off, replaced by pure rage. His heart began to race, and he could feel the heat rising. Timothy's track record worked against him. He had screwed his ex-wife—and now Christine?

Derek clenched his jaw, squeezed his eyes tight, and crumpled the tabloid in his hands. Christine had left him for Timothy? Half in disbelief and half in fury, he opened his eyes and slammed the article on the desk. Standing abruptly, he focused on Gregory, his expression thunderous.

Gregory remained motionless; he had anticipated Derek's reaction, of course. Given his ties to Timothy, he expected an interrogation. Derek was so in control of his emotions that it was rare for him to lose his temper. Gregory had only ever witnessed it once, over a lost deal, and he recalled feeling very sorry for the employee on the receiving end. Now, as Derek strode around his desk and came face-to-face with him, the assistant couldn't help but feel like he should recoil. However, he held his eye contact with Derek, not challenging him but instead offering him sympathy.

"Did you know?" Derek snarled at him.

"No," Gregory answered him quickly.

Derek didn't look away. "He's your brother, damnit; you had to have known something." His tone was dangerous, and he clenched his fists.

Gregory remained calm. "I didn't know," he repeated evenly. "Derek, I'm on your side."

Derek considered Gregory, then his expression relaxed slightly as he knitted his brow and closed his eyes, a look of sorrow crossing his face. He turned away from Gregory.

"I know, Greg. I'm sorry," he said, then walked back to his desk.

"You don't know that the article is true," Gregory offered now, noting how defeated his boss seemed.

Derek reached over the desk and smoothed out the tabloid, making a face as he studied it again.

"Pictures don't lie," he said tightly, the rage beginning to build once again. *How could she do this?* he thought, his features distraught. *How long has it been going on?*

The thousands of questions now burning in his brain were suddenly interrupted by his office intercom.

"Mr. Landino, sir?" Derek looked at his desk, recognizing the voice of his head security officer.

"Yes, Jeff," he answered, turning back to the tabloid, the same menacing expression on his face.

"There's a Courtney Metcalf in the lobby here to see you." Derek snapped his head back to the intercom, shock and dread now coming over him.

"What?" he demanded. "Get rid of her immediately."

The security officer continued in a hurried voice, "I told her very firmly that you would not see anyone without an appointment, but she is being extremely persistent." He paused and lowered his voice. "She insists that you will want to see her," he added in a suggestive tone.

The revelation dawned on Derek that she had threatened his security officer with the same story she had given him at the conference, and he looked up to meet Gregory's eye. Gregory was the only person Derek had confided in about his last encounter with Courtney. The assistant was looking very intently at Derek in response but said nothing.

"This has got to stop," Derek seethed under his breath. With his anger over the tabloid still boiling, he felt the need to lash out at something, or someone. Feeling reckless, he punched the intercom button to answer Jeff. "I'll see her," he said, "but not in my office. Down in the lobby. She can wait there." He looked back at Gregory. "Where there are witnesses."

Courtney paced in the lobby. She just knew Derek would consent to see her. After all, it had been a month since that woman had gone—surely he had realized by now that he still loved her. She had specifically waited to come to see him to give him some time, but she could wait no longer. Following the media posts and tabloids, she could see what many could not. She knew his features so well that it didn't matter how much he tried to look put together for the cameras; she could tell that he was broken.

Seeing the change in him had delighted her at first. It meant her plan to destroy him and cause him agony had worked, which gave her an initial sense of victory. But now she longed to put him back together. She realized that she shared in his anguish, and regardless of how much satisfaction she felt in making him suffer, her own pain had returned.

She turned when she heard the elevator doors open behind the security desk. Derek exited, his assistant close behind. Her heart raced when she saw him. Tabloids were one thing, but seeing him in person was different. Unable to contain herself any longer, as he rounded the security desk, she rushed toward him.

Without warning, she threw her arms around his neck in embrace. The sudden movement caused his security to close in, but Derek was faster. Grabbing both her arms, he wrenched himself free from her grasp.

"What are you doing?" he hissed at her, holding her out now at arm's length. "And what the hell are you doing here?" His look was ominous and threatening, his eyes narrowed, his jaw clenched.

Courtney opened her eyes wide in innocence.

"I came to see you," she replied, perplexed by his reaction. Why wasn't he happy to see her, she thought.

"You're not getting another dime out of me," he responded. His voice was dangerously low, and he was careful not to draw too much attention to their conversation. The atrium of his building was buzzing with employees heading home for the day, and he was grateful for the public setting, but he didn't need anyone unnecessarily overhearing compromising details.

Courtney smiled dismissively at his comment. "I don't want money!" she exclaimed. "I came here for you. I love you, Derek," she said as if it were the most natural thing in the world. She looked at him adoringly. "And I know you love me too." She tried to reach for him again, but he held her arms firmly, keeping her from him.

Noticing that it didn't require much strength to restrain her, he felt as though he could snap her in two. Her words completely bewildered him, and he realized she was delusional, filled with an unhealthy obsession. Deciding that he no longer had the patience and that directness was best, he looked her square in the eyes.

"I don't love you," he said coldly. "I never have, and I never will. You need to leave now and never attempt to contact me again." With finality in his voice, he released her arms, confident that she had gotten the message. He turned away from her back toward the elevators.

"No!" She suddenly screamed at his back, causing him to spin around, surprise on his face. "You do!" She cried at him, tears now burning in her eyes. "That night..." she said, chokingly, "you loved me..." She started to feel panic. *He couldn't be saying this,* she thought frantically. Feeling as though the breath had been knocked out of her, she staggered slightly where she stood. How could he say this to her?

His rage now becoming nearly uncontrollable, already having been fueled by the tabloid, he knew he was about to snap. No longer concerned about manners, being socially correct, or any kind of hurt feelings, he squared his shoulders and stepped close to her.

"I fucked you," he said quietly, his eyes boring into hers. He turned then to Jeff. "Escort her out of the building," he instructed. Not looking back, he headed to the elevator. As the security guard grabbed Courtney's upper arm to guide her out, she twisted to free herself, covering her face with her hands as she walked out.

———•———

One witness to the entire scene watched her wipe away her now streaming tears as the guard followed her to the door. Amid her blurry eyes and forced exit, Courtney hadn't noticed that he had been standing right there observing everything and every word that she and Derek had exchanged. Meaning to stay out of sight, James had kept his hat low and his nose down to the magazine he had been pretending to read.

Ever since Courtney had been let go from the symphony, he had become obsessed with Derek Landino. His hatred for the man compounded daily; he knew that Derek was to blame for Courtney's deranged behavior. He had made himself familiar with Derek's routines and habits, watching him from afar whenever he had the chance. As such, he spent a good deal of time around the headquarters of Land Corporation. Posing as a potential client, James was able to observe a lot of what happened at the company, who came to visit, and he was very close to pinpointing Derek's routine.

Today, as he stayed inconspicuous in the atrium, he had been shocked to see Courtney enter the building. Moving to position himself just behind a large pillar so he could hear the conversation unobserved, he had been enraged at Derek's continued abuse of her. Even if he didn't have feelings for her, he didn't have to treat her like that, James had thought, like she was garbage he could just throw away. She deserved so much more than that, and James knew he could have given it to her. If she had only given him the chance. But he didn't get his chance, and it was all because of Derek.

He continued to watch sadly as she exited the building, sobbing, broken. *Don't worry, Courtney*, James thought. He made a commitment to himself: *I will bring him down for you.*

Chapter 15

Two Months Later

Derek sat pensively in the main conference room on the twenty-third floor of Land Corporation headquarters. He had been dreading this day, the day he would announce his resignation to his vice presidents and the rest of the leadership team. Mixed emotions ran through him, and he inhaled deeply, thinking through how this meeting needed to go. He had made the decision regarding his successor several months prior, and soon it would be made known—to that person and others.

Looking out across the table at the expectant faces of those he worked closely with and had shared a great deal with over the previous ten years, he had made another decision, for his own personal peace of mind.

"This month's executive meeting will be brief," he started. "I have only two key announcements regarding the future of our company." He paused, noting the raised eyebrows across the room. "However, before I get to that, I understand there are a couple of items that need to be addressed." He turned to his left to his chief financial officer, Daniel. "Daniel, I understand you have an urgent matter to discuss?" The CFO straightened his tie and cleared his throat.

"Yes, sir," he responded. "There is a discrepancy on the Land Foundation account," he paused, "of one million dollars."

"What?" Derek responded in disbelief.

"It's in our favor," Daniel replied quickly. "When I looked through the ledger, it appears there was a check made payable to the New York Symphony for one million about three months ago now," he narrowed his eyes at the bank statements in front on him, "but it never cleared the foundation account."

Derek knew immediately which item was outstanding. Looking to his right, he caught Gregory's eye. Realizing that Courtney never gave the check to the New York Symphony, he reasoned that they had refused to support her proposed nonprofit outright.

"Call the bank, and place a stop payment on that check," Derek said, "then balance the foundation ledger." Daniel nodded in response, making notes on his paperwork.

Turning to the blonde in a well-tailored suit seated near the end of the conference table, Derek now addressed his vice president of external affairs. "Taylor, what's on your agenda today?"

"Sir, there are two businesses in which we hold a large controlling stake that are not reporting profits," Taylor responded in a clear and confident tone. Derek nodded, encouraging her to continue. She glanced through a file in front of her. "The first," she started pulling out a paper, "is the Galerie d'Art de Paris. I've reviewed their financials and spoken to the curator there, Elliott Leblanc. He states that attendance is down and their last three exhibits failed to bring in new buyers." She looked back up at Derek. "He's asking for your advisement."

Derek stood up from the table, thinking. The Paris Art Gallery—struck with inspiration, he pushed up his already rolled shirt sleeves and placed his hands on the back of his chair.

"They need to find a new artist to draw attendance," he murmured, "someone with a very different approach, something never seen before."

Taylor raised her eyebrows at him. "Sounds right sir, but—" She started to speak, but Derek cut her off.

"Tell the curator to contact the dean of academics at the University of North Carolina regarding the work of Ms. Christine Dayne." He exhaled slowly. "I'm sure he'll find the artist he's looking for."

Taylor didn't respond to his suggestion, and no one moved. The room was still for several moments. Hesitantly she finally spoke. "Christine Dayne, sir?" she asked timidly. Derek's expression remained stoic, and his eyes fell upon the head attorney to the far right of the table. "Timothy?"

Timothy looked up from his portfolio to meet Derek's eyes, the tension in the room mounting uncomfortably. "Yes, sir?" he responded stiffly.

"You are clearly familiar with Ms. Dayne's work," Derek stated formally, but his eyes were menacing. "Don't you agree she will bring great success to the Paris Art Gallery?"

Timothy's expression faltered, and Derek didn't miss the blankness in his face, giving away that he had no clue in regard to Christine's work. "Yes, sir, of course," Timothy responded evenly.

Derek smirked slightly, amused at making his attorney uncomfortable. He turned back toward Taylor. "There you are," he said with a finality. She nodded her agreement and started to make notes. "One more thing, Taylor," he added.

She looked up at him. "Yes, sir?"

Derek narrowed his eyes. "There's been some recent bad press regarding my involvement with the University of North Carolina." His gaze fell once again on Timothy, who refused to look up this time. "When you make the recommendation to the gallery, make sure my name and Land Corporation are not disclosed to the dean."

"Of course," she replied. "I will ensure extreme discretion with the recommendation of Ms. Dayne to the gallery."

Derek paced slightly behind his chair. "What is the other business?" he asked.

Taylor opened another file in front of her. "Gable Ranch, in Texas," she replied. "It seems they are overextended on their line, and the bank is calling it. They don't have the means to make the payment, and they haven't reported a profit in several months." She paused, flipping through some pages in the file, then looked up at Derek. "Sir, I recommend we send someone down there immediately to oversee their operations. If we can't turn this around quickly, we will have to sell. It's pretty dire."

Derek considered the ranch, remembering how he had promised Fawna he'd visit and how proud she had been of her work there. Helping the ranch get back on its feet was suddenly very appealing to him, and it presented the kind of distraction he felt he might need. Also, this was a part of his job that he truly enjoyed, and it would be the last chance he got to make a trip into the field to straighten out a struggling company.

"I can go, Taylor." Scott Matthews, Land Corporation's senior CPA, offered. "I can free up my schedule for the next couple of days." Taylor looked expectantly at Scott, then to Derek, who shook his head resolutely.

"Actually, no, you can't, Scott," Derek replied. "You, as well as the entire senior leadership team, will be needed here over the next couple of weeks." He paused, then made the decision. "I'll go."

"You, sir?" Taylor asked. "You're much too busy, Derek," she stated, perplexed by his choice.

"Yes, I'll go," he repeated. "In fact, I may be the only one here with the additional time on their hands, which is a nice segue into my announcement."

He made eye contact with each of his team members. Taking in a deep breath, he picked up a small stack of paper and proceeded to pass one sheet around to each executive. "This is a confidentiality agreement," he explained, "which I need you all to sign right now, because what I am about to share with you could not just be considered insider information regarding Land Corporation but also a security threat to some, if it is breeched." At the severity of his words, many heads snapped to look at Derek with very confused expressions. Derek waited to say more until he had seen each and every member sign the document and had collected them back.

Now standing at the head of the table, he continued.

"In three weeks' time," he started, "I will be resigning from my position here at Land Corporation as president and CEO." Jaws dropped, eyes opened wide, and several gasped at his statement. "I have been preparing for this company transition for months now, and it is time for me to step aside. I have named a successor to my position, whom I will announce in a few minutes."

"Sir…" Daniel responded, unable to contain the question everyone was burning to ask. "Why?"

Derek paused for several moments before responding. Only Gregory and Timothy even knew where he was from, let alone his birthright.

"I am the crown prince of Calina, a microstate in Europe," he said slowly, digesting the expressions on the faces around him, which included complete shock. "In just over three months," he continued, "I will be coronated as their monarch." He paused. "As I stated, confidentiality is crucial." Not wishing to go into more detail at this particular time because he knew the questions would never end, he changed the subject.

"Now, I'd like to announce the individual I have selected to lead Land Corporation" He smiled slightly, knowing that he had made the right decision; his intuition had never failed him. "I believe you will all have a great future with this successor. In fact, I can say with certainty that many of the tough decisions are already being made by this person, and I've never had the privilege of working with someone who was more dedicated or passionate regarding the success of this company." Derek paused, then looked down at the man seated directly to his right. "Gregory," he said, smiling.

"Yes, sir," Gregory responded automatically, looking up from his note-taking, unaware that the entire room was looking expectantly at him.

Derek smirked at him, and it dawned on the assistant that his mentor had just handed him the company. His eyes flew open wide.

"Me?" he asked as Derek continued to smile at him.

"You are my right hand, Greg," Derek replied, "and you handle business better than me." He paused, thinking. "You're also much smarter than me," he added, laughing lightly. As Gregory stood, Derek placed his hand on his shoulder and looked him in the eye. "You are the best man for the job, and I have complete faith that you will lead Land Corporation to new and even greater heights."

Gregory shook his offered hand. "I won't let you down, Derek," Gregory responded confidently, now smiling broadly.

Derek nodded in return. "I know," he said.

He looked out across the room, again making eye contact with each executive. Knowing how much the company had come to value Gregory, he wasn't surprised at the smiles of acceptance at his choice. All except for one.

"Meeting adjourned," Derek stated. As everyone gathered their notes and pens and began to rise from their seats, Derek zeroed in on his attorney, now needing to execute the second decision he had made. "Timothy," he called across the room. Timothy looked in his direction and just raised his eyebrows. "I need to see you in my office."

Derek made his way to the conference room door, shaking hands with those he passed, Timothy following close behind. The main conference room was only a short walk down a hallway from his office. Derek's stride was quick and confident, and his mind was determined. Just before reaching his office door, he addressed the attorney.

"Effective immediately, I am terminating you," he stated clearly as he entered the office, stopping now, facing his desk.

Timothy's mouth dropped open in shock. "What!" he exclaimed, but before he could say more, Derek rounded on him quickly.

"And one more thing," he said through gritted teeth. As he turned to face Timothy, his fist came with him in full force, the physical blow of his rage finding its mark on the left side of Timothy's face.

Caught unaware, Timothy stumbled backward onto the floor over the office threshold. Giving Timothy a last glare and preparing to exit the office, Derek stepped over his ex-attorney and ex-friend.

"I told you to stay away from her," he said as he walked out. Timothy shook his spinning head and touched his jaw, blackness and spots blurring in front of him.

"Derek, wait." He mustered the words as Derek entered the hallway. But refusing to listen or care further, Derek didn't stop.

He made his way to Gregory's office and rapped on his assistant's open door.

"I'm heading out to Texas," he informed Gregory. Having heard the commotion and the distinctive "thud" coming from Derek's office, Gregory knew what had transpired. He also knew that at some point Derek would snap and go after Timothy. Deciding it best not to question his actions at this moment, he instead picked up his cell phone to make a call.

"I'll have the jet waiting," he responded, preparing to dial, but Derek shook his head.

"No, I'm going to drive," he said matter-of-factly.

Gregory looked at him in surprise. "It's at least twenty-four hours to Texas," he said, but he knew arguing with Derek was of no use, and Derek didn't respond. "How long do you think you'll be down there?" Gregory asked, changing the direction of the conversation.

Derek shrugged. "A couple days, I suppose," he said, "as long as it takes to straighten them out. Then I'll be back."

Gregory considered this. "Maybe you should take your time," he said, looking at Derek with concern. "You need a break, and once you take on your new responsibilities, who knows when your next chance will be," he paused. "A change of scenery might do you good."

Derek ran a hand through his hair, not wanting to even think about what his life would look like in four months, and he knew Gregory had a point. But he didn't feel comfortable committing to anything either. "We'll see," he responded. He turned to leave, but Gregory called after him.

"Don't forget your boots," he said, knowing that Derek would not be thinking about the proper attire for staying on a ranch. Looking back at him, Derek knitted his brow. "You can't wear loafers or oxfords" he explained with a smirk. "And jeans," he added. Derek half smiled, shook his head slightly, and turned to make his way down the hall toward the elevators.

His mind reeling from the confrontation, Derek made himself refocus. He made mental notes of what needed to be done in Texas as he emerged from the elevators into the atrium. His eyes zeroed in on the private exit, outside of which his car was parked, and he strode toward it, thinking that if he left now, he'd beat rush hour.

———◦———

Every time James caught a glimpse of him, he hated the man even more. He thought of Courtney as he watched the billionaire make his exit from the building. Unsure of how to help her, James continued to stalk Derek at Land Corporation, wondering if (and even hoping that) she might show up again. He had it in his mind that if she did, he would confront both of them and rescue her from this madness. He wasn't afraid of Derek, and really what other choice did James have? He had to save her.

She refused his calls and attempts to see her. He had even tracked her down to where she was living now in the Bronx, but she wouldn't even open the door for him. He was convinced that if he didn't do something, she would end up harming herself, or worse. So her obsession became his obsession, and every day he monitored the building, hoping that she would return and he'd get his chance.

James put down the magazine he was pretending to read and prepared to go home for the day. He sighed, thinking to himself how much better his life, Courtney's life, and possibly the world would be if Derek Landino just didn't exist. He stopped midstride as the thought continued to resonate with him. Was it possible for Derek not to exist anymore? Could he make that happen? Courtney would surely see James for the man he was if he were to get Derek completely out of the picture. For good.

A grin formed on James's lips as he strolled out the exit, a new and improved mission on his mind.

One-twenty, one-thirty-five, one-forty miles per hour. It was 3:00 a.m., and Derek pressed on the accelerator, shifting the gears of the LaFerrari. Thinking that the long drive would do him some good, clear his head, he enjoyed the adrenaline rush of pushing the limits on the freeway. Putting physical distance between himself, his business, and Timothy felt liberating to him. He had been driving for nearly nine hours now, and having chosen to drive straight through, he figured that would put him at the ranch just a bit after 6:00 p.m.

He was looking forward to the task ahead of him and had already begun to run through the most likely business reasons for the company's financial crisis. Driving for so long had given him time to do nothing except think, and although this made him extremely confident he could repair the ranch, he also couldn't stop his mind from wandering to thoughts of Christine.

He thought of her face, her laugh, her perfume. He sighed as pain coursed through him, a very familiar feeling to him now. Usually the feeling was followed by anger, and this instance was no exception. Because thoughts of Christine always led to vivid images of her with Timothy. He glanced at his right hand and gripped the wheel, his knuckles bruised from their contact with Timothy's face.

Punching him had given Derek a momentary, needed sense of satisfaction, but it had not taken away the facts. The fact that Christine had left him for Timothy, and that they had both betrayed him. He shut his eyes tight just briefly in an effort to block out rage-inducing mental pictures of them together; of him holding her, kissing her. Taking several deep breaths to control his senses, he backed off the accelerator, down-shifting to a reasonable speed.

Shaking his head to clear it, he turned up the radio—a classic rock satellite station—and forced his mind back to the ranch and his agenda. He was familiar with their operational structure, having set it up personally. He knew the bank they worked with and their expectations, and he felt quite certain that Fawna had made too many aggressive decisions in an attempt to grow the business. *If it grows too quickly, you find yourself needing capital and maxing out convenient debt vehicles like credit cards and bank lines of credit,* he thought. When the bank sees that happening, they get nervous that payments can't be made.

Derek was fairly sure he could call in a favor, straighten out the books and get the business back in the black. He grimaced, though, knowing that in doing so, certain things may have to change, including proposed projects being halted, expenses being cut, or employees being laid off—this was the ugly side of making bad business decisions, and he hated being the bearer of bad news. But, he reasoned, it needed to be done if she wanted to, yet again, save the ranch from being sold.

———•———

Fawna Gable paced around the great room of the ranch's main house. It was her home, her office, and where she was expecting to receive Derek Landino. When she had taken the call from Land Corporation, she had felt certain they would be sending an accounting executive. She had been shocked to learn that he was personally coming down to review the ranch's business operations and finances. She was embarrassed that she had not been properly running the business, to the point that it was nearly in worse shape than it had been when her father had run it, and having Land Corporation's CEO dig through all her mistakes humiliated her that much more. Not to mention the immense amount of pressure it added.

She twisted her hands together as she paced and glanced at the nearby clock on the mantel: 6:15 p.m. She was expecting him to arrive at any moment. Unsure what to expect, she had made dinner and had had her staff prepare rooms in both the main house and guest house, hesitant to decide where he would be the most comfortable. There was a large desk in the great room, just outside her personal office, and on it she had set all the books, records, ledgers, and bank statements, ready for his review. Regardless of what he wanted when he first arrived, Fawna made sure she would be able to accommodate any request.

Derek maneuvered his car down the winding dirt road leading up to the ranch, arriving at nearly the exact time he had anticipated. He made a face as he realized the filth that was now covering his precious automobile, but he also couldn't help but feel satisfaction over the large dust cloud behind him; he had been incapable of resisting punching the accelerator. He pulled up in front of the large main house and parked the car. Opening the door, a young man of about thirty wearing a cowboy hat and dusty jeans greeted him.

"Mr. Landino, sir, welcome to Gable Ranch," the young man said, smiling as Derek emerged from the car. Derek shut the door and shook the man's outstretched hand in a firm shake. Then he removed his sunglasses.

"Thank you," he replied. "You are?"

"Trey Adams," the man replied. "I work for Fawna, of course. I help with the horses." Derek nodded his understanding. "Fawna's waiting for you up at the house," Trey continued. "Would you follow me please, sir?"

As Derek followed Trey toward the house, he took in his surroundings. The sun was low in the sky, turning the horizon pink. As the ranch was off the beaten path, it was quiet and tranquil, save for the sounds of chirping crickets and an occasional horse bray. He took inventory of the layout, noting several buildings, including guest houses, barns, and stables. He didn't recall nearly as many structures, and the ranch had quite clearly been extensively developed.

Having seen the car pull in, Fawna waited by the front door. Upon hearing the two men on the front porch, she opened the door in anticipation, sudden nerves coursing through her.

"Mr. Landino," she smiled, holding the door for them to pass through. "It's very nice to see you. Welcome to the ranch." Derek shook her hand as he entered the house.

"Derek," he replied. "And it's nice to see you again, Fawn." He emphasized the mistake, smiling playfully. Her smile grew at his recollection. She had wondered if she had left any impression on him at all from before. Indeed, she remembered in detail her last encounter with the famous billionaire during the anniversary gala. She had not been able to stop herself from being quite taken with his charm and humility then, and her stomach flipped upon seeing him again now.

She cleared her throat slightly in an effort to shake her anxiety.

"I wasn't sure where you'd feel most comfortable," she said as she led him through the foyer and into the great room. "There's room here, in the main house, of course. But you're welcome to stay in one of the guest houses." She couldn't help but secretly hope he'd choose to stay with her.

"Well," he said, looking around, "where is your office?"

"Just around the corner. There," she responded, pointing.

He nodded and noticed the large desk, part of a built-in wall unit including cupboards and book shelves.

"Do you work here too?" he asked, motioning toward the desk.

"Sometimes," she replied. "It can be more comfortable, and I can access the grounds more easily than when I am tucked away in the back office."

"It seems logical for me to stay where I will be working with you," he said sensibly. "Your office and files are here. Do you mind if I take over this desk?"

"Of course not," she assured him. "Whatever you need." She turned to the ranch hand.

"Trey, why don't you see to Mr. Landino's things and set him up in the bedroom down the hall?" Trey nodded in response, then left back out through the front hall.

Derek walked toward the desk, inspecting the work space more closely, pleased to see the piles of financials awaiting his attention. Having had many suspicions and thought through possible solutions and outcomes during his long drive, he felt anxious to actually see the numbers.

"Shall we get to it then?" he asked, picking up the top tax return. Fawna blinked at him, and her face fell slightly. She had hoped that he wouldn't want to get to work right away.

"Um, we can," she replied. "Wouldn't you like to have dinner first, though?"

"I'm not hungry," he said absently, scanning the document. The silence that followed made him look at her. He raised an eyebrow, noticing the disappointment on her face. Realizing that she had gone out of her way for him, he put the return back on the desk, giving her a half smile.

"I suppose this can wait until tomorrow morning," he said. His grin widened. "What's for dinner?"

Her face lit up, and he saw the relief wash over her. "Fajitas," she replied. "They're my specialty." Suddenly, he did feel hungry.

Appraising her for the first time since he had arrived, he couldn't help but see her as the girl next door. Her hair was honey blond and curly, with bleached highlights from her being out in the sun. Her skin had a tanned glow, and her large blue-gray eyes were innocent-looking. Her attire was simple—a red T-shirt and jeans—and although she was rather petite, her toned arms gave him the impression that she didn't mind hard work.

"My favorite," he said, following her into the kitchen.

Three days later Derek held his head in his hands; his eyes were dry and tired as he tried to muster, yet again, more patience. Fawna paced behind him as he sat at the desk, practically glaring at him as she crossed her arms.

"I won't do that," she insisted for what felt like to him like the hundredth time. Checking his phone, he noted that it was after 1:00 a.m. He sighed, realizing they had been arguing about this one issue for over an hour.

What he had originally deemed to be simple and easy he soon discovered was difficult, mostly because he had concluded that Fawna was just about the most stubborn person he had ever encountered. Fighting him at every turn, she was strong-willed and determined to keep certain plans for her business intact, offering very little compromise. More than once it had occurred to him to throw in the towel and declare that they should sell, but this was his last opportunity to help in this capacity, and it just wasn't in his blood to admit defeat. Continuing to muscle his way through her demands and having called in multiple favors, he was now at the point where he could see light at the end of this long, dark tunnel.

"It's simple math, Fawn," he said, growing weary of repeating himself. "Either you find a way to gain more revenue or expenses get cut. We've exhausted avenues to grow revenue, and your plan there going forward is solid. There is no other option."

"But you've already cut employee benefits, and I've given up half my salary for the next two years," she argued. "I won't lay off anyone, especially not Trey."

Derek ran a hand through his hair and stood up, needing to stretch. She wasn't being reasonable, and his nerves were raw.

"If you don't, you will not be profitable and I will be forced to sell this company," he said sternly.

"But he needs this job!" she cried. "He has a family. It's not fair. You have to find another way."

"Is saving his job more important to you than keeping your ranch?" The lateness of the hour, lack of sleep, and mounting stress had caused a rare rise to his voice. Beyond frustrated, he could no longer hide his irritation.

She opened her mouth to rebut him, but closed it again and simply walked away from him into the kitchen. It wasn't the first time she had walked away from him when she hadn't liked what he had had to say. Unappreciative of the disrespect, he growled and crashed heavily back into the desk chair. Stifling a tired yawn, he squinted his eyes at the profit and loss sheet. She came back a moment later and set a mug down on the desk in front of him. He gave the cup the side-eye.

"What's that?" he asked sharply.

"Coffee, of course," she replied, the former sharp emotion in her voice now replaced with pleasantness. "I figure if we're going to come up with another option, we need more fuel." He knitted his brow in disbelief, prepared to continue the debate, but eyeing the black liquid caused his thoughts to drift to Christine. He wondered briefly what she might be doing now. Was she with Timothy? He felt nauseated as the tabloid pictures pushed their way back into his mind.

Deciding that the caffeine would probably help, he picked up the mug and took a drink, unconcerned at the moment with the bitter taste. He felt the fog in his brain clear slightly and took a breath, ready to retackle the current issue.

"I'm sorry I've been so difficult to work with," Fawna said behind his back after a few moments. He turned in his chair and gave her a pointed look, raising his eyebrows.

Considering her, he rose and approached her, placing his hands on her shoulders. "You are just like you father," he said calmly. "You are very spirited and stubborn, and it's clear you love this ranch more than anything. But if you love it, you have to take care of it financially as well. Otherwise, everyone will be out of a job. Not just Trey." She looked up at him with wide, sad eyes, but he could also feel an attraction radiating from her as she held his gaze.

It occurred to him that he could kiss her and she would respond to him with enthusiasm. But would that help? Even if slept with her, would he feel better? He thought again of Christine and Timothy, and his rage boiled; he wanted nothing more at that moment than to release his tension with a physical abundance of passion. But he knew, as he removed his hands from Fawna's shoulders, that was all it would be. He felt nothing for her except physical attraction, and a momentary escape from his torment was not an answer.

He let the moment pass and turned from her, breaking eye contact so as not to see the disappointment cross her face. Absently, he picked up the cash flow statement.

"You've left off any discounts from your suppliers," he mentioned, his voice fatigued, assuming an oversight of the software.

"What do you mean?" she questioned him, stepping forward to take the document from him.

He narrowed his eyes. "Your supplier discounts," he repeated. "They're not on here." She gave him a blank face. "Don't you receive supplier discounts?" he asked her slowly, unwilling to believe that she could possibly have missed such a crucial step to effective cash flow. Her embarrassed expression told him all he needed to know.

"I...I didn't know," she said quietly. He took the paper back from her, took his place back at the desk, and began jotting down notes, rifling through her ledgers and configuring percentages.

He worked in silence for what seemed like forever, but Fawna didn't dare interrupt him, on edge and hoping that he had found a viable solution. Finally, a slow smile spread across his face as he set down a pen. Turning, he looked at her.

"This will work." He grinned. "I know I can get you at least a fifteen percent discount, saving you just enough to get you out of the red and"—he paused—"allowing Trey to keep his job."

Satisfied that the grunt work of the job was finally done, he stood, ready to call it a night. Immediately he felt her arms thrown around his neck as she embraced him tightly.

"Thank you," she said, muffled against him. He froze, expecting her to release him. When she didn't, he patted her back then reached up to pry her arms loose. She gave a quick laugh and a sniff, and he realized she had become so emotional it had brought tears to her eyes.

"I'm sorry," she said, letting go of him. "I'm just so grateful, but I feel so dumb now." She lowered her eyes. "You probably don't think I'm much of a business owner, do you?"

"You made a rookie mistake," he said, "but that's how you learn. If you never fail, you'll never succeed." He offered her an encouraging smile, which she returned, then promptly yawned. He laughed. "Why don't you turn in. I want to double-check these numbers one last time, and in the morning, we'll get everything wrapped up." She wiped away a stray tear and nodded. Giving him a last smile of gratitude, she turned and headed toward the back hall and her bedroom.

He shook his head slightly as he watched her walk away, thinking briefly how she both intrigued and frustrated him, which left him slightly amused. Reaching over and grabbing the profit and loss statement, he wandered over to the couch in the middle of the great room. Suddenly feeling more exhausted than he had ever felt before, he sank into the couch, attempting to focus on the numbers in front of him, quickly becoming aware that he could no longer see them. His temple throbbed, and his vision blurred. Closing his eyes as he leaned against the back of the couch, he felt sure he couldn't move his limbs if he wanted to. The overwork, sleep deprivation, and pressure were finally catching up to him, and Derek's last thought was of Gregory's warning, wondering if this was what "crashing" felt like.

Chapter 16

After packing away the last painting, Christine decided she needed a break. She walked out of her studio and into the kitchen, grabbing an apple and turning on the coffeepot. As she munched on the piece of fruit, she thought in amazement about how much had changed in the last couple of days.

Christine had been informed via a phone call from the university that a prominent gallery in Paris was looking to showcase a new, cutting-edge artist to draw buyers. The dean had some connection with the curator, Elliott Leblanc, and had recommended Christine's work. Hardly daring to believe what the dean was telling her, Christine had only hesitated for a second when he asked her if she would be interested in meeting with the curator.

It had been two months since the scandal had broken surrounding her and Timothy, and hoping that it would have died down by now, Christine was continuously disappointed to notice the side-eyes and whispers behind her back. It seemed as though everywhere she went, people were staring, talking about, and even sneering at her. Timothy had done nothing to counter the stories circulating in the media, and Christine had the sinking suspicion that he enjoyed everyone believing that she had left Derek for him. So, the rumors persisted and grew more outrageous.

Even the dean, when presenting her with this opportunity in France, had taken on an insinuating tone when commenting that this might "be in her and the university's best interest." He didn't come out and say he was glad she might be resigning from her position as art program director, but she could read between the lines. Christine even wondered if the dean had used his connection with the curator to set this all up so she would leave.

The only person she was able to continue to confide in was April. She knew she had a faithful friend for life in April, but even she wasn't enough to keep Christine rooted to the university. Only a week ago, her friend had given Christine the news that she wanted to move back to New York, and Christine knew it was to be with Gregory. So in approximately three months April would be gone, and Christine would have nothing left in North Carolina.

The coffeemaker done, Christine reached over and grabbed a cup, pouring out the steaming black liquid. She took in the aroma as she sipped, thinking what her life could possibly look like in a month's time. If the curator liked her work and agreed to the exhibit, she would be staying in France to prepare and finish her pieces. If the exhibition was successful, she might consider moving there and starting a new life. A life she'd always dreamed of, doing what she truly loved, finally fulfilling her purpose of being a successful artist.

She set down her cup and prepared to get back to her packing, smiling slightly at her prospects, feeling grateful that the dean somehow knew this curator in Paris.

———◆———

Having arisen at 6:00 a.m., Fawna emerged into the great room expecting to see Derek already at work, which seemed to be his norm. Surprised to find his desk unoccupied, however, she shrugged, concluding he must have chosen to sleep in this time. After all, the hard work was done, and she felt they both deserved a break.

She had spent the better part of the last three days with him poring over numbers, spreadsheets, and business plans, working until the early hours of the morning. She smiled as she thought of working so closely with him, and although she had never been through such a grueling process and vowed to never get into this situation again, she felt sad that it was finished. She didn't want him to leave. In awe of the way he had been able to not only turn her company profitable but find ways to do it without her having to give up too much, she felt she owed him everything. He had saved her employees, her livelihood, and, most importantly, her father's legacy, which was now her own.

As she walked through the great room toward the kitchen, she spotted him on the couch. Confused at first, she realized he must have fallen asleep out here after she had gone to bed. Walking up to him, she noticed the profit and loss statement still in his hand. She smiled softly and gently removed the document. He didn't stir, sleeping deeply. Considering waking him so he could rest more comfortably in his bed, Fawna quickly decided against it. She had seen so much strain on his face in the past days, and his jaw was always set as if he carried the weight of the world on his shoulders. But now his breathing was slow and even; his features were peaceful and relaxed. She stared at him, her gaze transfixed, having always been convinced that she couldn't become more attracted to him than she already was. She was wrong. She sighed, reminding herself that it was futile to develop any feelings for him. His job here was done, and he was going to leave soon, possibly even today.

Unable to bring herself to ruin his peace, she reached over him for the throw blanket on the back of the sofa and laid it across him. Giving him one last adoring glance, she proceeded to the kitchen to start the coffee. She knew he wanted to finalize the business plan and present it to the bank as well as Land Corporation first thing this morning, but then she thought excitedly of being able to get out to the stables today and possibly even go for a ride. Besides, she thought, she wasn't going to wake him, and what was the hurry anyway?

Fawna spent the entire day outside, feeding and grooming the horses, taking several out for exercise, cleaning the stables and tending to general building maintenance. It felt good to be out in the sun, and it was a nice break from the dull monotony of paperwork. Moving from one duty to the next, she kept an eye on the main house porch for a sign of Derek, dreading the possibility of him calling her back in or announcing his departure, but he never emerged.

Now, a bit after 4:00 p.m., as she worked with a couple of horses enclosed in the paddock just outside the stable, she finally saw him appear and walk in her direction. As he approached, she couldn't stop her heartbeat from quickening. She noticed he had showered, shaved, and looked at home on the ranch wearing a simple black T-shirt and jeans. As he neared the paddock fence, she was happy to see he appeared well rested and healthier than she had seen him since he had come, which was something she couldn't help but take credit for. When he first arrived, she had noted that he seemingly had not eaten or slept in days. Ensuring that he never missed a meal, Fawna had dismissed his objections to working continuously, and although they had both endured a serious lack of sleep over the past couple of days, she took pride in knowing that he was finally able to rest at the ranch.

He smiled in greeting and rested an arm on the fence rail. In the process of grooming the mare in front of her, entranced by his image, Fawna faltered and dropped the brush.

"Look who's finally awake," she laughed lightly, covering her clumsiness, bending forward to recover the brush.

"I've never slept that much," Derek replied. "It must be the fresh air out here." He paused, reflecting. "Why didn't you wake me?" Fawna shrugged.

"You clearly needed the sleep," she said as she resumed brushing the mare's coat. He watched her for several minutes, slightly intrigued by her task.

Fully aware that he was studying her and feeling a bit apprehensive that he would scold her for not yet presenting her business plan, she stopped her chore and looked at him.

"Are you hungry?" she asked tentatively.

His grin widened. "Not really," he responded, giving his usual answer to that question. To her relief, he didn't mention work. "That's a beautiful horse," he said, eyeing the mare. She smiled and gazed at the horse lovingly.

"This is Honey," she replied, giving the mare's neck a stroke. "And that," she said, pointing to the stallion on the other side of the paddock, "is Dante. Do you ride?" Prior to his arrival, she had intended to go riding herself. Now, fearing that her afternoon was shot, she caught a glimmer of hope in continuing her plan if she could convince him to come with her.

But Derek knitted his brow and shook his head. "No," he said. "I don't know the first thing about horses."

Refusing to be deterred and excited at the prospect of doing something enjoyable with him, she made a proposal. "I could teach you?" He looked at her with surprise. "It's the least I can do," she insisted, smiling playfully. "You saved my business, so you receive one lesson free of charge."

Derek regarded her with uncertainty. Horses were completely foreign to him, and he typically did not engage in activities that he knew nothing about. But, he thought, what would be the harm in learning something new and taking a break from the norm? Fawna had been openly vulnerable and embarrassed in showing him her lack of business knowledge. It would be enticing to see her confident and in her element.

"Just one, huh?" he asked dryly. "I guess I'd better take you up on such a generous offer."

She beamed at him as he opened the gate and entered the paddock. "Well, my silent business partner doesn't like it when I don't watch my expenses," she said coyly. "I can't give away too much for free."

He laughed in response. "Ok," he said, catching his breath, "how do you ride a horse?"

Two hours later Derek found himself walking the stallion with ease next to Fawna on the trails surrounding the ranch. Not having known what to expect, he was pleased to find he actually enjoyed the experience. Of course, Fawna had made the learning process seamless, and he gave her credit. It was impressive to watch her teach and handle the horses with grace and confidence, further securing his belief in the value of the ranch and that she was the right person to run this business. She belonged here.

Taking in the surroundings, he let out a slow breath, grateful for the serene quiet and tranquility around him. Holding the reins gently as she had shown him, he allowed himself to become slightly mesmerized by the moment, appreciating the sun, the slight breeze, and the soft sound of the horse hooves kicking up dust from the trail. Unable to remember when he had felt more at peace, he suddenly realized this feeling was attributable to the fact that practically no one knew his location or what he was doing. There were no tabloids reporting on his activities, no paparazzi, no agendas. It was liberating.

Walking slightly behind Fawna, just off to her left, he glanced at her, taking in her form and posture, noticing how the soft curl of her hair swayed slightly to the rhythm of the walking horse and how the sun seemed to glow on the skin of her shoulders. Temporarily lost in his gaze, his stallion veered slightly in her direction. He shook his head and pulled the rein, bringing the horse back, remembering that she also told him to keep his eyes focused on where he wanted the horse to go.

Sensing that he was watching her, Fawna glanced back and slowed her horse so they were side by side. Derek had turned out to be a quick study, and she couldn't remember a more pleasurable afternoon.

"You're quiet," she observed, now in gait with him.

"I was just thinking how peaceful it is here," he replied. "I keep looking for photographers or racking my brain for when the next meeting is, but there's nothing." He smiled slowly. "It's nice."

Fawna considered his position thoughtfully, her pulse suddenly quickening as a bold offer occurred to her. "You don't have to leave," she said slowly, then unconsciously held her breath. He remained silent, and she stared straight ahead, afraid to look at him. "I mean, if you need a break," she added, "you're of course welcome to stay as long as you'd like."

"That's very considerate of you," he finally responded, but his tone held no commitment, and he offered no additional detail to his plans of departure. She chose not to probe further, fearing what he would say. "Tomorrow," he continued, "we really do need to finalize and submit your business plan." Fawna nodded absently, disappointed that the conversation had turned to work. But, she thought, at least he would stay one more night.

A half hour later, having finished their ride through the trails, they were guiding the horses back to the paddock.

"You must be hungry by now," Fawna said as they dismounted. "I'll have Trey see the horses back to the stable." Derek knew by now it was a waste of energy to argue with her when it came to meals, and admitting that she had a flair for cooking, he decided that he didn't mind too much.

He nodded. "I never seem to be able to turn down your cooking," he responded with a smile as he followed her back to the main house.

Having refused assistance of any kind, she made him wait while she prepared dinner. Deciding not to waste the opportunity, Derek worked on finalizing the numbers and presentation surrounding her business plan. As he was finishing up and refiling certain financials, he found himself thinking again about Gregory's advice to take some additional time before his life was thrown completely upside down. He had enjoyed his day, feeling well rested and better than he had felt in some months. It seemed as though Fawna also wouldn't mind his staying longer, but that caused him concern. He was not naive to the effect he had on women, and he wasn't prepared to explore the avenues of any kind of relationship. However, he thought in the back of his mind, Christine seemed to have moved on quite easily.

Wandering back toward the kitchen, he found her just finishing up setting the table and bringing out the dishes. He leaned against the door frame, placing his hands in his pockets.

"What's on the menu tonight?" he asked. Fawna looked up at him and flushed slightly. His ask had seemed so natural, as if making him dinner was a common occurrence.

Wiping off her hands on a towel, she motioned toward the table. "Roast chicken," she replied. "Have a seat."

He took the chair opposite her as she prepared their plates. While in the kitchen, she hadn't been able to stop her mind from thinking about the possibility that he might stay longer with her. After all, he had moved to North Carolina to be with Christine; he could choose to make similar arrangements and stay with her. As she set his plate in front of him, she noticed he was watching her intently.

"What is it?" she asked, taking her seat across from him.

"I was just thinking about what you said," he replied, holding her gaze.

Her heart began to race. Was he going to stay? She raised her eyebrows, anticipating what was next. "And?"

"You said last night that I probably didn't think too much of you as a business owner," he explained. Pursing her lips slightly, she couldn't help the heart-falling sensation. Of course he was talking about business, she thought. Nevertheless, she put a look of interest on her face and widened her eyes at him. "While it's true you may not have a knack for the financial side," he continued, "it's very clear to me that this is what you were meant to do."

She broke into a genuine smile. "Really?" she asked.

"Absolutely," he said in confirmation. "Your brilliance is in the physical aspect, Fawn, and you know the ranch—how to run it, what needs to be done. You shouldn't be behind a desk or crunching numbers. You will serve your employees and your customers better being on the front lines." He paused and leaned forward, folding his arms on the table. "I think you should hire a finance manager or CFO. Someone who can take care of the cash flow while you bring in and service your customers."

She blinked at him. The thought had never occurred to her to hire a financial manager. Her father had never had one. She had always assumed it was her responsibility. He narrowed his eyes slightly, picking up on her excitement over the prospect.

"You can't afford it right now," he added quickly, seeing the grin spread across her face. "But maybe in a quarter or two, after you've shown you can stick to the plan we have come up with."

"That would be amazing," she mused, the thought of never having to look at another spreadsheet exhilarating her.

He laughed at her dreamy response. "I'll make you a recommendation," he said absently, turning his attention to the meal. After he said the words, he paused, realizing that in one to two quarters from now, he'd be knee-deep in the mess that was the country of Calina and would not be around to make that recommendation. He shook his head, clearing his mind and choosing not to think about Calina.

Throughout dinner he noticed her gaze was continuously in his direction. Guessing what was on her mind, he ignored the tension. After they'd finished dinner and he had helped her with the cleanup, he followed her back into the great room.

"We'd better get some rest," he said and then smiled. "No sleeping in tomorrow."

She laughed lightly. "That was you, not me," she said teasingly. Her smile faded as she thought of ending their work in the morning. Her face grew serious. The look she gave him was enough to make him apprehensive; he knew she was about to cross the line. "I don't want you to leave," she said quietly. He regarded her pensively, preparing to give her an easy letdown speech, but before he could, she stepped toward him, wrapped her hand around his neck, and pressed her lips against his.

She had to stand on her toes to reach him, and he let her kiss him, deciding that her lips were sweet. Placing his hand on her back and holding her to him, he began to return her kiss, allowing the physical need to swell inside him. His mind soon overpowered his hunger, however, and almost as abruptly as she had kissed him, he ended it, grabbing her by the waist with both hands and pushing her gently from him.

"Fawn," he said as he broke apart from her, "I can't." The look on her face was one of confusion, and Derek winced. If the stubbornness she had shown him over the past couple days were any indication of how she handled rejection, this was not going to go smoothly.

"I don't understand," she said. "I can tell you're attracted to me." He looked away from her. Sure, he was attracted to her. But she wasn't Christine. "Do you think she's going to come back to you?" Fawna asked strongly, reading his mind. "Isn't she with Timothy now?"

Knowing that they both knew the answer to both questions, he met her eyes. His anguished expression matched hers, but for different reasons. He remained silent, and after a moment, she sighed, her eyes softening.

"I'm sorry, Derek." Her voice was almost at a whisper. She stepped toward him again, this time embracing him. "I'm sorry you're hurting," she said now, pulling back. "I like being with you. I like having you here." She looked up into his eyes. "I wish I could help you forget her." She lowered her eyes and turned from him, walking away toward her room.

He heard the click of her door being closed and briefly shut his eyes tight. Yes, he knew Christine wasn't coming back—she wouldn't even speak to him. And why? Because of Timothy. His jaw clenched, and he suddenly wished he could punch the smug attorney in the face again. Staring at the place from which Fawna had departed, he allowed himself to entertain the idea of moving on. Maybe this didn't have to be complicated. The images of Christine with his former best friend suddenly flooding into his mind pushed him over the edge, and he strode after Fawna, pausing as he reached her door. He knocked softly, and she opened the door after just a brief moment.

"Can I come in?" he asked her, his eyes darkening. Her expression held surprise at seeing him, but she nodded, stepping aside, allowing him to enter. He closed the door behind them, then turned to face her.

"Is this what you want?" he asked her seriously. Not allowing her to answer right away, he continued. "I cannot offer you any sort of commitment or relationship. It must stay simple and uncomplicated." He stopped for a moment, attempting to read her expression, which was blank except for her large, alluring doe eyes. "I cannot stay."

Her mouth opened slightly as she attempted to understand what he was offering her. A one-night stand? A casual fling every now and again? Prior to Christine, she knew, as everyone knew, that Derek had not engaged in relationships after the end of his marriage. And if he was trying to get over her, it was understandable that he did not want any obligations. Deciding that she could handle a casual affair with him, she nodded again.

"I understand," she said quietly.

He held her eyes with his, watching them fill with desire. As he approached her, he reached for the back collar of his T-shirt, pulling it off over his head and dropping it to the ground. Her breath caught in her throat as her eyes devoured his body, which was only inches from her now. His gaze never leaving her face, he hooked his fingers through the belt loops of her jeans and tugged her to him. The anticipation of his next move was almost unbearable to her. Unfastening the button and zipper on her jeans, he let his hands explore her, one bracing against her lower back while the other dipped inside her panties. Her eyes closed as his fingers expertly found their mark, slipping inside her. She gasped slightly with his touch, and as he began to work her body, she let out a moan, her breathing now becoming labored. Soon, she felt like she was melting onto him, becoming drunk on her lust along with the pleasure he was giving her.

Sensing that her knees were weakening and her legs would no longer support her, he removed his hand, sliding out from her depths. Reaching down, he gripped the backs of her thighs just below her ass, easily lifting her light body as she wrapped her legs around his waist. He laid her down flush against her bed, and his mouth seized hers with a physical yearning.

Fawna felt lost in a frenzy of emotion and passion, having never before experienced the way her body responded to him. As he peeled away the rest of their clothes, she could only think about how much she wanted him. She was giving herself up to him completely now through the fog of intense lust; his words echoed somewhere in her brain. She was half thinking about his resolve to not enter into any commitment and his not wishing to stay with her. Her last lucid thought before she succumbed to mind-numbing abandon was that maybe she could change his mind.

Chapter 17

Three Weeks Later

"I know I recommended that you take your time," Gregory said through the phone, "but you need to publicly announce your resignation." Derek furrowed his brow; he knew that Gregory was right, and his choosing to extend his visit in Texas was cutting his time down to the wire. He needed to leave.

Fawna had made it easy for him to stay as long as he had. Having kept to his terms, she never put any pressure on him or even brought up anything pertaining to an actual relationship. He had been able to see to the last-minute details of the succession of his business over to Gregory remotely, and he couldn't deny enjoying the freedom he had gained from prying eyes and tabloids. He had simply been able to disappear for the last three weeks, but he knew it was time now to begin his journey.

"By the way," Gregory said, "I'm sending you an email. I thought you would want to see this."

Derek rotated in his chair to face his laptop on the desk off the great room in the main house. Having clicked open the email Gregory had just sent, he saw it was an announcement, written in French, from the Paris Art

Gallery. The announcement declared to Land Corporation that the gallery would be opening an exhibit the following week featuring the work of a brilliant new artist, Christine Dayne. The letter went on further to inform Land Corporation that the previews had already produced a strong turnout and several interested potential buyers.

He gave a small smile. He had always known that she would be successful, as she deserved to be. As he stared at her name, his features turned sad. She was in France now. She couldn't still be with Timothy, could she? He frowned as it struck him how badly he needed to hear from her why she had done what she did. He would be traveling to Europe soon himself, and suddenly the thought of tracking her down consumed him.

"Derek? Are you there?" Gregory's voice brought him out of his thoughts.

"Greg," he stated urgently, "get me a ticket to that exhibit, will you?" He paused. "And find out from the curator where she's staying."

"Are you sure that's—"

"Yes, I'm sure," he said matter-of-factly. "And set up a press conference. I'll be back in New York tomorrow night."

"You're leaving?"

Derek ended the call with Gregory as he heard Fawna's voice behind him. He stood to turn and face her. He had been dreading telling her he had to leave for days now, putting it off, but he could pacify her no longer. Regarding her with an apologetic expression, he wasn't entirely sure how she would take the news of him leaving. Although he had been upfront and completely honest about his intentions, he wasn't blind to the signs that she had begun to form feelings for him.

Their relationship had entered a new crossroads just two nights ago, when she had asked him to stay with her all night as opposed to sleeping in his own room, his preference. She had asked him with such earnestness that he hadn't been able to bring himself to leave her, at least not until she had fallen asleep. She had not addressed the incident with him the following day, but he knew the signals of attachment, and it was clear he needed to leave before things with her entered a realm he didn't want to go to.

"It's time, Fawn," he told her now. "I have to return to New York." Her face held an expression that he wasn't sure would turn angry or tearful, and he glanced away from her, not looking forward to either response.

"I thought that maybe…" She started speaking but trailed off, unable to finish the sentence. Part of her knew it was foolish to cling to the idea that he would change his mind and stay, but she hadn't been unable to prevent herself from hoping it would happen that way. "Can't you come back?" she asked, not wanting to let him let go of her so easily.

His face remained stoic as he shook his head slowly. "No," he answered her quietly. Her desperation began to rise at his simple response, and she couldn't help the tears that pricked at her eyes or the anger that began to swell.

"But why?" she insisted, fighting both emotions. "You moved to North Carolina before. Why couldn't you make similar arrangements to stay here with me?"

He closed his eyes briefly, battling an internal pain. His expression held empathy as he met her eyes again.

"That was different," he told her softly. She fought the tears now as the realization of what he was telling her became clear.

"Different because you loved her." She finished for him. *And you don't love me.*

Her eyes left him and looked to his laptop on the desk. The art gallery notice was still open, and anger flooded through her now at the sight of Christine's name.

"You're still in love with her, aren't you?" she said accusatorily. Fawna knew she had no right to chastise him, but at the moment she didn't care. Feeling rejected, she only wanted to hurt him back. He didn't reply, which vexed her more. "She doesn't love you anymore. Why can't you move on from her?"

Derek sighed, noting the rise to her voice. "This conversation and these questions are not going to help matters for you," he finally replied. "All it will do is force me to say things that will end up hurting you more." Tears streamed down her face now.

"Please don't go," she whispered. He approached her and placed his hands on her shoulders. Narrowing his eyes, he locked his gaze on hers.

"Regardless of where my feelings lie," he told her, "I have no choice." He had not been prepared to divulge his future obligations, but if it somehow helped her to accept the situation, he now considered telling her who he was. "Tomorrow night, I will be publicly resigning from my position at Land Corporation," he explained to her. "I'm moving to Europe, to my home country of Calina." He watched her expression carefully as her eyes widened and her mouth opened slightly. "In approximately three months, I will be coronated as their monarch."

She swallowed an internal sob as she listened to his words, disbelief and heartbreak spreading through her. *How can this be?* she thought, almost frantically. He was leaving and never coming back? The prospect of never seeing him again was too much to bear.

"Why do you have to do that?" she cried out now, despair to her voice. "I can make you happy here. You could have a peaceful life here."

Derek couldn't disagree that he had never felt more relaxed and at ease than he had in the past couple weeks. With no pressures from deadlines or press, it felt liberating to say the least. Even if he wished to turn his back on those who were depending on him, he couldn't. He couldn't forget about his country, and as much as he had tried, he couldn't forget about Christine.

"You've been great to me, Fawn," he said, "and it's been wonderful to stay here. I didn't know what it felt like to just breathe." She searched his face, knowing there was a "but." "But going to Calina is not just my duty and birthright." He paused for emphasis. "It's my purpose. I could never feel any sense of fulfillment or true happiness unless I was living out my reason for being here."

"I love you," she told him quietly, looking up into his eyes. "If you asked me, I'd go with you."

Stunned by her response, Derek could only regard her again with empathy. He shook his head slightly.

"No, Fawn," he said, a sadness to his tone, "we both know you belong here." He leaned forward and gently placed a brief kiss on her forehead. "I have to go pack," he told her, then turned and walked away, back down the hall.

Left alone, Fawna glanced through her tears again at his open laptop, gazing at the gallery announcement. As she let the words of the notice resonate with her, she realized the exhibit was actually in France. Christine was in Europe. She blinked and shook her head with an increased understanding. He wasn't just going to Europe for his own reasons; he was chasing after Christine as well.

———— • ————

At the edge of the Bronx, James knocked on the door of the small, shabby home he knew belonged to Courtney's cousin. Having still been unable to contact her successfully up to this point, he had to try just once more. He had never been so focused on what he was going to do, and he needed her to know he was doing it all for her. To free her, once and for all, from the powerful spell that bastard had her under.

He knocked again, more urgently, and after a moment a small, dark-haired woman answered the door.

"Can I help you?" she asked as she opened just the inside door, leaving the screen door closed in front of him. Her tone wasn't exactly friendly, and her expression was no-nonsense, one eyebrow raised at him.

"I'm here to see Courtney," James replied, a bit awkwardly. "You're her cousin, right?"

The woman examined him closely, as if determining whether or not he posed a threat to her.

"I'm Dana," she said. "Yes, Courtney is my cousin. What do you want with her?"

"I came to check on her. She's my friend." James paused, his heart racing at the thought that she may be inside. "Is she home?"

Apparently having decided that his intentions were innocent, Dana opened the screen door for him and allowed him to enter.

"Yeah, she's home." She sighed heavily. "She's always home. She never leaves, never goes anywhere, never works." She emphasized the last sentence, with animosity. She studied James. "Funny," she added, "I didn't think she still had any friends. If you care about her so much, maybe you'll consider taking her in. I'm just about done with letting her freeload here."

James frowned at Dana's description of Courtney's condition, and he feared she was in a worse state than he had imagined. Dana gestured toward the hallway. "She's in the back bedroom if you want to go see her. I was just on my way to work." She gave him a last up-and-down glance, then grabbed her keys off the table and left through the front door.

Making his way down the short hallway toward the bedroom Dana had indicated, James took a breath, apprehensive of what he would find. He knocked on the door lightly.

"Courtney?" he said. Upon receiving no response, he pushed the door open. His eyes roamed over the room, taking in the debris and stench. Clearly, she had been shut up in here for some time. Laundry was piled on the floor, as well as countless empty liquor bottles. The shades were drawn, letting in very little light, and he could barely make out a limp, huddled figure on the bed. She sat upright, her knees pulled right up to her face, her bony arms wrapped around them, clutching them for dear life. Her long hair was greasy, unwashed, and fell lifelessly around her. She didn't look up when James entered. He moved toward her tentatively, wishing he could open the window as the air hung heavy and stale.

He reached over and touched her shoulder. Slowly lifting her head, she squinted at him. His eyes opened wide at the sight of her face. She was so pale, almost ghostly, her dark eyes practically black and bloodshot. Her lips were dry and cracked, and she was so thin James couldn't help but wonder if she was deliberately starving herself. She attempted to focus on him, her eyes working to open wider.

"James," she mouthed at him, barely audibly.

"It's ok, Courtney," he said softly as he sat next to her on the bed. "I'm going to help you." He placed his arm around her small frame, and she leaned in toward him. She was too weak to struggle or push him away, so she allowed him to hold her. Still hugging her knees, she began to weep. Unable to cry real tears anymore due to severe dehydration, she could only dry sob.

"He doesn't love me, James."

James pursed his lips as pain crossed his face. Pain he felt for her. But a sense of relief flooded through him as well. If she was willing to admit that, then maybe there was hope that he could bring her back. He hugged her more tightly.

"I'm going to take care of it," he told her, his voice set in a serious tone. "He's going to pay for what he did to you."

She lifted her head and looked at him, her eyes wide now. "What do you mean?" she asked. Her voice cracked and sounded rough, as though she hadn't used it in some time.

In response, James reached into his jacket pocket, pulled out a nine-millimeter automatic pistol, and set it on the bed in front of her.

She stared at the weapon. "You'd do that," she said weakly, "for me?"

James nodded slowly, his pride swelling, knowing that he finally had her attention. "Once he's gone, you'll be free."

Is this the way out of my torture? she thought. She considered how she would feel if Derek were dead. She realized the concept made her feel surprisingly better. If he didn't love her and she couldn't have him, then why should anyone else? Yes, the idea gave her a sense of peace, and if James was willing to do the dirty work, then why not? A new hope and light filled her, but almost as immediately as it had come, it vanished as she remembered the news that had just come out today.

"You're too late," she said solemnly now. "He's leaving the country."

James pulled back from her sharply. "What are you talking about?" He asked sternly. She slowly reached over and grabbed her phone from the nightstand, showing him the article that had just come through that evening. "Derek Landino to Become the Future King Of Calina; Resigns from Land Corporation"

Panic rising within him, James struggled to make sense of the news. No, he thought, this can't be. He couldn't have missed his opportunity, not now, just when Courtney seemed to be responding to him. This was still his mission, still his goal, and he committed to it with a determination stronger than it had been before. Derek wasn't gone for good; he would still come back at some point. He just had to be patient. He would get his chance, and nothing would take that away from him now.

"Don't worry," he told her, his expression sincere and resolute. He brushed strands of her hair clinging to her face back over her shoulders as he looked into her eyes. "I promise you, Courtney, if it's the last thing I do, I will not rest until Derek Landino is dead. In the meantime," he added, her newfound dependance on him fueling his confidence, "you're going to stay with me so I can make sure you're taken care of." Courtney nodded, allowing her head to once again rest against him. She wasn't in any place to argue, and she had no strength or will to live. If James was willing to help her, she would gladly accept. A small smile crept onto her face. *Who knew James could be so useful?* she thought.

———◆———

Derek had landed in Paris two days before Christine's exhibit was to open. He was expected to settle in Calina within the week, but first he needed see

her, address and confront her. Hoping to find either an answer or closure—
if that's what it came down to—he needed to put the matter behind him one
way or another so he could focus completely on his next task. Having spent
his first day in Paris visiting the gallery, speaking to the curator and checking
in with important contacts, he now sat in the rented Mercedes across the
narrow street, looking up at the flat the gallery had set her up in.

For the first time, he realized he didn't know what he was going to say
or how he was even going to feel seeing her again after so long. Deciding
that stalling any longer wouldn't bring him any kind of new revelation, he
climbed out of the car and crossed the street. Ascending the front stoop,
he paused for just a second before knocking sharply on the door. He heard
footsteps within the flat, then a moment later the door swung open. She
stood before him, her eyes opened wide, a look of complete shock on her
face. He didn't smile, only took in her presence, observing that she was likely
in the middle of a project. Her hair was piled up in a loose bun, and she
donned her signature glasses and work jacket. A smudge of grayish-green
paint appeared on her right cheek.

"Derek," she found her voice after a moment. "What…what are you
doing here?" She stammered, and he could tell that she had been thoroughly
derailed by his sudden visit.

"I'm traveling to Calina," he told her matter-of-factly, then added, "as
you know."

She blinked at him. "This is France," she replied flatly, still in disbelief
that he was standing in front of her.

It was the first time she had spoken to him since walking out on him
four months prior. She had no intention of seeing him again, and she wondered how he had finally found her but then realized he had just about endless resources in multiple countries. Her breath caught in her throat as she
thought of all the things left unsaid; all the memories came rushing back. So
many times she had wondered what might have been.

"Can I come in?" he asked, his eyebrows raised. Suddenly registering that they were standing in the doorway still, Christine nodded, feeling rude. She stepped aside, allowing him to pass her into the flat. It was a simple studio apartment, and her paintings were set up throughout the airy space. She hadn't had time to unpack; the flat was simply a workspace in which she also slept.

She moved over to the opposite wall as she felt the need to put space between them. She hated that upon seeing him again, she had instantly felt the same magnetic pull toward him. His appearance still gave her heart the same thrill it always had, and she surmised she had been right to avoid him.

"What do you want?" she asked him rather timidly, refusing to bother with small talk or feigned innocence. If he was here, it was most certainly for a reason.

"You left me a note," he stated bluntly, following her lead and getting straight to the point. "You didn't say goodbye or give an explanation. Then, I find out you were with him? My best friend? You left me for him, didn't you? How long was it going on?" His voice sounded strained as he was now able to vocalize all the questions that had been circulating in his mind for months.

She stared at him. Left him for his best friend? Concluding that he believed the awful rumors and scandal surrounding her and Timothy, she opened her mouth to argue with him and set the record straight. But she stopped. *What good would it do?* she asked herself. Her expression turned pained. He knew damn well why she had left. Was he actually going to act like his affair with Courtney never happened? Like this was her fault? She regarded him with sorrow, and her chest began to ache. Why had he come here now? Just when she was beginning to move on and find good in her life again.

The silence between them lengthened. No longer able to endure not being answered, he suddenly strode across the room to her. Caught between anger and a yearning to be close to her again, he locked his gaze with hers, reaching for both her hands. As he laced their fingers together, he stepped forward, and she instinctively backed up against the wall. Dropping his head slightly, he rested his forehead against hers briefly. Her eyes closed in the intimate pose as tears began to sting.

"Derek, I—"

"Shh," he whispered. She felt so small in his presence, his broad shoulders hovering over her. His body almost threatening to touch hers. She could feel his warmth. Her heart was hammering as she struggled to maintain her composure so close to him. She ached to touch him, bring him completely to her. But he held her hands firmly. She felt a sensation of falling, falling into a void. Suddenly, bringing his head up, he lifted her hands and flattened them against the wall on either side of her head. Looking into his eyes, she thought he was going to kiss her. Her mind became frantic, unsure of what to do. She had not planned for this, and she had not expected to still feel so strongly for him. He wasn't supposed to ever come here. *I still love him*, she admitted to herself with a force that almost knocked her over, and she needed him back.

But, to her great dismay, he didn't kiss her. His eyes grew dark as they bore into hers. "How could you do that to me?" he whispered coldly.

Her eyes turned bright turquoise as they burned with tears, then he dropped her hands, turned away from her, and was about to walk out of the studio when she broke her silence, unable to maintain it any longer.

"I didn't do anything to you," she cried after him, now needing to say her piece, needing him to believe her. "Nothing happened with Timothy while you and I were together. I didn't leave you because of him. It was you who…" But her voice broke, unable to finish, to speak aloud his betrayal.

He stopped and turned around, facing her again, searching her for sincerity.

"But the tabloid," he said, the images coming into his mind. "Everyone saw you with him."

Christine clenched her eyes tight briefly, a tear escaping down her face. "What you saw," she began, "was all that ever happened between me and Timothy. Nothing more. And it was well after we were already apart. It was a mistake, and the press blew it completely out of proportion, spreading rumors and lies." She knew she didn't owe him an explanation. It was he who should be explaining. But, for the first time, she was able to share with someone the truth about Timothy, and she felt a small weight being lifted off her shoulders.

Derek's mind worked hard trying to make some kind of sense out of everything. If she didn't leave him for Timothy, then why?

"Was it Calina, then?" he asked. "You left me because of Calina?" The look on his face was one of complete confusion.

Christine couldn't believe that he was playing games with her. Was he just refusing to admit it, trying to save face? The whole situation becoming too much for her, tears began rolling down her cheeks. Having never before felt so conflicted about her emotions, she couldn't separate her love for him from her hatred of his betrayal. A sense of hopelessness taking over her body, she knew she had to confront him. He had offered her everything—love, devotion, trust—only to deceive her. She swallowed her tears and met his eyes.

"I would have followed you anywhere," she answered. She took a breath, preparing to finally address his infidelity. "You can act like you don't know," she said quietly, "but I know you had an affair. The day I found out was the day I left you. I know you slept with Courtney Metcalf."

At her words astonishment crossed his face. He opened his mouth to speak, but she cut him off.

"Don't deny it," she added. "I can't bear to hear you deny it. I saw the proof." He stood still for several moments, the same expression on his features; it seemed as though he was in shock.

"You believe I had an affair with Courtney Metcalf?" he repeated blankly. There was no more emotion left in his voice. Suddenly a look came across his face that she had never seen before. It was a look of apathy. "How could you believe that I would do that to you?"

Unsure how to respond, Christine shook her head slightly. She thought of the pictures Courtney had given her. The look on his face made her second-guess their authenticity. Had she been wrong this whole time? Was there more to the story than the pictures told? She averted her gaze, no longer able to look him in the eye. Had she made a huge mistake?

Derek became quiet, and he dropped his gaze to the floor. His silence now telling her he was no longer concerned with pursuing answers from her. She knew why he was shutting down. She had, in the harshest way possible, questioned his character, his intentions, and his love for her. Something that she knew he had tried so hard to prove to her. She realized she should have believed him, not the story she was told by some little bitch who may have just been trying to get even with him. As she looked back up into his eyes, she now saw a blank disinterest in them, and it became clear that she had come to this realization too late.

"Goodbye, Christine," he stated. He lowered his gaze, turned toward the door, and left.

———◦———

The following day Christine was surrounded by a sea of people at the exhibit. Her heart was practically beating out of her chest as she looked around the gallery, taking everything in. Art patrons, enthusiasts, and beautiful celebrities in formal attire were milling around gazing and murmuring about the artwork on display. Her artwork. Hushed, jovial conversations were being held amid the frequent clinking of crystal champagne glasses.

Her masterpiece seemed to be receiving the most attention. It was the centerpiece of the collection of four paintings signifying passion, lust, devotion and, finally, love—the last of which she now knew was her greatest work, inspired by a great love. A great love that, she now had to admit, was over.

Not being fluent in French, she could only make out a word here and there as most of the conversations were being spoken too rapidly for her understanding. It seemed, however, as though the mood was positive, and Christine couldn't help but feel elated in spite of her renewed broken heart. She needed this to be a success. She had to move on, start over—and on her own. This exhibit was her chance. It had been a huge risk—leaving behind everything she knew—but she needed the change to proceed with her life, especially after seeing Derek again yesterday, for the last time.

As she thought again of the expression on his face, she blinked hard to keep her emotions at bay. This moment should have been the most gratifying of her life, but she felt as though a dark cloud hung overhead. She would forever be haunted by him and the thought of what might have been. He was the love of her life, and she knew she would never recover from that loss. She had spent four months mourning, and just when she thought she was moving on, it was starting all over again.

As she made her way through the crowd toward her masterpiece, which was at the center of the exhibit, she noticed a tall, dark figure admiring her work. As she approached, she narrowed her eyes at the jacketed stranger. She was unable to make out his face; he kept his hat low. Suddenly, the stranger turned away from the painting and quickly walked into the crowd, disappearing from view. Christine's heart raced. Was that…? But before she could follow him, someone touched her arm.

"Mademoiselle!" Christine recognized the beaming face of the curator, Elliott Leblanc. Knowing she did not know much French, Elliott used English with her. "You must be *très* excited!" he exclaimed, and Christine couldn't help getting caught up in his infectious smile. "This has been the most successful exhibit the gallery has ever seen! Many of your pieces have sold, Christine, for top price! And many more buyers are looking for new paintings from you."

Christine's eyes opened wide at the news. Was he actually saying what she had always dreamed of? She had steady work as an actual artist, one whose work was in demand.

"This is amazing, Elliott," she replied as a glowing smile spread across her face. "I can't believe this is actually happening."

"Yes, I must admit I was nervous when His Highness the Crown Prince made the recommendation to exhibit your work here. After all, I did not know who you were! You were an unknown, and it was a huge risk." Elliott smiled slyly, "But I should have known! That man, he is never wrong."

Christine blinked as she listened to the curator. What had he just said?

"I'm sorry," she said, the smile frozen to her face as her brow furrowed in confusion. "I thought the dean of the university had recommended my work."

Elliott laughed. "Ah, no!" he cried out through laughter. "Is he taking all the credit? Of course he would try. But of course, mademoiselle, you must realize that it was Monsieur Landino who told me about you. He practically ordered me to exhibit your work. Given that he owns this gallery, I had no choice." At that moment, a patron grabbed Elliott's attention, and after giving Christine a brief kiss on each cheek, he excused himself from her, flashing her one more appreciative smile.

Christine stood stunned. She looked around the gallery, again taking in her surroundings, coming to terms with her newfound success. Her dreams were coming true after so long and so many failed attempts. And knowing that none of it would have been possible had it not been for him.

"That son of a…" she said under her breath.

"*Excusez-moi*, Mademoiselle Christine Dayne?" Startled, she turned sharply at the voice that addressed her. Standing behind her and looking at her expectantly with a dashing smile was a very handsome man. He was tall, with sandy, wavy hair and clear blue eyes. Dimples appeared below his defined cheekbones as he smiled broadly at her. He was most certainly French, and when he spoke English, his accent was heavy—and dreamy. He offered her his hand, and when she took his, he brought it to his lips in a brief kiss. "*S'il vous plait*, I am Sean Laurent."

Chapter 18

Two Months Later

Derek rubbed the back of his neck with his hand, trying to release some tension as he rode in the very back of the royal limousine. He was weary from the last few days worth of public appearances, and the hour was late. He glanced at the black tinted window, only seeing his own tired eyes reflecting back, while his personal security guard, Vincenzo Costa, sat across from him in the dark.

The limousine was headed back toward the old palace, where he was now settled. The palace itself was ornate and redolent of the past. Everywhere within its walls were tributes to past monarchs and their families—his family. Although this was all new to him, recollections from his childhood would arise, and he couldn't escape a sense of familiarity, of home. He knew he belonged here, that this was where he was destined to be, but he also couldn't help feeling emptiness or incompletion.

He closed his eyes briefly, resting against the headrest as he reflected on the past two months since his arrival back in Calina. There was a massive amount of curiosity among the people surrounding his upcoming reign, and he had realized quickly that many seemed frightened of him, assuming he would lead how the previous monarch had. Knowing that earning the peoples' trust needed to be one of his top priorities, he spent countless hours meeting and speaking with the citizens to gain their respect.

As he crossed his arms he glanced at the empty seat next to him, feeling melancholy. He had never before been surrounded by more people at one time, and yet he had never felt so isolated. He missed dearly those that were close to him; he missed Christine. Even his brother, whom he only ever saw occasionally, he found himself wishing for his company since he was family. Sadly, because Derek had chosen to prevent Nicola from taking over Calina, his brother had now refused to speak to him and had also chosen to remain in New York.

The limousine slowed as it pulled in front of the main palace entrance. Acting on instinct, Derek reached for the door handle but immediately heard Costa clear his throat. Derek drew back his hand and rolled his eyes. He was most unaccustomed to being waited on, and he hated feeling like he couldn't do simple things for himself. After a moment, his door swung open for him, and he stepped out, raising an eyebrow at the attendant who now bowed before his presence. Adjusting to the formalities with being a crowned prince was something he was finding great difficulty in. He greatly disliked the bowing, being addressed as "Your Highness," the formal attire. And he'd rather die before wearing a crown.

Almost immediately, Costa was at his side, following him closely as he made his way into the palace. Derek felt exhausted, and his nerves were raw. Pausing halfway down the main entrance hallway, he turned to face the security guard.

"I'm now safe and sound inside the palace," he stated. "I don't need an escort to my room." His tone made it evident that the guard was dismissed for the evening. Costa paused for a quick moment, clearly not in agreement of Derek's wishes, but he bowed respectfully.

"Yes, Your Highness," he replied. Derek suppressed a slight groan, then turned and continued down the vast hall. He needed rest; there was so much that needed to be done.

Early the next morning, Derek stretched his shoulders and focused on the proposals in front of him. Continuing on his mission to prove himself worthy to the people of Calina, he had determined that immediate action was needed. Now that he had met with all the key players and advisers, his next move was to weed out the corrupt officials. He had spent much of his time researching the backgrounds and prior decisions of many diplomats in high places, and he was confident that he knew exactly who must be dismissed. But he had also deduced doing so was potentially dangerous. There were few that he trusted here in Calina, and his very presence threatened the power and positions of many.

There was a knock, and Costa, who was stationed just outside the door, opened it and escorted the prime minister into the study where Derek was working.

"Ciao, Luca," Derek said in greeting. "Are all these guards really necessary?" He glanced up from the paperwork to see the grimace on Luca's face.

"With all due respect, Your Highness," Luca began after a brief bow, "you're continued preference of speaking English has upset some of the more traditional officials." Derek furrowed his brow and waved a hand dismissively in response. He thought his language choice should be the least of anyone's concerns. "I received word that you wished to speak with me," Luca continued. Derek rose and handed the prime minister a piece of paper.

"I wish to dismiss these members of parliament from all duties," he stated matter-of-factly.

Luca took the paper with curiosity and intrigue. Upon reviewing the list, his expression turned to one of horror.

"You can't be serious, signore," he said, astonished. "These are some of the most powerful men in the country." His voice became quiet and fearful.

Derek narrowed his eyes. "Exactly why they need to go." His tone was grave, and he spoke with conviction. "I have unearthed evidence of their corruption and fraud, both of which have been to the detriment of the people of Calina. I believe they were masterminds of the revolution, but their actions clearly show that their priorities lie only within their own interests." Derek rounded his desk and approached Luca, facing him, meeting his eye. "It intrigues me, Luca," he continued, "that it didn't take much digging to uncover these key players." He waited for the prime minister's reaction. "I suspect you've known as well but chose to turn a blind eye. Out of fear, perhaps?" Luca didn't respond, but his guilty expression gave him away. "You once accused me of not being strong enough for my position. I recommend that you take a look in the mirror in that regard. If you expect to keep your own rank, that is."

"I understand, Your Highness," Luca replied, his face now stoic. "However, you cannot exact executive power in your current position." Derek raised his eyebrows. Luca continued. "As a prince, you do not have the authority. You will have to wait until after the coronation tomorrow to carry out these wishes."

"That's fine," Derek replied. "I want you to have the guard standing by to ensure things are smooth." Luca nodded. "Speaking of the coronation, did you do as I asked?"

Luca knitted his eyebrows and suppressed a small sigh.

"Yes, signore, I ensured that Monsieur Sean Laurent was sent an invitation to your coronation." Luca regarded Derek with caution, as if debating whether to ask a question. "Although many celebrities will be in attendance tomorrow, it is really an event more for politicians and diplomats. I really don't see why the need to invite a French model. He's not someone I would have considered among the elite." Derek didn't respond and took his place behind his desk. He agreed that no, Sean Laurent was definitely not elite nor extraordinary in the slightest, and he clenched his jaw thinking of the headline that had popped up on his phone a week ago now: French Supermodel

Sean Laurent and New Art Sensation Christine Dayne Engaged! A Match Made In Heaven."

"I have my reasons," he stated.

———•———

Christine fought her nerves as she entered the palace grounds in Calina the following evening. She grasped onto Sean's arm as he led her through the hall; they gave their names to the guards stationed at the entrance and made their way into the ballroom along with the other guests. She hadn't actually wanted to attend the event; however, Sean had insisted they go, claiming that the press coverage alone would help his career. It wasn't every day a monarch was coronated, let alone someone like Derek Landino. The event was all anyone spoke about and all the press cared to report on.

Sean hadn't bothered to wonder why he had even received an invitation but had been elated at the prospect of attending. Christine knew it was her connection to Derek that had secured the invite, but she wasn't sure why. What could his intention possibly be in having her attend his coronation? As such, she thought it best not to divulge to Sean why they were going.

The ceremony itself had taken place much earlier in the day. Only a few select diplomats and officials had been invited to the crowning of the new king. The celebration that was to take place in the ballroom, the afterparty, was to be the social event of the year—and possibly many years to come. It shook Christine almost to the core to think that the very next time she saw Derek, he would no longer be just a man, but a king.

Feeling dwarfed in the massive space, she attempted to take in her surroundings amid the crowd that was gathering. She had never been in such a large and ornate room. The floor and wall accents were completely made of marble. As she looked up, she noticed enormous chandeliers and decorative carved paneling with hand-painted detailing. At the very front of the room was a double spiral staircase that ascended on both sides up to a balcony overlooking the room from the upper floor, and just below the balcony an orchestra was beginning to play traditional and classical music. All along the walls of the room there were numerous doors and exits, with guards posted at each one.

Christine looked up at Sean; his dashing face held a grin and he was clearly in his element. She could see his eyes scanning the crowd, scoping out possible connections. She sighed under her breath, foreseeing how the evening would go. Sean was very sociable by nature, and at such an event, surrounded by so many opportunities, she saw him doing his best to rub elbows with the right people, which usually left her to her own devices. She was rather unsurprised when he soon began mingling with several celebrities that he was acquainted with, then dragging her further through the masses, making more and more introductions. However, it was Sean who had the connections, and therefore he was the interested party. Feeling like just an arm ornament after a while, Christine began to grow bored and restless, tired of presenting the same smile on her face.

She longed to find some relief from the crowd, and so she slipped her arm out from his and moved away. Glancing back briefly, she saw that he hadn't even realized she had left his side. And thinking that some fresh air would be helpful, she searched the doors lining either side of the expansive room. Would she even be permitted to pass through any of them? Spying one at which no guard was currently stationed, she gathered the folds of her ball gown and walked quickly toward it. She looked over her shoulder to see if anyone was going to stop her, then opened the door quickly, slipping through it.

The door opened into a long corridor. With the music and buzzing of the crowd now shut out, the silence in the hallway felt deafening, but the air was certainly more breathable. Christine attempted to inhale deeply, but then cursed the tight bodice of her gown, which constricted her rib cage. Standing still for a moment to take several short breaths instead, she began to wander down the hallway, away from the ballroom. Her heeled footsteps echoed amid the marble flooring, muffled only when she came across large ornamental rugs.

She became mesmerized looking at the walls, noting the various precious artworks displayed. Doing a double take in awe at some of the pieces, she concluded that they were all, of course, original, and many had been done by some of the most famous artists in history. Impressed by the collection and anxious to view more, she continued down the corridor, around a corner, taking another left, then a right. She stopped, coming to an intersection of hallways, where two life-size portraits hung in the center.

Looking up at the first, she stepped back to view it more clearly. It was Derek. No. She narrowed her eyes. The man portrayed had the same build, tousled black hair, and sapphire blue eyes. But the jaw was squarer, and his features were not as refined. She could not imagine this man smiling or giving an expression of gentleness. He was standing straight and tall, posing proudly and commandingly. He was clearly someone who demanded authority. This was Derek's father, she concluded. Then the other portrait must be of... Turning her attention to the woman pictured next, she saw his mother. She was indeed a beautiful woman, with lighter brown hair and dark eyes. Her face held a kindness that made Christine instantly like her, and looking upon her smile, Christine couldn't help but notice the dimple in her left cheek. She stared at the portraits for a moment longer, seeing visions of Derek in both. Turning from them reluctantly to make her way back down the corridor, she realized she had lost track of time and needed to return to the ballroom.

As she turned to glance down both hallways, it became clear to her that she was unsure of the way back. Choosing the larger hallway that led away from the portraits, she began to walk quickly, but something caught her eye as she passed by an open doorway. Backing up a step and pausing to peer into the room, her eyes flew open wide as she recognized something very familiar.

The room was a cozy sitting area with velvet sofas and chairs, beautiful glass lamps, luxurious carpets, and a multitude of bookshelves. Clearly meant to be a lounge or reading area, it had a large fireplace made of dark marble as its centerpiece, setting the tone of the room, and above the fireplace hung…her painting, *Love*.

She approached it slowly, transfixed by its presence, appreciating again the work she had poured into it and how beautiful it looked in its new home. It only took her a second to piece together how it had gotten here as she recalled the jacketed stranger admiring the work during the exhibit. At the time, she had felt confident it was Derek. But the mere fact that he purchased the piece left her feeling unsettled. Why would he want it? She had to admit that although she felt an immense amount of pride at the work, it also caused her an immense amount of pain. This was why she had agreed to sell it in the first place. Surely, Derek had realized what it represented?

She heard footsteps approaching, and she froze, her heart skipping a beat. Would she be in trouble for being here? How would she even begin to explain herself? She breathed a sigh of relief when the steps passed, but a second later she heard them pause. She had been seen, and he or she had now entered the room. Still facing the fireplace, she closed her eyes briefly, then, holding her breath, she turned to face what she assumed was most likely a guard.

"Christine." Derek stared in disbelief at her; it felt surreal to see her standing casually in one of the lounges. She stared back at him with a look of shock that mirrored his own.

Her heart leaped to her throat at seeing who had entered. Never expecting to see him in this way, so privately, it occurred to her again that he was now a king. She took in his formal attire, noting the royal blue sash under his tuxedo jacket. He walked farther into the room toward her, and she suddenly wondered what she should do. Bow? Curtsy? What did she even call him now? As if reading her mind, he gave her a slight smile and held up a hand preventing her from those actions.

"You don't need to bow," he said quietly.

"I got lost," she explained in response, knowing that he must be wondering how she had arrived here. "I'm sorry," she added quickly, "I didn't mean to intrude."

"No," he replied, "it's fine. I'm just surprised to find you here."

He couldn't help but continue to gaze at her, as though she were just a vision or figment of his imagination. She was striking in her deep red satin ball gown. Her hair was swept up in an elegant twist, leaving her neck, collarbone, and shoulders completely exposed. A single dainty diamond pendant hung around her neck, matching the diamond studs in her ears. She looked at him with such an intensity, her red lips slightly parted, and he determined that she had never before looked more beautiful. The sight of her nearly tearing him in two as his eyes moved to the other diamond she wore, the one on her left hand.

"You bought my painting," she said now, not taking her eyes off him. He looked up at the painting and nodded, allowing himself once again to feel all the emotions it represented when he was with her. "Why?" she asked, and he could tell she was genuinely curious.

"It brings me a sense of peace," he stated. Surprised by his response, Christine looked at him in confusion. "I see the pain, the torment," he explained as he turned his eyes from the painting back to her, "but I also see you. It allows me to remember what it's like to feel…you."

Her eyes widened at his intimate explanation. How could she have doubted that he loved her?

"You didn't have an affair, did you?" Her voice caught in her throat, and she practically whispered the words. Sadness crossed his face, and in response he placed his hand in his pocket and pulled from it a ring. She stared, awed by the brilliant diamond.

"You have to ask, don't you," he stated, disappointment flooding his features. "I wanted to propose to you that night. I wanted you to come to Calina with me, not as a guest lost in the halls but as my queen." He paused, again eyeing the ring on her hand. "But I guess that doesn't matter now." He placed his ring back in his pocket and gestured back toward the painting. "I wasn't lying to you when I told you that you were my purpose. At least I have a remembrance of a time when I felt complete." As he looked back at her, he reached out and touched her cheek. "Complete, and the happiest I had ever been."

She began to feel dizzy, and she realized she had been unconsciously holding her breath, attempting to keep from becoming emotional. As she exhaled slowly, though, a deep-seated pain ran through her. What had she done?

"I'm sorry, Derek," she said softly. "I'm so sorry." She cast her eyes down as tears dropped from her lashes. "If I could go back and make different choices…" she trailed off, knowing that nothing she said now would help. Nothing would change what happened.

"I wish things had been different," he replied. His tone was gentle, but she could hear the regret. "And you've moved on, it seems." She met his eyes, then looked down at her own ring. "Are you happy?" he asked. "It's important to me that you're happy." Christine studied his expression, which appeared sincere.

When Derek left her flat that day, she knew the door had forever been closed to his heart, he would never forgive her for walking out on him. She had begun her relationship with Sean soon after meeting him during the exhibit, and she could admit that things had progressed quickly with him. Desperate to put Derek behind her, she had tried to think of Sean as her second chance at some kind of happiness or love. She knew that what she had with Sean would never rival the feelings or passion she felt for Derek, but what good would it do if that was never going to be a reality for her? So, she had decided to settle and take a chance.

"I'm trying to be" was all she could think to say.

Her lack of a direct answer and her expression, which was laced with sadness, told Derek what he needed to know. He had invited Sean to the coronation to see for himself whether Christine had truly found happiness. Inevitably she had not, and he knew this would plague him until the day he died. He knew in his heart that she belonged with him, but he just couldn't see past her lack of faith or trust in him. He couldn't ask for her back, and they both now needed to find a way to move froward with their lives.

"You need to get back to the ballroom, and I have an appearance to make," he told her. "I'll escort you to the main hallway, and you should be able to find your way back from there."

She nodded, glancing at him briefly but unable to meet his eyes any longer. All she could think of was how much she wanted to reach for him, embrace him, and beg for his forgiveness, her harbored anguish needing to be somehow extinguished. And her torment helped her to admit how wrong marrying Sean would be. Even if she was destined for a broken heart, it would not be fair to him. She could not make him happy, and he deserved that as much as anyone did.

Derek turned from her to walk toward the door, but suddenly he stopped. Having begun following him, Christine almost collided with him as he turned around quickly. He reached for her, wrapping his hand behind her head, and pulled her to him; his lips crashing against hers. His sudden kiss was shocking and intense. Her breath caught in her throat, and her knees almost gave. Nothing had ever before felt so right, and her heart wept knowing that this was not a reunion but a final kiss goodbye.

He released her, backing away but staring into her eyes. She saw something there she had never before seen, a glassy mist, and she couldn't stop the screaming voice inside her mind: *I love you.* Never before had she so desperately wanted to hear something: needing to hear him return the statement of love. But he remained silent, and so did she. Turning away from her again, he left the room, this time allowing her to follow him out and down the hallway. She kept her pace slightly behind him as he guided her around the corner toward the ballroom.

"I need to go in this direction," he told her, gesturing as they reached the main corridor. "But just follow this hall straight down and to your left. That will take you back."

There were no words left to say as she nodded, gazing at him. Respectfully, she closed her eyes lightly and bowed her head slightly to him.

"Your Highness," she addressed him softly. He gave her one last pensive look, then turned and walked away. She watched him until he had rounded the corner and was out of sight.

"Christine?" She turned sharply at Sean's voice behind her. "I've been looking for you," he said, a cautious expression on his face. "Was that the king I just saw you with?" Christine dropped her eyes and nodded. She knew it would be futile to attempt to deceive Sean. He was well aware of her past relationship with Derek. "I thought it was over between you," Sean said quietly, his thick French accent making every "th" sound like a "z."

"It is," she replied quickly, but he noticed the hint of sadness in her voice. He took in an uneasy breath.

"You know I love you, Christine," he said, sounding defeated. "You said you loved me too..." he trailed off, searching her face for some kind of affirmative response. She finally brought her eyes up to meet his, her gaze betraying her feelings of remorse.

"Sean, I..." she began, but he cut her off.

"Not here," he said. "This is not the time," he sighed, "let's just get through this reception." She nodded, agreeing that this was not the most opportune time to have this discussion, although her gut clenched tight knowing what she had to do. He reached for her hand, grasping it perhaps a bit too tightly and proceeded to lead her back into the ballroom. As she passed him through the entrance, he leaned into her ear, speaking lowly. "Your lipstick is smeared, my dear."

———◦———

A little after 2:00 a.m., Christine arrived back at her flat. Anxious to remove her restrictive gown and heels, she immediately headed toward her closet in the darkness, practically colliding with the stack of packed up boxes in the middle of the room. As she stumbled, reaching down to grab her shoes to remove them, she grimaced, realizing that now she needed to unpack.

She had planned to move in with Sean following their engagement, but now there was no need for that. She threw her shoes in the closet and grabbed the zipper on the back of her dress, inhaling deeply as she let the gown fall to the floor. Pulling a comfortable tank top on over her head, she fell back against her bed. She was emotionally drained and couldn't stop the playback of the evening in her mind.

After she and Sean had rejoined the reception, she had stayed by his side until the event had ended. Remembering in detail the moment when Derek had appeared on the upper balcony, she couldn't help but smile. He had waved, grinning proudly as he had been presented to the crowd as the king of Calina. She had not been able to glimpse much of him after that as the masses monopolized him entirely, each person eagerly waiting their turn to greet the new monarch. But in spite of her own heartbreak, she felt a happiness for him knowing that he was fulfilling his destiny. She knew he would go on to do great things for his country and for his people.

Following the reception she had boarded Sean's private jet to begin their journey back to Paris. It was during the three-hour trip back that she had broken their engagement. He had argued with her, tried to reason with her, and she had shed more tears. Sean had expressed his love, saying all the things she had wanted to hear, only not from him. And she could no longer deny that.

She yawned, exhausted, as she removed the pins from her hair and tossed them on the nightstand. She knew she just needed to rest, and in the morning, she would have to deal with the aftermath of her decisions. Then she would focus on her work. She pulled a pillow up next to her, and her final thought was of Derek's last kiss, how it felt so perfect to be with him and so wrong to say goodbye.

———————◆———————

One Month Later

In the days following his coronation, Derek had begun to put his new plans into action. Working endless hours, the days turned into weeks. Through more public appearances, announcements, and new policies, he promised much-needed change, and feedback from the people was turning favorable as they now trusted he would bring them necessary relief. The only point of friction had been the dismissal of several officials in parliament. He had chosen to not publicly announce their corruption, wishing to keep the scandal as low-key as possible, but even so, they had not gone quietly and rumors persisted that they swore revenge. Unconcerned, Derek had forged ahead. Making enemies was not new to him.

As he worked now, intensely concentrating on new proposals surrounding tax reforms, his study door suddenly burst open, with three men striding in carrying looks on their faces of the utmost urgency. He stood as they approached him and turned his attention first to the man to his right, Antonio Esposito, the head of the King's Guard. Calina was too small a country to house its own military, and the guard held authority over potentially dangerous conflicts and threats.

"Signore," Esposito began, bowing his head before continuing. "Intelligence has informed us that there is a small but silent uprising being led by the families of the politicians you've dismissed. Plots have been uncovered surrounding potential assassination attempts."

Derek raised his eyebrows at the news.

"One month in and I've already got people wanting me dead," he said dryly. "That's got to be some kind of record."

The three men did not seem to share his amusement.

"For your safety, Your Highness, we feel it would be best if you left the country for a short time," said the director of intelligence, and Derek regarded him with a bewildered expression.

"Are you telling me I should run and hide, Romano?" he asked sternly.

"Signore," Esposito interjected, "I feel very confident that the guard will be able to apprehend those behind the plot and deal with them swiftly and quietly. However, I agree with Romano—for the short while it will take us to get the situation under control, it would be in your and the people's best interest if you were unreachable." Derek studied him closely. "The threats are viable."

"What do you think, Luca?" Derek asked, turning to the third man.

"I agree with them, Your Majesty," the prime minister replied firmly. "The people now have a good leader, one who has been desperately needed for decades. Our main priority is to protect you." He paused, thinking. "It would only be natural for you to travel aboard. However, at least at first, you must maintain a low profile. It will not take long to stabilize affairs here, but in the meantime, you will be safe." He met Derek's eye. "I do not want to see history repeat itself."

After a moment Derek reluctantly nodded his agreement.

"Where can you go, signore?" Esposito questioned. Thinking of his car in storage back in the States, Derek immediately knew where he could go.

"I know of a place," he said.

Chapter 19

The sun was setting into a mass of colors across the horizon. Fawna rocked slowly in the chair on the porch, lost in thought. The chair creaked to a rhythm on the wooden floor. It was hot, but a cool breeze was blowing in with the setting sun. It had been a peaceful day on the ranch, and she was happy to have spent a good deal of time riding Dante, the black stallion.

Unfortunately, riding the stallion had just brought back memories of him and the last time they had ridden together. His face flashed in front of her blue-gray eyes as she looked toward the sunset. The tears stung and threatened to start once again. She fought them back, gazing out, looking to draw strength from some unknown place, but to no avail. She scanned the ranch, taking in all the things she loved most. As her eyes fell upon the paddock, the horses grazing, she imagined him standing there, just as he had when she had first shown him how to ride. He had seemed so happy that day, and she had thought she could make him happy like that forever. She inhaled deeply, thinking back to that evening after their first ride together, the way he seemed to need her, the passionate first kiss and what it led to throughout the night.

Of course, he did not love her. She accepted this now. He loved Christine. Christine. Her eyes narrowed into slits. She hated that name. But Christine was in Europe now. As France's hot new artist, she was now famous in her own right and attached to the hip of the French supermodel Sean Laurent. She may have been a fool, but so was the man she pined for, and the thought gave her a bit of satisfaction, if only for a second.

She sighed, and she couldn't help but see his face again. Those eyes, that smile; one hot tear spilled over onto her cheek. Anger rising within her, she clenched her eyes tight. *Stop shedding tears over him!* she commanded herself. *He's gone.* She knew she would never see him again. He was also in Europe, having gone there to chase after his precious Christine.

He used me, she thought now. *He used me to get over her.* But she wasn't as disappointed in him as she was in herself. She knew he was using her; he had practically told her so, before the affair had even started. She had agreed to the "uncomplicated," "no strings attached," "don't expect more from me" relationship, thinking that she could deal with it, only to realize she had been ignorant, that she was in love with him, almost from the start. She would have agreed to anything just to be with him. But he couldn't get over Christine; he never would. Of course he would eventually leave to go after her.

She didn't know whether he had ever found her, but regardless, he had also needed to stay in Europe to travel to his native country of Calina. Recent news from Calina revealed that a new monarch had been named. She swallowed hard, reminding herself again that he wasn't coming back.

She broke from her reverie, and off in the distance she heard a low roar. Thunder? No, it was getting gradually louder, and there wasn't a cloud in the sky. The roaring was turning into a low, rumbling hum. Then she saw the dust kick up on the dirt road approaching her ranch. She stood from her chair and narrowed her eyes to peer into the distance. She could just make out the source of the dust; a low red sports car. It maneuvered around the bend to her road, slowing as it turned onto the long drive.

There was no mistaking the red LaFerrari, and her heart caught in her throat as the multimillion-dollar car rolled up to the side of the house. She stood frozen, wondering if she might be dreaming or even hallucinating. Had she obsessed over him so much that her mind was now playing tricks on her?

Deciding this must be real, she stepped toward the car, not daring to believe it could possibly be him. As she reached the end of the wraparound porch next to the driveway, the car door opened. He stepped out casually, dressed in khaki slacks, a white linen shirt with the sleeves rolled up, and his signature black Versace sunglasses; he took her breath away. His black hair was tousled, as usual, and as he turned to face her on the porch, he radiated confidence and grace, but he regarded her with his famed unreadable expression.

He waited for her reaction, placing his hands in his pockets. Her eyes took in the sight of him—his six-two stature, the chiseled features, strong jaw, and broad shoulders. His skin was olive-tanned, and he had what she knew behind those sunglasses to be electric sapphire-blue eyes, the most mesmerizing she had ever known.

She struggled to believe he was standing there, afraid if she blinked or said anything, the spell would be broken and he would vanish. After what seemed like forever, he finally broke the silence.

"Fawn," he said in acknowledgment. He was the only one she knew who called her "Fawn." She walked down the porch steps toward him.

"Derek," she replied, "I can't believe you've come back." She spoke slowly, with an icy tone she couldn't keep at bay. "I didn't expect to ever see you again," she added, almost choking on the words. Her mind began reeling, trying to understand why he was here. She could only come up with one answer—he was running. Running from his responsibility in Calina? Or running from not being able to deal with Christine being with another man? Running away was not part of Derek's character, so his appearance here was a complete mystery. Refusing to be a fool twice, she knew he was not here to stay.

As she appraised him, his expression remained unchanged. He removed his sunglasses and met her gaze. As he looked into her eyes, her icy exterior melted instantly, and at once he knew he had control.

"I will need to return to Europe," he said. "However, I still have business to attend to in the States."

Fawna mustered her courage and took a deep breath, deciding to call him out. "You've come back to me because she's with someone else now, is that it?"

He stared at her, neither acknowledging nor denying the claim. Ignoring her question, he stepped closer to her. She could breathe in his scent, and it made her light-headed. It suddenly became very quiet. The breeze stopped, and she could no longer hear the rustling or buzzing, the typical ranch sounds. She could only see him, hear him, and smell him. *He's too close*, she thought. Snapping out of the spell, she placed a hand on his chest to prevent him coming any closer. The muscles under his linen shirt tensed when she touched him, sending shivers down her spine. Containing her composure, she steeled her blue-gray eyes at him.

"I'm not sure if I want to laugh at you, strangle you, or just let you have me," she hissed at him. His eyes grew dark, but he couldn't help feeling slightly amused at her attitude.

"Well?" He raised an eyebrow. "Which is it going to be?"

"You can't have her, so you think that you can just waltz back here?" she said accusatorily.

Again he refused to respond. Disregarding her attempts to maintain her personal space, he stepped closer to her still. A strand of soft blond curl escaped across her face. He reached up and brushed it away, letting the backside of his hand trail down her cheek until it came to rest on her bare shoulder. Her skin was warm to the touch. He could tell she had been riding; she was wearing her traditional ranch-hand clothes, ripped jeans and a simple tank top. Her honey blond hair was down and fell in wavy curls around her shoulders. Her skin was sun-kissed bronze and glistened in the last rays of the downing Texas sun.

Not having considered too much what he would do when he arrived at the ranch, he had become consumed by the thought of taking comfort in Fawna again. He had chosen the ranch primarily because it was the perfect place to lie low as he had been instructed, but as he had continued to ponder the situation during his travels back to the States, he had arrived at the conclusion that there could be other benefits to coming here as well.

He needed relief—from his pain, the newfound stress and dangers in Calina, and the loss of Christine. He had to forget Christine, and he knew Fawna would not be able to resist him. Did he love her? No. He knew he didn't. She knew he didn't. He could rationalize being with her knowing that he'd been honest with her from the start, about everything. She knew the risks. He let his hand slide down her bare arm, stopping at her waist. Bringing his other arm up around her, he pulled her to him, their bodies touching, his face only an inch from hers.

She met his eyes.

"Don't do this to me," she whispered, her voice strained. Narrowing his eyes at her, he released her. She was right, he thought to himself. She had confessed her love for him, and he knew she would be incapable of putting aside her feelings. It wouldn't be fair to take her back down that road. Casting aside his yearning for physical comfort, he refocused on his primary reason for returning. Taking a step back from her, he spread his hands.

"I'm sorry, Fawn," he said. "I don't want to hurt you."

She nodded solemnly, loving and hating him at the same time. "That's very considerate of you, Your Highness." The formal reference came out almost sarcastically, and although she hadn't really meant it to be, the extent of her resentment was clear.

"That's really why I'm here," he told her, and she raised her eyebrows, expecting him to continue. "It was imperative that I left Calina for a short time." He paused. "I needed to go somewhere I could trust I wouldn't be found."

"Where's your entourage?" she asked dryly.

He smirked. "I left them at the airport," he replied. "They will find refuge elsewhere. I've been told to lie low, and massive amounts of security would just draw attention, don't you think?"

"I suppose so." She studied him carefully, fear suddenly crossing her face. "Are you in danger?" she asked.

He gave her a smile. "No," he said simply. "I would not come here if I thought there was any risk to you."

She nodded again, then sighed heavily, crossing her arms, coming to the defeated decision to let him stay.

"Well," she said, "why don't you come in? Do you want some coffee or something?" She turned to head back into the house, and he followed close behind as his smile broadened.

"No," he replied, "but I wouldn't say no to your fajitas later if you asked." She glanced back at him and gave him a half-amused smile.

———◦———

Three days later Fawna entered the kitchen to make coffee, then, having realized it was already made, she peered into the dining room to see Derek there. He appeared to have been up for some time and was concentrating heavily on several documents. Knowing that it was just going to be for a short while, she had agreed to let him stay at the ranch. While he was there, she had resolved to keep him at arm's length, and he had also not approached her again. She knew it was better this way, even if he did still tug at her heart.

He continued to work tirelessly even at the ranch, she noticed, checking in with his security constantly, receiving updates on the situation in Calina, obtaining status reports from advisers and making urgent decisions. She secretly wished he could take a break, but she understood the weight of responsibility within his role, and she did not envy the monarch.

Having grabbed her coffee from the kitchen, she joined him in the dining room, taking the seat opposite him, across the table. Burning to ask him something that had been weighing on her mind since he had shown up (really since he had left her), she stared at him silently, willing him to look up at her. Sensing her gaze, he put down his pen and document and met her eyes. He raised his eyebrows expectantly and waited for her to speak. She hesitated for a second but knew this was her chance if she wanted to know.

"Derek, what happened with Christine?" she asked.

He didn't react immediately, then knitted his brows as a sadness crept into his features. "I decided that I couldn't be with her," he replied.

His answer shocked Fawna. What? She questioned. Wasn't he trying to get her back? "Why?" she replied, astonished. "Don't you love her?"

He picked up the pen again and began making notes on the document. "Very much so." He answered simply.

Unwilling to let him dismiss the topic so easily, especially when his response made no sense, she persisted her questions.

"I don't understand," she stated. "If you're in love with her, why can't you be together? What did she do to you?"

He sighed and met her eyes again. "She chose," he began, "to believe that I had an affair with someone despicable. Something I could have never done." He took a breath. "She didn't trust me, Fawn. She walked away from me because she didn't trust me."

Fawna thought back to the news at the time.

"I thought she left you for Timothy," she stated.

Derek shook his head. "No," he replied. "I thought she had too, at first."

"So, she left you because she thought you had an affair…" Fawna said slowly, trying to make sense of the timeline. "Why did she think that in the first place?"

Derek narrowed his eyes slightly. He hadn't put too much thought into why Christine had thought he had had an affair; he had been more focused on the fact that she had chosen to believe it. But she had said something—that she had proof. He had dismissed the comment at the time, knowing that there was no such evidence. His silence intrigued Fawna; she could see he was pondering the question.

"Didn't you ask her why she thought that?"

"It's not important to me why she thought that." Derek replied. "What matters is the fact that she did think that and she assumed lies about me were true without even talking to me."

Fawna frowned. "So, who does she think you had an affair with?"

"Courtney Metcalf," he replied, a scowl crossing his face. "She's a deranged lunatic obsessed with believing that I'm in love with her."

"Does she know Christine? How would Christine even know about her?" Fawna couldn't stop the questions, which kept coming to her mind. Something didn't seem right, and it didn't seem to her that Derek had considered certain points of the matter.

"She doesn't...they've never met," he said slowly. He blinked. Why *did* Christine think that he had slept with Courtney? Why her of all people.

"Derek," Fawna said, reaching across the table and touching his hand. "You blame Christine for not trusting you, judging your character. But what do you know about her character? Is Christine the type of person who would believe something without hard evidence? Would she have walked away from you without due cause?"

Derek turned angry. "If you're insinuating that I actually—"

Fawna shook her head quickly. "No." She interjected. "I'm not saying there's real proof of any infidelity." She paused. "But it sounds like this Courtney is pretty unstable? Did she feel like she needed revenge? Maybe she fed Christine the lies?"

"But, even if she did, Christine wouldn't have believed it, like you said, without proof. And there wouldn't be any." Derek objected with a finality to his voice that indicated he felt the matter was closed.

"Then she must have had something to show Christine to prove it," Fawna continued thoughtfully. "What could it have been?"

She sat in silence for a moment, thinking. There had to be something he didn't yet know. Derek turned back to his paperwork, the dialogue causing deep concern lines to appear on his chiseled face.

"When was the last time you actually saw Courtney?" she asked him suddenly. "Were you seen with her recently?"

"Yeah," he said, not looking up from his task, "not long before I came here to the ranch. She came to my building, and I told her to fuck off."

"But that was after Christine had left you. What about before?" she asked insistently.

He put his pen back down hard on the table. "Damn it, Fawn, I can't deal with this right now," he said irritably. Why wouldn't she let this go? Why did it matter to her? He had more pressing concerns, and talking about Courtney put him in a very foul mood. "Why are you being so stubborn about this?"

"Because there's something not right about all this, Derek," she exclaimed. "Don't you see that? And you're misplacing blame on Christine when you don't have all the pieces of what really happened." She sighed. "I know you need her; she can make you happy. I just want you to have that. You deserve it, and you owe it to yourself to know the truth."

His features softened at her, appreciating her genuine care for him. Giving her line of questioning his full attention, he began to process alternatives. The previous time he saw Courtney was at the business conference in New York, where she threatened him, asking for money. His expression turned to stone. Money she had never cashed, he realized. Was money her real objective during that interaction? Or were there ulterior motives. There was a lot of press at that conference, and any paparazzo could have taken a picture of them together. He recalled her manner that night, the way she had spoken to him and her insistence that he follow her to the Bronx. Had she set him up then provided Christine with misleading photos? He had been so caught up in her extortion and threats, he hadn't considered that maybe that wasn't her real goal.

Realization hitting him hard, he ran a hand through his hair, feeling suddenly sick. Photos. He thought of the pictures he had seen of Christine with Timothy and how easy it had been for him to believe there was more to it. Pictures don't lie. Or do they?

"You look pale," Fawna said, noticing the dramatic change in his expression. *He's figured something out*, she thought to herself.

"You're right," he said slowly. "I had been seen with Courtney. She could have set me up." An immense amount of guilt began to engulf him. Christine could have been a victim. He stood up suddenly, adrenaline coursing through him. He needed to find out what Courtney told Christine.

"Thank you for helping me see this, Fawn," he told her sincerely. "Excuse me, I have a call to make." She smiled slightly, watching him exit the room, knowing that he was now going to do what he needed to do.

———◦———

Hours later, and unbeknownst to his security, Derek had boarded a private jet to New York. Alerting Gregory of his presence in the States and explaining everything to him, he used his connections to arrange travel and track down Courtney. Although now a powerful CEO in his own right, Gregory was more than happy to oblige and support his former mentor, allowing Derek complete access to Land Corporation's resources.

When he arrived in New York, a car was waiting for him, one that was at his disposal so he could continue to move anonymously and freely. He wasn't sure where he would be going or staying, his only thought was of getting answers from Courtney. Once he knew the truth, it would determine his next course of action. Gregory was standing by and would offer him refuge if need be.

It was evening by the time he pulled up in front of her apartment, having learned that she had moved back to the Upper West Side. His face was set in a determined glare as he prepared to face the person who had single-handedly destroyed the most valuable thing in his life. Now knowing that she no longer played for the symphony and having found no trace of other employment, he felt confident she would be in. Striding quickly to her building, he entered and climbed the three flights up to her door. He knocked sharply. There was no answer; he made a fist and pounded on the door, his aggression rising. A moment later, the door swung open and she stood facing him.

Her eyes tried to focus on him, as if she weren't actually seeing him. She appeared dazed, and she reeked of whiskey.

"You came back," she whispered. "I always knew you would." He gave her a menacing stare.

"I know what you did." He seethed at her. Then, because she didn't respond right away, he grabbed her shoulders, shoving her back into the apartment, forcing his way inside. Releasing her, he closed the door behind him. "I know you had me set up and then gave false information to Christine. I want to know what you told her and what evidence you gave her." Still she didn't answer, just gazed at him. She swayed slightly. "You didn't want money from me, did you?" He interrogated her. "You just wanted to get close enough so someone could take pictures of us together." She appeared to not know what to say, but the way her eyes wandered, the way they opened wide in fear at his accusations, he knew it was true.

Having taken time during his flight to New York to think further about these events, Derek had begun to wonder just who her accomplice had been. She had to have bribed someone to take the photos. He enlisted the support of trusted Land Corporation team members to do some digging based on the timeline and location, and it didn't take long for them to find what he was looking for

"You really crossed every *t* to make sure your scheme wasn't uncovered, didn't you?" he said coldly now, removing a piece of paper from his jacket. He slammed the cut-out article on the nearby table so she could see the headline: "Local Photographer Found Dead: Accident or Suicide?" "Once I knew what game you were playing," he said, "it wasn't too difficult to find this rather uninteresting bit of news to the world. But this photographer died the day after the conference…just outside the Bronx. What did you do? Push him off that bridge?"

If there was no fear in her expression before, he definitely saw it now. He continued to glare at her, waiting for a response, but she only opened her mouth as if to speak. Her lack of confession enraged him further.

"You fucked with my life," he told her, his tone dangerously quiet. "Now I'm going to fuck with yours. I will get my hands on those photos. I happen to know someone who has them as well." He walked closer to her, invading her personal space, looking her dead in the eyes. "I will expose you for extortion and murder. You will go to jail." Giving her one last hateful glance, he turned away from her and left, slamming the apartment door behind him.

Left alone, Courtney began to shake violently, panic flooding through her, making her feel dizzy and nauseated. Of course, James had not been home, and now it was too late. She sat on the edge of the sofa in the seating area and placed her spinning head in her hands. There was no way out of this, she knew—there never had been. She thought back to that day on the bridge, before she had ever met Paul, and she wished she had just jumped then.

She had been foolish to try and find comfort in James and his empty promises; he couldn't take down Derek. And now it was all over for her. Her thoughts swimming through the sea of whiskey, she consented to the only path she had left. Rising and making her way to the kitchen, she removed a pen and piece of paper from the drawer and began to write.

Once she had finished writing, she paused to reread her note. Yes, she thought, it was perfect. She took another swig from the bottle of whiskey, having already gone halfway through it. Her mind was now completely made up. This was the only way. Her only way out of the dark depths of her misery, and the only way to make him experience the pain in the way she had.

Taking the note, she continued into her bedroom, where she removed an envelope from her purse, lying on the desk. In the envelope was a check written to her for $1 million, as well as a picture of her and Derek, the one she had shown Paul. The picture had been taken during the charity event. His arm was around her, and they were both smiling for the camera. It had been the happiest day of her life, and he had made love to her that night. She stared at the picture, his sapphire eyes sparkling. On the outside of the envelope she wrote the name Derek Landino.

She thought of how her scheme to ruin his life would die now with her, and it brought a slight smile to her face. This was her only solace, and her only sense of peace, however miniscule it was. She staggered through her small room, from the desk over to the mirror that hung above her bedroom dresser. As she gulped more whiskey, she took a last glance at her reflection. Her long, dark hair was limp; her brown eyes were dull and sunken, making them look abnormally large. Although James had been making her eat some, she was still extremely malnourished and pale.

Her eyes were blurry, and her head was still spinning as she sat down on the bed. She needed to finish this now. She knew that with his power and resources, it would not take long for him to return with authorities and charge her for what she had done. The note she'd left, along with the check, was the only way left to ruin him. Without him, there was no point to this world anyway, and a fleeting smile crossed her face as she thought that maybe one day she'd see him again in hell.

She heaved a sob, and with despair consuming her, she reached for the pill bottle sitting on the nightstand—the pills she used to help her through sleepless nights. She twisted the cap off and proceeded to swallow the pills three to four at a time, washing each handful down with the other half of the bottle of whiskey, until both were gone. She was taking no chances, and her decision to end her life was resolute. She had chickened out once before, but this was different. There was no going back. Dizzy and nearing unconsciousness, she collapsed onto the floor. Her eyes felt heavy and dark, she could no longer see, and she was simply slipping away into nothingness. She was cold. The last image in her mind was of his face.

———•———

Later that night James returned home. Walking up to the apartment door, he took his key out, then realized the door was already unlocked. He sighed and shook his head slightly, knowing he would need to remind Courtney, yet again, to keep the door locked. As he walked into the apartment and set his keys on the table, he couldn't help but sense an eerie silence.

"I'm back, Courtney," he called. There was no response.

Making his way slowly toward her bedroom, he rounded the door frame and peered into her room. Noticing that she was splayed out facedown on the floor next to a bottle of whiskey, he immediately concluded she had drunk until passing out, which was not uncommon for her. Then he saw the overturned, empty pill bottle on the nightstand.

"Courtney!" he screamed, now rushing over to her and lifting her lifeless, bony form from the ground. Turning her over, her head lolled, and he couldn't ignore the coldness of her body. As he unsuccessfully checked for a pulse on her neck, he concluded she was gone.

As he continued to hold her, he pulled out his cell and dialed 911. His voice was shaking as he gave the operator his address, then he clicked off, still staring at her dead face. Tears flooded his eyes, and he sobbed freely as he set her gently back on the ground, brushing her hair away from her face.

"How could you do this, Courtney?" he cried at her. "I told you I would take care of everything. Why now?" *Why now?* he repeated to himself.

Standing, he tore his gaze away from her and scanned the rest of the room, his eyes falling on the envelope sitting on the desk. Seeing who it was addressed to, he tore it open; the check fell out along with the photo. His eyes flew open wide at the sight of the check, and he unfolded the note, scanning her last words feverishly.

My darling, I can no longer suffer, living with your harsh words and cruel dismissal of me, even if you have decided that you no longer love me. I need you to know that our last night together in New York, right after the business conference, was both my happiest memory and the most sadness I have ever felt. I thought that you had finally agreed to acknowledge our love, only to discover afterward that I was just a game to you. If you had just asked me to stay quiet about the affair, I would have, because regardless of how you've treated me, I still love you. But attempting to buy my silence drove your knife that much deeper into my heart. I've left behind with this letter your check for $1,000,000. If you'd be so kind, please donate the money to a suicide prevention charitable cause in memory of me.

He stared at her words for what seemed like an eternity. James's shock at Derek's cold-hearted maliciousness subsiding, rage was the only feeling left in him. *He* was the reason Courtney was dead. James set the note back on the desk as if in slow motion, looking back at Courtney on the floor. He asked himself again, *Why now?* A look of hatred crossed his face as he realized Derek must be in the States.

It was well into the night by the time the paramedics, the police, and the coroner began to wrap up in James's apartment. Sitting on the living area sofa, as though all feeling had been drained from his being, he watched as

Courtney's body was rolled out of the door, a white sheet covering her from head to toe.

There were two policemen working at the scene. They approached James now for his statement or any additional information. As they went through the basic questioning surrounding her mental state and other family members or friends who may need to be notified, James noted they did not ask him about the note or the check. Unwilling to accept that they were going to possibly turn a blind eye to Derek's involvement because of who he was, he spoke up.

"I read her note," he said bluntly, "and I'm very much aware of her relationship with Derek Landino. I've witnessed him bullying her psychologically, and the money is proof that he was involved with her. Seems to me like he was bribing her. Are you going to ignore that he is responsible for her death?" His questions were stated without emotion, so matter-of-factly that the two cops exchanged uncomfortable glances.

"Well, this seems like a pretty clear case of suicide," the first cop explained. "She was clearly infatuated with him, and the money does seem suspicious...but Derek Landino is not even in the country."

"He is in the country," James insisted, "and I guarantee you he's in New York. The only reason Courtney would have done this now is if he had contacted her and somehow pushed her over the edge." He paused, deep sadness crossing his face. "She was getting better," he added quietly.

The second cop looked at his partner.

"If that's true, and if Derek Landino is here, we need to make some inquiries," he said, a regretful tone to his voice. "And we can't just dismiss this check without knowing it's true origin." He paused, as if coming to a decision. "Call the detective and see if he wants to open an investigation."

Chapter 20

"What are you going to do now?"

Derek shook his head slowly.

"I don't know," he answered. Sitting across from Gregory in his former office on the twenty-third floor of Land Corporation headquarters, Derek now confided in his colleague. It seemed surreal to see someone else seated behind his old desk, and he couldn't help the sentimental feelings that came over him as he thought of his former life. But Gregory was also excelling in his new role, adapting and forging ahead as Derek had expected him to, and he couldn't have been prouder of the man who was once his personal assistant. "Courtney wouldn't confess to me when I confronted her," he continued. "Although I could see in her face that it was all true, without a confession, I don't know if there will be enough evidence to arrest her. Especially for the murder of that photographer." He took a deep breath. "I guess it would be best to bring in the authorities. I'm sure I could get them to open an investigation. Maybe they could even get a confession out of her."

Gregory nodded his agreement when the intercom buzzed.

"Mr. McKenzie, sir?" It was Jeff, the head of security, and Derek couldn't help but smile.

"Yes, Jeff," Gregory answered.

"There are several very official looking men here bearing flags looking for Mr. Lan—I mean, His Highness." Jeff's voice sounded stressed, and Derek could only imagine the scene his security guards were causing. Slightly amused, he broke into the conversation.

"Tell Costa to come up," he told Jeff, not about to allow the entire entourage to intrude.

"Yes, sir," Jeff replied, sounding relieved, then clicked off.

Gregory raised his eyebrows. "Your secret service, I assume?"

Derek grimaced and nodded. "In a manner of speaking," he replied. "It's more of an annoyance than anything."

"It seems they've caught up with you." Gregory smirked and stood from the desk as the office door opened. Rising as well, Derek turned to address the head of his security.

Vincenzo Costa took his charge to protect the monarch very seriously, and as such, he was not pleased. He radiated intimidation, standing tall and broad and dressed in an all-black suit. A Bluetooth device was clipped to one ear, and he spoke into it as he entered the room.

"I've located the king," he said quietly. Derek just raised an eyebrow at him as he approached.

"Signore." Costa greeted him in a low bow. "Your safety is our top priority. You must understand that your location and movements have caused concern, and your mere presence could raise alarm. It is crucial that you remain in contact with your country."

"I had business to see to," Derek replied simply.

"I understand, Your Highness," Costa responded, "but your travel must go through channels, to alleviate any risk." He took a breath and changed the subject. "You'll be happy to learn, signore, that I've received word the situation in Calina has stabilized. The plot has been uncovered, and those responsible have been arrested." He paused. "They now await trial for treason, and no further uprisings have been noted."

"That is good news," Derek said. "But I cannot return to Calina just yet." He glanced back at Gregory. "As I said, I have business to see to."

Costa recovered a bewildered expression quickly, knowing it was best not to question the monarch.

"As you wish, Your Highness," he said, lowering his head in respect. "I will make the arrangements and alert the relevant parties of your presence here in New York."

"Fine," Derek told him. "I will inform you when I've completed my meeting here."

"Of course, signore." Costa gave one last bow before turning to exit the room.

As the security officer reached the door, it swung open. Jeff entered, escorting a man of about forty-five wearing a light gray suit, a white dress shirt, and tie. He carried a plain manila folder, and a badge was clipped to his belt. Costa stopped midstride, almost colliding with Jeff.

"Jeff, what is going on here?" It was Gregory who spoke, not taking kindly to the revolving door treatment of his office.

"I apologize, Mr. McKenzie," Jeff replied, "but this is Detective Robert Morrence of the NYPD." The detective stepped forward in front of Jeff, while Costa immediately retraced his steps back further into the office, toward Derek.

"Forgive the interruption, Mr. McKenzie. I'm afraid I insisted on being let up. You see, it is Mr. Landino that I need to speak with, and it was pretty clear based on the men in the lobby that His Highness was here as well." He paused, looking at Derek and bowing his head briefly. "Although, I must say, we were surprised to discover you were in our city, sir."

Gregory nodded at Jeff, dismissing him.

"It's all right, Jeff. Please go back downstairs." Jeff nodded and left the office, shutting the door behind him.

"My trip here was unexpected," Derek said, acknowledging the detective. "Why are you looking for me, Detective Morrence?"

"I was hoping you would permit me to ask you a few questions, Your Highness. I am investigating the suicide of Ms. Courtney Metcalf." Derek blinked, and Gregory narrowed his eyes slightly. Morrence turned to Gregory. "Mr. McKenzie, this does not involve you, sir. If Mr. Landino does not object, I'm sure we can settle this conversation at the station."

Derek walked over to the office's sitting area.

"Actually, I do mind," he said with eyebrows raised. "My appearance at the station would only draw attention. We can talk here. Gregory and I were just discussing Ms. Metcalf, so it's rather convenient that you're here. However, your news is quite surprising to me. She committed suicide? When?"

The other men followed Derek's lead toward the chairs; Costa remained standing behind Derek with his hands folded behind his back, silent. Once he was seated, Morrence answered the question.

"Late last night," he replied. "Boyfriend came home and found that she had swallowed a bottle of sleeping pills. She was gone by the time he found her." He watched Derek's expression carefully; he kept his eyes pensive and wore his usual poker face. He knitted his brow.

"I'm sorry to hear of this," he replied. "But it seems like a very simple case of suicide. I will say that from what I've personally experienced with her, she was rather mentally unstable." He folded his hands. "What are you investigating exactly?"

Detective Morrence leaned forward and removed a flat plastic bag from the folder with a single sheet of paper inside.

"It's been implied," he said, his eyes on Derek, "that you are the reason she committed suicide." He said the words slowly, anticipating a reaction. Derek only frowned slightly, but he sensed a stir from Costa.

"Who implied that?" he asked, his tone even. Morrence passed him the paper.

"She did," the detective responded simply. "The last words of someone willing to commit suicide are not usually to be taken lightly. Had you seen her recently?"

Ignoring the question for now, Derek took the paper and began to read the note, disbelief passing through him at her audacity.

"These are lies," he said calmly, handing the note back to the detective.

"Like I said," Morrence responded, "these were her last thoughts before she killed herself. It seems unlikely that she would lie. Are you saying you didn't pay her one million dollars to keep silent about your affair with her?"

"Unless that someone was Courtney Metcalf," Derek said, his eyes darkening. "No, I did not bribe any silence from her, and no, I did not have an affair with her." Removing from the envelope another plastic bag, Morrence passed the additional evidence to Derek.

"Is this your handwriting, sir?"

Derek's eyes widened in shock upon seeing his check, the one he had given to Courtney to fund her nonprofit, the one that had never been cashed. But the payee line no longer said New York Symphony. She had altered it to her name, and she had somehow forged his penmanship. He looked up from the check and caught Gregory's eye, the look saying all it needed to for Gregory to understand.

"I gave Courtney this check," Derek explained slowly, "but I made it payable to the New York Symphony to fund a nonprofit project of hers. She has clearly forged this."

Morrence reached over and took the check back, examining it with feigned scrutiny. "Interesting," he murmured. "If so, that's quite the job." He paused, then looked back at Derek. "That's rather a large sum of money. Why would you so willingly invest with her? A friendly gesture, perhaps?"

Derek clenched his jaw, unappreciative of the suggestive way the detective had used the word "friendly." He remained silent, eyeing the detective, who seemed to be waiting patiently for his response. He did not trust Morrence, and this was not how he had foreseen his dealings with Courtney

Metcalf concluding. But with her dead, there was no longer any opportunity for a confession. His only option was to share his side.

"Over a year ago now," he began, "I made the vast mistake of making the acquaintance of Ms. Metcalf, escorting her to an event, and, yes, sleeping with her. Since that incident, she had become quite obsessed with the idea that I was in love with her. Because I do not share her feelings, she sought to seek revenge against me. During this conference that she references in her note, she cornered me and threatened to go public, saying that I took advantage of her"—he scowled and sighed—"unless I agreed to fund her project." He shook his head slightly. "I regret it now, but at the time, it seemed best to pacify her and avoid a potential scandal."

"I see," Morrence replied. "And did you? Take advantage of her, I mean."

Derek narrowed his eyes menacingly. "Of course not," he said, seething. The detective spread his hands.

"I mean no disrespect, sir," he said, seeming apologetic. "I have to ask these questions, you understand." He remained quiet for a moment, appearing to process the story. "So, she blackmailed you for money, over something that you didn't do. And then she never even used the money…" He trailed off, the unanswered question not needing to be asked, and it was clear to Derek that he was right in not trusting this detective. Seeing that Morrence was bent on drawing conclusions that painted Derek as the "bad guy," he surmised that a quick end to this discussion would be in his best interest for now.

Looking Morrence in the eye, Derek decided to cut to the chase. "Why don't you just go ahead and tell me what you'd like to say, detective?" he said evenly.

Frowning slightly, the detective shrugged. "There is reason to believe that you are responsible for this girl's death," Morrence replied simply. "The note, the check…and there are witnesses who have seen you emotionally abusing her." He paused for effect. "You may not have shoved those pills down her throat," he declared, "but the evidence shows you drove her to commit the act. By the way, where were you last night?"

"Derek, don't answer that." It was Gregory who interjected.

Costa had cleared his throat loudly at the same time. "Do you understand who you are speaking to, sir?" he asked the detective, his tone defensive and threatening.

Morrence sighed and smiled slightly.

"Yes, of course. I beg your pardon, Your Highness. I understand you have diplomatic immunity and all that. I also understand you are a US citizen...the situation is highly unorthodox. But"—he took a breath—"justice is justice, and a girl is dead. I would not be doing my job if I didn't explore why. If someone else is responsible, then that person should be arrested and punished according to the law."

Derek rose from his chair, indicating that the discussion was over.

"Don't worry about showing me out," Morrence smirked as he also stood. "I'm sure we will talk again soon." Picking up his folder, he straightened his tie and left the office, closing the door as he walked out.

"I think you would do well to have representation," Gregory said thoughtfully. His eyes glued on the point from which the detective had exited. Derek nodded his agreement.

———◆———

Two weeks later Derek found himself once again face-to-face with Timothy McKenzie. Since Timothy's dismissal from Land Corporation, he had opened his own practice in New York, taking on several partners. Already a well-known attorney from his stint at Land Corporation, Timothy had now risen to a new level of success and was highly regarded as one of, if not the, most sought-after attorney in the state.

Derek had not spoken to nor seen Timothy since his fist had made its mark on the lawyer's face, and he had greatly objected to seeking his help now. But, unfortunately, the press had gone ballistic due to leaks surrounding the new monarch's alleged involvement in Courtney's death. The story of how a billionaire turned king had seduced, taken advantage of, and then rejected an innocent girl, driving her to commit suicide, was too juicy to not make sensational global headlines. Add in rumors surrounding blackmail, bribery, and hush money to the tune of $1 million, and Derek knew he was caught dead center in the scandal of the century. The pressure from the media had caused authoritative channels to act, and despite the fact that no charges were presented, it was clear they were trying to cut through the red tape.

Although the formal proceedings were inconvenient as hell and his reputation was going down the drain, Derek felt confident that there was no real evidence against him. However, he needed this to end quickly, and he had to admit that regardless of their disagreements, Timothy McKenzie was the best man for the job.

Gregory had first approached Timothy about taking the case, and though Derek was unsure of how the attorney would respond, he was surprised to learn he had agreed without hesitation. Concluding that Timothy also viewed this case as more media smoke and mirrors than anything, Derek was sure it would be a simple win for the shrewd lawyer, and with such a high-profile client, it would be a major feather in his cap.

Having spent the past week learning the details of Derek's relationship and encounters with Courtney, digging into the evidence, and meeting with judges, Timothy now sat across from the monarch and his security guard, prepared to give them the outcome of the latest court decision.

"There's going to be a hearing," he said, noticing the immediate look of displeasure on Derek's face. "It's just a formal way of putting this to rest," Timothy insisted. "I'm sure no charges will be or can be filed. The strongest evidence is the check, and we've brought in an expert who can prove it was washed. Everything else is circumstantial at best."

"Then why is this hearing even necessary?" Derek questioned.

"Only because the media has drawn so much attention to the case, because of who you are," Timothy explained calmly. "You should look at the hearing as a good thing. Once the matter is resolved and the public can hear the truth for themselves, your reputation will be restored." Derek gave him a look of uncertainty. "You have nothing to worry about."

"My image is very important to my country right now," Derek commented. "This whole affair has caused questions to arise regarding my character, which is impacting an already delicate situation in Calina. If this hearing will address the allegations toward me, then of course I will proceed."

Timothy nodded and offered a comforting smile. As the three men rose to take their leave, Derek turned to Costa.

"Please wait for me outside; I'll be right with you."

"Yes, signore," Costa replied, bowing before leaving the room.

Now alone with the attorney, Derek regarded Timothy closely. "Why are you helping me?" he asked.

Timothy lowered his eyes, then sighed. "Guilt," he replied. "I'm sorry for what I did, Derek. For Cynthia, for Christine, for not considering or appreciating our friendship." He met Derek's eye. "If I can help you now, I figure I owe you."

Derek nodded. "I appreciate that," he said, "and I accept your apology."

"I want you to know that nothing really happened between me and Christine," Timothy added. "As with your current situation, it was mostly hype. For what it's worth to you, I believe she still loves you."

At the mention of Christine's name, Derek couldn't stop a yearning that swept through him, one that he had been suppressing since the detective had first walked into Gregory's office. Since learning the truth, he had been longing to contact her, tell her he forgave her and beg her forgiveness of him in return. She hadn't trusted him, but he had also refused to listen to her, and he had been just as wrong to judge her decisions. Knowing that he needed to settle this chaos before he was free to reach out to her, the urgency within him practically choked him daily. Urgency because soon it would be too late, and he could only hope that she hadn't yet married Sean.

Subconsciously, he placed his hands in his pockets, one enclosing around the ring he kept, gripping it so hard the diamond began to hurt his palm.

"Thanks, Tim," he said sincerely, and he turned to depart. A thought occurring to him, he looked back at his friend. "Have you called her?"

Timothy raised his eyebrows in confusion. "Who?" he asked.

Derek smiled. "Cynthia," he replied. "I'd call her if I were you." He then opened the door and left, closing it behind him.

Timothy stared after Derek for a moment, partially in shock and partially feeling suddenly nervous. He had not reached out to Cynthia since she had broken off the affair with him all those years ago as he had always been afraid of what Derek would think of him if he did. But he thought of her every day. Now it felt as though he had Derek's permission, which freed him from his guilt.

Taking a seat behind his desk, he opened the drawer and pulled out a photograph he kept of her, a sad smile crossing his face. Coming to a decision, he set the picture down and pulled out his phone. Hesitating for just a brief moment, he took a deep breath and hit "Call" when he reached her name in his contacts. She answered on the first ring.

"Cynthia, hey. It's me, Tim…I know it's been a long time…" He smiled. "Yeah, I've missed you too."

———◦———

Deep in concentration over her current piece, Christine didn't hear her phone vibrate on the stool beside her, next to the easel she was working on. Her new project had consumed her day and night; she called it *Regret*. As she stood back, a large paint brush in her hand, she became once again distressed, feeling as though she was not capturing her emotion fully. She began to think it wasn't dark enough, knowing that it needed to fill her with a complete hollowness, a hole that could not be filled. Darkness, she thought, all she could feel was darkness.

She closed her eyes briefly to recenter her thoughts, and the buzzing caught her attention. Snapping her head toward her phone, she reached over and smiled upon seeing who the caller was.

"Hi, April!" she exclaimed.

"Christine, what are you doing?" April's voice was quick and blunt.

A look of bewilderment crossed Christine's face. "Well, it's nice to hear from you too," she said, amused at her friend's dramatic flair. "I'm working."

April sighed. "I should have known you would shut yourself off from the world."

"Ok," Christine said slowly, unsure what April was getting at. She cleared her throat. "So, how are you, April? How's Gregory?"

"Oh, forget about Greg! He's fine," April replied, frustrated now. "Christine, I called you because of Derek. Haven't you seen the news?"

Christine's face went blank. "No, I…April, what's going on? Is he ok?" Panic began to rise within her.

"That bitch, Courtney? Christine, she's dead," April began. "She committed suicide and basically her dying words were that she did it because of her affair with him. She left behind the money he gave her…it doesn't look good for him. The media's painted a very ugly picture."

Christine's eyes widened as she listened to the story April was sharing. She shook her head.

"That doesn't make any sense," she said evenly and took a breath. "April, I don't believe Derek had an affair with her."

"No," April said in agreement. "Greg knows that the check she showed us, the one that looks like hush money—it was forged." She paused, and both women were silent for a moment as Christine attempted to digest everything.

"She only wanted me to leave him," she said quietly, understanding Courtney's motive now. "The pictures?"

"I don't know," April replied. "But Greg said he was set up, and he made mention of a photographer that died. I guess Derek believes she killed him, but there's no proof. And now that she's dead…"

"The truth died with her," Christine finished the sentence sadly. "What's going to happen? They can't arrest him."

"There have been a lot of rumors," April said. "Most of it is just nonsense. But there is going to be a hearing. Greg is hoping it'll just put things to rest because there's no real evidence."

Christine was quiet again, thinking about Derek and what he was going through. She knew now that Courtney had plotted against him and had gone to great lengths to destroy their relationship. Even in her death, she was still trying to ruin his life.

She cursed herself once again for not believing in him; her guilt was almost overwhelming. She glanced back at her painting. She had so many regrets. She narrowed her eyes, knowing what she needed to do.

"I'm coming there, April," she said, determined. "The first flight I can book. When is the hearing?" She could practically hear April smiling through the phone.

"It's about time," she said. "In two days."

"Ok, I'll text you the details," Christine replied hurriedly. "Can you meet me at the airport?"

"Of course!" April exclaimed. "I'm glad you've finally come to your senses."

Christine ended the call with April but couldn't take her eyes off her painting. It was so black, so dark, so desolate. So regretful. But it wasn't what she wanted. Acting on her instincts, she grabbed a new brush and soaked the bristles in white acrylic. Adding the new color and texture, she continued to pile on lighter colors in shades of the palest pink. Standing back to admire what she had done, she realized that the piece was not *Regret*, but *Hope*. She knew that she needed to forgive herself in order to move forward, and she made the decision to stop dwelling on what she had done and focus on him.

She needed to be there for him, now more than ever, and she was resolved to do whatever it took to show him how much she needed him too.

———————————

The hearing was held at the courthouse in Lower Manhattan. As the car escort approached the large white-pillared building, Derek groaned and sighed at the volume of press and gawkers. *There seems to be more people crowded here than at the Academy Awards*, he thought to himself, not that he had anticipated anything different. The car stopped, and as he emerged from the vehicle, he was instantly surrounded by his security, who ushered him into the building. He moved quickly, completely ignoring the flashes, shouts, and questions coming at him from all directions. The hearing itself would be closed to the public, but Derek knew that the outcome would soon be worldwide news.

The following six hours were grueling as statements were made, questions were asked, and evidence was presented. Timothy had done his job well in verifying with certainty that the check had been washed and altered, which corroborated Derek's side of the story. In the end there was nothing to prove that Derek had coerced Courtney into committing suicide; unfortunately, she was simply a mentally unstable and obsessed person. The photos that Courtney had staged had never surfaced, and therefore there was no evidence of an affair. Nor would there be any justice for Paul, who's name was never brought up. Although Derek felt certain he knew what had truly transpired, unfortunately, there would be no means of proving it. And with Courtney now dead, there was no one who could take responsibility. By the time Timothy had given his closing statement, there was a deep sense within the courtroom of foolishness, and after a short deliberation, the court dismissed the case with a sincere apology to His Highness.

Word was already on the street as to the outcome of the hearing by the time Derek, his security, and Timothy started to make their exit. The crowd had become even more dense, and he was lucky to move at all down the vast number of stone stairs leading from the main entrance to the car waiting as his security pushed their way through the reporters.

Timothy stopped to answer a few questions from the mob in an effort to distract attention away from Derek, but most of the crowd continued to buzz around him, anxious to get a statement.

"Derek!"

Derek stopped, hearing a familiar voice call his name. Looking to his left, over the edge of the crowd, he saw her rushing up the steps toward him. Christine? Wondering if he was imagining her, he blinked. No, she was real and now pushing her way through the mass, seeming desperate to get to him. He moved to his left to find a clear opening among the throng of people. He knew it was reckless to move away from Costa and his security, but he had to get to her. She was close now; he could see the expression on her face, which was laced with relief and love. He smiled as she drew near.

A sudden commotion and several shrieks from the crowd made him tear his eyes away from Christine. A man was shoving people aside, then he pulled out a gun. There was a shout.

"You bastard!" Costa immediately dove into the crowd toward the man, but not before he was able to pull the trigger. Two shots rang out in quick succession in Derek's direction. People seemed to scatter in all directions, and his eyes widened in terror as comprehension of what was happening hit him too late.

Having also seen the man pull out the gun, Christine had reacted, throwing herself in front of Derek. He caught her as she fell into him, his expression one of horror as he realized the first bullet had pierced her in the back. Suddenly he collapsed onto the steps, still holding her in his arms. His adrenaline had caused a delayed reaction to his own injury as a deep-seated pain ripped through his shoulder, the second shot finding its mark on his body.

Trying to forget about the blood now gushing from his arm, he looked down at Christine, lying still in his arms. He let out a slow breath as he saw her eyelids flutter. She was alive.

"Christine," he choked out softly, "it's going to be ok." He flinched, knowing he was losing consciousness, but he couldn't slip away, not until he knew she was safe. There were continued shouts, struggles and swarms of people all around him, and in the distance, he heard sirens, but he could only see her. She blinked and slowly lifted her hand to touch his face.

"Forgive me," she whispered, "I love you...I've always loved you."

His eyes misted, and tears freely fell from his face onto her. Her hand dropped lifelessly to her side, and her eyes closed.

"No! Christine!" He mustered his strength to cry out. "Open your eyes..." He begged her, but she remained still.

Now he vaguely felt tugging and pulling as paramedics attempted to remove her from his grasp. Unwilling to let her go at first, he ran out of strength to hold her any longer.

"Save her," he pleaded as he watched her being carried away and felt himself being lifted. The last thing he saw was the blood. He was unsure whether it was hers or his—it didn't matter. All that mattered was that she live. As he blacked out, he knew he wouldn't survive, and even if he did, without her his will to live was dead. After all, she was his purpose.

Epilogue

Derek winced in pain as he tried to adjust his shoulder sling. He stood, staring at the headstone that marked her grave, the one he had commissioned himself. His expression was of remorse, and he couldn't stop the replay of events in his mind. He had asked Costa for solitude, and the security guard waited at the cemetery gate, ensuring no one else entered.

"If I could do things differently..." he murmured to himself.

He wasn't sure how long he had been there, having become lost in his thoughts, and the uneven, staggering footsteps approaching him from behind startled him. Spinning around to see who his intruder was, he couldn't suppress a small smile.

"You shouldn't be here," he said softly, "you should be resting."

She returned his smile as she stopped, nearly to him, her hand adjusting the grip she had on the cane she used to help her walk.

"You're the one who should be resting," Christine replied. "It was a miracle you survived. I heard the bullet hit one of your main arteries. You almost bled out immediately." She regarded him with concern as he met her eyes. "I had a feeling you'd be here though."

329

Her eyes wandered to the inscription on the headstone: Courtney Metcalf.

"You have to stop blaming yourself," she said quietly.

He sighed heavily. "It's my fault," he said, looking away from her. "If I hadn't threatened her that night, she wouldn't have gone to these measures." He paused, looking at Christine. "There are many things I could have done differently, and you almost died because of my actions."

She narrowed her eyes, thinking. "Who was he?" she asked.

"His name is James Fulton. Courtney was living with him when she died, so I assume they were close. His statements to the police indicated that his motive was to avenge her. He blames me for her delusions and her death."

Christine frowned.

"You had no way of knowing that, Derek," she said. "And you only confronted her because of what she did to you." She paused. "To us."

He reached for her face with his good arm and brushed her hair back behind her ear. "I thought I had lost you," he whispered. "Why did you do that, Christine?" Tears began to well in her eyes.

"I had to," she said earnestly, her brows coming together. "I couldn't let you die."

With his hand still in her hair, he pulled her to him, embracing her.

"You saved my life," he said quietly. Releasing her, he looked into her eyes. "I love you, Christine. I never stopped loving you." His eyes wandered to her hand, still gripping the cane she leaned on for support. "You're not wearing his ring," he observed.

She shook her head slightly. "I couldn't do it," she said, and her voice cracked. "I didn't believe you would ever forgive me, but I'm in love with you." She paused and glanced down. "I was so foolish, about so many things."

"I'm the one who needs forgiveness, Christine," he replied, his voice barely above a whisper. Silence followed, her eyes were still glassy, and he took a step back from her, knowing it was time to go. "I have to return to Calina," he told her. "Costa's been waiting for me, and this trip to the States ended up being quite a bit longer than expected."

She bit her lip and nodded quickly, unable to speak as her throat began to seize up at the thought of parting from him again. But before she could turn from him, he reached into his pocket and pulled out the diamond ring.

"So, are you going to come with me this time?" he asked.

She could no longer hold them in, and tears streamed down her face as she stared at the ring. Closing the distance between them, she gingerly lifted her arm, wrapping it around his neck, unable to stop the smile and joy coming out through her tears.

"Yes," she said as she rested against him. "I'll go anywhere you want me to."

He pulled back from her just enough so his mouth could capture hers. As he broke the kiss, he placed the ring on her finger. "Let's go home."

He wrapped his good arm around her waist, letting her lean on him as he helped her walk down the path toward the gate. He smiled upon seeing Costa waiting for him, thinking about what lay ahead and happy to be starting the next journey of his life with this woman by his side.

CPSIA information can be obtained
at www.ICGtesting.com
Printed in the USA
LVHW030425200221
679375LV00001B/21

9 781649 907257